Single d

# Dat
# SINGLE
# DAD

Three sensational novels from Ally Blake,
Donna Alward and Natasha Oakley

Special treats for February.
Want a date with a gorgeous man?
Look no further!

# Date with a
# SINGLE
# DAD

ALLY
BLAKE

DONNA
ALWARD

NATASHA
OAKLEY

MILLS &
BOON

Mills & Boon, an imprint of Harlequin (UK) Limited, Eton House, 18-24 Paradise Road, Richmond, Surrey TW9 1SR

DATE WITH A SINGLE DAD

*Millionaire Dad's SOS* © Ally Blake 2010
*Proud Rancher, Precious Bundle* © Donna Alward 2010
*Millionaire Dad: Wife Needed* © Natasha Oakley 2006

ISBN: 978 0 263 90282 2

011-0213

Harlequin (UK) policy is to use papers that are natural, renewable and recyclable products and made from wood grown in sustainable forests. The logging and manufacturing processes conform to the legal environmental regulations of the country of origin.

Printed and bound in Spain
by Blackprint CPI, Barcelona

# MILLIONAIRE
# DAD'S SOS

## ALLY BLAKE

Having once been a professional cheerleader, **Ally Blake**'s motto is "Smile and the world smiles with you." One way to make Ally smile is by sending her on holidays, especially to locations which inspire her writing. New York and Italy are by far her favorite destinations. Other things that make her smile are the gracious city of Melbourne, the gritty Collingwood football team and her gorgeous husband, Mark. Reading romance novels was a smile worthy pursuit from way back, so, with such valuable preparation already behind her, she wrote and sold her first book. Her career as a writer also gives her a perfectly reasonable excuse to indulge in her stationery addiction. That alone is enough to keep her grinning every day! Ally would love for you to visit her at her website at www.allyblake.com.

This one's for Veronica,
my constant companion through the writing of this
book—from bump, to blinking into the light, to
becoming my beautiful
smiley girl.

# PROLOGUE

*News just in...*

*The cameras were out, the paparazzi waiting, seamstresses across the city ready to copy whichever designer frock they were about to be dazzled by, yet all were sorely disappointed when so-fabulous-it-hurts, thinking man's It-Girl Meg Kelly—the youngest, and we think most adorable, offspring of one-time uber-financier, some-time squillionaire, KInG of the corporate jungle Quinn Kelly—failed to show at the opening of hot new nightclub Bliss.*

*But wait, there's more!*

*Sources close to the family say she hasn't slept at her apartment or her folks' pad, the stunning Kelly Manor, the past two nights. And her familiar classic red convertible, often seen parked out front of Kelly Tower—the home of titanic family biz the Kelly Investment Group—is nowhere to be seen.*

*Where has Brisbane's favourite daughter disappeared to?*

*Could she be—gasp!—in hiding, nursing a new nose job? Has the nicest girl in town finally shown a kink in her squeaky clean armour by—eek!—blowing off her host? Is her vanishing act a sign that her Herculean father is not as recovered from recent heart problems as the family would have us believe?*

*Or—bless her little heart—has she run off with the studly Texan oil baron seen visiting the family manor last week? Oh, please, let that be it! Can we possibly hope this means the last of the Kelly kids has finally found true love at last?*

*Take our online poll for a chance to win a copy of bestseller* Long Live the King: An unauthorised biography of Quinn Kelly!

# CHAPTER ONE

'OF ALL the resorts in all the world, why did she have to walk into mine?'

Zach Jones stood in the shadows of a lush potted palm in a dark corner of the Waratah House lobby, narrowed eyes locked on the figure skipping down the wide stone steps leading away from the main building of the Juniper Falls Rainforest Retreat.

There weren't many reasons why his resort staff would contact him directly, *ever*, his reputation being that he was akin to a bear with a sore tooth at the best of times. That was as kind a character reference he could have hoped for, considering his years of unequivocal lack of co-operation with the press.

Despite all that, the rumoured arrival of the woman currently whipping off her cap and trying and failing to tuck her mass of dark curls beneath it had been deemed important enough to give the bear a nudge.

The bear was thankful they had.

After his daily run, he'd lain in wait for her to show her face. In the end he'd missed out on that privilege. She'd scooted through the lobby, head tipped down. Nevertheless, he'd recognised her in an instant. There wouldn't be many a red-blooded man in this corner of the world who would not.

Even though she was dressed down in shorts, vest top,

sneakers and cap rather than her usual society princess razz-matazz of designer frocks and diamonds, there was no mistaking her. Not with those sexy dark curls, that hourglass silhouette in miniature, the kind Zach couldn't help imagining just begged for fifties-style dresses and high heels to make the most of it, and the ridiculously confident, rock-and-roll sway of those infamous hips.

The woman who'd sent his staff into a tizz the moment she'd zoomed up to the front gates of the resort earlier that week in a growling red convertible filled with designer luggage and equally designer friends was none other than Meg Kelly.

'Dammit,' he said loud enough a group of guests heading out the doors gave him a sideways glance. He slid deeper into the shadows, a place he'd always found far more comfortable than being under any kind of spotlight.

Much less the kind of spotlight Meg Kelly seemed to carry on her person, such was her magnetism for the kind of rabid media attention usually reserved for royalty and rock stars. That kind of attention made her exactly the kind of guest most resort owners would give their right arm for.

*Not him. Not now.*

She disappeared for a moment behind a fat spray of red Waratah flowers and he felt himself leaning to catch her coming out the other side. He rocked himself back upright and planted his feet into the marble floor.

She popped out eventually only to bend from the waist to tug at the heel of what appeared to be brand-new sneakers, her shorts curving tight over her backside, her thigh muscles tightening, her calf muscles lengthening.

He glanced away, but not soon enough to stop the quickening in his blood. He ran a hand over his mouth, his palm rasping from the effects of three days' worth of stubble growth, and told himself it was the after-effects of his run.

He glanced back out of the window only to have his gaze catch on the sliver of pale, soft skin that peeked between the back of her shorts and her top… Was that a tattoo?

His eyes flicked to the heavens and he drew in a deep breath through his nose, attempting to temper the swift kick of attraction.

*Not her. And most certainly not now.*

The little-known truth that he'd stayed put in the one place for the past few months, rather than jet-setting about the globe in a constant effort to exponentially expand his empire of international resorts, would be enticing news for the kind of gossip-hungry media for whom Meg Kelly was the poster girl.

As far as he was concerned they could all go jump. Not since he'd jumped off the merry-go-round of foster homes and orphanages he'd grown up in had he let anybody tell him who he was, who he was not, how low he might fall, or how high he dared reach. His successes and mistakes were only his own to judge.

And of all the successes and mistakes he'd ever accomplished in his life the reason *why* he was now stuck in the middle of nowhere was the most inviolable yet.

In fact, he'd missed a call from his 'reason why' already that morning, and now she wasn't answering the mobile he'd bought her specifically so they could *always* be in touch.

Then his man on the ground in St Barts had left a message saying the government was playing hard ball on signing off on the final inspections of his latest resort site. And then there was Meg. All that before the day had even officially begun.

He didn't see how this week could get any worse.

Meg couldn't imagine how her week could get any better.

'Ouch, ouch, ouch!' she barked as a blister spontaneously popped up on her right heel.

Okay, so a handy supply of Band-Aids might have made it

ever so slightly better, but everything else was heavenly. She simply shifted her stance to compensate and breathed deep of the glorious fresh air, sunshine and fifty acres of beautiful resort and her world was close to perfection again.

The breath turned to a yawn, which turned into a grin, which she bit back lest she be caught laughing to herself in the middle of the patch of lawn in which she'd come to a halt. Apparently she'd already been declared AWOL by the gossip hounds today—she didn't need to add loony to the list.

A funny sensation skittered down her back. Years of experience gave her the feeling she was being watched. She did a casual three-sixty-degree turn, but in the early morning, the resort grounds were quiet and still and she was all alone. It was probably just the rising sun sending prickles over her pale skin, and teasing her curls into damp springs on the back of her neck.

Another deep breath, another blissful smile as she skipped onto the immaculate lawn, which she figured would be kinder on her feet.

If her big brothers could see her now—up and at 'em before the birds, in a jogging outfit of all things—they'd be in hysterics. She wasn't exactly built for the great outdoors and her way of life meant that the only time she ever saw a sunrise was when she'd yet to go to bed the night before!

But this week she wasn't Meg Kelly, socialite. This vacation was not about to turn into some last-minute Kelly Investment Group junket in disguise. This week, thanks to her angelic best friends, she was just a girl on a summer holiday.

Sure, when Rylie and Tabitha had turned up on her doorstep two days before, told her they'd cleared her schedule, shoved her into her car and demanded she drive them to a wellness resort high in the hills of the Gold Coast Hinterland, she'd had a moment or two of panic.

Events had been planned. People had been counting on

her—dress designers she was meant to be wearing, charities whose events she was attending, local businesses she was turning out to endorse, the several staff she kept in gainful employ, the women and children at the Valley Women's Shelter. There was such inertia to her life it was almost impossible to bring it to any kind of halt.

But even after Tabitha had explained that the 'wellness' in wellness resort was more about detoxing one's life by way of eating granola and valiantly trying to put one's left ankle behind one's head while meditating thrice daily, and not so much code for cocktails, chocolate fountains and daily massages at the hands of handsome Swedes she'd soon begun to warm to the idea.

As the city lights had dropped away from her rear-view mirror and the scent of sea air had filled her nostrils the idea of getting away, of having one blissful, dreamy, stress-free, family-free, paparazzi-free, drama-free week had almost made her giddy.

Not that drama, paparazzi and family issues bothered her. They'd been par for the Kelly course from the day dot.

Though, when she thought about it, the past few months had been particularly dramatic even for her family—engagements, elopements, near-death experiences. The kinds of things that made the paparazzi that touch more overzealous, and a touch harder to avoid when she tried to sneak away for much-needed private time.

Meg shook off the real-life stuff creeping up on her and glanced back at the main building. Still no sign of the girls. Her girls. Her support crew. The ones who'd obviously sensed she was floundering just a very little even if she hadn't uttered a word. Girls who were right now both probably still fast slept in their snug, warm beds.

'Cads.'

She headed off; this time with slower, shorter steps in the hopes the girls would catch up. Soon. Please!

A resort staff member passed, smiling. 'Good morning.'

'Isn't it just?' she returned.

His smile faltered and he all but tripped over himself as his neck craned to watch her while he walked away.

Meg's smile turned wry. So the cap and sunglasses and still-so-white-they-practically-glowed sneakers she'd bought from the resort's well-stocked shop the night before might not fool everybody as she'd half hoped they just might.

It had been a long shot anyway.

Meg stood happily at the back of the morning jogging group— primarily a group of middle-aged strangers in an impressive array of jogging outfits—collected on the track that ran along the edge of the overhang of thick, lush, dank, dark rainforest.

In an apparent effort at warming up, Tabitha lifted her knees enthusiastically high while jogging on the spot. Rylie, the Pilates queen, stretched so far sideways she was practically at a right angle. Meg, on the other hand, tried not to look as dinky as she felt without her ubiquitous high heels.

'Now that man is worth the price of admission all on his own,' Tabitha said between her teeth.

'Shh,' Meg said, only listening with half an ear as she tried to make out what the preppy, bouncy 'wellness facilitator' at the front of the large group was saying. 'Please tell me she didn't just say we're jogging four kilometres this morning!'

'She said five.'

Meg slid her sunglasses atop her cap and gaped at Tabitha. 'Five?'

'Five. Now pay attention. Hot guy at six o'clock. He's been staring at you for the past five minutes.'

'Not news, hon,' Rylie said, touching the ground with her palms and casually glancing between her legs before letting out a long, slow 'I take that back. This one is big news.'

Meg rolled her eyes. 'I'm not falling for that again.'

'Your loss,' Rylie said.

A husky note in her best friend's voice caught Meg's attention. 'Fine. Where?'

'Over your right shoulder,' Tabitha said. 'Faded T-shirt, knee-length cargo shorts, sneakers that have pounded some miles, cap he ought to have thrown away a lo-o-ong time ago…'

Rylie laughed, then gave Meg's leg a tug so her knee collapsed, turning her whether she wanted to or not.

Meg didn't even get the chance to ask Rylie what was so funny. She didn't need to. There was no way any woman under the age of a hundred and twenty was going to miss the man leaning against the trunk of one of the massive ghost gums lining the resort's elegant driveway.

He was tall. Impressively so. Broad as any man she'd ever met. His chin was unshaven, the dark curls beneath his cap overlong. With the colour of a man who'd spent half a lifetime in the sun and the muscles of a man who hadn't done so standing still, he looked as if he'd stepped out of a Nautica ad.

She tucked a curl behind her ear and casually bent down to tug at her ankle socks, not needing to look at the guy to remember exactly what she'd seen. Her hands shook ever so slightly.

He was the very dictionary definition of rugged sex appeal. For a girl from the right side of the tracks, a girl who was a magnet for stiff, sharp, striving suits, a girl whose planner had become so full of late she had to diarise time to wash her hair much less anything more intimately enjoyable, he was a revelation.

She glanced up as she stood. He hadn't moved an inch.

The skin beneath her skimpy clothes suddenly felt hot, and the fact that it was thirty-odd degrees and muggy had nothing to do with it. She was a Kelly, for Pete's sake. It took something *extra* extraordinary to make a Kelly sweat.

Though she couldn't see his eyes beneath the brim of his

soft, worn cap, she could feel them on her. Her right shoulder tingled. The sensation moved up her neck. It finally settled in her lips. The urge to run her fingers across them was so strong she had to curl them into her palms.

Then he finally moved. He pressed away from the tree and shifted his cap into a more comfortable position on his head before crossing his arms across his chest. His strong, tanned, brawny arms. His broad chest.

She breathed in deep, releasing it on a long, slow, deliciously revitalising sigh.

What if *this* was what she needed more than even a holiday right now? More than granola or t'ai chi. More than early-morning jogs or internal reflection classes. A little bit of something for herself.

Could she? Should she? Considering every step and every misstep she experienced outside the walls of her family home somehow ended up being known by the whole country, it took something *extra* extraordinary for her to put herself out there. The lanky stranger who would not take his eyes off her was exactly that.

She took another deep breath, faced him square on and gave him an honest, inviting, unambiguous smile.

Needless to say, after all that build-up, it was more than a bit of a shock when she didn't get one in return. *Nada*. Not a twitch, a nod, not any kind of acknowledgement that he was paying her any attention at all.

Her cheeks heated from the inside out, her fingernails bit into her palms, and her lungs suddenly felt very, very small.

Meg fair leapt out of her skin when Tabitha leant on her shoulder and sighed. 'Imagine,' she said, 'if we hadn't kidnapped you to this place this moment never would have happened.'

'I'm trying my very best to imagine it right now,' Meg said on a mortified croak.

Pathetically late though the attempt at saving face was, Meg let her gaze glance off Mr Tall Dark and Silent Rugged Man, then up into the sky as if she were pondering the time and using the sun as her guide.

'I might well be seeing things,' Rylie said, finally upright and now staring brazenly at the silent stranger, 'but isn't that Zach Jones?'

Meg grabbed Rylie by the hand and spun her around to face front. All the while her wits began to return and synapses connected in the back of her brain. 'Why do I know that name?'

Rylie said, 'He was a rower years back. Olympic level. Keeping it up too, by the looks of him. Now he's a business-man. Big time. Owns this place, in fact, as well as a dozen-odd of its like all 'round the world. Self-starter. Self-made. Rene-gade. Refuses to list his company on the exchange. Not all that much known about him otherwise. He somehow manages to live under the radar.'

'Single?' Tabitha asked.

'Perpetually,' Rylie said with a grin.

'Perfect.' Tabitha grinned. 'Your dad'll hate him.'

Meg turned on her. 'So?'

Rylie said, 'She has a point. You don't have to limit your dating schedule to charming, skint, ambitionless, undemand-ing men to get back at Daddy.'

Meg's right eyebrow tweaked to a point. 'I actually *prefer* to spend time with men who don't consider bragging about that day's corporate buyout fit for pillow talk, thank you very much. I get enough of that around the family dinner table to find it in any way an aphrodisiac. The only way my father comes into it is that at least men not on their way up the corporate ladder never try to get to him through me.'

Tabitha mirrored her expression. 'Whatever you say.'

Meg poked a face, then looked decidedly back to the front of the group.

What she didn't say was that the men she favoured also weren't the types to press for any kind of commitment. They weren't in any rush to start families of their own. One less pressure to concern herself with.

Besides, it had been a long time since she'd bothered doing anything extreme in order to get through to the big man herself. What was the point? It had never worked anyway.

Rylie pushed in tighter, her voice a secretive stage whisper. 'It has to be him. Zach Jones. He's notoriously impossible to pin down. He's one of those ungettable interviews that would take a girl like me out of Sunday morning fluff TV into the big leagues. I wonder what he's doing here rather than flitting around the world buying up great wads of prime real estate like it's going out of fashion? I smell a scoop.'

Meg shook her escaping curls from her cheeks and peeked out of the corner of her eye one more time.

He'd tilted his head up ever so slightly. Sun-kissed skin was smoothed over the most immaculately masculine bone structure Meg had ever seen. The shadow of three-day growth covered a jaw that just begged to be stroked. And his lips were so perfectly carved she struggled to take her eyes off them.

All that perfection somehow managed to pale in comparison when she finally saw his eyes.

They were locked on hers.

Dark, dangerous eyes, too far away for her to make out the colour, but she had the feeling she could have doubled the distance between them and still been hit by the thwack of awareness behind them.

She sucked in a breath, thick with tropical humidity that caught in her throat. And a trickle of what was most definitely sweat ran down her neck and between her breasts.

Zach Jones.

His name buzzed about inside her head in her father's most frosty voice as he flapped the *Financial Times* in a way that meant he was not happy. '*He got too big, too quick. Stubborn fool is overreaching. One of these days he'll land flat on his face. Mark my words.*'

Meg didn't know about overreaching, but she did know that her father didn't give a damn about *anyone* below a certain level of accomplishment—client, competitor, offspring…

She swallowed.

There was no flirtation in Zach Jones's gaze. No measure of awe about who she was. Just copious amounts of brooding intensity centred in those unfathomable dark eyes. Despite it all, the backs of her knees began to quiver.

He blinked. And rolled his shoulders. The first sign he wasn't as nervelessly blasé as he was making out.

The very thought made way for an unimpeded rush of sexual attraction to slide through her, like a waterfall breaking through a dam of knotted foliage that had held it back a decade.

The ferocity of her reaction had her literally taking a step back. The blister on her heel popped, again. A hiss of pain slid through her teeth as she hopped madly on her good foot.

The man took a step towards her, a hand appearing to flicker in her direction. The tension curling inside her ratcheted up a notch and a half and she knew her sudden breathlessness had far less to do with her stinging foot, and more to do with the stranger in her midst.

Thankfully she caught her balance all on her own, and the man unclenched from his ready-to-pounce position.

She spun back to face front. 'When are we going to start running, for Pete's sake?' she whispered through her teeth.

Rylie reached out and pinched her hot pink cheek. 'Look who's suddenly Miss Eager Exerciser.'

'You bet,' she said, shuffling from one foot to the other as though she had ants in her pants. 'Bring on the lactic-acid burn!' Better that than having to endure the feel of the man's burning eyes on her back.

She shook out her hands, attempting to shake off the fidgets. It wasn't as though she hadn't been rebuffed before. It came with the celebrity package as much as being excessively adored. It just thankfully generally happened from afar. By strangers. Whom she didn't have to look in the eye and pretend it didn't sting.

'Meg, he's coming over!' Tabitha said so loud those straggling nearby must have heard.

'We'll leave you to it, then,' Rylie said cheerily. 'I'm counting on you to get me the exclusive!'

'No, no, no!' Meg begged.

But it was too late, they were off—Rylie the runner, and Tabitha the gym junkie. There was no way Meg was keeping up with them, even with the amount of adrenalin pouring through her body as she stood all alone in the middle of the dirt track, Zach Jones making a beeline her way.

# CHAPTER TWO

MEG jogged for almost five minutes before pulling up to a walk. By then she was already wishing she'd brought a better bra, a hairband and a scooter.

The rest of the stragglers passed her by, including the wellness facilitator who had been bringing up the rear.

All bar one.

She could feel a male presence tucked in behind her. She could hear the heavy pad of his large feet on the compacted dirt path. Dragging in deep, unfit breaths, she caught his scent on the hot summer breeze—expensive, subtle, and wholly masculine.

All this from a man who'd managed to get under her skin in half a second flat. A man who'd rejected her come-hither smile in even less time. Sheesh. The sooner she found out what he was after and got rid of him, the better.

She said, 'Are we there yet?' just loud enough he could have no doubt she was talking to him.

'Do a U-turn and ask me again,' a deep voice rumbled beside her. A voice that matched the rest of him so perfectly that if she wasn't gleaming with perspiration from the effect of it she deserved some kind of medal in self-control.

Meg pinched her side with the hopes of fending off an

oncoming stitch and the slow burn of attraction that was infusing her in one fell swoop, and turned.

At a distance Zach Jones was something. Up close and personal he was too beautiful for words. Her breath shot from her in a discombobulated *whoomph*.

She concentrated on the slight bump of a once-broken nose, the different angles each of his dark brows took above his hooded eyes, the stray sun-kissed flecks within his dark hair, lest she be overwhelmed by the whole.

'Please don't hang back on my account,' she said, oft-practised casual smile firmly entrenched. 'My pace is purpose-ful. Those chumps up ahead don't realise how much more one can appreciate the scenery by walking.'

He said, 'I'm fine right here.'

If she didn't know better she could have taken those words a whole other way. As it was she had to give her heart a mental slap for the unwarranted little dance it was currently enjoying.

'Excellent,' she said. 'We'll walk together. Scenery is always more enjoyable when you have someone to share it with.'

And then neither of them said another word for a whole minute. The unmistakable tension was almost enough for Meg to start jogging again, despite the fact that she'd barely caught her breath.

'Would I be right in thinking you're not a big runner?' he finally said.

After Meg's laughter died down she waved her hands in the direction of her well-tended curves. 'Do I look like a runner?'

Given the invitation to do so, the man's eyes travelled down one side of her body—over her borrowed hot-pink short shorts and black T-shirt with sparkly designer name splashed across her chest—and up the other. Given the chance, she looked into his distracted eyes.

Deep, dark, soulful brown they were, with the kinds of

creases at the edge that she just knew would make a girl's heart melt at ten paces when he smiled. *If* he smiled, which she realised he still was yet to do. In fact, he carried with him the distinct impression of a frown.

Finally, and none too soon, Meg managed to duck out of the heady cloud of attraction to hear cymbals crashing inside her head. They warned of impending doom.

There was no doubt he was intentionally at her side. He'd had to have waved the wellness facilitator on to get her alone. But it was becoming increasingly clear he wasn't exactly over the moon to be there. On both counts she was clueless as to why.

She worried the tiny chip in her front right tooth with her tongue, an old habit that re-emerged only when she felt as if things were slipping out of her exacting control. An old habit she worked hard at keeping at bay.

She curled her tongue back where it belonged and answered her question herself. 'Between us, running's not my forte. I'm more of a yoga girl.'

Sometimes. Every now and then. Okay, so she'd taken a couple of lessons with Rylie once.

'Yoga,' he repeated, his eyes finally, thankfully, leaving the contours of her body and returning to hers.

She shouldn't have been so thankful so soon. For in those dark, deep, delicious brown eyes she saw that he had seen the equivocation in hers.

She dropped her gaze to the fraying collar of his T-shirt lest he see the surprise in her eyes as well. She'd had a lifetime in which to perfect the art of being Meg Kelly, public figure. Her front had been demonstrably shatter-proof. *Two minutes* after meeting her, Zach Jones had seen right through it.

*Who was this guy and what did he want with her?*

'Downward dog? Upward...tree?' she shot back, arms swinging in what she knew was a terrible impression of some-

thing she'd seen on TV once. 'Okay, so I'm not a yoga fanatic
or a runner. I'm more an eat-chocolate-for-breakfast dance-it-
off-in-your-living-room kind of girl. Either way there is no
way on God's green earth I'll be catching up to the others any
time soon. So please go ahead. Jog. Be free.'

'Between us,' he said, leaning in, his voice dropping to a con-
spiratorial tone that sent her blood pressure soaring, 'I've
already run five K today.'

'Oh.' Oh, indeed. 'So what brings you out here again?'

All she got for her blunt question was an out-held hand. 'I'm
Zach Jones.'

Meg twisted her body to slide her smaller hand into his. Even
the coolest of customers usually gave themselves away when
shaking her hand. A nervous vibration here, a sweaty palm
there. She was extremely adept at ignoring their nerves.

With Zach Jones they never eventuated. His grip was warm,
dry, strong, masculine and wholly unmoved.

*Remarkable*, she thought. More than remarkable. The man
was perspiration-inducing, utterly gorgeous and wholly unsmiling even though he had the kind of warm, open, likable face
purpose built for the function.

*And don't forget*, she reminded herself, *beneath the casual
curls, the sexily shabby clothes, and the body of an Olympic
god, Zach Jones is an alpha in beta camouflage. So not worth
worrying about.*

So why was she still holding his hand?

*Because it really is so very warm, dry and blissfully envel-
oping, that's why.*

'I'm Meg,' she said, pumping once more, then letting go.

At the last second she held back her surname. As if there was
a slim chance she'd been reading too much into every cheek
flicker, or lack thereof, from the very beginning. Maybe he was
just some cute guy too shy to chat her up even though he had

a thing for girls with impossibly curly hair and a glaringly obvious lack of sporting prowess.

'It's a pleasure to meet you, Meg,' he said, his mouth quirking at her omission.

Argh! What was she thinking? He knew. Of *course* he knew. She'd have to go further than the Gold Coast to find a man who didn't know who she was. A man whose mind wasn't already made up about her before they even met.

She squeezed her eyes shut a moment. Using a technique they'd encouraged in internal reflection class the day before, she searched for her centre. Patience thin, she failed miserably. Instead she went with what worked in the real world: she summoned her inner Kelly and looked the guy dead in the eye.

'So, Zach Jones, from what I hear around the traps you own this joint.'

The full-frontal approach brought out a combative glint in his darker than dark eyes. If possible it only made the guy more tempting. Warmth curled through her empty stomach.

But rather than doing the polite thing and answering her charge, he ignored it and asked, 'How long are you planning on staying?'

Frustration began to war convincingly well with attraction. In response, her practised smile only grew wider.

'A survey?' she said, lobbing it right back in his corner. 'Aren't you the hands-on boss?'

The most sensuous mouth she'd ever laid eyes on kicked into a sexy almost-smile, creating an arc in his cheek that hinted at so much more, but still it never quite reached his eyes. He didn't believe her devil-may-care performance for a second.

'How long?' he repeated.

'We're here the week.'

His eyes skimmed the empty path ahead. 'We being?'

Something in his tone gave her the sense the impending doom wouldn't be impending that much longer.

She casually lifted a foot and stretched her…whatever the muscle that ran down the front of your thigh was called. 'Two of my closest mates gave me this holiday as a present. Rylie Madigan and Tabitha Cooper.'

At the last second she threw out their full names on a gamble, for Tabitha, with her ex-Prime Minister dad, and Rylie, with her job on TV, were almost as recognisable as she was.

Her fishing paid off. He breathed deep, his fists bunched at his sides, and the sexy hollows in his cheeks grew their own hollows.

'So you go home…?' he said.

'In a few days.'

He nodded, breathed out deeply, apparently most satisfied that she'd be out of his sight as soon as that.

Whoa. That was harsh.

Even though beneath the bright smiles and fancy clothes she was a tough cookie—she had to be in order to survive being a Kelly—it turned out she was still just a girl whose pride could be hurt like anyone else.

Okay, so there had been a time before she'd toughened up. A time when she'd been in danger of imploding under the relentless pressure. A long time ago, a lifetime really, in some perverse effort to get her father's attention she'd let things go far too far. It had scared her enough to buck up and take control over her image, her life. To figure out how to use the process that used her.

Any naivety she might have had was lost for ever, making a certain amount of cynicism unavoidable. On the upside she was no longer easily fazed. By anything.

*Yet somehow this guy was getting to her.*

Frustration finally won out, bringing with it a desire to share the pain. She lifted her chin and breathed deep of the tropical air. 'I have to say you picked a gorgeous spot here. I could really get used to it. Who knows? We may stay longer yet.'

His eyes slid back to hers; dark, gleaming, shrewd.

She raised both eyebrows. *Now what are you going to do about that?*

What he did was smile.

Naturally it was everything she'd imagined it might be and so much more. The latent vitality his physique hinted at shone from his eyes when he smiled. It made him appear playful, warm, engaging. Her knees turned to jelly. Her resolve turned to mush.

She opened her mouth, ready to ask him outright what the hell was going on when he placed his bare hand in the small of her back and gave her a light shove. She was so surprised she gave a little yelp.

Through the thin cotton of her T-shirt his fingers were hot. Insistent. Touching her without fear or favour.

Only when she looked up to see a small tree in the middle of the path did she realise he was merely stopping her from thwacking into the thing.

And even after his hand moved all too easily away, and even while he was making her feel more and more out of step with every step in his presence, she could still feel the hot, hard press of Zach Jones's hand against her skin.

Now why did he have to go and touch her?

A simple, 'Watch out for the tree,' would have sufficed. Instead, constant glimpses of that tattoo peeking out from the rise of her shorts had been like a magnet.

Now he had to do this thing with the sensation of that soft warm skin imprinted on the tips of his fingers.

Zach curled said fingers into his palm and took a small step to the left to add a little more physical distance between himself and the woman at his side. The woman whose very proximity could expose everything he'd worked so hard to keep pre-served. Protected. Pure.

He stretched out his shoulders and shot her a sideways glance. He had to concede that for a woman who appeared to bloom under the spotlight like an orchid in a hothouse, in person she was smaller, more low-key, and more approachable than he'd expected her to be. Funny, mischievous, switched on...

He actually had to remind himself her father was Quinn Kelly, one of the most patronising men he'd ever had the displeasure of dealing with in the early stages of his business career. No doubt there would be a good dash of spice beneath the sweet. That kind of bite had to be genetic.

As for the rest of her?

His gaze lingered on her mouth before skimming over her pale bare shoulder, down her slim arm, over her Betty Boop hip, before being drawn back to that mouth.

Surely lips that lush could not be the real deal. Soft, pink, curving up at the corners even when she frowned as she was doing right then. Those lips alone were enough to make sure half the men of Brisbane thought themselves in lust with her. The other half simply didn't read the right papers. And as it turned out *his* body didn't give a hoot if they were genuine. Saliva gathered beneath his tongue. He swallowed it with such force his throat ached in protest.

His gaze moved north only to be reminded of those infamous blue eyes. The colour was mentioned every time her name was spoken aloud. The second she'd turned them his way he'd known why. They were startling—glinting, bright, sapphire blue. The kind of blue that looked as if it could cut glass. The kind of blue that could make even the most disinterested man dive right in and not care if he drowned.

Luckily for him the fact that his hormones had so spectacularly tuned into Meg Kelly's siren song was not going to be a problem to add to the reasons why he needed her as far away from there as possible. He'd long since been wise to the barb of wanting someone that would never be his to have. He had the relentless dislocation of his childhood to thank for that vital life lesson if for nothing else.

There was no getting away from the fact that she was trouble. Add friends who were of all people a TV reporter and an ex-Prime Minister's wild child to the mix and his day had just got a whole lot worse.

It was time to turn things around.

'Ms Kelly,' he said, making sure she knew without a doubt he knew who she was, 'I need you to tell me what you and your friends are really doing here.'

Her hands clenched so tight at her sides her knuckles turned white. Whatever else she was, Meg Kelly was smart. She had clued onto the fact that he wasn't about to roll out the red carpet.

'Whatever do you mean?' she asked, her spicy core all too evident in her tone.

'Wouldn't you all prefer somewhere more…rousing in which to spend your vacation?'

She afforded him a glance. There was nothing he could pinpoint to say it wasn't a perfectly amiable glance. Yet he felt the smack of it like an arrow between the eyes.

'I'd say a five-thirty wake-up call is about as *rousing* as I like things to get when on holidays,' she said.

His cheek twitched. He corralled it back into line. 'Perhaps. Yet neither you nor your friends fit into our usual demographic of guests looking to shed a few pounds, get back to nature or affect a mid-life change of life.'

He turned to find she had come to a halt. Hands on hips. She said, 'Now why would you think that we aren't here to replenish our emotional wells just as it suggests on the brochure? Is my jogging prowess really that atrocious?'

Her answer was entirely reasonable, her tone playful even.

But in the end it was those most famous of eyes that gave her away. Inside she was readying for battle. A battle he had no intention of letting her win.

He took a slow step inside her personal space, forcing her to tilt her head to look up at him. He could feel the breath from those sweet lips brushing over his chin. His blood accelerated with the kind of urgency it hadn't felt in a good many months.

'A private island off the Bahamas,' he said. 'A yacht on the Mediterranean. Las Vegas. You could be in any of those places within twenty-four hours and no jogging would be required.'

'Well, now, *Mr Jones*,' she said, her voice low and deliciously smooth. 'I'd think twice before making that your new resort motto.'

Again his cheek twitched, and again he caught it just in time. He leaned in as close as he might without risk of contact. Her chin shot up, her jaw clenched, her stunning blue eyes flashed fiercely.

His skin warmed, not like a man with a serious purpose, but like a man in heat. He pulled hard at a hunk of leg hairs through his shorts.

'Then what do you think of this one? My resorts are places of private contemplation and rejuvenation, not celebrity hunting grounds. If I see one film camera, one news van, anything that looks like a long lens glinting through the underbrush—'

'Then what?' she said, sitting on enough steam to cut him off. 'You'll assume it's somehow our fault and kick us out?'

God, how he would have loved to have done just that. But negative publicity would bring as much attention to the place, and to him, if not more.

'Of course not,' he said, turning down the heat. 'I'm only concerned that your privacy remains upheld as much as I am concerned for the privacy of all of us staying on the resort grounds.'

She watched him for a few moments, her eyes flickering

between his as if she was trying desperately to figure out his angle. She could try all she liked. She would never know. Her jaw clenched tighter again when she realised as much.

Then with what appeared to be an enormous amount of effort she breathed in, breathed out and smiled so sweetly his whole body clenched in anticipation.

'So no drunken nudie runs across the golf course. No demanding that everything we eat is first washed in Evian. No insisting a documentary crew follow our every move for a new reality TV show. Then we can stay?'

He lifted his eyebrows infinitesimally in the affirmative. 'That works for me.'

She lifted hers right on back. 'Truly, Mr Jones, the further away you stay from the marketing side of your businesses, the better.'

Then *she* took a step closer, this time purposely invading *his* personal space. He dug his toes into his shoes to stop himself from pulling away from the rush of her body heat colliding with his.

'This is your lucky day,' she said. 'Because I am here for a holiday, not to be caught out in my bikini for next month's *Chic* magazine gossip pages. This is my first real vacation in a little over two years, and I need it. I really do. So for the next few days I have every intention of having a fun time with my friends. Right here.'

She pointed at the dirt and looked up at him, daring him not to believe her. But even though she appeared to be the very picture of candour, he had too much at stake to care.

'And your friends—?'

'Exist entirely independently of me.'

It was not an ideal answer, but he'd done all he could do without holding her down and forcing her to give him her oath in blood. He said, 'Then I bid you have a wonderful stay for the remainder of the week.'

She nodded. And when she finally took a slow step back he

felt as though a set of claws was unwinding from his shirtfront. The waft of hot summer air that slid into the new space between them felt cool. Cooler at least than the remnant reminder of her body heat.

She started to walk away, talking back to him as though expecting him to follow. 'You know, there is something you could do to make sure my stay is wonderful.'

Negotiation? This he could do with far more panache than stand-over tactics. In three long strides he was back at her side. 'What's that?'

'The mini-fridge in my room is stocked with nothing but bottled water. I'd re-e-eally like you to add some chocolate to the menu. And coffee. I'm not fussy. Instant's fine. Not you personally, of course. You still have to catch up to the group ahead to survey them as to why they're here and to wish them all a nice stay too. They are already about a kilometre ahead of you so you'll have to run your little heart out to catch them up.'

And then Zach laughed, the sound echoing down the unoccupied tunnel ahead. Well, that was the very last thing he'd expected he might do after he'd first answered his phone that morning.

While her forehead frowned, her mouth curved into a smile. A smile with no artifice or strategy. A smile that reminded him of one she had aimed at him while he'd been standing in the shade of the gum trees awaiting his moment to strike. A smile that even from that distance he'd recognised as being loaded with pure, feminine summons.

He swallowed the last of his laughter and cleared his throat before saying, 'If you *had* read the brochure you might have discovered that this here's a health resort.'

'So that's a no?' she asked.

'Unfortunately, that's an absolute no.'

'Oh, well. I guess it never hurts to just ask nicely. Right?'

The hint in her tone—that he might have caught more flies with honey—was as subtle as a sledgehammer, but by the time he realised it she'd lifted her feet and jogged off along the trail, her dark curls swinging, the small muscles of her thighs and calves contracting with each charmingly wonky step. If she made it back to the main house before lunch he'd be very much surprised.

Zach slid his mobile phone from his pocket, called the resort's manager and asked him to contact the wellness facilitators to send someone to escort her back to the resort.

He flicked to his inbox. No new messages. No more missed calls. His frown lines deepened so severely he wasn't sure they'd ever fully recover.

Then he turned tail and ran in the opposite direction.

He concentrated hard on the *whump whump whump* of his feet slapping against the compacted dirt. Better that than let himself get caught up in that earlier moment of unmistakable invitation. Or the lingering spark.

He pushed himself harder. Faster. Till sweat dripped into his eyes. It didn't help.

Maybe if she'd lived down to his expectations and been the ditzy powder puff he'd fully assumed she'd be, that'd be the end of that. Instead he couldn't let go of the fact that despite her reputation she'd been out there at six in the morning with no entourage, no make-up, no airs and graces, no expectation of special treatment.

A woman who hid a sharp tongue behind her soft lips. A woman whose wickedly intelligent eyes could make lesser men forget themselves.

Zach pushed till his muscles burned.

Forgetting himself was not an option. It would mean forgetting a little girl who had no one else left in the world to protect her bar him.

His daughter. A daughter only a handful of trusted people even knew about.

No one else *could* know. Not yet. Not now.

She was so very young. Her life so recently upheaved. It was all he could do to keep her safe.

To do that he had to keep her from those in the media who would carelessly make bold, loud assumptions about her future before she ever had the chance to find her footing in the present.

He knew full well how even the most innocent of comments at that age could influence how one thought about oneself. He'd met more than one person in a position of power who'd taken some kind of sick pleasure in telling a lonely orphan kid that he was nobody and would grow up to be even less. Decades on he still remembered each and every one.

He'd never forgive himself if that happened to her because of her relationship to him. And that meant keeping her identity concealed from those for whom Meg Kelly was their most prolific source of sustenance.

Eyes on the horizon, he ran until his shins ached, his heels felt like rock, and his body was drenched in thirty-five-degree sweat.

He ran until the ugly faces from his past became a blur.

He ran until it no longer mattered how long he'd now been in lock-down in this middle-of-nowhere place trying to make his round life fit into a square hole.

He ran until he was too exhausted to be concerned that he was trying to be a father when, having never had one himself, he had no real clue what the word meant.

He ran until he could no longer quite remember the exact mix of colours it took to make up the most bewitching pair of feminine blue eyes he'd ever be likely to see.

# CHAPTER THREE

POST-BREAKFAST, post long hot shower, make-up done, hair coiffed, and changed into a vintage pink designer sundress— the exact kind of body armour she'd have preferred to have been wearing when meeting the likes of Zach Jones—Meg's skin still felt all zingy.

Not good zingy either. Uncomfortable zingy. Miffed zingy. It didn't take any kind of genius to know it was all *his* fault.

Standing in front of Waratah House she held the resort map in front of her, turning it left ninety degrees, then right. Rylie and Tabitha thought she was taking a nap, as they were. All the zinging made that absolutely impossible, so she'd snuck out.

'Excuse me?' she said to a passing couple. 'Do you happen to know which way's north?'

The gent pointed without even thinking. Amazing. Then his hand remained outstretched, his mouth agape even after she'd hit the bottom of the wide steps and was heading north towards the bulk of the resort, her ballet flats slapping against the stone path.

Her calves were so tight she winced with every step. The blisters on her heels stinging as if they were teaching her a lesson for not wearing high heels.

Message well and truly heard, she wasn't going to push her luck by going the week without her beloved caffeine as well.

She was going to find something sweet and dark and rich and bad for her if she had to hike down the mountain, flag a passing truck and barter her shoes for some at a local milk bar.

The fact that what she craved sounded a heck of a lot like Zach Jones only made her walk faster.

It really was the strangest thing. She was used to people bending over backwards to get her endorsement, to have her wear their product, mention their charity, look sideways at whatever they were touting. Not that she ever agreed unless it was something she'd advocate even without being asked.

Zach Jones, on the other hand, had all but suggested he'd really prefer it if she and her friends would just clear off. To Las Vegas, no less. As far, far away from his resort as possible seemed to be his main point.

*Far, far away from him.*

Yet there was no mistaking the zing of electricity when he'd touched her. No denying the way the tension vibrating throughout him had melted away when she'd made him laugh. No confusing the way he'd taken his time getting to know her body when she'd unthinkingly told him to take his fill.

And absolutely no doubting, whatever beef he had with her, it was very *very* personal.

She was nice, for Pete's sake! She worked her backside off. She was kind to small animals. She gave everyone a fair go. Why shouldn't she expect to be treated the same way?

It was as though the guy had been given a torch and a map pointing him right towards her Achilles heel—a terminal relic of a childhood spent doing whatever it took to get even a hint that her father cared. *That* heel couldn't be soothed with antiseptic cream and Band-Aids.

'Grrrrr!' she shouted to the wide-open sky.

When she glanced down a group of guests in matching pale green Juniper Falls Rainforest Retreat brand tracksuits doing t'ai chi on a mound of grass were looking her way. From nowhere one of them pulled out a mobile phone and took her picture.

It shouldn't have surprised her. It happened every day.

But being on holiday she'd been silly enough to let down her guard. Enter one tall, dark, handsome businessman and her usual cool had gone up in smoke. She had to pull herself together quick smart.

The kind of attention that followed a down-and-out It Girl was far worse than for one who went about her business with cheerful grace. Not only would that adversely effect the family—God, the horror of ever being on the end of *that* conversation—the one part of her life that was truly her own, her one beautiful unspoiled secret, her time volunteering at the Valley Women's Shelter, would be gone.

Zach Jones was a very lucky man. They both seemed to want the same thing—for this next week to be drama free. She'd just have to keep Rylie away from Zach, Zach away from Tabitha, and herself aware of the whereabouts of all three so that she could relax. Ha!

Meg picked what felt, and tasted, like birdseed from between her teeth. If she was looking for a reason to really not like him she realised she had one. It was his fault her belly was full of nothing bar raw oats bathed in pale soy milk, bite-sized chunks of some mysterious organic fruit and a green drink so thick and speckled it looked as if it had been scooped out of primordial ooze.

She needed chocolate. And coffee. And bad.

She pulled herself together and waved cheerfully to the group. 'Good morning, all!' she called out.

A few people waved back. Several more mobile phones went click-click before the wellness facilitator clicked his fingers loudly and reminded them it would be best to leave their mobiles in their rooms while working towards a mind free of distractions.

Then she skipped up the path as fast as her sore muscles and flat shoes would carry her.

Skirting the eastern edge of the resort grounds, Meg passed an array of cosy guest bungalows peeking out of the edge of the rainforest. One was completely covered in creepers, the next had been built on stilts above a bounty of ferns. Another bungalow had obviously been built around an existing tree. Each was more charming than the last. But unless the gingerbread house from Hansel and Gretel appeared next she wasn't slowing.

*Coffee, chocolate, coffee, chocolate*, chugged in her mind along with each step. The large outbuildings she'd seen on the map had to contain food for the staff. Food she planned on sweet-talking her way.

A handful of minutes later Meg's foot slipped a tad and she realised she was no longer on the white stone path that guided guests everywhere around the resort. Thicker, less perfectly trimmed grass slid underfoot. And the rainforest encroached more tightly on all sides.

She was so hot she was puffing like a steam train. Her brow, her underarms, and the spots behind her knees were slick with sweat. And she realised she had no idea where she was.

A gap appeared in a moss-covered rock wall peeking through the underbrush ahead. A faint path had been beaten into the grass at her feet by regular footsteps so she did all she could think to do and followed.

Barely a dozen steps beyond she found herself in a garden—tiered, and lush with wildflowers in the most amazing, vibrant colours the likes of which she'd never seen.

And beyond that…

A house. But what a simplistic word for the structure crouching silently before her.

A large octagonal structure had been built tight against a rising embankment. It had a pointed thatched roof and more windows than walls. Rope bridges led from the yard up to the front door, and then again from the front door to several separate enclosed rooms scattered haphazardly about the hill face. A meandering creek ran beneath, and a wide deck wound around the lot.

Her brother Cameron, the engineer, would go absolutely nuts for the place. She just stood there and admired the heck out of it, not noticing a rhythmic squeaking sound until it stopped.

She glanced towards the space where the noise had been to find a young girl staring at her. Her small hands were wrapped about the handles of a swing, legs locked straight as she used her feet as a brake to halt her progress through the air. Her long dark hair was pulled back by a yellow headband and flickering in the light breeze.

She must have been six or seven, around the same age as her brother, Brendan's eldest girl, but with her loose footless pink tights and pink floral shoes browned by mud she was deliciously messy where Violet and Olivia were always picture perfect. As always happened when unexpected thoughts of her favourite girls came to her, Meg's heart gave an anguished little skip. The skip was always part love, part fear.

Right now they were such innocents. But without their mum around any more to give them balance they were becoming deeply indoctrinated into the Kelly way of life. Meg's greatest hope was that somehow, some way, they would have a choice in how their lives turned out that she'd never had. And that being the granddaughters of Quinn Kelly didn't eventually smother those sweet natures for good.

'Hi,' the young girl said, and Meg blinked to find herself on the other end of a long, flat, intense stare.

Shoving her concern for the next generation deep down inside where it couldn't shake her, she took a deep breath and smiled.

'Hiya,' Meg said.

The little girl shuffled her feet through the muddy ground till her legs dangled beneath the rubber swing and her hands slid down the chains. 'I'm Ruby,' she said.

'It's a great pleasure to meet you, Ruby. I'm Meg.'

Ruby's mouth twisted as she fearlessly stared Meg down. Meg bit back a smile. She was being sized up.

When Ruby came back with 'I'm seven and a half,' she knew she'd come up to muster.

'Seven and a *half*? That's impressive. I'm a tad older than seven too, and I'm lost. Any chance you can read a map?' Meg waved hers back and forth.

Ruby merely blinked at Meg, giving her time to work out the answer for herself.

'No?' Meg slowly tucked the map back into the front of her dress. 'Fair enough. I couldn't read a map at seven any better than I can now.'

From nowhere her father's voice came to her. *How simple do you have to be not to be able to tell up from down, girl?* She placed a hand over her thudding heart and begged it to calm down.

And for good measure found herself, once again, cursing Zach Jones.

It was *his* fault the resort menu contained nothing remotely normal, thus sending her out into the blinding heat in search of sustenance. It was his indifference that had made her crave comfort chocolate in the first place. He'd started the chain reaction that was bringing up long-since-buried feelings now fanning out like a swarm of angry bees whose nest had been poked with a really big stick. She had no idea what one was meant to do to mollify angry bees, but as for her...

Her hand fell limply to her side as she sniffed the air. 'What's that heavenly smell?'

'Chocolate muffins,' Ruby said. 'My nanny cooks them. I don't like muffins much.'

'You don't like muffins? And you call yourself a seven-year-old!'

Ruby's mouth quirked ever so slightly. Her eyes narrowed for several moments before claiming, 'My dad likes them so I get her to make them for him so he can take them to work and I just eat the leftovers.'

'I see.' Meg licked her lips and looked to where the smell was coming from. The sight of that dramatic dwelling reposing peacefully, silently, privately within the forest had her letting out a long, slow, soothing breath. 'That is one amazing house you have there, Miss Ruby.'

'It's not mine. It's my dad's.'

Meg's eyes swerved back to Ruby to find her toes had slunk together, her chin had dropped and her whole body had curled into itself.

With Violet and Olivia firmly in mind, Meg made sure she had the girl's full attention before she said, 'You have your own bedroom, right? Fridge privileges. Access to the TV remote.'

Ruby thought a moment, then nodded.

'Then that means it's your house too.'

Ruby looked up at the house thoughtfully. Meg did the same, wondering how close the kitchen might be. And if she might be able to outrun the nanny. Then it occurred to her—it was mid-morning on a weekday.

She spun back to Ruby. 'Shouldn't you be at school?'

Ruby's mouth puckered into a defiant little pout and her chin lifted a good two inches. 'I have a sore throat.'

Meg's eyes widened as she let her gaze run over the swings, and the Frisbee resting next to them on the lawn. If the kid had a sore throat she'd give up chocolate for ever. Still, Ruby's rebellious streak hooked her. Maybe the kid was more like her than her nieces after all.

'A sore throat, you say.'

Ruby nodded, then added a couple of terrible attempts at a sniffle for good measure.

'You know what?' Meg said, tapping her chin with her finger. 'When I was seven and a half and got a sore throat, I found the days went so much quicker if I actually went to school. I know, sounds crazy, huh? But truly, by the time I got home I'd forgotten all about my throat and why it felt sore in the first place!'

Ruby eyed her down a moment before admitting, 'It has been a very long day.'

Meg laughed before hiding it behind a cough. 'Okay, now the lesson's done, you didn't hear this from me. But if I did stay home from school I let my mum smother me with ice cream and tuck me up with blankets on the couch while I watched daytime TV. That way she knew where I was and I felt better at the same time.'

Ruby blinked, but her expression didn't change a jot as she said, 'My mum's gone.'

'Gone?'

Ruby nodded.

And then Meg knew from the look in the kid's eyes 'gone' meant she wasn't coming back. She took a step towards the small girl and knelt down in front of her. 'Oh, sweetheart.'

Why God let some kids grow up so quick she'd never understand. Now she *did* understand.

Now she did understand the sore throat all too well. Classic 'get Daddy's attention' manoeuvre. But come on, what kind of father didn't give his little girl attention when he was the only thing she had left?

The guy obviously had no idea Ruby's attention-seeking behaviour could escalate so fast and in ways more dangerous than he would ever believe possible. Then again, maybe he knew, and maybe he simply didn't care.

Meg nibbled at her bottom lip as she glanced back to the

house. This wasn't some shell-shocked urchin at the Valley Women's Shelter happy to have a pair of warm, comforting arms around her no matter who they belonged to; this was a spunky, healthy-looking kid, surrounded by toys in a multimillion-dollar home. A home Meg was currently trespassing on.

She stood and took three steps back. 'Sweetheart, I'm sure your dad knows where the ice cream is kept too.'

This time at mention of her father Ruby sat bolt upright. 'He's busy. He has an important job with lots of people counting on him. He works all week while I'm at boarding school and only comes home weekends when I come home. But I could go get him now if I really wanted to. To tell him about my throat and all. I just don't want to.'

'He works at the resort?' Meg asked. The imaginary huffy bees were back, swirling about her head with increased volume and intensity.

Ruby said, 'He owns this one and lots more all over the world. He's going to take me on his plane and show me all the others one day. He promised. Just not right now. I have school when I'm not sick. But some day.'

Meg heard not much more than *blah blah blah* as she stared down at Ruby. The dark hair, the wary dark eyes, the natural intensity that even a supposed sore throat couldn't dampen. Once she saw the similarity it was so blaringly obvious she felt like a fool for not noticing it sooner.

Her blood pounded so loudly in her ears her voice came out rather more flat than she would have liked when she said, 'You're Zach Jones's daughter.'

Ruby's eyes flashed with the first spark of real enthusiasm and Meg knew she was right even before the girl said, 'Do you know my dad?'

Did she know Ruby's dad? Not a jot.

*Zach Jones had a daughter. A daughter whose mother was gone.*

Hang on, he had a daughter with a mother Rylie hadn't even known about and Rylie was such a proficient muckraker she probably already knew who really killed JFK and was awaiting the right moment to reveal all.

He had a daughter who was at home sick, or pretending to be. And the only reason Meg saw that Ruby might not want him to know was in case he only proved to her he didn't give enough of a damn about her to care.

Meg's fists clenched at her sides, a scene to end all scenes threatening to erupt from within.

She'd seen it time and again listening to stories told by countless women at the Valley Women's Shelter—men, focused on themselves, on their work, on their local bar, who blithely disregarded their children's need to be loved. Hell, she'd seen it with her own eyes. She'd felt it with her own heart.

Thankfully she'd taken measures in order for it never to happen to a child of her own. Conclusive measures. Unfortunately none of that helped her from feeling threadbare watching neglect happen to someone else.

Her gaze cleared to find Ruby was still looking up at her with her father's uncompromising gaze. And while she knew the second she'd found out who Ruby's dad was she should have walked away, she still said, 'As a matter of fact I met your dad only this morning.'

'What did he say about me?'

*What did he say? Well, he was actually pretty darned arrogant. He said back off. He said lie low. He said...*

Meg's fingers unfurled from her palms. He'd said he was determined that the privacy of *all* staying at the resort remained upheld.

He was talking about himself. Him and his anonymous daughter. A daughter who no longer had a mum.

She closed her eyes to hide the mortification that she had

beamed her flirty little smile at a man who'd lost his…wife? Lover? Ex? What did it matter? He'd lost the mother of his child.

Far too many adult-only concepts to share with a seven-and-a-half-year-old.

Instead, she gathered up her cheeriest smile and said, 'I'm such a yabberer I'm sure I didn't let him get a word in edgewise. If he'd had the chance I'm sure he would have said plenty. How could he not? A daughter who lets her nanny make chocolate muffins even though she doesn't like them but her dad does. You're a gem!'

Ruby tried for a smile herself, but her slight shoulders drooped, giving her away. Meg's heart twitched far harder than she liked for the little girl. She couldn't let herself get attached. There was no way it could end well.

She opened her mouth to say her long-overdue goodbye when something out of the corner of Ruby's eye had her springing from the rubber seat like a jack-in-the-box. 'I have to go!' she shrieked.

Meg glanced up at one of the small detached rooms to see the wooden blinds snap shut. A flash of silver hair, not dark and curling, meant her heart didn't stop, but it certainly thundered hard enough for her to know she'd pushed her luck far enough.

Ruby took a last quick step forward. 'You won't tell my dad I was on the swings, will you?'

Meg laughed. 'Not a chance.' Probably best for her continued health if she didn't bring any of this up with the man at all.

'I won't tell him you were here either, okay?' Ruby said.

Meg laughed again. 'That would be fine with me.'

Ruby gave a quick, sweet, girlish wave, and then ran off towards the flickering blinds and freshly baked chocolate muffins, her long hair swinging behind her as she skipped up onto the longest rope bridge and was soon consumed by her astonishing home.

Meg spun on her heel and vamoosed back along the make-shift path, through the gap in the rock wall and out onto the manicured grass of the resort proper. She headed in a direction she thought was probably south. If it wasn't, someone would put her to rights soon enough.

Her breaths shook as the adrenalin she'd held at bay finally spilled over.

What if when she'd smiled her flirty little smile Zach had smiled back? What if when she'd made him laugh she'd let herself join in? What if when he'd touched her he'd liked it too much to let her go? What if things had happened between them and she'd gone in deep before he'd decided to let her know that he had a little girl?

It had taken her nearly thirty years to get to the point where she finally felt as if she had a handle on her celebrity. There was no way she would knowingly expose a child to it.

It gave her the perfect excuse to wash her hands of the whole situation, get on with her holiday, and forget the lot of them even existed.

Damn him! He'd started this. By including her in his convoluted duplicity he'd made her a part of it. And having met Ruby, talked to her, looked in her eyes and seen herself mirrored right on back she couldn't let it go.

He might not know it yet, but Zach Jones needed her help. And for the sake of a bright, sweet, adoring little girl who needed him it appeared he was going to get it.

# CHAPTER FOUR

MEG rushed to find the Wellness Building to meet the girls for that day's internal reflection class. While they tried to locate their *chi* she had every intention of pretending to meditate while dreaming up the perfect way to broach the subject of his daughter when she bumped into Zach Jones again.

With an objective in sight, despite the flat shoes and sore muscles, she had a decided spring in her step when she rounded a thick bank of head-high reeds.

Until she came face to face with a human rear-end.

Male it was, bent from the waist. Knee-length khaki cargo shorts sculpted a magnificent rear belonging to a tanned, solid man fiddling with something in a cooler. And even though she couldn't see the colour of his hair, or the breadth of his shoulders, or the shape of his arms or any of the other bits that seemed to be permanently imprinted on her mind, she knew it was Zach Jones.

Her heart hammered in her ears, and her palms grew slick. She and *chi* might well be incompatible, but there was simply no denying this man's life force was so potent it radiated from his very pores.

He stood, stretching out his limbs. Sunlight glistened lovingly off the expanse of perfectly sculpted muscle, as he was naked from the hips up.

His large hand was wrapped about a condensation-covered bottle of beer. He tilted his head and downed half the bottle in one slow go.

Meg's gaze remained stuck on the muscles of his throat, pulsing with each large swallow, with each heavy thud of her heart against her ribs.

Once done, he let out a deep, satisfied *ah-h-h* that seemed to echo across the distance between them, then he wiped a tanned, muscular arm across his forehead. He might as well have been sliding that arm around her waist for the reaction that shuddered through her.

'I must have done something horrible in a previous life to deserve this,' she murmured beneath her breath.

As though the slow, hot, summer air carried her whisper to him too, he stilled. Then his body twisted at the waist until his eyes locked on hers.

The colour of expensive dark chocolate. The colour of strong espresso coffee. Right there in those eyes she saw everything she hungered for. Unfortunately half a second later she also caught the full force of his disapproval simmering beneath the urbane surface.

Then she remembered why.

She'd been seriously kidding herself in thinking she might be able to convince this man he needed her help. If he had any idea she'd stumbled upon his daughter he'd probably already decided which exact spot in the surrounding rainforest would be the best place to hide her cold dead body.

Her tongue darted nervously out to slide along the chip in her tooth. His gaze slipped to watch the movement, his dark eyes turning almost black.

She was pinned to the spot, unable to move as he reached out and grabbed a T-shirt from beside the cooler, then slid it on in that particular way men did such things. The soft cotton casually sculpted his muscles and if at all possible he was even more intimidating fully dressed.

When Meg finally found her voice again she said, 'This isn't the way to the Wellness Building.'

'No,' Zach said, his deep voice rumbling through her very bones. 'It's not.'

She frowned. 'Where am I exactly?'

'The lake.'

'There's a lake?' she asked. 'Wow, I really don't know how to read a map.'

'I'll give you a hint,' he said. 'It's the big blue bit at the bottom with "Lake" written in the middle of it.'

Her cheeks, if possible, grew warmer still. Her voice was dripping with sarcasm when she said, 'Thanks. You are as ever the gracious host.'

'Was there something else you wanted from me?'

'Look, you can relax. I really didn't mean to invade your beer-drinking time. Stumbling upon you was pure accident.'

'Obviously fifty acres isn't quite as much room as it sounds.'

'So it seems.' She began to back away. 'If you'd be so kind as to point the way—'

'I was just about to head out for a row. Want to join me?'

Her feet stumbled to a halt. 'Excuse me?'

While his eyes seemed to skim the view behind her in search of prying eyes, he waved an inviting arm towards the end of a jetty that was shrouded in tall reeds wilting in the heavy heat. 'After many months of wrangling with a guy on the end of the phone, my old row boat has finally arrived from a storage lock-up in Sydney and I'm taking her for a spin. You game?'

Game for *what*? Concrete shoes? A speedboat containing Rylie, Tabitha and their ready packed bags? Or worse, an intimate boat ride with a man whom she couldn't want; who didn't much like her; who still managed to give her uncontrollable stomach flutters that only grew more intense with each and every meeting.

A whimper from her self-preservation instincts had her licking her lips in preparation to say thanks but no thanks, until her mind filled with the memory of a sprawling house in the forest, and a lonesome, brown-haired girl with his eyes.

The most decisive reason for her to walk away was the one reason she finally could not.

'Sounds lovely,' she said with the distant but polite smile she used on those who shamelessly accosted her in the fruit and veg section of her local supermarket asking for an autograph.

His eyes darkened all the more, as though he knew it too, but he still slipped the strap of the cooler over his shoulder, then turned and walked towards the lake.

Meg did all she could do and followed.

Once she rounded the thick reeds she saw a small, fat, wooden boat bobbing merrily on what turned out to be a massive lake. The boat's mission-brown paint was faded, the red floor was scratched and fatigued, and the benches had seats worn into them from a lifetime of accommodating bottoms.

It was ancient and imperfect. So not the kind of sea-faring-type vessel any of the men in her family would be caught dead in. She loved it.

She crouched down and ran a hand over the stern to find it smooth and soft. 'She's really yours?'

She glanced up to find Zach watching the rhythmic movement of her hand. She curled her fingers into her palms and pushed herself back to standing.

He had to bend past her to unhook the rope from the jetty. She leant back to give him room, but not far enough not to catch his scent. She breathed it in. She couldn't help herself. It was drinkable.

He wound the rope around his hand and elbow, muscles

contracting with every easy swing. '*Marilyn*'s been a faithful companion since I was about eighteen.'

'*Marilyn*? Are you serious?'

His cheek twitched into one of those almost smiles that gave a girl unfair hope there might be more to come. 'She came with the name.'

'Sure she did. You haven't thought to trade her in for a fancy schmancy yacht with all the trimmings?'

'I've got one of those too. A hundred footer moored off St Barts right now.'

'The *Norma Jean*?'

And there it was. The holy grail. His mouth tilted into a slow smile complete with brackets that arced around his beautiful mouth and creases fanning out from the edges of his delicious dark eyes. Boy, were they worth the wait.

'I called her *Lauren*.'

'Bacall?'

'It was my mother's name.'

Of course it was. Meg looked down at her shoes instead of into those too discerning eyes. 'And a tad extravagant to use for a paddle about the lake.'

'Just a tad.'

She glanced up, and for a brief moment Meg swore she saw a glint warm his dark eyes before it was gone. He ought not to bandy those about unless he meant them. It was hard for a girl not to get ideas.

Zach threw the rope into the boat, then held out a hand. Unless she wanted him to know her mouth turned dry at the thought of him touching her again, she had no choice but to take it.

A slide of natural warmth so out of sync with the constant cool in his eyes leapt from his hand to hers. She gripped on tight as she stepped into the wobbly vessel, but the second she had her backside planted on a bench she let go.

He stepped in after her and tossed her a cosy, red-checked, woollen blanket. It was too soft to be freshly washed, too fluffy to be new. It was the kind of thing a man might keep at the end of his bed, or the back of his couch. She imagined it covering his long bare legs as he lay back—

She cleared her throat. 'What exactly am I meant to do with this?'

'Slide it beneath your backside or you'll get splinters,' he ordered. 'That or that dress of yours will be shredded.'

Of course. So what if it carried a faint lingering scent of him—he hadn't given it to her as some sort of come-on. It was near forty degrees out! She lifted her backside and planted it back on the folded blanket.

'This too,' he demanded, throwing her a soft khaki fisherman's hat, which was frayed to the point of falling apart.

She gripped the hat between tightly coiled fists. All that commanding was beginning to get on her nerves. Her voice was sugary sweet as she asked, 'And where, pray tell, am I supposed to put this?'

His hands stilled. He glanced up. The smile hovered; the glint loomed.

And it hit her as if the lake had suddenly thrown up a tidal wave over the boat. Zach Jones might prefer her to be far, far away, but a certain part of him took a purely masculine pleasure in having her close by.

She licked her suddenly dry lips and blinked up at him. The smile faded and the glint disappeared without a trace.

'Just stick the thing on your head, will you?' he growled.

'Aye aye, Captain,' she muttered.

The hat smelled like the sea and fitted over her head like velvet. Atop her sateen cocktail dress it must have looked a treat.

He slapped an old cap atop his curls, shoved a foot against the jetty, pushing them off before easing down onto his own bench.

She tucked her knees tight together and pretended to pay attention to the ripples fanning out through the flat silver water, and not how close his knees were to hers, as he picked up the oars and pushed them effortlessly out into the lake.

Within seconds the wilting reeds shielded them from the rest of the world and they were alone.

The sun beat down upon Meg's back, making her glad of the hat. The soft swish of the displaced water created a slow, even rhythm. And as Zach built up a sweat every breath in gave her a fresh taste of his clean cotton clothes and some indefinable heat that was purely him.

Like this, all easy silence, all effortless masculinity, it was hard not to imagine he might be exactly the kind of guy she could happily spend oodles of time with. A beautiful sailor who slept in late, didn't believe in making plans, and just went with the flow.

It was hard to believe he owned and ran a huge multinational business that no doubt took long hours away from home. That took the kind of relentless ambition that meant everything else in life came a distant second. Family included.

Her brother Brendan was trying to do the single father thing. Running the Kelly Investment Group and raising two young daughters. And though she'd never tell him so to his face she knew in her heart the half of his life he was letting slip from his grasp was his girls.

Zach's eyes slid from some point over her shoulder to find hers. His dark, deep, unfathomable eyes. Their gazes held a beat longer than polite. Two beats. She held on, trying to sense regret, bereavement, concern for his little girl. All she got for her trouble was the sense that *she* was getting more entangled by the second.

She breathed in slow and deep through her nose. Could she ask him about Ruby now? Should she? Would she be doing it to be helpful? Or did she know he'd react badly, so she could use Ruby to save herself from feeling the way she did when he looked at her like that?

In the end she lost her nerve and said, 'So you've been on two runs today and now rowing. I feel tired just thinking about it.'

He went back to staring at the water. 'I like to be on the move. Eyes forward, nothing but the wind and the sun to keep me company. It clears the head. If you don't run or do yoga, what do you do?'

Mmm. She had proven that day that exercise made her hurt, and wobble and crave sugar.

'To clear my head?' she said. 'Disco music.'

One dark eyebrow rose and his hot, dark gaze slid back to hers. 'Disco?'

'Blaring from my iPod directly into my ears. Ten seconds into any Donna Summer or Leo Sayer song and the rest of the world fades away.'

They said music soothed the savage breast, and so it had done for her, many a time in her teens when she might have otherwise given in to mounting frustration with her life and done something she'd later regret. Ultimately disco could only soothe so much hurt.

'Even if you're lying on the couch your feet can't help but bop. Your head clears of everything but the music. It's kind of like exercise only more relaxed.'

When he merely blinked at her she gave him her 'greeting line' smile, with a full showing of teeth, twinkling eyes and dimples. 'You're going to give it a go the moment you go home, I can tell.'

And while most people, even members of her own family, could no longer tell when she was 'on' and when she was just being herself, the slow rise of the corner of his mouth told her she hadn't fooled him for a nanosecond.

How did he *do* that? How was *he* able to see straight through her? Again she felt exposed, as if she'd walked into a ballroom with her dress tucked into the back of her undies.

He stopped rowing and the boat's sleek glide slowed so that she rocked forward on her seat.

'I'm game. I'll give disco a go,' he said. 'But only if you take the oars right now.'

She imagined splinters. She imagined aches in even more as yet undiscovered muscles. She imagined her hands brushing against his as she took him up on his offer.

'I'll pass.'

Zach laughed. The column of his throat moved sexily beneath the sound. It faded all too soon in the wide-open space, and his eyes once again grew so dark they drew her in while they pushed her away.

She wondered if he could see the same impulse in hers.

She wondered what might happen if they both pulled at the exact same time.

His large hands curled back around the worn old wooden sticks and he slid the oars back into the water, pushing off with such grace and power Meg was sent to the back of her seat. Smart move. Pushing was much more sensible.

A cooling wind fluttered past her warm face. Streaks of gold dappled the rippling silver water where the sun burst through fluffy white clouds. The edges of the lake were completely obscured by the thick, green rainforest spilling into water.

Time stretched and contracted. She realised she had no idea how long she'd been gone. Or why he'd taken her out there onto the lake alone in the first place.

'I don't mean to say this isn't entirely pleasant, and so generous for the owner to give me such a personal tour of the blue bit on the bottom of the map,' she said, 'but how long were you planning for this outing to be?'

'We can turn back now if you're getting too hot.'

Only then did she even consider that, while he looked like a sun god, she must have looked an utter treat—in his floppy hat, her hair plastered to her face after her hike to the end of the resort and back, her Irish skin pink as a rose.

She wasn't used to feeling so discomposed; her voice was rather sharper than she intended when she said, 'I'm only thinking of you.'

He raised a solitary eyebrow. 'You're thinking of *me*?'

*More than you know.* 'Many a poor fellow has ended up reportedly engaged to me after spending far less time in my company, and I have been made quite aware how highly you regard your privacy.'

'I do at that. Which is why I have not left any stones unturned in an effort to protect it. You needn't worry on my behalf.'

'I need not?'

His cheek twitched. 'The forest has eyes. Trackers flushing out the perimeter in search of poachers.'

'Poachers? There's nothing for miles bar a few birds, some lizards and a bunch of resort guests in matching tracksuits.'

And then she got it. Her jaw dropped. 'Are you saying you have people posted about the place to ward off anyone turning up here to take a photo of *me*?'

'We both know it's not you I am trying to protect.'

His gaze was steady. Not a hint of humour. Not a hint of a smile. While Meg's cheeks grew so flushed even her teeth began to feel hot.

*Ruby*.

Of course. This, *all* this, the thoughtful blanket, the helpful hat, the beautiful scenery, the long brooding looks, were all about his daughter.

He wasn't thinking of her at all.

Zach couldn't remember a time in recent history when he'd been so furious. And mostly with himself. For since the moment he'd turned and found Meg Kelly standing on the jetty in her completely inappropriate pink party dress he'd thought of nothing but her.

He hadn't been exaggerating when saying he rowed to clear his head. The sport had saved him from being just another scrappy, angry kid with a chip on his shoulder and had turned him into a man who knew how to focus, create goals and push himself to the absolute limits to achieve them.

He needed a clear head now more than ever. The St Barts government was still playing hardball with the building inspections on his latest site. It was balanced on a knife's edge with his only achievable contributions controlled by the whims of local telephone operators. Because he was trying to run a multimillion-dollar international business from a laptop and a three-room bungalow in the middle of nowhere.

For Ruby. So she could be in a familiar place. So she knew her world was solid and secure. Ruby, who, despite his best intentions, had been compromised.

When Ruby's nanny had called to say she'd had a visitor he'd almost popped a gasket, believing the woman had blatantly gone out of her way to punish him for not bowing and scraping and rolling out the red carpet. When he'd calmed down he'd realised the only way she could possibly have found Ruby in such a short amount of time was by stumbling out of the forest in one great cosmic accident.

Either way, rather than putting himself as far from Meg Kelly as he could, he now had no choice but to be on her like a rash until the day she left.

So as far as he was concerned Meg Kelly could sit out in the hot summer sun all day, her knees knocked in chagrin, her ridiculous dress getting splattered with water spray, his dilapidated green hat sloping low over her face, leaving only her down-turned mouth in sight.

Except of course it had only given him enough time

studying that mouth of hers to know it was all natural. And so was she. Her skin was as pale as it ought to have been with a smattering of freckles across her nose make-up couldn't, and needn't, hide. Her curves were as God gave her with apparently a little bit of help from occasional disco. The woman was pure, wholesome femininity and irrepressible audacity and ingenuous sex appeal.

He was beginning to wonder if she'd been sent to test him. After dedicating his entire adulthood to purely selfish pursuits, was he really man enough, strong enough, self-sacrificing enough to resist her? To put aside his needs for the needs of one girl?

When Ruby had landed on his doorstep, her small hand held tight in the hand of a weary-looking social worker, she was alone in the world, orphaned and in shock. She'd been on the verge of replaying his cold, lonely, disjointed past through her future. There was no way he could let that happen to her and look himself in the mirror ever again.

But had he been the right person to save her?

He let out a long, hard breath and realised that beneath the brim of his hat Meg was watching him. Those sharp blue eyes constantly calculating.

He should have known better than to believe what he'd heard about her in the press. Assuming she'd be a lightweight adversary had been a huge tactical error. It served him right that it had come back to bite him where he'd feel it most.

The ante had been upped. It was time he showed his cards.

He used the oar on the starboard side to head the boat back to civilisation. 'So, Ms Kelly.'

'Yes, Zach.'

'What possessed you to trespass inside my private residence this morning?'

'Your yard,' she shot back as though the words had been waiting to explode from inside her. 'I never went any farther than the very, *very* edge of your yard. Once I knew it was yours I was out of there.'

'I don't give a flying fig if you were sitting on my rooftop. What the hell were you doing so far from the boundary of the resort that we now have to have this conversation?'

'Please,' she scoffed, her voice cool, her eyes electric. 'It was an honest mistake. It's not like there's a ten-foot-high electric fence separating the two.'

'There's a rock wall and a whopping great big gate!'

'A gate? Not today there wasn't.'

Zach swore beneath his breath. That meant Ruby had been out again. What would it take to make the kid understand that it was for her own safety that she stay put and not gallivant about the resort? Hell, all he wanted was to keep her clear of those who would have her believe that because her childhood had not been perfect she was damaged from the start. He was fast running out of ideas.

The boat rocked beneath them as he pulled harder on the oars. Meg's hands whipped out to the sides and held on tight.

'For a woman who thinks lying on the couch listening to disco is a form of exercise, the hike to my place makes no sense.'

'Fine,' she said, throwing her arms in the air, rocking the boat so that he had to steady them with some fancy flicking of the oars. 'I was casing the grounds in search of chocolate.'

'Give me a break—'

She lifted her chin as though a haughty bearing could make the words seem less undignified. 'I warned you. Caffeine is a staple in my diet. And I never expected to have to go cold turkey this week. So actually it was all your fault that I ended up there.'

His laughter again came from nowhere and again surprised the hell out of him. And a few local birds that screeched as they scattered from the treetops nearby.

Gorgeous, plainspoken and stimulating. Delilah herself couldn't possibly have been more tempting.

Thankfully he'd long since proven himself invulnerable to the lure of apparently easy promise. He'd learnt early on not to trust the feeling as far as he could throw it. So long as the bright, breezy, easy warmth in this corner of the world hadn't rotted away his indoctrinated dubiousness he'd be just fine.

# CHAPTER FIVE

'ZACH,' Meg said, and by the tone in her voice Zach wasn't sure he'd be keen on what came next.

'Okay,' she continued, 'I was hoping to get around to the fact more gracefully, but since I have no idea how long you intend to keep me hostage out there let's get to the point. You have a seven-year-old daughter named Ruby who, it seems, nobody knows anything about. There. Now it's out there. So what do we do from here?'

Zach slapped an oar into the water at such a rough angle it covered them both in wet spray. 'Don't get cute, Ms Kelly.'

She waved a hand across her face as though swatting away a fly. 'Stop being so formal. I've practically been in your house, I'm on first-name basis with your daughter, and you've seen me in this hat. Call me Meg.'

Through gritted teeth he said, 'If you saw yourself in that hat you wouldn't be half so concerned.'

She blinked up at him. Hell. So much for proving himself invulnerable. Now she was sitting there gawping at him as if he'd outright told her how lovely she was.

'Okay then, *Meg*,' he said, his voice coarse, 'if formalities are now to be tossed aside, then I'll be blunt.'

'All this time you were being polite?' Something in his expression must have made her catch her tongue. She mimed zipping her mouth shut. That mouth…

'I want you to tell me in avid detail about every second you spent in my daughter's company. And don't miss a moment.'

She blinked at him. 'Relax, Zach. We didn't talk about sex, drugs or rock and roll if that's what you're worried about.'

Sex? *Drugs*? He ran a hard hand over the back of his neck, which suddenly felt as if it were on fire.

'She's seven, for Pete's sake. The *High School Musical* soundtracks are as extreme as her rock and roll tastes go.'

She hooked a thumbnail between her teeth and looked up at him from beneath her thick dark lashes. His gut sank so fast he pressed his feet into the bottom of the boat. What wasn't she telling him?

By age seven he'd already stolen his first pack of cigarettes, he'd kissed his first girl, he'd been hit so hard by one so-called parent he'd gone to school with a hand print bruised into the back of his thigh.

He'd known Ruby barely seven months. There was a fair chance he didn't know his kid at all. His voice was unsteady as he said, 'Ruby's situation is…sensitive, therefore it's imperative that I'm kept informed.'

'Just informed? Not present? Not available? Not her first port of call?'

The riddles finally became too much and his frustration got the better of him. 'Meg, I'm her father. If I don't know everything I'm going to imagine the worst and then go quietly out of my mind.'

A smile spread across her face—a radiant thing that made the sun beaming down upon the lake pale into insignificance. 'Well, now, that's just about the best news I've heard all day.'

He shook his head, hoping for clarity. None came. 'What on earth are you talking about?'

'The fact that you *want* to know is a good thing. A wonderful thing.'

She even reached out and patted his hand, as if he'd accidentally given her the password to a treasure he didn't even know existed. It wasn't the kind of touch he wanted from her.

'Then hurry up and tell me.'

'I'm not going to break her confidence that way. Come on.'

Zach glanced at the clouds above Meg's head. Who in heaven had he screwed over to be made to live through this day?

'Trust me,' she said, 'every girl needs her mysteries, especially from her father. It's character building. So long as she knows you care enough to *want* to get to the bottom of them, to the bottom of her, then you have nothing to worry about.'

*Nothing to worry about.*

She couldn't possibly have known that of all the four-word combinations that could placate his exasperation with her, that was it.

Still, time and again in his life, just when he'd begun to get comfortable, that was when fate pulled the rug out from under him. Foster families he'd felt as if he'd connected with had let him go. His knee had given way a week before the World Championships and he'd been forced into early retirement from competitive rowing. The momentum and success of his resorts had him finally living his life in such an easy groove, then along came Ruby.

He couldn't accept things could be that simple. That certain. There always had to be a catch. What was he missing?

*Aw, hell.*

'What did you tell your friends about her?'

'Nothing!'

'One thing I've learned from Ruby is that girls like to talk to their friends. A lot. About everything.'

'We do. A lot. But here's the thing—I have the feeling the

reason you accosted me this morning was tied up with wanting to keep your private life separate from your working life. And Ruby would naturally be a big part of that. Right?'

He didn't say no.

'If so, believe me, I'm not going to be the one to out her. She's your only secret kid, I assume. Lone heiress to all this?'

Zach still didn't say no.

Meg said, 'Well, I know better than anyone what she'd have in store for her if the world found out. I wouldn't bring it on any young girl.'

Crazy as it sounded, he believed her. 'Thank you.'

'My absolute pleasure.' She smiled. That lush mouth. Those stunning blue eyes. He had a sudden need to know what they'd look like bathed in moonlight as she spilled apart in sheer pleasure in his arms.

He hooked the oars back into their loops and aimed for the resort, and every stroke felt as if he were pulling them through wet cement. 'You seem perfectly comfortable in the limelight. Are you implying that's all an act?'

'Oh, no, did that just sound all woe is me? Please tell me it didn't. Don't get me wrong, I know I'm blessed in, oh, so many ways. And I am perfectly at peace with the contradictions that came with being notable. But I wasn't born twenty-nine and world wise. You haven't heard the story of my glittering debut?'

Zach shook his head.

'Well, here it is. I must have been three at the most. My father was giving a press conference to announce that he'd bought the George Street building in which the Kelly Investment Group was housed and was renaming the thing Kelly Tower. Mum had taken us all along to see him in action. All trussed up for the big occasion, my hair in ringlets, wearing my favourite navy velvet dress and black patent shoes, I got away from her. I made it to the podium mid-announcement, clambered up, tugged on my father's trousers and whistled through the gap in my front teeth that I needed to tinkle. Needless to say my father wasn't all that impressed at being upstaged, but the press ate it up. I haven't been able to tinkle since without the world knowing about it.'

Her smile was cheeky, but as he seemed able to do with this woman from the outset he felt the undercurrent stronger than the surface words. On the outside it was a cute story about a girl and her dad. For her it was a story of innocence lost.

He pulled the oars harder through the water. 'Just because a spotlight follows you doesn't mean you have to perform for it.'

She raised both eyebrows in challenge. 'You really believe that? Do you really want to know the God's honest truth? Or are you pushing my buttons in an effort to continue to punish me for the whole Ruby thing?'

He felt a smile coming, but this time didn't bother trying to put a stop to it. 'Both.'

'Fine.' She took a breath. 'The only reasons I am telling you any of this is recompense for Ruby. Okay?'

'Okay.'

'Fame is a funny old thing. It's not like I've done anything to deserve being remembered. I haven't invented something, or cured anything or broken any world records. But my name has brand recognition, which gives me not only a certain power, but responsibility as well. Say the name Kelly and what do you think?'

Wealth. Charm. Beauty. But also excessive influence. Secrets. Lies. Scandal. Everything he wanted Ruby nowhere near.

She didn't wait for him to answer. 'I had to figure out early on how to deal with all that baggage. I have no interest in running the company like Brendan. Or owning the city like Cameron. And the rush Dylan feels every time a new client is lured into the KInG net is a mystery to me. I wouldn't even begin to know what drives King Quinn himself. But what I can offer with a splash of perfume, a flash of designer skirt and a dash of feminine glamour is a much-needed counterpoint to the excess of testosterone my family exudes. A way to use some of that power for the greater good. And, boy, am I good at it. So good I could sell tickets. But unless you know a guy with a good line in wigs and fake noses it's twenty-four hours, seven days a week, barely a holiday in sight.'

'Why do it at all?'

She blinked, clearly thinking him obtuse. 'For them. For each other.'

'For your family?' That kind of self-sacrifice was something he was only just beginning to understand.

'Jobs change. Friends come and go. Family is where you begin and where you end. My brothers may appear to be the kings of the jungle, but deep down they have the hearts of big kittens. They need me as much as I need them. And no matter what part we play all of us are working towards the same goal.'

'The succecss of your father's business.'

'No. For our family to be happy. The business success is a side effect. I certainly don't dance to my father's tune, if that's what you mean.'

'Is that what I said?'

She frowned deeply. 'It's what you intimated, isn't it? To be fair, I did once. Then a time came when I became a right little tearaway. The things I got up to would make your eyes water. Then I grew up. Took charge of my life. And decided making love and not war was the only way forward.'

'Who knew the life of a society princess was lived on the front line?'

Her frown faded away, but her eyes remained locked on his, a tad wider than normal, as though she couldn't quite believe she was telling him all of this. 'You can mock me all you like, but in offering a corner of myself to those who are interested,

I am able to use my money, my influence and my time helping some of the less trendy, less telethon-appropriate organisations I believe need all the help they can get, which is extremely satisfying.'

'I wasn't mocking you. I—'

What? *Envy you your infamously close family?* Like hell he was going to tell her that.

Not knowing how to ask, he instead said, 'Moving on.'

'Excellent idea.' She let out a deep breath and leant forward, just a touch, but enough that when her mouth curved into an all-new smile, a luscious, flirtatious, brain-numbing smile, he felt it like nothing else. If her life really was lived on a battle-ground, that mouth was as good a weapon as they came.

'Am I off the hook?' she asked.

He slowed his strokes, not quite ready to return to land. To real life. To the other side of the battle from her. 'Just one last thing. Tell me how you got the chip in your tooth.'

She crossed her eyes as her tongue slid to the gap. His hands gripped the oars for dear life.

'It's so tiny. How did you even notice it?'

'I happen to be an extremely perceptive man.'

Her eyes slid to his, warm, tempting, wondering just how perceptive he might be. Unfortunately he was perceptive enough.

As she slid her tongue back into her mouth her teeth scraped slowly over her lips and her nostrils flared as she let out a slow, shaky breath. He knew he wasn't the only one feeling the impossible zing between them. He also knew she was wishing with all her might that he hadn't noticed a thing.

She tilted her chin up a fraction before shaking her hair off her shoulders in a move meant to distract him from the fact that for the first time since he'd met her she was no longer looking him in the eye. 'How else would a party girl chip a tooth but on a glass of champagne? On the upside, it was truly excellent champagne.'

He laughed softly as he was meant to do. Her eyes flickered to his and her smile was grateful.

After a few long, loaded moments, Meg asked, 'I just... I'd like to know one thing too. Did Ruby tell you I was there?'

He shook his head. 'Her nanny.'

She nodded, then looked down at her paint-chipped finger-nails with an all-new smile on her face. A secret smile. An honest smile. One reserved for Ruby.

And from nowhere Zach felt something the likes of which he'd never felt in his entire life—the most profound kind of pride that a woman such as her thought so highly of his little girl.

Meg's tongue kept straying to the itty-bitty chip in her tooth.

What had she been thinking, fessing up to all that guff in some great unstoppable stream of consciousness? Nobody wanted to see the workings behind the wizard. It ruined the fantasy. It seemed all she needed was a man who looked her in the eye and asked about the real her, and it was fantasy be damned.

Thank goodness she'd been rational enough to pull back when she had. There were some parts of her life not for public consumption.

If she wanted to continue volunteering at the 'less trendy, less telethon-appropriate' Valley Women's Shelter she had to keep it underground too. Every woman needed her mystery, and every public figure needed their sanctuary, even if it meant she had to truss herself up in a blonde wig, red liptick, brown contacts, and tight second-hand acid-wash jeans circa 1985.

If she was to remain Brisbane's favourite daughter she had to pretend the part of her life in which she'd attempted to leave the spotlight had never happened. She felt lucky much of her memory of that time was a blur of flashing lights—from the nightclub, the police car, the hospital.

As to the way she had finally taken control of her life? If she planned on going through life with a spring in her step and a smile on her face she knew it was best not to revisit the choices she'd made back then ever again.

It was done. It was for the best. Move on.

So Zach Jones—stubborn, pushy, scarily insightful Zach Jones; the guy who saw through her so easily that every time they met she had to chase him deeper into the darkest recesses of herself in order to drive him back out—could just take a step back.

Besides, her big mission had been to sort him out, not the other way around. *He* was the one with the rebellious daughter. *He* was the one who'd lost someone close. *He* was the one who needed help.

As she'd seen real social workers do, she started slowly, easing her way to the point so as not to scare him away.

'So Ruby was home sick from school,' she said. 'Does that happen a lot?'

Zach's cheek clenched and the look in his eyes made her wonder if he might not be deciding whether Operation Dispose of Meg might have to be put into action after all.

'I ran away from home once when I was a little older than her,' she pressed. Though she kept back the part where she got to the corner of the street, sat there for a good hour before she went home, only to find nobody had even noticed she was gone.

'She told you she had a sore throat?' he asked, taking baby steps her way.

'She sure did.'

She bit her lip. Argh! Had she broken a confidence? No, she'd told Ruby she wouldn't tell her dad she was home from school, and that had been taken out of her hands by the nanny. Phew. She'd make sure the kid knew it the next time…

Only then did it hit Meg there wouldn't be a next time. She believed Zach wasn't kidding when he said he'd hired security to case the perimeter of the resort, so he'd probably already commissioned twenty-foot-high fences around the house as well.

If she were in Zach's shoes she'd keep his kid as far away from her as she possibly could.

Still, the thought of never seeing Ruby again made her heart give an all too familiar little twinge. But this wasn't about her. Then again, maybe, just maybe, as a nice little side effect, if she helped Zach get Ruby on track then she could stop those darned heart twinges for good.

He watched her with those clever dark eyes that made her feel as if she were melting from the inside out and he rowed.

She merely sat there and waited.

It paid off.

He took a deep breath, narrowed his eyes, then with all the enthusiasm of a man with a knife pressed to his ribs to make him talk, he said, 'She rang Felicia this morning, claiming a sore throat. Felicia called a cab to bring her home. When I heard my first thought was that it was a ruse. Then I wasn't sure. Do you think…?'

He shook his head and pressed the oars deeper into the water.

It more than paid off. Had Zach Jones just asked her for advice? She was shocked it had come so easily. But boy, was she ready to—

*Who the heck was Felicia?* Another woman in Zach's life? Meg wrapped her fingers around the bench to stop from tipping right off. 'Felicia is…?'

'The nanny.'

She all but laughed with relief. When Zach's eyes narrowed, she babbled, 'I had a nanny once. I told her I was adopted. She told a friend, who spilled the news to the press. Wow, I'd completely forgotten about that. Mum was so upset. And my father...' She shook her head to clear that image before the rest of the memory filtered through. 'Let's just say no more nannies came through the place.'

Zach's eyes widened a fraction. He really had no clue that young girls were as much about sugar and spice as they were about snakes and snails and puppy dogs' tails. It only made her more determined to make him see.

'Don't get me wrong. Other kids adored theirs,' she continued on. 'Tabitha still sends hers cards on Mother's Day. Does Ruby get on with Felicia?'

He waited a beat then nodded. 'She taught at Ruby's school for over twenty years. She's seen it all. I poached her earlier this year when Ruby came to live with me.'

'Well, that's great, then,' she said, her finger fiddling with her bottom lip as she frantically thought through what tack to take next. 'A girl needs firm boundaries as much as she needs her space.'

And then it hit her. Ruby hadn't always lived with him.

Where had she been? With her mother? Had they divorced? Had they never married? Had they been in love but couldn't live together? Was he still in love with her now? Was that where his innate darkness sprang from? There was no denying her heart hurt just thinking about it. It hurt for Zach. For Ruby. It was much easier letting it hurt for them than in any way for herself.

Now Meg needed to know the whole story so badly she could taste it. She held her breath.

'That's enough,' Zach said, and Meg's finger stilled. 'I have no idea how we started talking about this in the first place.'

*Enough*? They'd barely begun! She didn't have half the information she wanted—no, *required*—in order to help.

'You brought it up,' Meg shot back.

'I— What?' His oars paused mid-air.

'If you'd been sensible enough to ignore the fact that I happened upon your backyard, then we might never have had to have this conversation.'

'Why do I get the feeling you're used to getting your own way?' he growled.

'Ha! I have no idea because it certainly ain't true. I have three bossy older brothers and a father who thinks everything I do is a complete waste of time.'

Meg's eyes slammed shut and she bit her lip, but it was far too late. She'd said what she'd said. Somehow he'd done it again—given her all the rope she needed to hang herself.

She opened one eye to find him sitting ever so still, the oars resting lazily in their slips, dripping lake water over the bottom of the old wooden boat.

He was quiet for so long Meg could hear the sound of wings beating in the forest, the soft lapping of water against the side of the boat, and her own slow, deep breaths. Then he put the oars back where they were meant to be and pushed off.

He said, 'Ruby attends a local weekly boarding school.'

Meg could have kissed him. Right then and there. She had no clue why he'd let her off the hook when she'd been pressing herself into his personal life with barely concealed vigour. All she knew was that if he looked her in the eye rather than at some point over her shoulder she would probably have gone right ahead and kissed him.

'Where Felicia used to teach,' she encouraged, her voice soft, her words clearly thought out before she uttered a single word.

The muscle beneath his left eye twitched. Then as he pulled the oars through the water he said, 'It's barely a ten-minute drive from here. The same one she was attending before her mother passed away a few months ago.'

And there it was.

Meg's hands clasped one another so tight her fingers hurt.

Ruby's mum had been gone only a few months. Oh, that poor little creature. No wonder he wanted to keep Ruby wrapped up in cotton wool. The fact she was able to go back to school at all was amazing. As for Zach…

She opened her mouth to ask how he was doing, when he cleared his throat and pushed the oars deeper into the water, sending them spearing back towards shore.

He said, 'This isn't the first time since she moved in with me that she's had a sore throat, a finger that twitches so hard she can't write, a foot so itchy she can't walk. So far all she's needed is a day at home and she's been right for another few weeks. So all in all I think we're doing okay.'

Doing okay? He cared. He considered. It was important to him to be a good father. In her humble opinion Zach was doing everything in his considerable power to do right by his little girl. And just like that all sorts of bone-deep, neglected, wishful, hopeful feelings beat to life inside her.

'Zach, I had no idea,' she said as she tried to collect herself. 'Truly. I'm so sorry about your wife—'

He cut her off unceremoniously. 'Ruby's mother and I knew one another for a short time several years ago when I was visiting with a view to building this place. I didn't even know Ruby existed until after Isabel died.'

'So you weren't—'

*So you're not still in love with her*, was what she was trying not to ask.

'We weren't,' he said, insistent enough Meg had the feeling he'd heard all too clearly nonetheless. 'I was in Turkey when my lawyer contacted me with the news. After much legal wrangling I met a social worker here, at the house. And I met Ruby. She had one small suitcase and carried a teddy bear wearing a purple fairy dress under one skinny arm. I never expected her to be so small—'

Zach came to an abrupt halt, frowned deeply and glared down into his lap.

The backs of Meg's eyes burned. It took her a few moments to recognise it was the sharp sting of oncoming tears.

She never cried. Ever. Never sweated, never blushed, never cried. The moments she'd let herself succumb to her emotions were the times she'd been most deeply hurt—by careless whispers of envious types, by stories of horrendous depravity at the Valley Women's Shelter, even by herself. But this guy tugged shamelessly at hidden parts of her that didn't know the rules.

She blinked until the sensation went away.

'We're both trying to get used to our new living situation. To each other,' he went on, his voice raw, his eyes staring at some point on the bottom of the boat as it drifted steadily on. 'The last thing we need at this point is for her existence to come to the attention of the press. You obviously do know what they can be like. She needs to find her feet without constantly looking over her shoulder. She'll trip. She'll fall. She'll be hurt even more.'

He lifted his dark eyes to hers. There was a newfound lightness within them that came with getting everything off his chest. But the second he remembered he'd been divulging his story to her, it was gone.

'Meg,' he said, his voice rough, beseeching.

She breathed deep to calm her thundering heart and said, 'I know I haven't done much to make you believe this, but you really can trust me. I'm exceptionally good at keeping secrets. You have no idea how good, which only proves my point. I'll not breathe a word.'

'I truly hope so.'

She smiled. He managed to do a shadow of the same. And in that moment of silent communion something rare and magical was forged between them.

It felt a lot like trust.

# CHAPTER SIX

THE boat bumped against solid ground.

Meg flinched, her flat shoes slipping on the wet wood, but she caught herself in time. She'd been so engrossed in Zach, in his story, in the man, she hadn't even noticed the head-high reeds encroaching.

Zach tied them off. He threw the cooler onto the wooden deck, then leaned over and held out a hand.

She took it, the loaded silence of the lingering moment of amity still making her feel all floaty and surreal.

Once on the jetty she took off his hat, ran a quick hand through her messy curls and handed it to him along with his blanket. He wrapped his hands around both, but didn't tug. Meg looked up into his dark eyes.

Her heart felt heavy in her chest. Her body felt heavy on her legs. The only thing about her that felt light was her head. Which was probably why she said, 'Now that I know everything there is to know about you, are you finally going to give in and stop stalking me?'

His dark brows rose. His voice, on the other hand, deepened. 'Is that what I've been doing?'

She said, 'Either that or fifty acres *really* isn't quite as much room as it sounds.'

From nowhere his head rocked back and he laughed. The sexy sound reverberated deep in her stomach, leaving it feeling hollow. As it faded to a smile in his eyes it left a new kind of warmth in its place she wasn't sure what to do with.

'I like you better this way,' she admitted.

'What way?'

'Not bossing me around. You should try that more.'

He gave the blanket and hat a tug. She shuffled forward a step before letting go and he threw them lazily onto the cooler.

He looked back at her. The earlier glints in his dark eyes had been mere imitations of the glints glinting at her now. The kind of glints she now wished she'd not wished for. They were dazzling, they were blistering, they were completely incapacitating.

His voice rumbled, low and deep. 'By that logic if I continue that way you'll only like me more.'

'You can't argue with logic,' she said, trying to sound pithy; instead she sounded as if she was flirting. Which, of course, she was.

How could she not? He was glinting and smiling, and somehow, whether by her brilliant psychological tactics or by his choice alone, she'd been allowed to see a little of the man behind the mask.

What she saw there she liked.

And by the look in his eyes what he saw in front of him right at this moment he liked right back.

Meg licked her lips. His hot gaze trailed slowly down the curves of her face until it landed square upon her mouth. His eyes turned dark as night and he breathed out. Hard.

Despite knowing that what was about to happen was reckless and pointless and born of nothing more concrete than the ephemeral connection of confidences shared, Meg just stood there, her entire body vibrating in anticipation.

Zach slid his arm gently around her back, with such little pressure she had time and room to curl away.

She knew she should. She thought to the very last she would. She was *always* the one to back away first before anything truly serious came to bear. But her toes curled into her shoes and she held her ground.

Zach's brow creased for the briefest of seconds as though he was surprising even himself before a small smile eased onto his mouth. Hers lifted in its image.

Then he pulled her in close. The warmth of his sun-drenched body pressed through her dress until every inch of skin, exposed and concealed, felt as if it had begun to glow.

Her hand fluttered up to rest against his chest to find it hard, fit, unyielding, everything she'd thought him to be. Only now she knew that beneath the tough exterior beat the heart of a man whose primary goal was the protection of a little girl.

He leaned down and moved his lips over hers. He tasted like chocolate muffins. She was toast.

The kiss was slow. Dreamy. As if he had no intention of missing out on experiencing every single nuance.

It took about three and a half seconds before Meg slid her arms around his neck and pressed up onto her toes to get closer to him. Sinking against him. Soaking up every bit of him that she possibly could.

With a groan that reverberated through her body like a little earthquake, his strong arms wrapped so tight around her he lifted her off the jetty as though she weighed nothing at all.

The kiss deepened. And deepened again.

His tongue eased into her mouth, caressing the edges of her teeth, sliding over the tiny chip in her front tooth, sending delicious shivers through her, touching her tongue for the briefest of moments before it was gone.

She was breathless and hot. Her skin hummed. Her insides

ached. Her toes curled. Her lungs burned. And the kiss continued as beautifully indulgent and unhurried as it had begun.

Until her flat shoes slid from her feet, landing on the jetty with a soft slap, leaving her feet bare, and leaving her feeling exposed. Completely at his mercy. And finally her senses came swarming back.

She pulled away. Ever so slightly. But he felt it. Slowly, gently, he placed her back on the jetty. And they uncurled their limbs from around one another.

Only once there was enough space for a summer breeze to slide between them did Zach say, 'I'm not sure where that came from.'

'I am,' she said, her cheeks pinking the second the words left her mouth. But it was the truth. She'd wanted to do that since the moment she'd first seen him.

It got her a slow, easy smile and a nod. The moment of accord, of finally admitting to each other what they both felt, was even more formidable than the kiss itself.

'I'd better go,' she said. 'My posse will be moseying back to camp any time soon.'

She reached out and rested her hand on his arm. His skin was so warm, the energy coursing through him so vital, her heart rate rose in direct response.

'I'm really sorry about Isabel,' she said.

His mouth quirked, but he didn't smile. And she wondered if he'd been hoping the kiss would wipe everything else from her mind. She wasn't about to tell him how close it had come.

Instead, she squeezed his arm again, and said, 'But I'm not worried about Ruby. I have no doubt she's in good hands. She's really lucky to have you.'

She lifted her hand in a small wave, then gathered her shoes and jogged up the jetty, her mind already playing over the fib she'd have to create for Rylie and Tabitha to explain where she'd been, what she'd been doing, and why she was floating an inch off the ground but couldn't quite remove the frown from her forehead at the same time.

Later that night, once Rylie and Tabitha were snoring lightly in their rooms Meg lay on her bed, wide-awake, her mobile phone warm in her palms.

She'd been tossing it from hand to hand for a good couple of hours, ever since she'd got off the phone from saying good-night to Olivia and Violet, Brendan's girls.

They'd sounded bright, cheery, happy. What had she expected? They were seven and four, and they had ponies, ballet lessons, piano, rock climbing, Chinese and French lessons, summer trips around the world with their grandmother, twenty-year-old nannies who spoilt them rotten, and a dad who clearly wrestled with the amount of time he spent at work while they grew up without him there to see it.

But as she lay back on her bed, the pale summer moon spilling light through the far window creating a hypnotic play of light and shadow on the ceiling, the fairy dust cleared from her eyes and Ruby's small face looked back at her instead.

She'd seen so much of herself in the kid's mutinous streak. That spark could be so easily deflated. Or worse, it could spin out of control. She hoped not. With all her might. Not just for Ruby. But also for Zach.

Big, bad, daunting, noble, solid Zach Jones.

Growing up in her family, the only kind of masculine strength she'd understood till she met him had been overt. Overpowering. Uncompromising.

Zach's strength came from somewhere much deeper. A place he didn't feel compelled to proclaim to the world. The fact that she'd been allowed to witness it in the revelation of how he'd changed his life for his little girl made it that much more compelling. It was like seeing a fireman rescue a kitten from a tree.

She'd hate to see all his good work go to waste. But since Zach's parenting skills were now obviously nothing like her father's, Ruby might not need the intervention her adolescent mutiny necessitated after all. She struggled with deciding what to do.

One thing she knew had been a bad decision on both their parts had been that kiss.

Her fingers lifted to stroke her lips as they must have done a few dozen times that afternoon. She could still taste his sweetness, sense his warmth all around her, feel his hardness imprinted on every inch of her body as if it had happened mere moments ago.

Soft, dreamy, luxurious, deep, unguarded, magic.

And indefensible. Because Zach Jones had a child.

When she'd ruled out any chance of having kids of her own, kids who—just because they were hers—would never live up to her father's expectations of them, it had never occurred to her that she might one day meet a man who came with kids of his own. Her usual types were never that proactive.

Then Zach had to come stomping into her life, shaking loose old choices she'd never thought she'd have to revisit again.

But no. Her nieces were living proof of why she'd done the right thing.

They seemed fine, now. But they were little kids. They ought to wear gumboots and get into mud-pie fights, not wear dresses and tights and patent leather shoes when playing in the backyard.

The pressure for them to live up to her father's unwavering ideal of what a Kelly had to be was mounting. And soon they'd be old enough to feel it. Soon they'd be old enough to know.

There was no way she'd wish that pressure on any child. Not by blood, and not by association. Because she knew the consequences.

She threw her phone across the room and it landed with a thud on a couch in the corner.

She tried humming Stevie Wonder to clear her head, but it didn't work. Zach's deep voice rang louder still.

She liked the guy. She adored how he kissed. She was smitten with his efforts to do right by Ruby. And she was in his debt for letting her get away with the unforgivable slip about her exceedingly private dealings with her father.

But she wasn't any good for him any more than he would be good for her. He might not see it yet, but he had the natural inclination to be some kind of dad. He'd want more kids down the line, and with her insides the way they were she could never give them to him.

Meg turned on her side, tucked her thighs against her belly, and slid her hands beneath her pillow. The sheer curtains over the ceiling–to-floor windows—chosen especially to *not* let a girl sleep in when there was jogging to be done—flapped under the soft push of air-conditioned air.

Out there, in that big, rambling, amazing house of his, Zach would soon be asleep. She wondered if he dreamt. What he dreamt about. And more importantly, who.

It had long since been dark by the time Zach stepped foot in the place he'd called home for the past few months. He was humming as he shut the front door. It took a few moments until he realised it was KC and the Sunshine Band. Classic disco.

Throwing a full set of keys onto the sideboard rather than a simple hotel card still felt strange.

Being shuffled from foster home to state institution and back again, he'd hit a point where he'd simply stopped feeling connected to places, to possessions, to people. Living in this large, rambling house, sleeping in the same bed every night, seeing the same faces every day, he felt the return of the natural desire to preserve those connections. Along with that came the niggling fear that it all might yet be taken away.

'Good evening, Zach,' a voice called out to him in the darkness.

He jumped. 'Felicia. You took a year off my life.'

'Working to all hours will do that to you far more quickly,' Ruby's nanny said. 'I'd say you are a prime candidate for attending one of those wellness programmes that are so trendy nowadays.'

Zach gave her shadowy figure a flat stare. 'If I'd known you had such a funny bone I'd have left you in that draughty old school.'

The older woman patted him on the arm.

He glanced down the dark front hallway towards the bright haven of the warm family kitchen, his nose catching the delicious concoction of homey smells that meant there were leftovers waiting for him in the oven. 'Is she still awake?'

He felt her shake her head. 'Out like a light the minute her head hit the pillow.'

'Have you heard any—?' He stopped, hoping he wouldn't have to put into words the wretched sounds she screamed out every few nights.

'Not a peep. What with her sore throat I'd say she needed the rest.' She tossed her large book bag over her shoulder. 'Goodnight, then. I'll see you in the morning.'

He heard her meet up with one of the rotation of night staff who escorted her back to her own bungalow down the way, their voices trailing into the distance until he was left with silence.

Rather than heading for the beguiling scent of zucchini quiche he took a left. The light from the kitchen faded the farther he moved through the house.

He reached Ruby's bedroom door and stared at her name spelled out in big pink letters, his ears straining to hear the sound of her sleeping breaths.

He could have been home hours earlier. Certainly before her bedtime. Instead he'd remained shackled to his workstation in the Blueberry Ash Bungalow he'd taken as his office, telling himself Ruby wouldn't have expected him home as it was still officially a school night. The truth was the thought of having to question her, to chastise her even, for skipping school had left him in a cold sweat.

She was seven, for Pete's sake. He was thirty-five and operated a massive multinational company. There wasn't anyone on earth who had a hope in hell of intimidating him. Yet from the day he'd first looked into those all too intelligent brown eyes he'd lived with the fear that, though he'd *never* abandon her, there was always the chance she'd decide she did not want him.

He ran a hand over his face, the pads of his fingers rasping against the day-old shave, before resting his palm on the cool wood of her bedroom door.

The instinct to press open the door, sneak in and check on his daughter, to let himself believe she slept because *he'd* made her feel safe, was so strong. Yet every night he managed to talk himself out of it.

He might wake her. She might see him and expect her mum and become distressed. He might get used to her being there.

Yet this night the urge felt different. Not nearly so complicated. Today his knowledge of what a girl needed in order to feel safe had been increased tenfold in one short conversation with the most unlikely source—Meg Kelly.

She'd been so confident that Ruby needed her space. And just as sure that it was okay for him to impulsively not want to give it to her. And even more than okay that Ruby knew it. His instincts were spot on. Maybe he did have it within him to do this right after all.

He wrapped his hand around the door handle.

*Good hands*, Meg had called them, and with enough vehemence he'd let himself believe it too.

He went in. Even in the darkness there was no mistaking the big white bed jutting out into the centre of the largest bedroom in the house. He might have gone overboard with the rocking horse, the padded window seat, the library stacked with *Saddle Club* books, the tea-party table, the twenty different dolls, but he'd taken note of every lick of advice from Felicia and her other teachers who'd known her the past couple of years and let his International Resort Decorator go crazy, no expenses spared.

He took a few steps into the plush-carpeted room until moonlight spilling through the faraway window gave him enough light to see that beneath the pink-and-white lacy bedcovers lay a skinny, young girl.

A handful of days had passed since she'd been home for the weekend, but he was sure she'd grown. Her dark hair splayed across her pillow with such perfection it was as though someone had brushed out every strand. Her face was smooth and unlined. Her breathing even and unworried. Her throat not bothering her a bit.

Before he knew it was coming he smiled wide. Cheeky kid. She even had her nanny fooled. But Meg, considering her more recent experience being a daughter, had seen through the subterfuge in a second.

He took another step closer until he was near enough he allowed himself the small gesture of wiping a long, straight lock of hair from across her eyes.

Ruby stirred. Mumbled a bit. He froze. But she soon resettled—taking up the whole bed, one arm flung over her head. Exactly the way he'd always slept.

His heart slammed against his ribs. This creature was his daughter. His responsibility. His only family. If anyone did anything, said anything, printed anything that made the authorities even *think* about denying her to him...

Before his throat clogged so tight he couldn't breathe he spun on his heel and walked from the room.

'Daddy?' a soft voice called when he was a metre away from being home free.

He turned; Ruby was sitting up, a shadow in the darkness, as he must have been to her. He found his voice for her. 'Yes, honey?'

'Nothing. Just checking.'

Checking to see he was real.

Checking to see he was still around.

Checking to see he hadn't disappeared right when she was getting used to him being there. God, how he knew that feeling. That loathsome, sinking, hollowness when someone you trusted to love you left without looking back.

'I'm here,' he said, his voice gruff. 'I'm not going anywhere. You can go back to sleep.'

By the slow, even breaths coming from her bed, he knew she already was.

He closed her door and paced into the kitchen where he leant his hands on the island bench in the middle of the huge room.

Felicia had left out his newspapers. Beside them sat a permission slip from Ruby's school for an upcoming field trip, and a spaghetti jar overfilled with a mishmash of local wildflowers. He imagined Ruby picking them for Felicia as an act of contrition, and Felicia falling for the sore-throat stunt all the harder. Smart kid.

He played with the rubbery, cream petal of a waxflower. Working in solitary, coming home late to a dark house, eating leftovers, keeping his weekends completely free to spend them at Ruby's beck and call within the confines of a handful of safe places; this was the inflexible life he'd chosen. This was how things were going to be for the next dozen-odd years. No more hands-on business, no more travel, no more adult company?

Meg Kelly's lovely face swam all too easily back into his mind.

For the first time since he'd set foot in the door—but certainly not the first time that day—he remembered the kiss. God, the delights he'd found within that mouth. It had drawn him in like a siren song he could no longer resist. But her warm skin, and her goddess curves and her instant response had made it impossible for him to tear himself away.

He pushed away from the island and moved to the oven to grab his dinner. Oven mitts the last thing on his mind, the ceramic quiche tray burnt his fingers. He let go and it smashed to the floor. Egg and zucchini and cheese flew everywhere, splattering the wooden cupboards and embedding themselves in every bit of slate-tile grout it could find.

He swore at the great mess profusely but sotto voce, always remembering Ruby was asleep down the hall. He flipped on the tap and shoved his stinging fingers beneath the cold-water stream.

What the hell was he thinking? Kissing Meg. Confiding in her. Her pretty words might have sounded believable at the time, but Meg Kelly could yet bring down his carefully balanced house of cards with one word whispered in the wrong direction. Her best friend was a journalist, for Pete's sake! Dammit. That mouth of hers could prove to be his downfall in more ways than one.

He turned off the tap, wiped his hands down his trousers when he couldn't find a handy tea towel, and set to cleaning up the mess.

After cheese on toast for dinner he signed Ruby's permission slip with a flourish so fierce he tore the paper.

He'd let himself be wrapped around a female finger for the last time. The next time Ruby tried to pull a stunt like skipping school, he *would* talk with her. He would grow some backbone and set some boundaries.

Apparently boundaries were something young girls needed. Or so some would have him believe.

# CHAPTER SEVEN

IN LIEU of the dawn jog, the next morning Meg slid notes beneath the girls' doors saying she was taking the hike through the national forest instead and to meet her at the rendezvous point at seven.

After finally falling asleep some time after two she needed the extra hour to recuperate. But that wasn't why hiking was suddenly her new favourite pastime.

She was avoiding Zach.

After the dreams she'd had, G-rated dreams of white picket fences and yellow Labrador puppies with herself in an apron washing dishes while looking out a kitchen window at a yard full of kids, she needed to put as much of the fifty acres of resort land between her and Zach Jones as she could.

She stood at the back of the thankfully large hiking group, decked out in what seemed the most appropriate hiking attire she had, twisting her crazy morning hair into two thick plaits, determined not to let the humidity beat her, ready to put aside the past couple of days and start her holiday anew.

'Good morning,' a deep voice rumbled beside her.

She snapped her eyes shut, not needing to look up to know who the voice belonged to. That tone alone could make her skin hum no matter what it said.

'So where are the other two musketeers this fine morning?' he asked.

Thankful for the excuse not to look him in the eye, she glanced over her shoulder to find the path behind her empty. She said, 'Still snug in their warm beds, I expect. Who knew I'd turn out to be the energetic one?'

Who knew? They knew. And that was why they weren't coming. Oh, no...

In an effort to be honest with her best friends while still keeping from them everything she was unable—or not yet ready—to share, she'd been brief when mentioning her run-ins with Zach. Obviously too brief. Her insouciance hadn't fooled them for a single second. They knew something was up, and being her best friends they'd optimistically assumed her reticence meant true romance was in the air. They were leaving her alone so that it might flourish.

Being stuck with Zach looking all scruffy and gorgeous, with no buffer to keep her out of harm's way, was all she deserved.

She tied off her second plait then glanced at him causally from the corner of her eye, catching sight of yet more cargo pants, yet another sexily faded T-shirt, a tattered old backpack snugly attached to his back and the same well-worn cap she'd seen him wear before.

Her perusal ground to a halt when it reached his mouth. Her own turned as dry as dust as their kiss came rushing back to her in Technicolor. She licked her lips, then croaked, 'Please don't tell me I've accidentally done something else that would necessitate you tailing me?'

'Now what could possibly make you think my presence here has anything to do with you?'

Before she could come up with a succinct retort, the wellness facilitator called out, 'Today the crew heading up our new St Barts resort are joining us to see how we Aussies do it. So let's lift our feet, keep up a super pace, and ooh and ahh at the local flora and fauna like we've never seen anything so fabulous!'

'You're here to train your next crew?' she said, mostly to herself.

'Beautiful *and* brainy. Who knew?'

Zach tugged on one of her plaits, shot her a grin that was complete with the glint that made her common sense unceasingly fall to pieces, pulled his cap lower over his face then jogged ahead.

With the words *beautiful and brainy* ringing in her ears, she stared at his back until he was swallowed by the forest.

Amazing. He was well over six feet tall, with skin like bronze and the build of a world-class athlete, yet he clearly had no clue *that* was why half the people in the group would be wondering who he was. It wouldn't matter if she was sitting in his lap or a million miles away.

Meg hitched her shiny new Juniper Falls backpack into a more comfy position on her shoulders, took one last glance back at the empty path, then followed on as the group turned off the running track.

They soon found a network of wide wooden walkways with the kind of gentle slope built to accommodate every level of trail rambler and Meg was truly surprised to soon find herself contentedly lost in the rhythmic pace of her feet.

Before long they were ushered through a gap in the railing as they headed off the main tourist trail. The path became instantly less clear-cut, less regularly tramped, and the gentle path gave way to one in which they had to walk single file, at times grasping at vines to pull themselves up the face of a steep rise.

Sweat dripped down the sides of Meg's face, down her spine and behind her knees. She could feel spirals of her hair plastered against her cheeks and the back of her neck. When she licked her lips she could taste salt. She gave up trying to hear the guide over her laboured breathing and just climbed.

Meg wasn't sure if she'd picked up her pace or Zach had slowed, but somehow right when she needed leverage to step over a particularly slippery-looking rock as she picked a path across a slow-moving stream, his hand was there to help her leap across to the opposite bank.

'Thanks,' she said, her voice rough from lack of use. 'Are we there yet?'

From her view of his profile she caught his smile, this one complete with eye crinkles. Her heart skipped a beat, which, considering her fitness level and the uneven ground, was not smart.

'Not far now,' he said, his voice as clear as if he'd been standing still the past half-hour.

'If I have a complaint do I really have to write to management?'

'Hit me. I can take it.'

'Are the super-early starts entirely necessary?'

The smile spread to laughter as though it was the most natural thing for him to do. 'The days get hot very quickly around here.'

'I'm not sure I believe that makes a lick of difference to your sadistic timetable planners.'

The eye crinkles deepened. 'That's because you're too smart for your own good.'

'Mmm. So does that mean you actually believe in the stuff you're spouting? Inner health, inner happiness and all that.'

His eye crinkles faded as he gave her question consideration. The guy listened, seriously listened, to what she had to say. Most men in his position patted her on the head as if she were a clever puppy before deferring to her brothers, not caring that she might be a woman with ideas and opinions and more street smarts than they had in their little fingers. No wonder she was finding it harder and harder to pull herself away from this one.

He said, 'I believe that what you put into your life is what you get out of it. Treat it well, it'll treat you well. Surround yourself only with positive people and they'll affect your life positively. Fill your body and your mind with rubbish and rubbish is all you can ever hope to be.'

Meg let those pearls sink in and then kind of wished she hadn't asked. Because it shed a new light on how she must have appeared to others. And to him.

She attended parties to keep her profile current, so that meant she was a party girl. Nothing deeper. Nothing more. And it was entirely her own doing.

She kept hush-hush the best parts of herself; the truth about the number of women at the Valley Women's Shelter she'd secretly helped over the years. That way *nobody* knew the real her. Not her family. Not even her friends.

For years she'd thought she had the best of both worlds— public affection and private fulfilment. But Zach's words made her wish *someone* knew. They made her wish he knew. The urge to just blurt it all out then and there was a powerful thing.

But then what? He was too perceptive. He'd wonder why she needed to spend time with battered women and displaced children in particular, and why she'd even hidden the fact in the first place.

Nah. Better to keep things as they were. Best not to discover people might only be attracted to the light, bright, amusing, easily palatable version of herself. Zach included. She wasn't sure she was prepared to know the answer to that one.

Realising the silence was stretching on far too long, she forced a dazzling party-girl smile and said, 'So you are what you eat?'

His cheek lifted. 'In not so many words.'

'By that logic if I go home right now and marinate myself in chocolate and red wine, then at the very least I'll die tasty.'

He laughed softly, before saying, 'You can't argue with logic.'

Meg's breath caught in her throat. He'd just had to go and

use the last words she'd said to him before they'd kissed, hadn't he? Her heart beat double time. She breathed deep to control it before she keeled over.

Perhaps he hadn't realised what he'd said, because he just turned and followed the group. Or perhaps the kiss hadn't affected him nearly as much as it had affected her.

*Good*, she thought. *Fantastic even. Fan-bloody-tastic.*

Now they were descending again. Single file. Meg was caught behind Zach, so naturally while she ought to have been watching her feet she watched him instead. The spring of curls against his tanned neck. The athletic ease with which he strode the trail.

Surely he'd felt *something* when they'd kissed. She'd felt magic.

When her foot half missed a stepping stone, she stumbled and caught hold of his backpack for support.

'You okay back there?' he asked, snapping a hand behind him to cradle her hip.

She closed her eyes against the flow of feeling rushing through her that felt more tangible and immediate than mere magic. 'Mostly.'

'Take my shoulders.'

'Why?' she asked.

He glanced up at her, his dark eyes shadowed beneath his cap. And she was certain his voice dropped a note or two when he said, 'Because it only gets riskier from here.'

'I'll be fine,' she said, her voice husky.

'Meg—'

'I'm not completely inept, you know. I may not know which direction I'm heading, but I can put one foot in front of the other without falling flat on my face.' *Most of the time.* 'I can do this on my own.'

Ignoring her outburst, Zach simply took her by the waist and physically lifted her and placed her to the left of the path so that those behind her could get past.

Once they were alone with their group bundling down the descent in front of them, Zach said, 'Relax, Meg. I'm not offering you anything more than a hand down the mountain.'

Meg swallowed, the lack of saliva making her throat scratch so she winced. His dark eyes slid down her face to rest on her lips. His grip tightened. Infinitesimally. And she felt in his touch the same confusion of want and restraint surging through her body.

Triumph coursed through her. He'd felt every bit of enchantment in that kiss that she had.

Triumph fast turned to confusion. What was she meant to do with the knowledge that helping her down the hill wasn't all he wanted to give her any more than that was all she wanted from him?

In the quiet that followed Meg realised the group had moved far enough away that birdsong came back to the forest. The water in the stream they had crossed bubbled melodiously about the fall of rocks unable to completely block its path.

They were to all intents and purposes alone. Anything could happen. Like having photos of 'Meg Kelly and friend' getting up to no good being splashed all over the Internet within hours. For that he'd never forgive her.

She took his hands from her and pressed them back to his sides. 'Thanks for the offer, but I just slipped a little on some moss. I'll pay more attention to where I put my feet.'

His eyes finally, thankfully, skimmed from her mouth back to her eyes and his hands moved to grip the straps of his backpack. 'Just be careful, for my sake. I don't need you slipping and breaking a bone.'

'God, no. The press would be all over this place like a rash. Which is, of course, the last thing we want.'

'We want?'

'Yes, *we*. As in we agree that it's Ruby who's front and foremost in our minds when we happen upon one another.'

*Ruby who should be reason enough we never happen upon one another again.*

After one final dark glance he nodded, then turned and headed down the ragged path.

'Keep up,' he called without turning, 'before we have to send out a search party for you again.'

'A search party? Please,' she called back as she walked unsteadily down the trail.

*Had he just said 'again'?*

Five long, hot minutes later, the descent evened out and the path became made up of wide, neat steps carved into layers of grey rock.

The group spread out, walking in clumps. The scurrying, flapping, whistling noises of the forest had been overtaken by the nearby sound of rushing water. The overgrown forest cleared to reveal a vertical slant of wet rock that was so high Meg had to crane her neck to see the sliver of sunlight above.

'Hold onto the handrails, step carefully, and prepare yourselves for something fabulous!' the guide called out.

Meg followed Zach into a gap in the rock. And darkness. And sudden dank coolness. The sweat covering her whole body brought her skin up in goose bumps.

Bit by bit, step by slow step, Meg's eyes became used to the gloom. Up ahead, through the bobbing heads of her fellow hikers, there was light. Eerie, green light.

Then suddenly she stepped onto the edge of a high-domed cave. At her feet lapped a pool of bright green water clear enough to see the floor was made of a tumble of smooth stones of all shapes and sizes. Above, through a gap way up high in the ceiling, a stunning, glowing, white sheet of water splashed magnificently into the deep centre of the pool. It was literally one of the most beautiful things she'd ever seen.

'I give you Juniper Falls,' Zach said from somewhere to her right.

Meg couldn't think of a thing to say back. She just let it wash over her—the noise, the colour, the primal violence and beauty of it all.

'Worth the early start?' Zach asked some time later.

'And then some,' she said, drawing her eyes away from the spectacle to give him a quick smile.

A couple of nearby camera flashes went off. She took a step away from him, her eyes instantly scanning the crowd for the offender. But everyone was ogling the waterfall, not their blurry shapes in the semi-darkness.

'Photos don't do it justice,' he said. 'Just look, listen, absorb, get your fill. You won't forget. This moment will be with you for ever.'

While Zach kept his gaze dead ahead, and despite the splendour raging in front of her, Meg's remained locked on him.

As though he knew just what she was taking her fill of, he turned to look at her. His brows came together and his right cheek creased into a sexy arch, questioning her. She shook her head, shrugged. What could she possibly say?

His eyes left hers to rove slowly over her face as though he too was taking the chance to memorise every centimetre.

He was right—it was a moment she knew she would never forget.

The group spread out, some continuing around the other side of the pool, others finding patches of sunshine so they could sit and relax. A few game souls took off their shoes and waded into the shallows.

'Coming?' he asked, holding out a hand.

'How about you point the way to the best spot, then you can get back to work?'

His eyes narrowed, then he looked about and saw the camera flashes for what they potentially were. He took a slow step away from her. And even though she'd been the one to encourage the move, her heart clenched just a little in her chest.

He curled his hand back to his side as he pulled his old hat farther down over his eyes. Then he gave her a long, straight look. 'As it turns out I have a little time to spare for my guests if you'd care to follow me.'

She swallowed and nodded. Then followed him to a large, mostly dry rock on which sunshine dappled through the ferns above. Meg settled herself onto it with a thankful sigh.

'Is the water warm?' she asked.

He stood, towering over her. 'See for yourself.'

When she leant over and whisked her hand through the clear water the illusion firmed. It was warm enough to swim in, but cool enough to soothe her hot hands.

Zach filled his flask with water, then his tanned throat worked hard as he chugged it down. When Zach saw her eyeing his drink bottle with her tongue practically hanging out of her mouth he handed it to her.

Her lips hovered where his lips had been. She imagined she could smell chocolate muffins. She closed her eyes, all but groaning as the blissfully cool liquid slid down her scorching throat.

Zach's voice was loud enough for those nearest to hear when he went all 'tour guide' on her and said, 'The pool is fed by the falls and the overflow creates an underwater spring to the south, which feeds into a stream that heads off into the national park. With the constant pummelling, the floor at the centre of the pool is the softest sand you'll ever feel.'

She put the lid back on his flask and handed it to him, their fingers sliding past one another as they exchanged the bottle from her hot hand to his.

'So you've swum here?' she asked, looking back out into the pool, tucking her shaking hand tight into her lap.

'Once or twice.'

'I can't imagine when you'd find the time. What with running a trillion businesses and looking after you know who.'

She felt him draw back. She'd been discreet. But it hadn't mattered. The withdrawal of all that lovely warmth stung.

And shocked her sensible. Even though they were both on the same side in wanting to protect his daughter, while it was her wish, it was his mission in life.

She slung her backpack onto the rock between them, the most substantial wall she could mount on short notice, then said, 'I'm sorry. I won't bring that subject up again.'

His voice was low and intimate when he said, 'Meg, I wanted to—'

She flapped a hand between them. 'It's fine. I understand.'

'No, I don't think you do,' he said. 'I wanted to tell you... She made me pancakes.'

Meg's eyes slid to his, envy and delight spilling through her in tandem. 'She did? When?'

'This morning. Before she went back to school.'

'Jeez, she's an early riser. Like father like daughter, I guess.'

He glanced at her with an expression she'd never seen on him before. As if he'd thought the same, but couldn't be convinced that it wasn't just wishful thinking. It got to her, like an arrow straight to the heart.

'Were they any good?' she asked, her voice reed-thin. 'The pancakes.'

'Atrocious.' He laughed softly.

'But you ate them all,' she said, knowing the answer before she even asked the question.

He nodded once. 'I certainly did.'

The arrow in her heart stabbed a little deeper.

She tried to imagine her own father eating pancakes she'd made. Unless they'd been fit for the table of literal kings he would have taken one look and fed them to the dogs. And he would somehow have made sure she knew it too.

She swallowed down the heady mix of new good and old bad feelings rising far too quickly inside her.

'She asked after you, you know,' Zach said, glancing away from her to stare out at some vague spot in the distance.

Meg raised her eyes to the roof of the cave to hold back the encroaching sting. If he knew what was good for him, the guy should really stop talking. Now.

She knew what was good for her and still asked, 'What did she say?'

'Young girls need their mystery. Or so I've been told.'

'Hey now,' she laughed, taking a quick moment to brush a finger under her eyes, 'that's not fair. I was being nice giving you all that secret girls' business insight, and now you're using it against me.'

'Fair enough,' he said, 'then I will tell you that it was something you said to her yesterday that had her heading off to school today like she had the wind at her heels. So thank you for that too.'

Wow. She'd done that? She gave him a nod. It was either that or croak out, *You're welcome*.

'Mr Jones,' a woman's voice with a lilting foreign accent said from between them.

Meg flinched and dragged herself out of the cloud of intimacy that had wrapped itself around them like a slow, thick, enshrouding fog shifting across the pool.

She turned to find a stunning redhead, her hair neat as a pin, her Juniper Falls uniform pressed, not a lick of sweat anywhere.

Meg ran a quick hand over her fuzzy plaits and so wished she hadn't. It would have been better not to know.

'Claudia,' Zach said, his voice so cool and aloof Meg was surprised to remember when he'd last used that tone of voice with her. 'What can I do for you?'

'Sorry to interrupt, but the St Barts group had a few questions about the morning they wanted to run by you while we had a moment's respite.'

'Of course. Claudia, this is Meg, a guest at the resort. Meg, Claudia will be my St Barts manager,' he explained.

'St Barts? You lucky duck,' Meg said with the instant return of her practised smile. 'And thank you, Zach, for taking the time to explain how the waterfall works. It was most informative.'

Claudia gave her a short smile, then headed off to join the St Barts crew.

Zach looked across at her with a kind of smile she was having more and more trouble resisting. 'Most informative?'

'Well,' she said, 'it was.'

Zach stood, yet he lingered.

'Go,' she said, shooing him away. 'Please. I'm not going to fall into the pool and drown and cause you endless hassles. I promise.'

His brow furrowed, then he said, 'No, that's not... I was going to ask if I'll see you tonight.'

'Tonight?' Her heart beat so hard in her throat she was certain it must have been obvious to everyone in sight.

'You are coming to the luau, are you not?'

'The what?'

'There's a clearing at the west corner of the lake on which we've created a beach. The staff put on a controlled bonfire there once a week. Have you even read the brochure?'

'I glanced at it. Briefly.' Trying to find chocolate, trying to find the Wellness Building. Both times she'd only found more of him. 'Look, I'm not sure what our plans are for tonight—'

'The St Barts team will be there tonight so I was thinking about putting in an appearance. For their sake,' he said. Adding, 'There'll be marshmallows.'

She couldn't help herself. She licked her lips.

And he laughed. Throaty, loud laughter that resonated through her bones as though her marrow were a twanged guitar string.

'Real marshmallows?' she asked, her voice comically low, amazed at the cool she could still find within herself when she needed it most. Thank heavens for her years of training. 'Or soy-based, gluten-free, sugar-free sticky balls?'

'Real marshmallows. Bags and bags of them. Pink and white. Sticks supplied if you're a toaster.'

'Sure I'm a toaster. You?'

'All the way. But just in case you need something to keep you going until then...' He tossed her a small package wrapped in the ubiquitous Juniper Falls pale green. He tipped his cap at her, then bounded across the rocks to join the St Barts crew.

Meg tore it open to find herself holding a small packet of M&Ms. She laughed out loud, then pressed her finger to her mouth before her fellow hikers discovered her laughing to herself and realised they ought to have been paying more heed to the frizzy brunette in their midst.

# CHAPTER EIGHT

ZACH stood on a corner of the lake's beach not lit by the blazing fire, feet bare as the day he was born, dressed top to toe in linen he'd ironed himself, and a hot pink lei someone he didn't recognise had thrown over his head.

'You're a fool,' he muttered to himself for about the seventh time in the past ten minutes. 'You and Ruby might have had a good morning because of something *she* said, and maybe you can't get that kiss out of your mind, but by poking your head out of your perfectly adequate cave again and again just to get another glimpse makes you a damn fool.'

His hands gripped the lei, crushing the flowers, but before he had the chance to whip it over his neck the sound of female laughter split the night.

Glitter twinkled in the darkness. Three distinct voices wafted towards him, followed by three female forms. The other two must have been her friends. All he saw was Meg.

Her dark hair had been pulled back into a slick ponytail. Huge hooped earrings hung from her ears to her shoulders, encrusted with more diamond dust than most women would ever own. But it was the dress that had him clenching his fingers into his palms.

Fire-engine red it was, made of some sparkly material that clung to her torso like second skin, cinching tight at her waist then billowing all the way to her ankles. Her shoulders were bare, her décolletage on display within a deep V, and around the middle she was tied up with a big red bow.

Never had he been given a gift quite like that. He'd obviously kept the wrong friends.

She leaned in as a staff member explained the 'no shoes on the beach policy' for the luau, and without hesitation she rested her elbow on someone's shoulder, hitched her voluminous skirt as high as her knee and proceeded to uncurl a good metre of red leather strap wound about her calf.

Zach closed his eyes and prayed for mercy.

When he opened them it was to see Meg, barefoot, bouncing onto the sand with the exuberance of a puppy. Mid-twirl he got a load of the back of the dress—she was completely bare from a small clip at the back of her neck all the way to her waist. It wasn't quite low enough to give him a glimpse of the tattoo he knew was there, but low enough he ran a hand hard over his mouth.

He knew what it was about her that had him tempting fate. For the past twenty years he'd spent every waking minute dedicated to turning himself from a kid with nothing into a ruthless businessman. For the past several months he'd had to completely strip away that part of himself in order to pour all of his energy into becoming a father.

Meg Kelly simply let him feel like a *man*.

It was energising. It was addictive. It could so easily prove to be his undoing.

*Look at her*, he said to himself. *The diamonds, the flashy friends, the artless va-va-voom. She revels in the flash and flare of public life. And look at you, hiding in the shadows.*

In allowing this infatuation to continue he was setting himself up to lose too much—he'd certainly lose Meg, and there was every real possibility he might yet lose Ruby. As for the fact that he could look in the mirror and see a guy who'd learnt from the alienation of his past? Gone.

Convinced beyond a shadow of a doubt leaving was the right thing to do, he took one step in that direction when a local reggae band on the other side of the fire struck up their steel drums with a little 'How Deep Is Your Love' Bee Gees action.

His eyes searched for Meg's. She looked up and clapped, radiating pure joy as he'd known she would when he'd put in the request with the entertainment director.

Her gaze began flicking back and forth across the crowd and he knew too that she was looking for him. Instead of sliding deeper into the shadows where he belonged, his feet held firm until her eyes found his.

She smiled with her whole body—ravishing red lips, sparkling blue eyes, the happy shrug of her creamy shoulders. A deeply felt attraction slid through him like slow, hot lava. God, it felt good—like gut instinct, abandon and release. Feelings he'd never allowed himself to come close to feeling for another person his whole adult life.

She made a beeline his way, her friends following in her shimmering wake.

'Zach,' she said on a release of breath when she was close enough he could see the firelight flickering in her eyes.

'Good evening, ladies,' Zach said, purposely including all three. 'Don't you all look beautiful this evening?'

One gave Meg a small shove forward. 'Don't we just.'

Meg glared at her friend, while Zach pretended not to notice.

'Ready for a big night?' he asked.

'I heard rumours of a marshmallow roast,' said the brunette. Tabitha.

'Bring 'em on,' said the blonde, her voice wry.

The hairs on the back of Zach's neck twitched under the blonde's incisive gaze. That one was the journo. At the very least she knew that *something* was happening between her friend and him. She who probably kept a lipstick camera and microchip microphone on her person at all times.

Meg slapped her friend on the arm, which he approved of heartily. 'Don't pay any attention to Rylie. She doesn't understand that sweets belong to their own food group the way some of us do.'

When her eyes slid back to him, she let them flick to her friends and with a small shake of her head told him not to worry. He was safe. Ruby was safe.

Then a small smile hooked at the corner of her mouth. *Thanks for the M&M's,* her eyes said.

He blinked back, *My pleasure.*

'Are they actually serving drinks from coconut shells?' Tabitha asked, then she was off.

Rylie, on the other hand, had her hand clamped over Meg's arm as if they'd been soldered together.

Meg blinked at him, her mouth curving in apology. The St Barts crew were a hopeless cover. She knew he was there for her. And while she'd made it perfectly clear to him on more than one occasion that she understood why they should remain miles apart for Ruby's sake, she'd come. The both of them needed their heads read.

'I like the choice in music,' Meg said over her shoulder as Rylie pulled her away. 'Yours?'

'Disco,' he said. 'It's my secret passion.'

She grinned. It lit up the night. And then she was gone.

Zach slid his hands into the pockets of his trousers. He'd put in his promised appearance, meaning he could walk away. Ruby wasn't home so he could slink back to his bungalow and work himself late into the night till his eyes burned and his back ached and he was too exhausted to think about anything but sleep.

He could do that, but instead he decided to stay a little

longer. Listen to some Bee Gees. Drink some punch. Eat a marshmallow or two. See where the night took him.

Damn fool.

Meg sat on a straw mat next to Rylie, drinking a mocktail and pretending to watch Tabitha lead a conga line around the fire, but whenever she had half a chance her eyes sought out Zach.

The moment she'd first seen him standing with the fire at his back, feet bare, watching her with the kind of intensity that took her breath away, her skin had warmed as though she'd stepped too near the flames. Even wreathed in hot-pink flowers he was the most wholly masculine creature she'd ever known.

Dark hair slicked back, clean-shaven, and wearing a pale grey linen suit, he *finally* appeared how he should have all along—like the kind of man her father would know by name.

That first moment when she'd been allowed to dream he might be something he was not hadn't been fair. If she'd first seen him looking like this then maybe she would have had her guard up and have avoided this whole mess from the outset.

*Who are you kidding?* she thought to herself on a slow release of breath. In cargo shorts and a soft faded T-shirt he was beautiful. In a perfectly cut suit he was devastating. A woman would have to be made of far sterner stuff than she to skim past such a creation.

'You having a good time so far?' Rylie asked.

'Mmm?' Meg said, turning to Rylie with the straw of her third pineapple mocktail bitten between her front teeth.

'I feel like we've barely seen you enough to make sure you're actually relaxing as promised.'

Meg raised an eyebrow. 'If you actually turned up to any of the scheduled events rather than leaving me to fend for myself that wouldn't be the case.'

'I'm here now.'

Meg bumped her friend with her shoulder. 'So you are. And I'm glad. This is fun. Especially since Tabitha is so on form, and thankfully not trying to rope us into her insanity.'

'Too true. And, now that I am here, is there anything you'd like to catch me up on? The weather, perhaps? Petrol prices getting you down? Anything happen in the past couple of days you'd like to let off your chest?'

She knew what Rylie was asking. And it was fair enough. They were best friends. Had been since school. Maybe she could give her a little sugar, so long as she gave nothing away about Zach or Ruby. But to do that she'd have to give too much of herself away as well. The myriad reasons why she couldn't just throw herself at him and be done with it went deeper than even Rylie knew.

'The weather, then,' Meg said, tilting her head towards the heavens. 'Look at that sky. Have you ever seen so many stars? Hasn't this been the most beautiful night?'

Rylie paused a long moment before glancing across the fire towards the man they were both pretending not to be talking about. 'Absolutely gorgeous.'

On a sigh Meg said, 'You have no idea.'

A gorgeous man and a gorgeous dad. It was the second part that was making it so easy for her to fall for him, while also making it impossible for her to have him.

She'd never gone through the grieving process the doctors had warned her she might when she'd convinced them to give her the operation that would take away her chance of conceiving a child. All she'd wanted was to do whatever *she* could to stop her father from ever getting the chance to bully another kid again.

She was beginning to fear that was what the faint but now constant ache in her heart was—fissures that had existed in her happy facade since the morning she woke up in Recovery. Only now, as she understood fully for the first time what she'd given up, those fissures were turning into cracks big enough to split her in two.

'Can you do me a favour?' Meg asked.

'Anything. Always.'

'I don't want to be missing any more. In the press, I mean. Dylan texted me today. Apparently the snippet *Chic* ran online a couple of days back has grown legs. I'd rather not be hounded by people with mobile cameras any more than usual this week.'

'I'll get onto my contact at *Chic* and give them the word,' Rylie said. 'Where do you want to be instead of missing?'

*Here.* 'Anywhere but here.'

'May I ask why?'

Meg tucked her chin against her shoulder and glanced at her friend. 'I wish I could tell you, but it's complicated.'

'Okay, for now. I'm not so silly to think wheat-grass juice is the reason you're glowing like you are. Tell your man he can do as he pleases, I'm looking the other way.'

Meg gave Rylie a quick hug.

Tabitha chose the perfect moment to twist her way out of the line and head on over, laughing as though she could barely draw breath.

'You are a maniac,' Meg said, her voice still slightly ragged.

Tabitha slumped down onto the straw mat beside them. 'Every party we ever have from now on should be exactly like this.'

'With nobody we know as guests and no alcohol?' Rylie asked.

Tabitha shrugged. 'Why not? I know the wellness class we took the first day was all about finding balance, but sometimes I think you need to let yourself go completely *off* balance too. It's a yin and yang thing.'

*Off balance.* That was the term Meg had been reaching for to describe how Zach made her feel.

He was intensely private while her life was splashed about

the papers so regularly she might as well have been living in her own reality TV programme. He saw family as something to safeguard, not to flaunt. His life was so far removed from her own as to be completely foreign.

This was a man trying so hard to be worthy of his daughter, if he knew how low she'd sunk, how desperate a measure she'd taken in order to pull herself back out into the bright lights, would he understand? Or would he think her ridiculous? Hopeless? Weak? All the things she'd been told she was by the one man who ought to have been her fiercest champion. If even her father couldn't see the good in the real her, what hope did she have with anyone else?

He shifted in the firelight, all shadowy angles and dark good looks.

This man had given her chocolate when she'd needed chocolate. He'd given her disco when she'd needed disco. Would he, *could* he, be the one she could trust to accept her just as she really was?

'As much as it pains me to admit,' Rylie said to Tabitha, 'you may be onto something with this *off balance* thing.'

'I hear that,' Meg whispered.

When the party had well and truly wound down, Zach found Meg standing by the bar alone—a bright red firecracker amongst the few shadowy forms lingering till the end.

'Did you get your fair share of marshmallows?' he asked when he was close enough to breathe in her subtly exotic perfume.

She turned to him with a coconut shell curved into her palm and a straw in her mouth. That mouth. If Zach had ever had cause to believe in heaven and hell that mouth was enough to convince him of both.

'I've eaten far more than my fair share. But it's too late. There's no getting them back now. You had a good night?'

'Tonight hiding in plain sight finally caught up with me. My right hand is bruised from pressing local flesh all evening.'

Her eyes smiled as she sucked on her straw. 'So how was it being Mr Social?'

'One couple had me pinned for half an hour trying to get me to join their pyramid scheme.'

She laughed so hard she tucked her drink to her chest so as not to spill it. 'If you want I can give you some hints on how to extricate yourself quickly and politely so that they leave thinking you were lovely but somehow certain they'd better not go near you again.'

'You are a woman of many hidden capabilities, Ms Kelly.'

She raised one thin eyebrow. 'And then some. Now come on, you must have met some nice people.'

'I did.' Most were surprisingly decent. Warm, welcoming, enthused that he'd seen such value in their beautiful region to create the resort. He said, 'One local businesswoman had some fantastic ideas about marketing local produce around the country using the resort label. I might even look into it while I'm here.'

She grinned. 'I told you schmoozing had its perks.'

'So you did.' He glanced around. 'Where are your chaperones?'

'Rylie needed her beauty sleep and Tabitha practically had to be carried back to the room, she so wore herself out dancing.'

When she smiled at him she made him feel as if he were sixteen again with possibilities he'd never even imagined opening up before him. He felt as if he could take on the world. He felt as if he were standing on unstable ground.

He waved an arm away from the bright bar. Together they walked around the edge of the beach to a place the firelight didn't quite reach.

She slid her bare feet sensually through the sand. Her fingernails and toenails had been repainted blood-red. She smelled of jasmine. Her skin glowed warm and creamy in the firelight. Escaped tendrils of her hair flickered away from her lovely face in the light summer breeze. Heat curled deep within his abdomen.

His voice was rough when he said, 'I've had a question I wanted to ask you all night.'

She clutched her coconut shell to her chest and looked at her feet. 'And what's that?'

'Did you seriously have *that* dress in your suitcase this whole time?'

She laughed. 'A girl never knows when she's going to need a party frock. Besides, the girls packed my bags for me. You'll be shocked to discover coming to a wellness retreat was their idea.' She glanced sideways. 'You look very smart yourself.'

He puffed out his chest. 'I always do.'

'Mmm. But there's just something extra special about you tonight that I can't put my finger on.'

She put her finger on the fullest part of her bottom lip instead. The urge to drag her into the reeds and finish what they'd started the day before, to give in and let instinct and abandon bring release, was almost overwhelming.

Until she asked, 'So did you choose hot pink for your little necklace there?'

Zach glanced down at his shirt only to be reminded of the wilting lei. 'Give me a break—everyone got one coming in.'

'Do you see me wearing one?'

'They must have run out before you got here.'

'Likely excuse.' She slid the straw into her mouth and grinned.

*And now you're flirting*, he said inside his head. *Of course you're flirting. Just look at her. I mean, really look at her.* He did. She took his breath away.

They hit the far side of the fire and as one took up residence on an empty straw mat. The bonfire no longer blazed, but embers glowed red-hot at the base of the gently licking flames.

'It's very quiet out here all of a sudden,' she said, her voice soft.

'I think we may officially be considered stragglers.'

'Most socially uncool.'

'No need to panic quite yet. We won't be the very last. I'm told there's always one fellow hanging about ready to douse the fire once all's said and done.'

'Then our party reputations will live to see another day!' she said, but he saw in the flicker of her eyes that she heard what he'd really been telling her. They had a chaperone of sorts after all.

She crossed her legs frog style, sitting her drink on her far side and laying her hands in her lap—they fast disappeared into her ample skirt—as she looked into the fire.

Silence stretched between them. He wondered if she could feel the same electricity running up and down her arms that was creating havoc over his.

When she blatantly asked, 'So where's Ruby tonight?' he knew without a doubt that she was well aware.

# CHAPTER NINE

THE fact that Meg had to be the one to remind him of the participant in their relationship who wasn't there brought Zach solidly back to earth.

Habit had him slamming his lips shut tight. But then Meg tucked loose strands of hair behind her ear and shot him an encouraging smile. And he couldn't deny, even to himself, that talking to her helped. More than talking to Felicia, or the teachers at Ruby's school, or the social workers who came to the house once a week.

Maybe it was the fact that she would be leaving in a few days. Maybe it was because sometimes she seemed to understand Ruby more than even he did. Or maybe it was because he simply enjoyed talking to her.

For whatever reason, he said, 'She's sleeping over at her friend Clarissa's house. Her first sleepover since moving here. She was so excited when the invitation came through this morning I couldn't say no.'

'Did she tell you about the invitation before or after she made you pancakes?'

He thought back. 'After.'

Meg laughed softly. 'Getting you all nice and buttered up before going in for the kill. I love it.'

The affection in Meg's voice didn't surprise him, but again it moved him. Because of this woman, parts of himself he'd thought long since turned to dry ice had begun to melt. And he wasn't the only one.

He patted the chest of his jacket and felt inside the card Ruby had presented to him that morning. A card she'd made, addressed to Meg. He'd brought it with him with every intention of giving it to her. He even got as far as reaching inside and touching the pink cardboard before his fingers curled into his palm.

Even as he'd slid the card into his jacket earlier that evening, he'd known he couldn't *ever* tell Meg about the card.

Letting Ruby develop a fondness for her was a bad idea. A kid could only have the object of their affection snatched away from them so many times before they learnt it hurt less to simply never form attachments at all. It was his duty to protect Ruby from that kind of hurt as well. As such he could only in good conscience encourage friendships he knew would last.

Meg turned to him with a wide, lovely, genuine smile, and he wished he could be as conscientious with himself. He let his hand slide out of his coat pocket, empty.

She waggled a finger at him and said, 'If I didn't know better I'd think you've read the book after all.'

'Which book is that?'

'*How to Father a Girl.* It's extremely hard to track down and even more difficult to decipher. Lots of hieroglyphics and double talk. But you seem to be following along beautifully.'

'I don't always get that same feeling from Felicia.'

Meg raised an eyebrow. 'Do tell.'

He baulked. Then convinced himself that while keeping Ruby a step removed was one thing, sharing pieces of *his* experiences was fine. In fact, so far it had done him nothing but good. 'She seemed to think I ought to keep Ruby home from Clarissa's because a) she did have a sore throat, or b) she'd been hamming it up. Either way she should be spending the weekend in bed.'

'You overrode the nanny?' Her eyes widened. 'Brave man.'

Zach laughed. 'Letting Ruby have some fun felt right.' He scooped up a handful of sand and let it run slowly through his fingers as he remembered. 'Then after it was settled, for some reason I winked at her. I've never, not once in my entire life, winked. Didn't even know I knew how. And you know what the rascal did?'

'What?'

'She giggled. No more amazing a sound have I heard in my entire life.'

Meg pulled her knees back to her chest and wrapped her arms around them. 'I knew it,' she said on a sigh. 'You've so-o-o read the book.'

Zach brushed the sand from his hand and glanced at her from the corner of his eye. In the semi-darkness the angle of her body was outlined in gold from the dying fire—all curled into itself like a ball of shimmering red fabric. It wouldn't matter who her father was, or the size of her trust fund, she would draw the eyes of those who knew quality when they saw it wherever she went.

He took in a deep breath, wood smoke tickling the back of his throat. 'I may be faking it well enough to fool you, and perhaps even Felicia and Ruby. But the grim truth is I know next to nothing about kids, and less about girls.'

'Many, *many* eons ago little Zach was seven.'

'That is so. Yet my hope is that Zach at seven and Ruby at seven have very different experiences.'

'Why's that?'

The night was so quiet, the fire so mellow, the air so warm, Meg's voice and presence in the darkness so reassuring. The uncomfortable truth of his childhood balanced on the tip of his tongue for a moment before he swallowed it down. He didn't talk about it. Didn't even like thinking about it. If having stopped flying to the ends of the earth and back meant all that purposely lost baggage might yet catch up with him...

He said, 'She's a girl, for one thing.'

Meg laughed and it echoed through him hollowly. All that virgin trust between them had been built for nought if he could still feign his feelings so easily. But it was too late to tell her now. The moment had passed.

'To tell you the truth,' she said, 'what girls think, what we like, what annoys us, what we want isn't really all that different at Ruby's age or mine.'

'And that is?'

She laughed again. This time he was quick enough to close down the exposed parts of himself so, instead of it making him feel so cool and alone inside, her laughter skittered hot and fast across his skin like sparks from the fire.

Her knees fell towards him, her hand reached out to give her balance and he could see more of her face in the firelight. 'Better I don't say. The more you think you know about womankind, the more you realise you don't know. I'm not being any help to you at all, am I?'

'You are. More than you know.'

'Really?' The flicker of surprise in her voice caught him off guard.

'Really,' he said, infusing the word with as much gravity as he could.

She watched him for a few long, hot moments before finding the fingernails of her right hand unexpectedly intriguing. 'Well, of course I'm helping. I was a seven-year-old girl a lot more recently than you were a seven-year-old boy.'

'That'll be why.'

She smiled. He caught it at the fire-lit edge of her profile. A sexy curve of her mouth, a softening of her wide blue eyes.

Heaven help him, he could have kissed her then and there. In front of the lingering fire-douser and anyone else who'd cared to hang about once the food and drinks were gone.

Then she had to go and ask, 'Did you always want kids?' and it was as good as a cold shower.

'Never.' The all too illuminating answer shot from his mouth like some kind of penance for his earlier cowardice. But it was out there now. So he went the only way he knew—forward.

'My lifestyle was not conducive to kids. Or a family of any sort. I was on a plane twice a week. I've lived in hotel suites my whole adult life. The only real-estate I've ever owned was commercial. Any relationships I've had had to fit into that way of life, period.'

'And when you first found out about Ruby?'

'When my lawyer rang with the news I thought it was some kind of cruel joke. But when I hung up the phone it felt as though I'd been waiting for that call all my life.'

'Simple as that, she changed your mind?' she asked, her voice gentle.

'In a heartbeat. It's the strangest thing, but now I can barely remember my life without her.'

The fire crackled as a log split and those above spilt into the gap. Zach came to from far, far away, a whole other lifetime. He glanced across at Meg. Her face tilted to watch the sparks that fluttered up into the darkness. Without the play of expressions that continuously gave her away, he had no idea what she was thinking.

'How about you?' he asked on a whim.

She licked her lips and her brow furrowed for a moment before she turned to him with a breezy smile. 'Kids? Gosh, no. Wherever would I find the time?'

'You're just saying that to make me feel better for admitting I felt that way.'

'Not at all. I promise.' Again he thought he caught a hint of a frown, but it was too dark to really tell. Whatever it was it was soon swallowed by the kind of overbright smile he knew better than to trust. 'Don't get me wrong—my nieces are two of my favourite people in the entire word. I love them to distraction. But it's not on the cards for me.'

'Why?'

He could tell she was really looking at him, and he wished there were some way of turning on a light. Of looking into those bright eyes and knowing what she was thinking before she said it. Being a step behind felt…disquieting somehow.

She eventually said, 'Even apart from the whole cameras-outside-your-front-door thing, the life of a Kelly kid is not an easy one. The pressure to be the best, the brightest, every day a winner is immense. And that's not changing any day soon.'

'Your nieces are going through this now?'

Again she paused. *Come on*, he thought, *I could do it, so can you.* 'I find myself quietly sabotaging the process wherever I possibly can. I sneak them junk food when their dad's not watching. I teach them swear words in French, which my father doesn't speak. If I babysit I let them wear pyjamas all day. I let them be kids.'

'Talk about maternal instincts,' he said with two raised eyebrows.

She stared at him as if he had grown horns. As if he was missing the point entirely. Then her hand moved to rest on her belly. She scrunched her hand into a fist before looking away and reaching out to grab her toes.

'Instincts or no, unlike you I'm hardly going to have one appear out of the woodwork so that's the end of that.' She shook it off. Literally, her whole body gave one great shiver, before she said, 'Okay. Moving on. Here's something *you* can take to the bank. You ready?'

'Always.'

'Meg's crash course on Raising a Girl 101. Ruby will make friends you don't like, she'll see movies that'll make your eyes pop out of your head, listen to music that makes your ears ache, she'll diet when she doesn't need to, and eat ice cream for breakfast, and she'll meet boys you wish had never been born. Roll with the punches for your own sake. And for hers, let her know no matter what happens she always has a safe place to go home to.'

He nodded, though his head was reeling with points one and two, much less the rest. 'That's why I took on the house here. To give her somewhere near her familiar haunts to come home to.'

'Nu-uh, Mr Jones. By home, I mean *you*. This is the clincher, the one thing you should get tattooed to your arm. No matter what happens, no matter what she does, always, *always*, make sure she knows you love her. That's what will keep her coming home.'

Zach realised he was holding his breath. But he didn't let it go until his lungs began to burn from inaction.

Love. *Love*. Love? The more times he said the word, the less sense it made.

What did he know about love? He'd fed Ruby, clothed her, given her shelter, filled her room with trinkets, let her have her little rebellions as some kind of compensation for not having a mother. But love?

If his own childhood had taught him anything it was that love was a sham. A fickle fairy tale. If loving someone as much as he'd loved some of his foster parents didn't ensure they loved him back, what was the point?

He breathed deep and buried his face in his palms. What a hypocrite. He'd been busy convincing himself he was all about the fatherly care, when all the while he was actually dolling out the same kind of veiled neglect of his childhood without even realising it.

That poor, *poor* kid. Baking him pancakes, picking him wildflowers. At least she was trying to show him she loved him. While he hadn't given her a single clue that he loved her too.

*He loved her.* Of course he damned well loved her. He'd have been some kind of fool to have changed his life so completely had he not.

He blinked into the fire. Stunned. Apparently never being shown how did not make him as incapable as he'd always believed.

He glanced at Meg. Their gazes tangled a moment longer than could ever be considered merely friendly.

Meg raised her eyebrows. 'Are you okay?'

'Terrified,' he said before he could censor himself.

She laughed softly. Sadly even. 'Then you know you're not perfect. You know you have limitations. That's a good thing. Believe me. What happened to Ruby's mum?'

The last part came so out of the blue it shocked Zach right out of his funk. 'Cancer. It was quick. Ruby didn't even know till it was all over.'

'No! Oh, the poor pet. And Isabel had really never told you about Ruby?'

He shook his head. 'Our relationship had been casual. It ended as easily as it had begun. Still she was very clear in her will that she wanted me to have custody. For that one fact I have to forgive her the rest.'

'Was it really that easy? I know I'm speaking out of turn, but even I don't feel like *I'm* ready to forgive her and I didn't even know the woman.'

She hadn't even had to tell him so. He'd seen the fight in her eyes. Like a lioness protecting her cub. When had this fireside flirtation suddenly become so intense?

He said, 'Over something that important, it was either forgive or let it burn for ever. The choice was simple.'

One dark curl draped over her pale shoulder as she wrapped her arms tight about her knees again. And there they sat, in loaded silence for a good couple of minutes before she finally said: 'My father's sick. You've probably heard.'

He didn't nod. He didn't need to. A person would have to be a hermit, a far more dedicated one than he was, not to know Quinn Kelly had heart problems. 'How's he doing?'

She nodded vigorously. 'Exceptionally well, the old warhorse. So far as I know. He's retired. Plays golf a lot. Eats the kind of food your chef would applaud.'

'That's good news, then.'

She nodded, but it wasn't as effusive. She was a million miles away. 'It gets a girl to thinking.'

'About?'

She scrunched up her nose. 'Things far too blah to go into on such a beautiful night. I'm sorry. Where were we? Ruby.'

Back to Ruby. Always Ruby. It occurred to him then that she might be using his daughter as a shield as much as he had been. He couldn't help but wonder why.

'Meg.'

'Zach,' she said in a mock-sombre voice.

'Tell me.'

She focused on the flowers around his neck. 'It's just all this stuff that I haven't thought about in years that has shuffled up to the surface in the last little while. And then you sit there all noble, making forgiveness sound so easy when I just don't think I could—'

'Tell me,' he said again.

She blinked at him. All big blue eyes and down-turned mouth. 'I can't believe I'm about to... God, where do I begin?'

His voice felt unusually tight as he said, 'Wherever you see fit.'

'Okay,' she said with a hearty sigh. 'There's this one memory that's been playing on my mind. Years ago my father was given an Honorary Doctorate of Commerce by a university in Melbourne. He'd never gone to uni, never even finished high school, so it was a matter of immense pride. One of my brothers had scraped his knee or something equally boyish, so Mum waited at the hotel to be taken with them in the town car and my father drove himself, with me there, at my mother's insistence, to keep him company. This was years before GPS.'

She looked to him. Her eyes narrowed, almost pleading he get her to stop. He just nodded. *Go on.*

'Anyway, when he finally admitted he was lost he gave me the street directory and told me to show him how to get there. I'd never used one before, couldn't pronounce half the street names, so I read the map wrong and we were late. Less than five minutes, but late is late.'

She stopped again. Licked her lips. Her hands were shaking. The tension streaming off her was palpable. He could feel his pulse beating in his temples.

'What did he do?' Zach asked, half not wanting to know, half needing her to trust him enough to tell him.

'Before the engine had even come to a halt he turned on me. With such venom.' She shook her ponytail off her shoulder to hide the flinch as the memory came at her. 'I was careless, ridiculous, stupid and I had to find my own way back to the hotel to teach me to take heed of where I was and who I was with. By the time I made it to the hotel it was after dark, my mother was beside herself and my father had holed himself up in his room. His doctorate thrown onto the front table of the suite as though it was rubbish.'

Her eyes flickered to his—dark, grave, wounded. Eyes so beautiful they should never be made to look that way. His fingers curled into fists and adrenalin like he'd never felt shot through him.

'How old were you?'

'About Ruby's age. Maybe a little younger.'

He'd known it the moment she'd started telling the story. Hearing her admit as much still made him want to hit something. Or more particularly someone.

'It wasn't the first time,' he said matter-of-factly.

She shrugged and seemed to disappear even further inside her ample skirt. 'Ever since I can remember he'd always been distant. Working a lot. But the first time he took it out on me was the time I told my nanny I was adopted. I thought it was because I'd dare think not being one of them was a more attractive option.'

'And now?'

She let out a long, shaky breath. 'Now I wonder if I had it all backwards. There have always been rumours…' She swallowed, and looked at him, her big, blue eyes begging him to say the things she couldn't.

Zach said, 'You mean his affairs?'

'Not the kind of thing a parent can keep from their kid when even rumours make the papers.' Her mouth twisted, but a gleam had lit her eyes, as though her strength was returning now she wasn't the only one bearing the load. 'I've often wondered if I was an afterthought. A way to keep their marriage together. If so, it worked. But while my mother never gave a hint of it, the only way I could make sense of my father's behaviour was that I was a reminder of the worst time of his life. That he regretted it. And regretted me.'

'Even if that's true it's not your fault.'

She shrugged. 'I know. I do. And I don't even care any more. At least I thought I didn't. I don't even know why I brought it up.'

Zach understood all too well. 'You've made it very clear exactly why I need to always put Ruby first.'

'I did? I guess I did. And don't you forget it!'

Her soft mouth turned up into the echo of a familiar smile.

As they looked into one another's eyes the night stretched and contracted, and once again they communicated more in the silence than mere words could ever say.

Ruby's card began to burn a hole in his top pocket. If ever there was a moment for him to take a risk and give it to her…

And then she yawned. 'And on that note now seems like a good time to escort me back to my room.'

She flapped her hands at him. He pulled himself to his feet before pulling her after him. As they stood face to face her perfumed scent washed over him, delicate and delicious.

All he'd have to do was slide a hand around her neck and pull her to him and that mouth would be all his. The urge to kiss her, to take away the hurt, to give her something warm and wonderful to think about instead was overwhelming.

But she wasn't some gorgeous young thing putting her hand up for a one-night stand. She'd had an intense night. Her thoughts were so obviously still scrambled. He'd be taking complete advantage.

'One last question,' he said, his voice low and rough.

She raised one sexy eyebrow.

'It's about Ruby. I know, I know, I'm getting predictable.'

The corner of her mouth twitched as though she knew exactly what he was doing. 'Shoot.'

'Should I get her a pet? A rabbit maybe?'

She let go of his hands and backed away from the beach towards the resort, towards the end of the night. 'You can't get her a rabbit! They're a pest in Queensland. Start with a goldfish. Let her choose it. Let her name it whatever she wants. She'll be putty in your hands.'

He caught up in three long strides. 'You had a fish?'

'I was a terrible pet owner. I always forgot to feed them, and they had a habit of leaping from the tank in desperation to leave me. But Mum just kept on replacing them. A dozen fish must have died to save the poor woman from having to tell me what was happening.'

'What did you name your first fish?'

She bit back a smile. 'Luke Skywalker. I so-o-o wanted to grow up to be Luke.'

'And now?'

'Now I know better. Han Solo is the bomb.'

# CHAPTER TEN

MEG felt more than a little shaky as she walked slowly beside Zach up the white stone path leading away from the lake back to the resort.

What a mess. The things she'd said, the things she'd admitted. So many years she'd kept them deep inside. And then along came Zach and her tightly reined-in emotions were in a tailspin.

There was only one conclusion. She was falling for him. She might as well have been running around with a pair of scissors in her hand. It was only a matter of time before she got seriously hurt.

She had no idea if it was ten at night or three in the morning. The moon told her nothing as she had no sense of direction. The grass was grey and dewy, low cloud cover hovered higher up the path, lending a magical feeling to the place. If she weren't feeling as highly strung as a thoroughbred she might even be able to enjoy it. Instead all she could think about was the man walking silently at her side.

At the very least she knew he'd taken from her shambolic confession what she'd wanted him to—that the foundations of his whole relationship with Ruby were being forged *right now*. The good moments, the pancakes-for-breakfast moments, should be the ones she remembered too.

But even knowing she'd done a selfless thing didn't stop her from feeling like a bowl of jelly on a shaky table.

She slowed her steps before she tripped over her numb feet. Zach's slowed to match.

'Zach?' she said, her voice so croaky she cleared her throat. 'Can I just ask, the things I told you before, I—'

He shook his head and held up a finger an inch from her mouth. Her words dried up in her throat.

Zach's voice was deep when he finally opened his mouth to speak. 'My parents passed away when I was five years old. With no other family I grew up in a slew of foster homes and state-run children's homes—some fair, more atrocious. It didn't matter which, I was still pushed in and pulled out again months later, again and again, with no warning and no word as to why. I had no consistent contact with any one person—no supervisor, no parent, no other foster child—until the day I turned sixteen and I caught a bus to Sydney and began my life.'

Meg realised she was breathing heavily. 'God, you must think me a schmuck. Complaining about my father when yours wasn't even—'

'No,' he said with a stilling hand on her shoulder. 'Don't do that. No comparing. We each need to own what we've been dealt or we'll never be able to move on.'

She nodded. Then laughed softly to release the pent-up energy coursing through her starting at the point where his strong hand lay upon her bare shoulder. 'You're making me think I ought to have listened harder in wellness class.'

She shook her head, angry at herself for being flippant when talking about anything real. If there was ever a time to not go there, this was it.

She looked up at Zach—tall, dark, divine. 'Have you really owned your past?'

He made a clicking noise with the side of his mouth. 'Please.

Why do you think I keep building bigger and better wellness resorts? I'm looking to prove I'm better than my past as much as the next man. But in the past few days I have come to understand a little more about what my foster parents went through. Not taking me in with open arms had little to do with me at all. They would have had to have been masochists to have given that kind of emotional investment to a child they knew would never be theirs. Knowing there's even a minute chance is akin to emotional torture…'

His voice petered off.

'But Ruby—'

'Might still not end up with me.'

'What?' Meg said, her voice like air. 'How?'

'We have up to a year for the state to decide if I am a fit guardian,' Zach said.

Meg's heart squeezed as she remembered the look in Zach's eyes when he'd said his life had changed in a heartbeat when Ruby had come along. The look in Ruby's eyes when she'd proudly said who her father was. 'How long have you had her so far?'

'Seven months, eight days.'

Meg bunched her dress to keep her hands busy lest she do something stupid like hug the guy.

She couldn't even imagine the daily torture it must be to have something so wonderful within reach, knowing it might yet be snatched away. She glanced up at his beautiful profile. Okay, so maybe she could imagine it just the tiniest little bit.

She placed a hand on her heart. 'If there's *anything* I can do. Write a letter of recommendation. Talk to the judge. My family has connections the likes of which you wouldn't believe.'

Before he could be too proud to turn her down, she held out a hand close enough she could feel the warmth of his breath washing against her skin.

'Forget you're not a fan of hoopla. If you need to in order

to fight for Ruby, use me for all I'm worth. My notoriety has to be good for something more than invites to every party in town, right?'

He wrapped his fingers around her hand, sliding them through hers until they were intertwined. 'I was going to say thank you.'

'Oh. Well, then, you're welcome.'

She glanced at him, the dark silhouette striding alongside her in the near darkness. Things were even more complicated than she'd imagined. A little girl. A custody battle. And all remarkably hush-hush. How he did it alone, with no family support and with such integrity, she had no idea.

'Is that why you don't do press? You don't like talking about your background?'

'I didn't like being judged for something I had no control over then and I still don't.'

'Why?'

She looked up at him too late to notice how tight his jaw had become.

'If people tell you you're crap often enough, you begin to believe it.'

'You don't think I know that?'

'I say don't give them the chance.'

'I say find a way to negate it so that it can no longer hurt you. There's nothing at all shameful about it. Who you've become is amazing.' She looked down at her toes sticking out of her Grecian sandals. 'I mean, the story of how you got here is amazing. Think about all the foster kids you could help if they knew how you'd pulled yourself up by your own socks to become who you are.'

'Not going to happen. I have to think of Ruby.'

'And what about her?' she asked. 'Are you ever going to tell her where you came from? And if you do will you swear her to silence? Or keep her locked up here for ever to protect yourself from the sting of other people's opinions?'

'What about your father?' he shot back.

'What about him?'

He pulled her closer, until they came to a stop. 'He's a bully. Hell, Meg, he was emotionally abusive to you. Yet of all the parts of your life on show, why has that never come out? Why not show other young girls that their own expectations of themselves are the ones that matter, not what other people think they should be?'

She tried to expertly extricate her hand from his, a move she'd pulled a thousand times, but it was as though he had been waiting for it.

He took her other hand so she was stuck facing him when he said, 'Forget Ruby for a moment—what about all the other little girls who read magazines and look up to you as a role model?'

That was what her volunteer work was for! So what if the girls whose hair she braided and the boys she played cops and robbers with didn't know who the woman behind the bleached-blonde wig and brown contacts was? At least she was there.

She itched to tell him so. To say out loud that working at the Valley Shelter was the most rewarding thing she'd ever done and that every moment she spent flirting with a camera lens so that her rotten bloody father got the chance to muck about with someone else's hard-earned savings felt more and more like hard work.

Especially when even having looked death in the eye it hadn't once occurred to him to make retribution.

But the old fear of being thought ridiculous for thinking herself more valuable than she was rose up her ankles, her calves, her waist, until it reached her throat and she sputtered like an old car whose engine would never again come to life.

'I do think of them,' she said. 'I am doing what I can. In my way. Just not the way you mean.'

He closed his eyes a moment and took a calming breath. He was probably counting to ten. Her brothers did that all the time.

When he opened his eyes they were deliberately calm. As such she wasn't nearly prepared for his next words.

He said, 'So you're not simply filling the void of not being loved by your father with being loved by the entire world?'

She coughed out an incredulous laugh, and dragged her hands from his to slam them onto her hips. 'Are *you* trying to tell *me* that giving up your life for Ruby isn't your way of making *someone* in the world love you back?'

Silence stretched between them as taut and dangerous as an overstretched rubber band.

Until Zach said, 'Maybe you're right. Maybe that's how this all began. But I do love her. And as soon as she comes home from Clarissa's, I'll tell her so because it's important for a little girl to know her dad loves her. Or so someone I trust told me.'

Meg shook her head. This was backfiring big time. If he pulled when she pushed she was never going to be rid of him. Instead, he was being gorgeous and warm and understanding and a tower of strength and a wonderful dad.

With a growl at the moon she headed back up the path again.

'Meg,' he said from behind her.

She waved a go-away hand at him.

He jogged to catch up to her, this time spinning her to face him with the gentlest of pressure at her elbow.

'Thanks ever so much for being such an enchanting escort, but I'm sure I can make it back from here.' She glanced at her surroundings to discover they had gone a ways past the Waratah House turn-off and had found themselves outside one of the lovely little bungalows on the way to Zach's place. A light was on over the porch.

'I could do with a coffee right about now—how about you?' he asked.

She whirled to stare at him. The moon was now almost completely obscured by cloud and his eyes were nothing more than patches of black within his shadowed face. 'Now what are you talking about?'

He waved a hand towards the bungalow. 'I use it as my office. Some nights I stay over rather than heading back to the house. So the pantry is well stocked with all sorts of delights, including coffee.'

'Oh,' she said, his meaning not even the slightest bit obscured by the fact that she couldn't see his eyes. He'd been leading her here the whole time. To his cosy, empty, private abode. Which had a bed. And coffee.

She licked her lips as her mind whirled a million miles a minute. 'And you kept this from me the whole time? The coffee part, I mean.'

His mouth lifted so the preposterously sexy arc in his right cheek put in a surprise appearance. 'I wasn't prepared to share my coffee with you then.'

'And now?'

He lifted a hand to slide it into the hair at the base of her neck, the tug of his warm fingers almost too much to bear.

'I'd say things have changed rather dramatically over the past few days. My eyes have been opened in more ways than one. And I only have you to thank. Coffee seems a meagre place to start.'

Meg swallowed, her mouth dry, her blood thundering in her ears until she felt the slightest bit dizzy. There were reasons, good reasons why this couldn't happen, only she couldn't remember one.

He slid his spare hand into his trouser pockets. She imagined she could hear the soft tinkle of keys somewhere on his person.

'Zach—' she said, her voice half appeal, half groan.

'Enough talk,' he said.

He leaned down and kissed her. And she was on her toes, reaching up to him even before he gathered her into his arms.

The raging heat of his kiss swept her away, spiralling her into the cosmos until she could no longer feel her feet. Could no longer remember her name.

Or why they hadn't been doing this all along.

Meg lay on Zach's bed, white cotton sheets tangled about her, his long limbs trapping her in his warm embrace.

She glanced at the clock on the wall. It was only a couple of hours before sunset. Rylie and Tabitha would soon notice her gone. They'd assume where she was, and they'd be right. They'd known she'd end up here before she did. As apparently did Zach. It seemed everyone knew her better than she knew herself.

She tilted her head to watch Zach's sleeping face. The creases at the edges of his eyes had disappeared. His tanned skin looked radiant against the white pillow. A faint line curved down his right cheek, a reminder of the arc that grooved deep when he laughed. He was sleeping like a man with no worries on his mind.

She reached up and slid a curl from his forehead. He didn't stir.

Such gentle strength. She felt it infusing her more with every second she spent in his arms until she couldn't imagine when in her life she would ever have felt this kind of peace, this slowly budding confidence that if she looked deep inside herself she might not be afraid of what she saw.

The words spilled from her lips to his sleeping form before she even knew they were coming. 'I volunteer at the Valley Women's Shelter at least once a week. It's a halfway house for women who've managed to break free of abusive relationships but have nowhere else to go. Most have kids. Most have nothing with which to go it alone bar the clothes on their backs. Many are so battered and bruised they can barely talk.'

He shifted and she held her breath. He slid his leg along hers, wrapping his arm tighter about her, sending warm waves of pleasure all over her body. But his eyes remained closed. She waited until the sensations rolling across her skin dissipated, and his breaths were once again even and deep.

'I wear a blonde wig,' she whispered, 'contacts, the kind of make-up you'd see in a bad eighties movie, clothes I picked up in a bargain bin at a thrift store. I can walk through a throng of paparazzi in front of my building and they don't turn an eye. The guys at the shelter know me as Daisy. They've never asked questions, just appreciated someone giving their time to play with the kids while the mums have medicals, or to just sit and hold a woman's hand while they tell their stories to the counsellors.'

She took a deep breath and let it out on a wobble.

'Compared with the level of abuse they've been subjected to my dad constantly finding new weird and wonderful ways of letting me know he didn't consider me worthy of the name Kelly was a walk in the park. But I still see myself reflected in their eyes when they talk about how hard it was to finally say "enough". I give cups of tea, and a shoulder to cry on and secretly stashed envelopes full of money to help them start a new life. It's the most worthwhile thing I've ever done and my name has nothing to do with it.'

She let her gaze amble over Zach's beautiful nose, his strong jaw, the smattering of dark hair curling over his chest.

'So there you have it. That's what I do to really make a difference. I just don't shout it out to the world. Not because I'm not proud, or I don't realise it's vitally important. But because it's hard, and it's private, and I do it for myself and for them, not for him and not for the cameras.'

'Thank you,' Zach said, and had it not been for the knot of sheets and his heavy limbs keeping her in bed Meg might well have leapt a foot in the air.

She placed a hand over her thundering heart. 'How long have you been awake?'

'Longer than you have.'

She lay back and blinked up at the ceiling. 'So, just now, you heard everything.'

'Everything.' He snuggled in closer and kissed her on the cheek, right at the edge of her mouth. 'And thank you for telling me.'

She turned to face him. His dark eyes burned into hers. She needn't have searched so desperately for what he was thinking—it was written all over his beautiful face. He did not think her ridiculous. He did not think her a mere party girl. He thought her pretty amazing.

'Thank you for listening,' she whispered before leaning in and placing her lips against his.

And they made love again. Slowly, gently, not once taking their eyes off one another.

A while later Meg fell asleep, knowing without a single doubt that she loved him. Knowing she was never again going to meet someone who saw her, really saw her, as he did. Who made her wonder if the day might yet come when she'd be brave enough to let the rest of the world nearer than skin deep too.

She fell asleep knowing Zach cared for her. Knowing he respected her. Knowing he'd made *love* to her.

She fell asleep knowing that, despite all that, Zach Jones and his gorgeous blooming little family only reminded her with stark, heart-wrenching clarity what she could never have.

As the sun rose through the bay windows of the bungalow, Zach stood in the bedroom doorway in last night's trousers watching Meg dress.

She stood by his rumpled bed, tying the bow on her dress,

the muscles of her back working sexily, a small frown pinched
between her brows, and her top teeth biting down on her bottom
lip. He couldn't believe there was ever a moment when he'd
assumed the Meg Kelly the country adored was all an act. In
that moment she was so very, very real.

The diamonds, the flashy friends, the *va-va-voom*, they were
the trappings of her life, but not why she was beloved. It came
down to the fact that she was a warm, dynamic woman who
bled like everyone else, and spent her life making sure those
around her didn't hurt as much when they bled too. Whether it
was a woman running from an abusive husband, her complicated family, his young daughter, a complete stranger who
accosted her, camera in hand, while she vacationed, she had
time, she had a smile, she had a way of making them feel better
off for having met her.

His hands literally ached with the desire to haul her back into
his arms and soak up every bit of vitality she could spare. But
he needed to get home. To be there when Ruby returned. He
had things to do. Things to say.

He pushed away from the door and slid his hand down her
back, tugging at her dress until he could feel and see the trail
of wild daisies tattooed across her lower back.

At his touch her head fell back in pleasure, her hair spilling
over her bare skin.

'So what's the story here?' he asked, his fingers tracing the
daisy vine, his breath tickling her ear.

She shivered. 'I got it when I was fifteen. Daisies were my
favourite flower. Luckily they still are.'

'What? Fifteen? You need parental permission, right? Until
you're eighteen?' *Please, God*, he thought, *let that be true*.

She smiled over her shoulder at him. 'Of course you do. Unless
your father said no way in hell was his daughter getting a tattoo
and you were me. Then you find a way to get whatever you want.'

Her skin was warm and soft until the tattoo made it feel ever so slightly rough. 'Did it hurt?'

'Like hot needles into the bone for two straight hours. Yuh-huh.'

'You really were a tearaway.'

'I could tell you stories.'

He placed a kiss where her neck met her shoulder. 'So tell me.'

She moved so that her hair fell over the spot he'd just been kissing. 'Another time perhaps.'

He pulled back. A sudden chill had come from her direction. He shook it off. Mornings after were always at least some level of awkward. She'd be all right with some space to process it all.

He searched for his shirt from the night before to find it crumpled on the floor. 'Give me a minute to find a T-shirt and I'll walk you back.'

She plonked onto the corner of his bed as she tied the straps of her shoes around and around her calves. 'Best not. The forest has eyes and ears.'

It struck him she'd once again gone there, to Ruby, so fast, and before he had. But then again there was so much about this whole night that had surprised him. Including the fact that eyes and ears no longer seemed such a threat as they had twenty-four hours earlier.

She had been right in accusing him of locking Ruby away to save himself from having to face the demons of his past. And while he didn't want to see Ruby hurt, ever, surely he didn't want her living the kind of emotionally and physically isolated existence he'd lived all the years before she brought him back into the light.

Meg stood, smoothed down her dress, slicked her hair back into a fresh ponytail and looked around to make sure she hadn't left anything behind.

'Come over for morning tea,' he said before he could stop himself.

Meg glanced up at him in obvious shock. She licked her lips before saying, 'And what, skip DIY Colonic Irrigation class?'

He laughed, but he was not to be deterred. 'Let's say around eleven.'

She watched him a few long moments. Her back was to the sun, so he couldn't make out the expression in her eyes. For the first time in hours a familiar hollowness began to expand inside him. He didn't know what to make of it, he only knew he didn't like it.

'Why?'

*Good question.* 'I promised you coffee last night and we never quite got there.'

'You didn't promise me anything, Zach,' she said, her voice gentle.

'Come over. Drink coffee. The rest we can make up as we go along.'

Another few protracted moments passed in which she just looked at him. Though it felt more as if she was looking through him, her mind a million miles away. 'Should I bring anything?'

The hollowness went away. 'Just yourself.'

She ran her hands down her dress again. 'Okay.'

'We'll see you then.'

She caught the 'we' loud and clear. He could see it in her sudden stillness. In the duration of her indecipherable stare.

'Just you,' he said. 'Not your family. Not your father. In the privacy of my home. I'm asking *you* to break bread with my daughter and me under comparatively conventional circumstances.'

She nodded. Then said, 'Fine. Till then.'

She leaned into him, her hand pressing against his bare chest as she placed a goodbye kiss on his cheek. He could smell the scent of the lei he'd worn the night before on her skin.

She moved back just far enough to look into his eyes for one dark, hot moment before she walked away.

# CHAPTER ELEVEN

LATER that same morning Meg stood in the opening in the stone wall at the edge of Zach's backyard, her fingers gripped tight around a bunch of wildflowers she'd picked along the way.

'What are you doing here?' she asked herself out loud.

She couldn't answer that any more than she could figure out what Zach saw as the end play to all this. She'd made it clear kids weren't part of her life plan and that she wouldn't be the right kind of influence over his. Last night she'd let him off the hook in showing she understood why he would choose Ruby's privacy over any manner of relationship with her.

Last night…

She sighed. It ought to have been their swansong, and a beautiful swansong at that. If only he hadn't had some crazy idea she couldn't fathom. And if only she hadn't gone and fallen in love with the guy.

Her mobile phone buzzed in her pocket, scaring the bejeezers out of her, and fraying her very last nerves.

She ignored it as she had the last ten times it had buzzed that morning. The moment she'd got back to her room her family—who had mostly left her alone for less than half her allotted vacation time—had decided to rear their relentless heads en masse.

Dylan's voice message had appeared first, taking the edge off her long, luxurious, hot shower: 'Hey, kiddo. Tabby told me where she's taken you. Classic! By now you must be itching for something to take your mind off the boredom. Find a computer, RSVP yourself to the Shyler Benefit in KInG's name for the day you get back.'

No *goodbye*. No *if you happen to be free*. Just do it. She justly ignored him.

During breakfast Cameron's first text message came through: 'U have Dad's *The Iliad*? Urgent…ish. Rosie'd love to read it. What Rosie wants Rosie gets!'

From her newly mobiled-up mother: 'Love you. Miss you.' From her father? Not a whisper. All that water under the bridge and it still wounded.

Angry with herself for letting her father get to her by omission, when Brendan's number blinked on the screen five minutes later she ignored it. Voicemail gave her: 'Mum has a thing next Saturday night. The nanny's night off. You need to look after the girls. Confirm with my secretary ASAP.'

Dylan must have called again as his next message came through straight after: 'How do you feel about co-hosting the Queensland Fashion Awards? You love the idea. I knew you would. Call me ten minutes ago and I'll set you up with press to confirm.'

She'd somehow almost forgotten that this was what her life was like back home—non-stop motion, never saying no, doing everything to be appear cheerful and be inordinately useful. Everybody's favourite girl. She felt exhausted and underwhelmed just thinking about it.

Of course the fact she'd had less than two hours of uninterrupted sleep amidst one of the most stunning, tender, unsparing, magical, revealing nights of her life would likely have made aliens landing on her doorstep an underwhelming experience.

She looked through the brush to the hint of a house beyond. To Zach. She breathed in deep through her mouth and out through her nose, her heart racing as if she'd run five kilometres that morning rather than tucking herself up under the bed covers and hiding the moment she'd snuck back to her room.

As she walked through the backyard a flock of pink and grey galahs settled in a nearby tree. Discarded by Ruby's swing were her skipping rope and a pink bike with a white cane basket and streamers on the handle bars. Had it really only been days since she'd been there before? It felt as if weeks had passed.

The thing that ought to have her walking away kept her moving forward: the chance to see them together. To see if he was as natural a father as she'd trusted. To see if Ruby was as doting a kid as she'd suspected. It would be akin to self-flagellation, but she had to know. To see if that kind of relationship really could exist.

Her phone buzzed again. She whipped it out of her pocket, switched it off and shoved it out of sight.

She headed up the rope bridge that led to the largest structure amongst the string of thatched-roof rooms.

A grey-haired woman came out onto the verandah, and she jumped in fright at seeing Meg bundling her way. 'Aren't you just as quiet as a church mouse?'

*I'm as nervous as one*, Meg thought. But she conjured up her second-nature Meg Kelly smile, designed to put others at ease, and said, 'I'm Meg. I'm expected.'

The woman's cheeks pinked. She even gave a small curtsy. 'Of course you are, dear. I'm Felicia, Ruby's nanny. You may as well make yourself comfy out here. Zach won't be long.'

Meg handed the motley bunch of flowers over to Felicia, whose eyes widened a tad before a smile snuck into her already copiously creased cheeks.

'How charming. I'll put these in water, shall I?' Felicia then turned and headed along the balcony and across yet another bridge and out of sight.

Feeling like a flibbertigibbet, Meg tugged at her floral peasant top making sure it remained demure, and smoothed down her tight, cropped jeans.

Footsteps came from behind her. She spun around and had to cling to the railing for support against the rush of heat that swept over her as Zach walked down the hall inside the house towards her.

His feet were bare below faded jeans that fitted snugly to his long legs as though he'd owned them all his life. A just as faded coffee-brown T-shirt made the most of his bronzed skin and his dark hair was still wet, as though he'd had a recent shower.

Her heart felt so full it didn't know what to do with itself. Beat? Go bust? Leap from her chest and into his arms?

As Zach hit the sunlight angling into the house he saw Ruby was hiding behind his legs. How alike they looked. Long, lean, dark good looks, fierce intelligence swimming behind their guarded eyes. But it was their natural connection that hit hardest. If he took one short step she would have banged into him, but somehow their rhythm stayed in sync. It was mesmerising. And unbearable.

'You came,' Zach said when he spotted her.

She shrugged, feigning nonchalance she was nowhere near feeling. 'I had nowhere better to be.'

He laughed. 'I won't be putting *that* on the brochures, I can assure you.'

'Smart move.'

They smiled at one another awhile and Meg took solace in the fact that she wasn't the only one who was nervous.

'Now, Ruby,' Zach said, gently uncurling his daughter from behind him, pulling her around in front but keeping two hands on her shoulders. 'You remember Meg, right?'

Ruby's dark eyes stared back at her, testing, deciding whether it served her to admit as much. Meg's heart performed the greatest twitch of its life. Zach had his hands full more than he even realised.

She leaned down to Ruby and murmured out of the corner of her mouth, 'You didn't happen to save me any muffins from the other day, did you?'

Ruby shook her head.

'Mmm.' Meg held a finger to her mouth. 'I'm guessing that's because your dad ate the lot.'

Ruby glanced up at him with wide eyes.

'Men,' she said, rolling her eyes. 'Promise me you'll never make the mistake of thinking they're at all complicated.'

'I won't,' were Ruby's first words. Bright kid.

'On that note,' Zach said, his voice a rumble that skittered along Meg's arms, 'I'll be back in a minute with real food. No muffins. Behave. Both of you.'

Meg smiled back.

He gave her one last, white-hot look before heading inside, jerking her poor heart around all the more. How could he expect her to behave after that?

She sauntered over to a large square outdoor table sitting neatly in the shade of a massive cream, linen umbrella and perched her backside on the edge of a wooden bench seat.

'So, Miss Ruby,' she said, curling a finger at the girl, 'what's the plan for this morning?'

Ruby moseyed near and picked at a knot of wood in another chair. 'Since Dad got to choose who was invited over, I got to pick what we'd eat.'

'Fair enough. So what are we eating?'

Ruby eyed Meg down with wisdom beyond her years. 'I picked peanut butter on white bread. Dad thought you might like something else. I told him you'd like peanut butter on white bread.'

'Well,' Meg said, trying to keep her cool while the kid wrapped herself tighter and tighter around her heart. 'Would you believe that of all the food in all the world, peanut butter on white bread is exactly what I want?'

'I knew it. I liked your pink dress, so it made sense that if I liked peanut butter you would too. Ooh, wait there!' Ruby said, before tearing off inside.

'I'm not going anywhere,' Meg said to the empty doorway, her heart pressing towards the space where Ruby had been.

She shoved her face into her hands. She should never have come. She knew it would only make her love him more. Make her feel for his sweet kid. Make her wonder how she was ever going to go back to a life of smiling and pouting and pretending it was the greatest job on earth.

Unless this didn't have to end. Unless Zach had brought her here with completely non-altruistic intentions. Unless last night had meant exactly as much to him as it had done to her.

Ruby came running out of the house with something behind her back.

Meg sat up and physically wiped the hope from her face. 'What have you got there?'

'I asked Dad to give this to you yesterday but I found it on the hall table this morning. He must have forgotten,' Ruby said, sneaking up onto the bench beside Meg.

As Meg would have done with her nieces, instinct had her putting her arm around Ruby as she opened the gift. Pink cardboard was covered in scraps of cellophane, wrapping paper, leftover art-supply stuff. And inside Ruby had drawn a picture of a woman who could only be her. Brown curly hair. A pink dress. And a pile of chocolate muffins at her feet.

*To Meg*, it said in rainbow-coloured letters. *Love Ruby.*

Her breath got stuck in her throat. A gorgeous card that Ruby had made for her. A whole day earlier.

Zach hadn't forgotten to give it to her. He was so smitten with this kid there was no way. He was on a high from the smallest of advances they were making. He might even have believed he had her advice to thank for many of them. But deep down he had no intention of either he or his little girl getting too attached to her.

She breathed in and out and somehow managed to talk Ruby through all the delightful nuances of the present knowing Zach had never wanted her to have it.

It had been the smart move. The right decision. That still didn't stop her heart from shrinking until it felt three sizes too small.

'Are you both still in one piece?' Zach asked as he re-joined them.

Meg slipped the card beneath her backside, looked to Ruby, held a finger to her lips, and said, 'Shh.'

Thankfully, Ruby just giggled.

Zach's smiling eyes were full of questions. Of devotion to his little girl. Of so much promise to be the most complete man she'd ever known. Only Meg knew that the promise would never be hers to see fulfilled.

All this and morning tea had only just begun. If she was ever going to get through this she'd have to give the greatest perfor-mance of her life.

Zach placed the tray of drinks and a platter of fat fruit and gleaming cheeses and exotic crackers on the table. Her motley bunch of flowers had pride of place in a skinny glass vase in the centre of the tray.

Ruby snuck up onto her knees and pulled out a waxy white flower from the bunch, tore off the stem, and tucked it behind her ear. She did the same for Meg. Then a third for Zach, who leaned down and let her do it.

'They're Ruby's favourite,' he said, running a hand over his daughter's hair.

Meg could have cried.

'Wait here,' Ruby said. 'I have more to show you.' She took off back into the house.

Zach grabbed some loose grapes and threw them into his mouth. He looked at her as if he knew some great secret, when she was the one sitting on the greatest of them all.

'You look ridiculous,' Meg said, staring at the flower. Anywhere rather than in Zach's warm eyes.

He grinned. 'So what were you two up to when I came out here?'

Meg's eyes connected with his and got stuck in all that deep, dark, beautiful, chocolate-brown. 'I have no idea what you're talking about.'

He stared into her eyes. 'You're a terrible liar.'

She blinked, desperately hoping he wasn't as clever as he thought he was. She looked away, and took a couple of strawberries from the platter. 'Ruby seems really happy.'

'I think she just might be. In fact, I think we both are. At the very least we're both now on the right path to get there.'

Zach leaned forward in his chair. His hands slid across the table until they were almost touching hers. She tried to keep her breaths steady.

'When you get home,' he said, 'you should talk to your father.'

She curled her fingers into her palms. 'About?'

'Meg,' he said, looking deep into her eyes, his voice ever so slightly ragged. 'This is me you're talking to.'

She swallowed. She knew exactly whom she was talking to—the man who'd won her heart. She uncurled her fingers from her palms, slid her hand along the table toward his—

Footsteps sounded on the wooden balcony. They both looked up to find Felicia holding a landline phone. 'Sorry to interrupt, but it's Reception for Meg.'

Meg cursed Reception with every fibre of her being for their terrible timing. Then she realised she hadn't told anyone where she'd be. As if that would stop the Kellys. If this was Dylan trying to pin her down to a dozen PR jobs for the first dozen hours after her return she'd throttle him.

She took the phone, her tone cool as she said, 'This is Meg.'

'Oh, thank God.'

'Rylie?'

'Honey, you have to come back. Now.'

'What's happened?'

'It's Quinn.'

Meg's eyes slammed shut as wave after wave of anger rolled through her. Of all the moments the man could have picked to— The words clogged in her head and anger turned to guilt, which turned to too many emotions for her to keep up.

'Tell me straight,' she said, her voice astonishingly even. 'Is he—?'

'He's had another heart attack.'

'But he's alive,' she said.

'He is. Brendan called my mobile when he couldn't get through to yours. Tabby's packing your stuff and we can be at your car in fifteen minutes.'

'I'll be there.'

She pulled the phone from her ear and suddenly didn't know what to do with it.

Zach was already beside her, sliding it from her shaky grasp. Then his warm arms were around her, pulling her close, wrapping her tight.

'What do you need me to do?' he asked, her ear against his chest feeling the rumble of his words.

*I want you to love me. I need you to let me go.*

She said, 'I have to go home.'

Home. Her life. Her father. God, could this be it? She realised she had begun to tremble.

Zach, on the other hand, was in complete control. He had already eased her down the bridge and across the yard before she even knew her feet were moving.

'But Ruby,' she said.

'Felicia's looking after her. I'll explain later that you had an emergency and had to go early.'

'What about her peanut butter on white bread? She was so excited.'

His arm at her back slid around her waist until he was cradling her and pressing her forward at the same time. She let him. Let herself steal as much of his kind of strength as she could get while she had the chance.

'Felicia's a pushover,' Zach said. 'Ruby probably has that all the time and they simply don't tell me. Feminine mystery. I'm learning to live with it.' His voice grew deep and close as his lips settled on her hair. 'Now stop worrying about us, and just walk.'

When she tripped over her own feet for the third time, Zach picked her up and carried her. She wrapped her arms about his neck and snuggled in. If he didn't care who saw them like that, then neither did she. It cushioned the several kinds of dread inside her as nothing else could.

He put her down when they reached the garage behind Waratah House. Her momentum propelled her to Rylie, who gathered her up and swept her into the tight back seat of the already packed Jag.

'Take care of her,' she thought she heard Zach's deep voice rumble as the engine gunned.

Rylie said, 'Never fear, Mr Jones. We always do.'

The car backed out of its spot, and Meg looked up to find Zach was a silhouette already too far away for her to see his eyes. Already too far away to thank him. To tell him…anything.

Tabitha drove them out of the high white gates, while Rylie held her hand in the back seat.

It must have been a good deal over an hour later, though it only felt like minutes, when they rounded the final bend of the Pacific Motorway to see the towering silhouette of Brisbane's glass and chrome skyline.

Kelly Tower—the home of the Kelly Investment Group— stood out tall and majestic, a gleaming reminder that she was nearly home. That within minutes she'd be slung back into the frantic, high-pressure, achievement-driven life her whole family led. That once again her father—a man who likely would have preferred it if she weren't even there—was about to become the centre of her life.

If it weren't for the wilting white waxflower she cupped gently in her hand, she might have thought the past few days were all a dream.

# CHAPTER TWELVE

A WEEK had gone by when Zach drove up to the imposing wrought-iron gates of the Kelly family's Ascot home.

A week with no clue as to what was happening in Meg's life bar what he read in every newspaper he could get his hands on, hoping he could trust what they said. A week spent living with the memory of her warm body wrapped around his as he slept in his now lonely bed. A week spent remembering that even while dealing with her worst nightmare Meg had still worried that Ruby might be upset about missing out on her peanut butter on white bread.

The gates of Kelly Manor opened as a florist's van trundled down the long, imposing driveway. Mounds of press lurked outside, but none of them pushed into the grounds, showing a measure of respect that surprised him.

He stared them down as they peered into his car from a relatively safe distance. Him with his little girl in the back seat. His palms sweated so much he had to wipe them on his trousers.

He'd just have to get over it. The few months he was assured of having her all to himself he was no longer going to spend locking her away like some modern-day Rapunzel. The best thing he could do for her was to make sure she felt safe and loved, but also as if her future was one filled with boundless possibilities.

And while his little girl was blooming under his new philosophy, inside that huge house there was another woman in his life who was suffering. And he had no intention of abandoning either one.

He fixed the rearview mirror so he could catch Ruby's eye. 'Honey.'

'Yeah, Dad.'

'See all those people there? They're newspaper and TV reporters. They have cameras, and will get very close to the car. If you don't want your photo taken you can stick your head between your knees.'

'I don't mind.'

He turned to look over his shoulder. To look at his little girl. For a kid who had every reason to be as skittish as a newborn colt, she was one of the most gung-ho people he'd ever met. He could only hope that had a tiny bit to do with him.

'Okay, then,' he said, winking at her, 'here we go.'

He gunned the engine, turned into the driveway. Flash bulbs blinded him enough he had to drive with one hand over his eyes, but he made it through the gate and up the long curving drive in one piece.

'You all right, hon?' he asked Ruby once they were clear of the throng.

She nodded, her eyes wide, before she turned to peek through the tinted back window. 'Why did they want a photo of me?'

He smiled. 'Because you're just so adorable.'

She patted at the pink band around her head that Felicia had shown him how to slide into place in order to keep her long hair from her face. 'Can we ask them for a copy of the picture so I can take it to school? Clarissa won't believe me if I just tell her.'

Zach's smile turned to laughter. 'I'll see what I can do.'

Tracking down a paparazzo for a favour was one of the

crazier things he'd ever agreed to. Though when compared with the fortnight he'd had, maybe not.

He pulled his car in behind the red Jag that had taken Meg from him all those mornings ago. His hands gripped tight to the steering wheel as he remembered the haunted look in her eyes as she'd been driven away. He should have come sooner.

He was here now. He hoped that would be enough.

He held Ruby's hand as they walked up the steps towards the Georgian-style manor, passing two life-sized statues of Irish wolfhounds. He tilted his head at the dogs and poked a face. Ruby giggled. And he knew that he wasn't only here for himself—he was here for her.

Within seconds of his using the old-fashioned brass knocker, Meg's mother, Mary Kelly herself, opened the door. He saw Meg in her eyes, the shape of her chin, and the same inability to hide her true feelings from him behind her practised smile.

She was exhausted, she was anxious, but her husband was still very much alive.

Zach said, 'I'm so sorry to intrude, Mrs Kelly. My name is Zach Jones. I own the Juniper Falls Rainforest Retreat and was with Meg when she heard the news about your husband. I was hoping I might be able to check how she and your husband were faring.'

'Of course, Zach, please come right in,' Mary said, welcoming him, a veritable stranger, into her home. This time he saw Meg in her natural warmth.

Ruby tucked in tight behind him so close she might as well have been sewn to his trousers. When Mary saw her, a spark lit her tired eyes. It was Meg all over again. He looked past her, wondering how close Meg might yet be.

Mary bent from the waist, placing her hands on her knees. 'And who might this gorgeous creature be?'

'This is Ruby,' he said. 'My daughter.'

Mary held out a hand and said, 'I'm very pleased to meet you, Ruby. As will my granddaughters be. Violet and Olivia are playing outside in the rear gardens now with their uncle Dylan. Would you like to come and say hello?'

Zach glanced past Mary again and wondered if everyone was playing outside with Uncle Dylan. Then he crouched down to her level and held her hands. 'Would you like to go outside and play? It's entirely up to you.'

Mary held out a hand. Ruby took it. Trusting. Sociable. Like her mother.

'James,' Mary said to a liveried man Zach hadn't even noticed standing by the entrance to what looked like a large sitting room, 'would you kindly take Mr Jones to Meg. I believe she's in the upstairs media room.'

'This way, sir,' James said before heading up the wide, carpeted stairs.

Family photographs lined the staircase wall. Dozens, dating back generations. He'd never had any photographs of his parents, and kept none of his childhood now. The Kelly wall of fame was thoroughly intimidating.

The closer they got to the top of the stairs, the more familiar faces became. Quinn and Mary sailing with two young boys scampering at their feet. The three boisterous-looking brothers, late teens, playing cricket in the backyard. And Meg at the beach, younger than Ruby was now, her bottom lip sticking out while her double scoop of ice cream melted on the ground at her feet.

*And look at her now*, he thought, his eyes resting on a much more recent picture of her walking down a city street, gorgeous in a silver party dress, pale pink high heels, hair flying as she grinned back at the camera. There was a measure of confidence in her eyes, secret confidence. He alone knew the hard work she'd done to feel as if she'd earned the right to hold her head high.

He reached out to wipe a smudge of dust from the picture.

'Sir, this way,' James said from the top of the stairs, his face discreetly averted.

Zach shoved his hands into his suit pockets and jogged the last few steps.

'Miss Meg is in the room at the end of the hall,' James said. 'Shall I announce you?'

Zach shook his head, gave James a slap on the arm, then headed towards the slightly ajar double doors. He pressed one open. It made no sound.

The large room was filled with overstuffed chairs in old-fashioned plaids and florals, which mixed incongruously with the discreet silver surround-sound speakers, the wall-to-wall built-in bookshelves stacked with DVDs, and the state-of-the-art cinema set-up.

And at the edge of the room, curled up on a tub chair, staring absently out of the open double windows leading to a small balcony, sat Meg.

His chest clenched at the sight of her in loose jeans, red winter socks and a long-sleeved cream-and-red T-shirt that clung to her curves. She wore not a lick of make-up and her hair had been scragged back into a low bun from which several long curls had escaped. She played absently with her lower lip while some movie he recognised as having not even been released at the cinema played out quietly on the massive projector screen behind her.

Now he was there he realised it was testimony of his years of obstinate will power that he'd managed to go without sight of her for a full week. And now he was there, now she was so close, he couldn't wait a second more.

He planted his feet and cleared his throat.

She glanced up. Dark circles ringed her deep blue eyes, making them look bruised. They took a moment to focus. Then she frowned. 'Zach?'

He nodded, suddenly not trusting his voice.

She dragged herself to her sock-clad feet and slowly walked to him as though she might be imagining him. He dug his finger-nails into his palms to stop himself from taking the final steps and dragging her into his arms and kissing her for all he was worth.

'How's your father?' he asked.

She shook her head. Then nodded. 'He's had two more attacks this week. He's lucid, his blood pressure is stable, but he's fading and refusing to go to hospital no matter what any of us say.'

Her eyes flickered at that last part, and he wondered if she'd been one of the ones suggesting it, or if she'd stubbornly kept out of his way.

She waved a hand over her face as though swatting away a fly. 'What on earth are you doing here?'

'You left in such a hurry. You were so upset. I couldn't let you stay away without knowing…' *God, this was much harder than telling Ruby how much he cared.* 'Without knowing I've been thinking of you.'

Day and night. Night and day. He'd been sure he'd heard her laughter around the resort, caught her jasmine scent.

The sound of real laughter, children's laughter, spilled through the window and like a mother hen Meg upped and headed out through the French doors to check see. Zach followed.

From the small balcony he saw Ruby sitting on Mary's lap watching Meg's nieces, clad in fairy dresses and tiaras, running around the backyard flying kites. Below, sitting in matching white cane chairs and drinking iced tea, like something out of *The Great Gatsby*, a slew of other Kellys—brothers, sisters, uncles, cousins, grandparents—watched on.

'You brought Ruby *here*?' Meg asked, her voice thin, her hands gripping the concrete balustrade as if she were prepar-ing to vault down onto the lawn and whisk Ruby away from the clutches of her family.

He understood why she'd resisted the idea of having children. But she was made to be a mum. She was a natural protector, an instinctive defender of those who couldn't defend themselves. As a child she might not have been able to fight back when she was pushed down, but now? Now she was a warrior.

As far as he saw it, the only thing standing in the way of her fighting for her own happiness with as much purpose as she did so for others was fear. A broken-down ego was a fragile thing. Not easily repaired. He just had to make her see how strong she had become.

He said, 'She overheard me explaining to Felicia that your dad was sick. She wouldn't let me visit without her, or we would have been here sooner. She wanted to make sure you were okay.'

'Me? Is she okay?' Meg asked, her eyes glued to Ruby. 'I mean, is this making her think too much about her mum being sick? I'd hate to be the one to bring all that back up again.'

'She's fine. She's curious. She's amazing, really. Tough when she needs to be, and soft when she can be.'

*Just like you*, he wanted to say, but he knew she wasn't ready to hear it. Yet.

Meg spun on him, a ghost of her usual spirit flashing in her eyes bringing colour back to her cheeks. She shoved a finger into his chest, backing him into the shadow of the doorway. 'Do you have *any* idea how many reporters are camped out on the other side of your gate?'

'I drove in that way,' he said calmly, 'so, yes.'

'They're not as dim as they look, Zach. They'll have seen you. They'll have seen Ruby. They'll know who you are. They'll figure out who she is. She's cute, and funny, and female and your sole heir. They'll eat her alive. Didn't you hear a word I said?'

He reached out and held her upper arms; she calmed instantly, blinking up at him as if she were really seeing him for the first time. Her energy coursed through him like a wildfire and he wanted to kiss her so badly he had to grind his teeth to distract himself.

'I'm fully aware of all that,' he said. 'But I'm done hiding. I'm not going to teach her that's the best way to live because it's not. We've decided that life can come at us from any angle now and we'll take it on together.'

Meg blinked at him. She felt so small, but so warm, beneath his hands. She was his match, his inspiration, someone he wanted to know everything about, someone he wanted right beside him as he leapt into the new chapters of his life.

As a five-year-old his happiness had been in the hands of strangers; as a thirty-five-year-old his happiness was his to reach out and grab.

'So in that same vein, here we are,' he said, emphasising each of the last three words.

At the last second he held back from adding, *And we're yours if you'll have us.* She'd work it out. She had to. All it had ever taken for them to understand one another was a look.

He lifted a hand to run the backs of his fingers gently down her beautiful cheek. And saw the moment she understood when a flare of awareness lit her dazzling blue eyes. The same flare ignited in his stomach.

He swept a curl from her eyes. Then another until his hands cupped the sides of her face. He could practically taste her, feel the soft fullness of that mouth against his.

Suddenly she twisted out of his grasp, turned her back on him, and walked back into the room.

'Has anyone offered you a drink? Would you like some lemonade? James has made bucketloads and it's magic. Really. He could sell the stuff and retire rich and never have to open another door for any of us again.'

He took a step towards her, arm outstretched. She slid grace-fully behind an ottoman.

'Meg.'

She breathed deep and sank down onto the ottoman, as though she was so tired of fighting she could no longer stand.

He moved towards her. She held out a hand using the inter-national sign for *back off*, and it stopped him in his tracks.

Her voice came to him, husky and defeated, as she said, 'Last weekend my family had been trying to get through to me for half an hour but I'd turned off my phone. I was heading to be with you and Ruby and it was easier to pretend they didn't exist if I wanted to believe that I could have what you have—a clean, fresh, new start.' She looked up at him. 'But this is who I am. This is where I need to be.'

'That's nonsensical.'

'Excuse me? Now I'm *nonsensical*?' She turned on him with such rancour in her eyes he backed up a step.

'*You're* not nonsensical,' he shot back, not giving her a chance to break eye contact. 'You're a human dynamo. You're an inspiration. You care so much for other people I know you don't take near enough time to care for yourself. And you've been a small miracle in my life. But believing you deserve to suffer right along with your father is ridiculous. You're punish-ing yourself for his mistakes.'

She blinked at him, her lips thin, her eyes raging. But at least she was listening.

'You've given me enough words of wisdom—it's my turn. Family *isn't* a given. It wasn't for me, and in the end it's not for you. Family is a choice. Because deciding who to share your life with is a choice, and those you choose to spend your life with are your family. Love the Kellys you love. But just because they are a vital and somewhat Herculean force in your life needn't ever stop you from stepping away and creating your own family.'

'Zach, it's not that simple.'

He took a careful step her way. 'All that ever stopped me was me. Ruby came along. I chose to take her into my life. And look at me now. All that's stopping you is you.'

She swallowed hard, her chin tilting as he came closer. 'I'm not you.'

'And for that I'm eternally grateful. But I'm also not your father. Ruby's not you. Ruby's not your niece. And you're not your father either.'

He sank to a crouch close enough he could touch her if he just reached out his hand. But even though it killed to do so, he held back. 'Meg, sweetheart, I came here today because it has become all too clear to me this week that you are my family. I choose you.'

Her eyes softened. Hope sprang within them. Until she shook her head. 'Well, you can't have me. You don't want me anywhere near your daughter.'

Zach's jaw clenched. *Now* she was being nonsensical. 'Meg, I told you, I'm past that. You helped me get past that. And Ruby adores you—'

She shook her head harder. 'Zach, please. If she's anything like I was at sixteen you'll lose half a head of hair.'

'Let me worry about my hair.'

She spun on the ottoman so her knees faced him square on. 'Then worry about this. I ditched school at sixteen. I went clubbing every night. I drank daiquiris like they were lemonade. They let me in because of who I was, because of who my father was. When I chipped this tooth on a champagne flute I was sitting up front at a comedy bar, already on my second three-hundred-dollar bottle. *Sixteen years old.* That same night I was pulled over for drunk-driving, driving without a licence, under age, and a bag of pot was found in my glove compartment. I had friends in the car with me. Friends I could have killed had I not been stopped. Friends who for some reason are still my friends today. That could have been the end of me, but some-body put pressure where it was needed and I was let off with a warning. Somebody paid off every paper in town so that none of it ever came to light.'

'Somebody,' he said, still trying to filter the rest. 'Somebody meaning your father.'

She breathed in deep, ragged breaths. Her hands began to shake. He placed a gentle hand over hers, but he wasn't sure she even knew he was there.

Her voice sounded so small as she said, 'My trust fund wasn't meant to be mine until I was twenty-five. It was signed over at eighteen. I figured it was his way of finally washing his hands of me. That same day I approached my first doctor. But even I, with my glorious name, and glorious money, and batting baby blues had to wait until I had undergone six months of in-tensive therapy before a doctor would agree to—'

Her words ended on a choke and that was when his confi-dence took its first tumble. 'Agree to what?' he asked, needing to know even though he knew he'd regret it when he did.

'I've had my tubes tied, Zach.' She looked up at him then, at the end of her rope. 'It's irreversible. I can never have kids.'

Holy hell.

If Quinn Kelly weren't on death's door Zach feared in that moment what he might have done to the man.

Meg stared at him as if she half expected him to shake her senseless. Or run as fast as his shoes would carry him. But all he wanted to do was to take her in his arms and hug her. To hold her until she absolved herself. Until he got his head around what it meant to him. Until he stopped thinking what might have happened had Isabel done such a thing and Ruby had never been born.

'Aren't you going to say something?' she said, her voice tight, angry, desolate.

Zach ran a hard, fast hand over his face. What the hell could he possibly say?

'Zach?'

He stood and paced in a tight circle. 'I need a minute.'

'I should never have told you.' She shook her head so hard he was sure her brain must have been knocking against her skull.

'Hang on now, Meg. You know you've just thrown me a hand grenade there and I get the feeling you're certain I'm about to run for cover. I'm not, but I still need a minute.'

She stood and paced on the other side of the ottoman. 'You didn't have to know any of it. Nobody ever did! But you had to appear in my life and be all unimpressed by it and make me like you. And then you had to add Ruby to the mix. And then more and more and more of you. There. Everywhere. Not letting me have a minute to think about what we were doing. So if this—' she waved a hand over her chest '—is too hard for you to take, it's your own fault!'

'Meg, you picked the wrong man to try to push away. I'm not running. Not any more.'

'But see now, that's the thing. You are still running. You just don't know it,' she said, her voice suddenly so calm he wondered if he'd ever been in control of the conversation, even for a single second.

Zach brought his back foot to rest beside his front, feeling as if he needed to be upright for what was coming. 'This ought to be good.'

'That morning, at your house, Ruby gave me the card she'd made me.'

'The card?' *Oh, hell, the card.*

'The pink card with the chocolate muffin picture and the fur and feathers and glitter.' She swallowed before saying, 'The one you wouldn't give me yourself.'

Zach stood rooted to the floor as the import of that one

small choice sank in. At the time it had been a split-second
decision. An insurance policy, protecting his daughter and
himself, that one last, tiny little bit.

In the end it might have cost him everything.

When he said nothing, Meg continued, 'Last week was
something crazy. Something amazing and wonderful and I'll
never forget a second of it. But the card only proved what I
already knew—that you're nowhere near ready to take on the
likes of me.'

Zach shook his head. The both of them were so adept at
talking themselves into whatever they wanted to believe, this was
all about to go belly up on the back of circular conversation.

He shut down reason and went purely on instinct, knowing
if there was ever a moment to trust in the man he'd become this
had to be it.

'Watch me,' he said, then shoved the ottoman out of the way
with a foot and gathered her into his arms. As though she'd been
holding herself up by nothing more than will power she collapsed against him.

He kissed the top of her head. The edge of her ear. The lift
at the edge of her lips.

With a sigh she tilted her head and kissed him back, her lips
clinging so gently, so tenderly, so lovingly to his.

It took all of his strength not to lift her in his arms and carry
her to the couch and prove to her in the most basic way that he
was right and she was wrong.

Far too soon she pulled away, looking down so he couldn't
see into her eyes. He snuck a finger beneath her chin and made
her face him.

Her chest rose and fell. Her eyes were as wild and blue as
his lake amidst a summer storm. 'Why don't you hate me for
what I did to myself?'

'Because I know why you did it.'

'Remind me, please. Right now I'm struggling to come up with a good excuse.'

'You made sure nobody could ever reject you again as fully as you rejected yourself.'.

She swallowed and a big fat tear rolled down her cheek. He brushed her hair from her eyes and breathed through it lest he join her.

'God, you were eighteen,' he said, his voice rasping through his tight throat. 'You were still a kid. Those blasted doctors should be hung. But it would be impossible for me to ever hate *you*. How could I when I love you so very much?'

Her eyes glistened, flickering between his. He'd said it. He'd told her. He was her safe place to come home to.

He thought he had her. Until she held out her hands in supplication. He could see in the utter transparency of her expression how much it meant to her.

It just didn't matter.

He let her go as though his fingers had been burnt, rather than his heart. She wrapped her arms back about her body and headed back over to the French doors to watch the interplay below from a safe distance—the only family she thought she deserved, the kids she'd convinced herself she'd never have.

'Please stay as long as you want while Ruby's having such a good time,' she said, polite as could be. 'James will show you out.'

There was nothing more he could do or say. He did as she asked and walked away.

He'd spent his adult life protecting himself from just this situation, from blindly loving someone with no guarantee they'd love him back. But Meg had smashed through that wall with all the subtlety of a wrecking ball, convincing him he'd found someone worth the risk.

As he jogged numbly down the steps with generations of stubborn-chinned Kellys watching on he realised the one thing he hadn't considered was that for her the risk of loving him might yet be too great.

# CHAPTER THIRTEEN

As THE sun set Meg sat out on one of the white cane chairs looking over the now-empty back lawn, the divine sound of kids just being kids echoing in the back of her mind.

The rest of her felt like toast. Three-day-old burnt toast that had fallen butter-side down on the kitchen floor and been kicked into the dust-filled gap beneath the fridge.

Zach had come to her daunting family home and left his precious daughter playing outside with her nieces as though if they were her blood they could do no wrong. He'd looked more dashing and beautiful and terrified than she'd ever seen him look. He'd offered himself up to the press, he'd heard her last and most devastating of secrets, a secret that meant she could never give him the kind of family he was ready for, and he'd still told her he loved her.

There was nothing more he could have done to prove himself as the man she'd known he could be. And still she'd sent him away.

'Sweetheart,' her mother said, a hand curving over her shoulder. 'Are you coming in for dinner?'

Meg smiled up at her mother and stretched until her tight muscles began to feel useable again. 'I'll be in in a minute.'

She felt her mum's hesitation. 'Your father's alone right now if you wanted to have a chat. I'd noticed you haven't been in to see him since you came home, and I thought, perhaps, now might be a good time.'

Meg stilled, then tucked her feet onto the chair and wrapped her arms about her knees. Her mum was right about one thing: there was no time like the present. 'Mum, can you sit for a minute?'

Mary sat, perched on the edge of the seat as though ready to take flight. It made it easier for Meg to say what she needed to say, as she was almost sure her mum knew what was coming.

'Mum, I don't much want to talk to him. And I think you know why.'

Mary clasped her hands together until the knuckles turned white. 'Darling, he's so sick, surely you can—'

'Mum,' she said gently, but it was enough for her mother to close her lips.

Meg leaned forward and took her mum's hands in hers. 'You know how he treated me when I was a kid.' Even using the endearing term 'Dad' felt wrong. It always had.

Mary said, 'He's exacting, and puts as much pressure on all of you as he always has on himself. His work was so much more stressful back then. The business was in its infancy. His father was hard on him too. And everything he did was for the betterment of the family.'

Meg nodded along. She'd heard it all before. 'Is that why the two of you had me? For the betterment of the family?' She swallowed. 'To keep the family from falling apart when Dad had an affair?'

Mary opened her mouth to deny everything, then something in her changed, relaxed, as though she didn't have the energy to keep up the pretence any longer. She took a hand and cupped it under Meg's chin. 'You always were the most sensitive child. You were a blessing at a time we needed one most. But you can't only blame your father. We both did things we shouldn't have done.'

'*You* had an affair?' Meg asked, sitting up so straight so fast her back cracked.

Mary nodded, her eyes filling with tears. 'It was short-lived. It was foolish. But in the end only good came of it as it proved to both of us that we were where we wanted to be after all. We chose to be a family again.' She reached out and tucked a curl behind Meg's ear. 'Having you after that was the best choice I've made in my life.'

A choice. Meg had always wondered if she'd been a stopgap measure, never looking at it from the angle that she'd been a purposeful *choice*. The massive delineation rang so loud in Meg's ears she almost couldn't think. But it was fighting hard against the clang of another. 'Am I his daughter?'

Mary's eyes grew wide with shock. 'Of course you are. Look at you. You have his eyes. You have his pluck. You certainly have his temper. Your sweet temperament and endless capacity to forgive are definitely from my side.'

Her mother leaned forward and kissed her cheek. 'Now that's the last we need to hear of that. Don't be long. Dinner's on soon. And your father is still up there alone.'

Meg nodded, but stayed put as her mother walked away.

Forgiveness.

Zach had forgiven his foster parents for their weaknesses for the sake of his own family. Her mother had forgiven her father for his trespasses for the sake of her family. Her father had never forgiven himself and self-condemnation left only bitterness in its stead.

Meg had to forgive herself the unhealthy choices she'd made at sixteen. The desperate one she'd made at eighteen. Only then could she fully embrace the many exceptional choices she'd made since then. The keeping of friends she'd had since school. Being an integral part of her family's success. For unreservedly giving to those far less fortunate than herself.

For falling in love with Zach.

That had to be just about the smartest thing she'd ever done in her whole life. He knew her. He understood her. He loved her. But even more importantly, he'd helped her to realise how far she'd come in knowing, understanding and loving herself.

Could he ever forgive her for abandoning him? Could she ever forgive herself? Before she had room to find out, there was one last person who needed to see how far she'd come too.

Late that night, after a typically long, noisy, combative Kelly family dinner populated by her mum, all her brothers and their significant others, a dog-tired Meg made her way back up the stairs, past the wall of beautifully framed, lovingly tended family pictures, and she slid into her father's room.

Flat against the wall she could hear his uneven breathing. Flat against the wall she wasn't going to be able to do anything. She walked to his bed, and sat carefully on the edge.

He looked old. Frail. His skin was like rice paper. Even his eyelids were wrinkled. Like this he seemed so harmless.

He flinched, then looked into her face with his fierce blue eyes and turned a not too happy shade of pink as he bellowed, 'Jeez, child, could you have snuck in here any more quietly?'

'Don't shout!' she shot back, moving hurriedly to sit farther down the edge of the huge bed. 'You'll pop something and I doubt I'm the one you'd want trying to plug it up.'

He tried to sit up, failed, swore to the high heavens, and then slumped gingerly back onto the huge mound of pillows. 'What on earth are you doing here, girl? I was informed you were whooping it up on holiday.'

'I've been back a few days now.'

'Not for my sake, I hope.'

'No. Of course not,' she said, her voice droll. 'The girls

were one down on their backyard cricket side. I had to come back for the sisters.'

His eyes were entirely clear when he said, 'You've never been any good at cricket.'

'Mmm, so you've taken great delight in telling me on numerous occasions.'

Quinn scoffed. 'Would you prefer I butter you up? Resting on your laurels never helped anyone.'

'No,' she said. 'You've made well sure my laurels have never given me any rest.'

And there it was. Back to square one. The two of them watching each other cagily from opposite corners of the ring.

Meg flattened a sock-clad foot on the ground, preparing to get out of Dodge, when it hit her that heading out that door meant nothing would have changed.

Unless she could make the break from her past she'd end up playing the 'It-Girl' for ever. Brushing off her blonde wig every time she did the kind of work that really gave her satisfaction. Dating men who never challenged her. Trying to pretend that Zach Jones never existed. Trying to convince herself that sharing every piece of herself, her fears, her joys, her body, her soul with him had been nothing but a holiday romance.

Not good enough. Not any more.

'Dad.' She reached out and took his cool hand. It stiffened, but she didn't let go. 'It appears my Kelly blood runs deeper than I even knew. I do believe I'm going to miss you.'

'Gallivanting off again, are you?'

She almost laughed. Stubborn old fool. Instead she took his words at face value.

'I will, in fact. I'll be taking leave of my Kelly duties for a bit.'

She would? *Yeah*, she thought with an inner sigh of relief, *she would*.

He glared at her as though she'd said she was renouncing her name, her religion, and the old country just to be contrary. She raised both eyebrows and glared right on back.

'The thing is, Dad,' she said, 'I currently volunteer at the Valley Women's Shelter every week. Have been doing so for some time now. It's tough, it's terrifying and I love it madly. So much so I've decided my PR work for the family is going to have to slot in around that from now on rather than the other way around. In fact, I might even take a social work course, which would cut into that time even more.'

He opened his mouth, no doubt to cut her down twenty ways from Sunday. She held up a hand and said, 'Not this time. The decision's been made. And there's more. I'm in love, Dad, with an amazing man who knows everything about me—everything—and he loves me anyway. Can you believe it?'

She could hardly believe it herself, but saying the words out loud finally made it all utterly, beautifully, intensely real.

'I'm tired, child,' he said, turning away. 'Can't you have this conversation with your mother?'

'I will in good time. But I wanted to have it with you too. For *you* to know that I've reached a point in my life when I feel as though I might just be really, really happy.'

'And you need to tell me this now in case I don't wake up in the morning?'

She lifted an eyebrow. 'That's exactly why. So now you know. Your daughter has turned out just fine.'

He looked her in the eye, for the longest time she could ever remember him doing so. His eyes, so very like hers. His inability to forgive so far removed from hers. Then he settled deeper into his pillows and looked up at the fringing hanging off the canopy bed as though it held more interest than anything she'd had to say.

'Fine,' he said. 'Now I know.'

It wasn't congratulations. It wasn't an act of contrition. Yet Meg felt her oldest wounds beginning to mend.

A soft rap on the door was followed by James's face poking through the gap. James slipped into the room with a box of Krispy Kreme doughnuts.

She opened her mouth to rouse at James, then let it fall shut. She wasn't her father's keeper any more than he was hers. So without another word she just hopped off the bed and walked out, pretending she hadn't seen.

Feeling as if she were living a good inch higher off the ground than she had been her whole life, Meg floated into her old bedroom, grabbed her handbag, fixed her hair, swiped on some lip gloss, spritzed on some perfume and continued floating down the stairs.

She passed the library where the family had gathered for after-dinner drinks. Dylan called out, 'Get in here, kiddo. I want to run through next week's schedule. There's a dozen odd things I need you to do for me.'

Her shoes touched solid ground. Telling Dylan he'd have to find someone else next week would take all night.

She caught James the butler's eye as he eased silently into the room from another door. And seeing her escape, mouthed 'sorry' then said, 'Did you know James is feeding Dad doughnuts?'

Brendan made to scold, but Cameron got in first, laughing his head off. And as their collective attention was diverted Meg took her chance and escaped.

And then she was gone, jogging down the dark front steps of the manor two at a time, the rush of summer air blowing her hair off her face, making her skin tingle, making her lungs feel open and free.

Or maybe it was the thought of a man with dark chocolate eyes, adorable curls, warm, strong arms, enough chutzpah to put her in her place, and a capacity to love her despite knowing the worst she had to offer that had every sense feeling as if it was truly alive.

She hopped into her Jag and burned down the Kelly Manor driveway, spinning gravel in her wake.

Only when Meg hit the locked gates outside the Juniper Falls Rainforest Retreat did she realise she hadn't exactly mapped out any kind of plan.

She simply pressed the intercom. A sleepy voice answered. 'Juniper Falls Rainforest Retreat, how can I be of assistance?'

'Hi. Meg Kelly here. Can you, uh, by any chance, wake Zach Jones and tell him I'm here?'

After a pause the voice said, 'I sincerely wish I could, Ms Kelly, but you are not down on my sheet as being expected.'

'I know. And I'm sorry about that. But this is a surprise visit. Of sorts. A last-minute but long-overdue kind of thing. You see I'm here to…'

To what? Oh, to hell with it. Zach had laid himself bare for her, to her family, to the press, to his little girl. If she was ever going to prove to him she was right there with him, she had to do the same.

'I've come to tell him that I'm in love with him!'

The gates whirred open instantly. She crawled through to find two men grinning at her from their booth. One doffed his cap, the other blushed like mad.

'Take the route around the back of Waratah House past the garage,' one said, 'and keep on following the fence line. You'll practically drive straight into Mr Jones's private carport. Good luck!'

She gave them a jaunty salute and spun off, feeling high as a kite, and as terrified as if she were in the middle of one of those walking-down-the-middle-of-the-Queen-Street-Mall-naked dreams.

But there was no backing down now. Her secret love was out there for her father and all Zach's staff to know. There was nothing, *nothing*, stopping her but herself, and herself was pressing down hard on the accelerator.

Zach was waiting by the garage at the side of his house wearing nothing but thin, faded, cotton pyjama bottoms when Meg's noisy old car zoomed up, lights on high beam.

He hated to think what had brought her here, tonight, at such a time. He reached for her car door and opened it before she'd even come to a stop. 'Meg, don't tell me your dad—?'

She half stumbled out of the car. 'He's fine. He's the same. But we talked. Well, I talked, he pretended not to listen. And it felt like letting out a sour, stale breath I'd been holding for almost thirty years. The next breath in was…ecstasy. I could never have done that without your encouragement. So first I have to thank you for that.'

He opened his mouth to try to slow her down, but she kept on going.

'I talked with my mum too. Boy, did so many things become clear. Even you'll be shocked. Or maybe not. I've probably used up your shock quota for the year by now. Or maybe I'd just been locked up inside all week and what I needed was fresh air and sunshine to see things clearly. You taught me that too. So thanks again.'

She looked up into the sky, arms outstretched, breathing deep, then seemed to realise the velvet black sky was littered with stars. She frowned.

Worried Meg might be about to spontaneously combust, Zach took her by the elbow and walked her to the octagonal pool house around the side of his property. Once inside the snug room he turned on a lamp, and placed her on a bamboo love seat.

Her entire, beautifully nubile body jiggled. He clenched his hands at his sides and struggled to keep his eyes on her face. 'I hate to ask,' he said, 'but have you been drinking?'

She looked up at him, all big blue eyes and pink cheeks and red lips raw from being nibbled at. Or had she put on make-up since he'd last seen her? Lip gloss, rouge, mascara, perfume? Had she done that for him? His fingers unclenched a very little.

'Coffee,' she said. 'Loads and loads of coffee from a couple of drive-through places on the way. I haven't slept much in the past few days and I needed to be awake for this. And since I wasn't actually sure that you had coffee on hand, or if you'd merely been using the promise of coffee as a lure all this time—'

She shook her head, seeming to realise she hadn't taken a breath. Then she gingerly reached out and took his hand and gently drew him down onto the seat next to her.

His fingers gripped hers and pleasure flooded through him. It seemed that even after she had put him through one of the most gruelling and sobering afternoons of his entire life, his body was not nearly as immune to her as his brain would have liked.

'Meg,' he said, his voice gravelly, 'it's after midnight.'

'It is?' she asked, looking around as if she only just realised where she was.

'I'm usually used to functioning at this hour, but it's been a very long day.'

'Tell me about it.' Her eyes swung back to his. Warm, inviting blue. Calm, settled blue. Vivid with a great purpose blue. A tiny ray of hope split the night. At least it felt like hope. Hope wasn't something he'd experienced all that much of in his life, but it felt good whatever it was.

Not sure he could stand to have it dashed twice in one day, he asked, 'Did you have a particular purpose in coming all the way out here?'

She turned his hand over and placed her palm against his. It was cool and small and light. He ached to pull it to his lips and kiss it for the longest time. But the purpose in her eyes was something he did not want to divert.

'I don't quite know where to start,' she said. 'I feel like I'm on daylight savings time. It all made such perfect sense about an hour and a half ago.'

He took a calming breath. 'What did?'

'That you came to the house today to tell me that you loved me,' she said. 'And for some great daft muddle of a reason I tried to convince you that it wasn't the most glorious news I'd ever heard.'

Zach's heart lurched. Gloriously.

'You love me,' she said again, shuffling closer. 'You, Zach Jones, love me. You love me enough to give me the space I needed to confront my past so that finally I could see further than a designer-shoe-clad foot in front of my own face, which was as far as I'd dare look into the future for such a long time.'

He did. And he had. On the drive home he'd realised she needed more time. And that he'd wait for her as long as she needed. A half a day was as good as he could have hoped.

He did what he'd been aching to do since the moment she arrived and slid a hand around the back of her neck. 'I must be crazy, but I do truly love you.'

'You do?' Her voice was so soft and unsure, her eyes so big and bright, Zach did all he could do and laughed.

His heart felt like a rocket ready to take off. The countdown had begun inside him the moment she'd hopped out of the car and if she didn't reciprocate and soon he was going to explode. 'If you have any feelings for me whatsoever then you'll put me out of my misery and fast.'

Her blinking slowed and, as was her way, she looked him dead in the eye. At the same time she laid a gentle hand on his cheek and it was all he could do not to ravage her on the spot.

'I've lived with a debilitating fear of rejection my entire life.

I combated it by being whatever I had to be to be loved by as many people as possible. You made me feel like I actually had to earn your respect. And when I did my opinion counted as much as yours, if not more because it was fresh and new. For those reasons and about a trillion others I do love you.'

She needn't have said another word for the rest of time. But being that she was who she was, she kept on giving.

'I love that you own a million health resorts, but have a thing for chocolate muffins. I love that you push my buttons leaving me nowhere to hide. I love your eyes, your arms, your bare feet, and the crease that appears in your right cheek only when you laugh. But most of all I love that you are ambitious, and hardworking and wilful, but it took less than half a second for you to change your entire life for the sake of one small girl. You are a unique specimen amongst men. And I love you so much my heart is full to bursting with it.'

The rocket inside him went off, filling the last of the empty places inside him with nothing but warmth. 'You have no idea what it feels like to hear you say that.'

'So tell me.'

He laid a matching hand on her cheek, her softness seeping into him, melting away the last of his sharp edges. 'After so many years spent not believing love was in store for me, I'm still halfway stunned that I actually believe you.'

She nodded. Glanced at his lips. Licked her own. Then swung her legs so they rested atop his. His soft cotton pants did nothing to hide the stirrings beneath.

'So what now?' she asked, her voice a husky whisper in the darkness.

'Are you kidding me? Do you want a play by play?'

She pulled back and gave him a look he feared he was going to be on the receiving end of for a very long time. 'I meant we aren't the only ones affected by this.'

'How about we keep the press release in the drawer for a few days yet?'

'Don't be smart. I meant Ruby and you know it.'

'She made me pancakes, but she never made me a card. I have the feeling you're going to be a big hit. And as for your other concerns, you have to remember she comes from tough stock.'

She raised an eyebrow. 'You think the Kellys aren't tough? They suck you in and there's no getting out. Dylan and Cameron are intractable and they've both managed to convince perfectly lovely women to be with them. And you took one look at me and you were gone. Kellys are competitive, ambitious, opinionated, defiant—'

'Sweetheart, they're you.'

'Me? I'm a marshmallow.'

'Nah. You just do it prettier.'

'Zach—'

'She'll be fine. Honestly. And at the first sign she isn't then we'll deal with that then. Okay?'

She thought about it a moment, then nodded.

'Though,' he said, 'there is one other way to fix any concern you might have over your family's influence over our girl.'

'How's that?'

He twirled her hair between his fingers. 'Don't be a Kelly any more.'

She shook her head so hard her hair fell in messy waves over her shoulders. 'They may all be as mad as March hares, but I do love them too.'

'Of course you do. Anyone who stepped foot inside that be- hemoth of a house of yours would see that as a clan you're just about unbreakable. But that's not what I meant. I mean you wouldn't be a Kelly any more if you changed your last name to Jones.'

'Very funny,' she said, slapping him on his bare chest. He clutched her hand to him and her fingers curled against his bare skin. 'So is now a good time to admit you're not the first person I told?'

He waited for his offer to sink in, but she was obviously still too wired. 'That you love your family?'

'That I love you!'

'Dare I ask?'

'I kind of let it slip to the two security guards who let me in.'

Zach laughed. He laughed so hard the windows of the tiny thatched pool house shook. 'Then again,' he finally managed, 'what's the use of one more secret? Everyone's going to find out eventually.'

'They will?' she asked.

'Marry me and there's no stopping them.'

Her eyes grew as big as saucers and he knew this time she'd heard him.

'You can't just say something like that to a girl, especially one in my highly caffeinated state.'

'I can and I will.'

'You really want to marry me? Even knowing everything you know? Even though I can't...' She swallowed down an obvious lump in her throat. 'I can't give you any more kids.'

Zach knew better. He'd Googled like a madman the minute Ruby was asleep. The operation she'd had was irreversible. She couldn't conceive naturally. But it didn't rule out IVF. He knew she'd have no idea because she'd have been too terrified to check. But now wasn't the time for that. They'd get there when and if the time was right, as they seemed to get to everything else when they were good and ready. Only this time he'd make sure they'd get there together.

'Meg,' he said, running his thumb down the side of her face, 'I certainly don't want to marry anyone else.'

'Ah,' she said, her voice getting wobblier by the second. 'The last of the great romantics.'

'How's this for romantic?' He took her hand, lifted it to his lips and left a gentle trail of kisses up each finger and across her palm. Her eyes fluttered closed and her mouth fell open. He took advantage, pulling her to him and kissing her for all he was worth.

She melted against him, warm and languid, and he had not a clue how much time passed before they fell apart.

She gripped his upper arms for support and her famous blue eyes fluttered open, looking into his as if she'd just had some kind of religious experience. God, he was going to love being with this woman.

He asked, 'Tell me that's a yes.'

She snuck her arms around his torso and hugged him tight, her chin resting on his shoulder, her words sliding against his ear. 'Yes.'

Yes! He mentally punched a fist in the air.

He said, 'We are never going to be able to live this down, are we?'

'What's that?'

'Meg Kelly, heiress, society princess, only daughter of the Ascot Kellys, the Kelly Investment Group Kellys, marries orphan-made-good Zach Jones.'

'Did you have any idea I could be so magnanimous?' she asked.

He laughed. Warm all over now, and only getting hotter every second, she wiggled her body further atop his.

'But first,' she said, running a finger in circles over his bare chest, 'before we go one step further, we need to get some things straight.'

'Honey,' he said, sliding a finger along the neckline of her stretch T-shirt. 'Believe it or not I'm worth double what you are. A pre-nup wouldn't be worth the paper it's signed on.'

Meg breathed out long and slow and finished with a smile that hovered halfway between beatific and a threat. 'Kellys don't do pre-nups. Kellys do for ever.'

Zach's next breath matched hers. *For ever*. Never ever did he think he'd see the day when he believed in for ever. But as he let his hand slide over her shoulder and more firmly down her back until she curled like a cat, he couldn't wait for for ever to start. 'So what do we have to get straight?'

Her eyes fluttered closed. 'I've jogged my last. I refuse to let wheat grass touch my lips ever again. And there is no way I'm getting up before the birds every day. Not even for you.'

'And chocolate, and coffee…'

Her voice was breathy as she said, 'Will for ever be a staple in my diet. You want me, you take my predilections.'

'Oh, I want you all right,' he said, stealing a kiss on her beautiful pale neck.

She shivered. 'And are you sure you really understand that you get my family too. They live over an hour away, but they aren't backwards about dropping in unannounced.'

'I actually liked your family, those I met anyway. Your mum was wonderful with Ruby. Truly. And your brothers are all sporty types, right?'

Her eyes opened in time for her to roll them. 'They'll see you as manna from heaven. Thank goodness for Rye and Tabby and my new sisters-in-law, all sensible indoor-type women.'

'Thank goodness for indoor-type women everywhere.' He reached out and switched off the lamp.

'Well, what just happened there?' she said into the darkness.

'Just in case,' he said. 'Guests have been known to come wandering to this part of the resort on occasion.'

'How impolite.'

'How indeed.'

Thankfully the moon was not obscured by a single cloud so he could still make out Meg's shape, her soft curves, her smile. He kissed the end of her nose. The corner of her lush mouth. The curve of her cheek. When he found the edge of her ear lobe her head lolled back on her neck as though her muscles had turned to liquid. 'You're too easy.'

'Try playing me at any board game on the planet and you'll be singing another tune, my friend.'

Instead he chose another indoor game, which left them both winners.

And afterwards, scads of coffee or no coffee, Meg fell asleep on the floor of the pool house, wrapped in his old, warm, soft, favourite, red, woollen blanket and in his arms. Her face peaceful, the dark rings beneath her eyes gone.

Content. Happy. Home.

# EPILOGUE

SIX weeks after making Juniper Falls her home, and a little over a month after Quinn Kelly's colossal and extremely moving state funeral—attended by no less than three foreign heads of state—Meg stood waiting at the gates of the Juniper Falls resort. Her high ponytail bounced about her shoulders as she hopped on the spot, and her hot-pink high heels kept getting stuck in the grass.

She glanced down at her brand-new engagement ring—a pink diamond solitaire as chosen by fashionista-in-the-making Ruby—glittering beautifully on her left hand and thought for about the hundredth time that her life couldn't feel any different than it had two months before.

Quite apart from becoming more at home with her spectacularly beautiful new digs, her new man, and the new little girl in her life, she was still attending sporadic events as Meg Kelly, the face of the Kelly family, ones she had hand-picked herself. She was still volunteering at least twice a week at the Valley Women's Shelter, only now she did so without any kind of disguise, internal or external, and the satisfaction it gave her had increased a hundredfold.

But this day, at the beginning of the next to last week of the summer school holidays, she was going to work for her new family's business.

A big white bus finally came through the Juniper Falls gates.
It had barely pulled to a stop when what seemed like a thousand
kids spilled out. Bedraggled urchins the lot of them. With dark
eyes all but popping out of their pale faces as they took in
elegant Waratah House and the lushly encroaching rainforest.

Meg clapped her hands loud enough for the group to quiet
down. 'Okay, guys, I need you to do me a big favour and get
yourself organised in one long line, alphabetical by first name.'

'What if two of us have the same name?' a big kid with a
missing front tooth asked.

'Excellent question. Then the one with the longest big toe
goes up top. Right?'

A couple of kids whipped off their shoes and holey socks,
just in case.

Meg grinned. 'If you have it done in five minutes, there's
ice cream waiting for you in the restaurant.'

The loudest whoop she'd ever heard had her holding her
hands over her ears and running for the side of the bus as the
kids frantically introduced themselves to one another, which
was the actual point of the exercise.

After the bus driver, whom Meg waved up the hill towards
food, Zach was the last to hop off the bus. He looked as raggedy
and wide-eyed as the rest of them. After an hour's trip up the
mountain with this lot she wasn't surprised.

She sidled up to him and wrapped her arm around his waist.
'There's my big, brave, manly man. You survived.'

He said, 'The week's not over yet.'

Together they watched the Juniper Falls ground crew,
headed by Felicia—now the resort's official Children's Activities Co-ordinator as well as Ruby's some time babysitter—
keeping the kids whipped into an eager frenzy.

'I never thought I'd say this, but thank goodness Ruby's a
reader not a runner,' Zach said.

Meg bit her lip. She knew better. The first time she'd seen Ruby she'd been swinging up a storm, her clothes covered in evidence of further adventure. But that was another mystery her dad would never have to know about. Now there was an extra pair of eyes looking out for Ruby, eyes experienced in the ways of feisty young girls, those mysteries ought to become fewer and further between.

Meg laid a hand on Zach's chest. 'I've babysat Brendan's girls a thousand times. Believe me, let them run it out and they'll sleep where they fall come dark.'

'From your mouth to God's ears.'

They watched on in silence as the rowdy kids walked single file towards the restaurant.

'Can you believe they're really here?' she asked.

Zach shook his head.

An idea Zach had thrown out over dinner one night had become Meg's obsession. The whole week at the resort had been booked out for a hundred pre-teens, some treading water in the foster system, others from families who'd been through Meg's shelter.

Zach had put out word within the Olympic fraternity and several well-known athletes would run them ragged. The resort's staff would teach them things like how to resolve issues with words not fists. Rock-star mates of Meg's were to host a couple of dance parties, celebrity chefs to cook up healthy, fun food. And they'd be spoilt rotten.

But best of all, exposing these kids to Zach's story, and subsequent success, would broaden the horizons they dared to reach for. Exposing Meg to these kids had already broadened hers more than she'd thought possible.

She leaned her head on his shoulder as a mass squeal of delight echoed from the restaurant.

Zach said, 'I hate that Ruby's missing this.'

'She'll be back in a couple of days, so she won't miss much. I know I've said so a hundred times, but thanks for letting Mum have her. Ruby will be a brilliant influence on Brendan's girls, and having all three girls has been the highlight of Mum's month. She's promised not to mention croquet lessons, or Baroque appreciation classes or a course in *commedia dell'arte.*'

Zach nodded silently, his back ramrod straight.

'You've got used to having her home these holidays, haven't you?' she asked.

He slid a hand over her hair, tugging the end of her ponytail, and nodded.

'Yeah,' she said. 'Me too. We don't really have to send her back to school next week, do we?'

He kissed the top of her head. 'You're the one who came from the good family—how did you end up being the bad influence?'

'I'm Libran. I will do anything to make people love me.'

'Mmm, and there I was thinking people couldn't help loving you just because you're you. And all along it was the accident of your birth.'

'Happy accident?' she asked, looking up at him again.

He appeared to think about it for a moment. Then two.

Meg moved to pinch his arm, but he caught her hand in time and held it behind her back. Heat slid through her centre, the kind that still caught her off guard after all these weeks, the kind she didn't see herself ever getting used to.

And then he kissed her with the kind of sweet, sensitive, all-consuming passion she never planned on getting used to.

Eons later they pulled apart when the sound of big tyres crunching against the white gravel drive split the peaceful silence.

The next of the four remaining buses was pulling in, and Dylan's harrowed face was peering out the front window. Tabitha bouncing about next to him the likely reason.

Meg grabbed Zach's hand and pulled him inside the first bus.

They jogged to the back bench seat and hunkered down with Meg atop Zach's lap, her arms about his neck so that they could watch from a covert vantage point as Tabitha, Dylan and his fiancée, Wynnie, attempted to corral their group.

'You should have let Rylie do a series on her TV show about what we're doing here this week, you know,' Meg said. 'The publicity would have been amazing.'

'It would have. If we wanted publicity.'

The public figure and the private benefactor in Meg both struggled to be given free rein. 'But think of the fundraising opportunity—'

'I have more than enough funds to do this any time I want.'

She sat up straight. 'As do I. But I wish the world knew what an amazing man you are.'

'So long as you know, and Ruby has a vague sense of it, and your family suspects, then the world can think whatever it wants.'

'You know what else?' Meg asked, curling closer. 'This way I get to keep you all to myself. And talking of having you to myself, how many sleeps till we head off to St Barts for the Grand Opening?'

'Ah, twelve.' He ran a finger down her nose before sliding it beneath her chin. 'We still have time for it to be a honeymoon instead, you know.'

Though the idea felt just as thrilling now as the first time he'd suggested it, she knew that she wanted her family, her whole extended family, to be a part of the happy day when it finally came.

'A quickie wedding?' she said. 'A four-day honeymoon? Sometimes I think you don't know me at all.'

The finger beneath her chin moved to slide behind her ear and she struggled not to purr.

'Fine. Then when we get back,' he said, his voice gentle, 'can we continue that talk from the other night?'

She nodded. Her next breath in shook. And then she smiled.

'We can do better than that. I made an appointment with a fertility specialist at Monash IVF in Melbourne for not long after we come home. They practically invented the procedure, so if we're going to start finding out the possibilities of maybe one day having another child, then that's where we start.'

Zach leaned in to plant a kiss on her lips. Talk about heartwarming. 'No matter what happens, always know I'll always love you.'

She kissed him back. 'Always know I'll always love you too.'

He nodded. Promise sealed. He moved in for another kiss, when Meg stayed him with a finger.

'I just had a horrible thought,' Meg said, biting back a grin.

Zach's eyes narrowed. 'Do I really want to know?'

'What if Ruby asks for *commedia dell'arte* classes?'

'I'm not going to be the one to say no.'

'Yeah, me neither. They were actually kind of fun. Oh, look.'

The next bus pulled up and Cameron and his wife, Rosie, stood at the front clapping madly and singing some travel song they'd forced on the poor kids in their bus.

'You know what else is fun?' Zach said, nuzzling against Meg's ear.

She turned back to face him. 'Do I really want to know?'

Zach slowly pressed Meg down against the leather seat, waved at her the keys he'd used to lock the bus door, and grinned. 'Yeah, you really want to know.'

# PROUD RANCHER, PRECIOUS BUNDLE

## DONNA ALWARD

A busy wife and mother of three (two daughters and the family dog), **Donna Alward** believes hers is the best job in the world—a combination of stay-at-home mum and romance novelist. An avid reader since childhood, Donna always made up her own stories. She completed her arts degree in English literature in 1994, but it wasn't until 2001 that she penned her first full-length novel and found herself hooked on writing romance. In 2006, she sold her first manuscript, and now writes warm, emotional stories for the Harlequin Romance line. In her new home office in Nova Scotia, Donna loves being back on the east coast of Canada after nearly twelve years in Alberta, where her career began, writing about cowboys and the west. Donna's debut Romance, *Hired by the Cowboy*, was awarded the Booksellers Best Award in 2008 for Best Traditional Romance. With the Atlantic Ocean only minutes from her doorstep, Donna has found a fresh take on life and promises even more great romances in the near future! Donna loves to hear from readers. You can contact her through her website at www. donnaalward.com, visit her MySpace page at www.myspace.com/dalward, or through her publisher.

To my girly girls, Ash and Kate.
Love you.

# CHAPTER ONE

OF ALL THE MISHAPS that had happened today—stubborn cattle, broken gates, his ATV running out of gas—Wyatt Black definitely hadn't seen this one coming.

His boots scuffed in the dust leading to the sagging porch, his gaze riveted on the oddly shaped lump next to his front door. It was rounded and...pink. Pink? After a pause, he quickened his steps. A sound came from the bundle, a small squeaking sound.

Three steps later his heart pounded as his eyes confirmed his initial assessment. It was, indeed, a baby seat. For a few brief moments he'd nearly convinced himself he was seeing things. But there was no mistaking the pink canopy. He took the veranda steps slowly, confused. What the hell?

Two steps away from the seat he could see a small white chubby hand, the fingers curled in, delicate pink fingernails tipping the tiny digits.

And then there she was. A small mite of a thing, eyes closed and lips sucking gently in and out with her breath as her hands moved restlessly. A hint of dark fuzz peeked out from beneath a stretchy pink hat, and a blanket patterned with white and pink teddy bears covered all of her but her hands. *A baby.* And beside her a navy-and-white cloth bag, as if announcing she was staying for a while.

Wyatt's heart raced as the necessary questions flew through his mind. He put down his toolbox with a quiet thud. Who was this child's mother and, more importantly, where was she? Why had a baby been left on *his* doorstep?

It was inconceivable that this miniature human could be meant for him. There had to be some mistake. The alternative was momentarily staggering. Was it possible that she might be his flesh and blood? He stared at the lashes lying on her china-doll cheeks. She was so little. He counted back several months, then breathed out in relief. No, it was impossible. A year ago he'd been outside Rocky Mountain House working as a roughneck. There'd been no one. He had always kept his relationships on the unserious side and short. There'd been no sense letting a woman get her hopes up when he hadn't been in a position to settle down. He wasn't into playing games.

He exhaled fully. No, this baby wasn't his—he was sure of it. The core of tension in his body eased slightly, but not completely. The baby couldn't be his, but that still left the question—*whose was she?*

And what was he supposed to do with her?

As if hearing his question, she lifted her fringe of black lashes and he caught sight of dark eyes. The hands waved even more as she woke. Then, as if knowing he was the last person she should see, her face scrunched up pitifully and a thin cry pierced the silence.

He breathed a profanity in shock and dismay. He couldn't just leave her there crying, for God's sake! What should he do now? He knew nothing about babies. He glanced around the yard and up the road, knowing it was a futile exercise. Whoever had left her on his doorstep was long gone.

He reached out and grasped the white plastic handle of the car seat, picking it up with his right hand and tugging open the front door with his left. He certainly had to get the baby out of the September chill—surely it couldn't be good for her. He didn't even stop to take off his boots, just went straight through to the kitchen at the rear of the house and put the seat on a worn countertop. The thin cry echoed—seeming sharper, stronger in the confined space. Wyatt took off his hat and hooked it over the knob of a kitchen chair before turning back to the unhappy bundle.

He lifted the blanket, momentarily marveling that a creature so tiny and fragile could emit such a shrill, ear-piercing cry. A quick search of the recesses of the seat revealed no clues to her identity, and he ran a hand through his hair as the cries increased, feet wiggling furiously now as well as hands.

"Shhh, baby," he murmured, his stomach sinking beneath the weight of the situation. He couldn't just leave her this way. He reached out to unfasten the buckle strapping her in and pulled back once he caught a glimpse of his hands. He'd been herding stubborn cattle and fixing run-down fences all morning. Pulse still hammering, he rushed to the sink and the bar of soap he kept on the rim in an old chipped dish.

He scrubbed his hands in the water, all the while looking over his shoulder at the baby, his nerves fraying as the cries grew more impatient. Instinct told him that he should pick her up. Babies needed to be soothed, right? After all, he'd be pretty ticked off at being strapped into a seat all day. He threw the hand towel next to the sink and went back to the seat. "Shhh," he repeated, desperate now to stop the crying. "I've got you. Just stop crying."

He released the strap and reached out, took the baby, blanket and all, from the seat and rested her on the crook of his arm.

The red blotchy face signaled more crying, and the wee body stiffened with outrage.

"Hey," Wyatt cajoled, wondering now if he shouldn't call 911. Surely this was an emergency. How many people came home to find a baby on their doorstep, after all?

How had this possibly happened?

Dimly he recalled that a bag had been on the veranda along with the seat. It was his best hope for a clue, he realized, so, baby and all, he opened the sagging screen door with his hip and retrieved the bag. His boots thunked on the scarred hardwood as he went back to the kitchen and the counter, putting the bag on top. Trying to ignore the crying, he wrestled the zipper with one hand while holding the baby tightly with his other arm. Perhaps in here there would be a name, an address. Some way to sort out this horrible mistake and return the baby to where she really belonged.

He pulled out a handful of tiny diapers, then a pair of pajamas with soft feet, and a stuffed animal. One, two, three bottles…and a can of some sort of powder added to the collection on the counter. Then more bottles. He ran his hand along the inside of the bag. More clothes, but nothing else.

Irritation flared, now that the initial shock was fading away. This was craziness, pure and simple. For God's sake, what kind of person left a baby on a stranger's porch and walked away? What kind of mother would do such a thing? What if he hadn't come back for lunch and she'd been left there all day? He let out a frustrated breath. Okay. Without a doubt the smart thing to do would be to call the police.

And then he felt it. Something stiff near the front of the bag. He lifted a Velcro tab and reached into a front pocket. An envelope.

Adjusting the baby's weight on his arm, he opened the flap, went to a kitchen chair and sat down. Heavily.

His eyes scanned the page. As if sensing something important were occurring, the infant quieted and she plunged a fist into her mouth, sucking noisily and whimpering. Wyatt read the brief words, his back sagging into the chair, staring at the plain paper and then at the tiny girl in his hands.

Holy jumpin' Judas.

Her name was Darcy. He said her name, tried it out on his tongue, his throat closing as the sound of his voice faded away in the quiet kitchen. The answer that greeted him was a fresh wail punctuated by a sad hiccup.

The break had helped only to increase the baby's vocal reserves. Her crying rose to a fever pitch and Wyatt closed his eyes, still reeling from the contents of the letter. He had to make her stop so he could think what to do next. His stomach rumbled loudly, reminding him why he'd come back to the house in the first place.

Maybe *she* was hungry, too.

As the inspiration struck he grabbed one of the bottles off the counter where he'd unloaded the diaper bag. At the first touch of plastic nipple to lips, Darcy opened her mouth and frantically started sucking at the milk inside. That was it! A sense of pride and relief raced through him as he went to the living room, sitting on the old couch with its sagging cushions and wiggling arms. He leaned back, rested his feet on a wood box he had pressed into use as a coffee table. Blessed silence filled the room as she drained the small bottle, her tiny body nestled into the crook of his elbow. She felt foreign there, unlike anything he'd ever held before. Not unpleasant. Just…different.

Her eyes drifted closed once more. Had he actually put her to sleep, as well? Thank God. With some peace and quiet, he could take a look at that letter again, try to sort it out. One thing was for sure…Darcy—whoever she was—couldn't stay here.

The little lips slackened and a dribble of milk slid down her chin into the soft skin of her neck. He was struck by how tiny, how helpless she was. As gently as he possibly could, he slid her back into her seat and covered her with the blanket. Then he went to the fridge, got out an apple to substitute for the lunch he'd missed. He took a bite and returned to the letter he'd left open on the table.

He read it again, and again, and once more for good measure. Half his brain told him there was some mistake. The other half, the part that nagged and taunted him each day of his life, nudged him cruelly and said he shouldn't be surprised. The apple tasted dry and mealy in his mouth, and he swallowed with difficulty.

Darcy was his niece.

Born to a sister he'd pretended hadn't existed.

He rubbed a hand over his face. Oh, he'd known for a long time that his father wouldn't win any awards for parent of the year. But he recognized the name at the bottom of the plain sheet. Barbara Paulsen had been two years behind him in high school. All the kids had known that she had no dad. She'd borne her share of ridicule, all right. *Bastard Barb,* they'd called her. He cringed, thinking about the cruelty of it now. He'd never joined in the teasing. It would have been too easy for the tables to be turned. He'd deserved the name as much as she had. There'd been rumors back then, of his father having an affair with Barb's mother. Barbara's dark hair and eyes had been so similar to his—and to Mitch Black's.

He'd always hated that he'd favored his father rather than his mother in looks. He didn't want to be *anything* like his father. Ever.

He'd chosen to turn a deaf ear to the rumors, but inside, a small part of him had always taunted that it was true.

According to the letter, they shared the same father. It wasn't much of a stretch for Wyatt to believe her. It had been no secret in his house that Mitch Black had married Wyatt's mother to do the right thing after getting her in trouble. And it had been a disaster.

Wyatt scowled, staring at the wall behind the table. Hell, even dead, his father still created ripples of destruction. Now Barbara—claiming to be his sister—found herself in the same position, and was asking for his help. Temporarily. But asking for it just the same.

The fact that she had left Darcy on his step meant one of two things. Either she was as great a parent as their father had been, or she was desperate. Reading between the lines of the letter, he was leaning toward desperation.

But it didn't solve a damn thing where he was concerned. He was now in possession of an infant. And he was a single man, trying to run a ranch, who knew nothing about babies. Maybe he should simply call the authorities.

He ran a hand over his face, heaving a sigh. The authorities, though, would call child welfare. He knew that much. And if Barbara were truly his half sister, she'd already suffered enough. He'd made no contact with her since leaving Red Deer. It had been easier to pretend she didn't exist. Easier to ignore yet another symbol of the disrespect Mitch had shown his family.

No, if he called, Family Services would take the baby away. Not just from him, but maybe from her, too, and the thought made his stomach clench.

Once he made the call, there would be no taking it back. What he needed to do was buy some time. He needed to talk to Barbara. Figure out the whole situation and make a better decision.

An ear-splitting scream shattered the air, scattering his thoughts into tiny fragments and making his eyes widen with the sheer panic echoing in his ears. He looked over—Darcy's face was red and the cries had a new, desperate edge to them. What now? He walked the floor, holding Darcy in the crook of his arm, at his wit's end. Until today, he'd never held a baby in his life.

He needed help. Even to make it through this one day so he could figure out what to do next. Maybe he shouldn't, but he felt responsible. Even if it turned out not to be true, he felt an obligation to make the right decision. It wasn't Darcy's fault she'd been left here. If what Barbara Paulsen said was true, she was family.

You shouldn't turn your back on family. He'd always believed it somehow, but had never had the chance to prove it.

His muscles tensed at the persistent wails. He couldn't do this, not alone. Who could he possibly call? His parents had been gone nearly five years. He'd been in the house only for the summer, after drifting around the upper half of Alberta for years now, earning his fortune in the oil patch and never staying in one place for long. He was alone, and for the most part that was how he liked it.

Until now. Right now he could really use a helping hand.

And then he remembered his neighbor. Not technically his neighbor either. He'd met Ellison Marchuk exactly once. She was housesitting for the Camerons, and despite being incredibly attractive, had no more sense than God gave a flea. Whatever possessed a woman to go traipsing through a pasture housing his bull—in search of flowers!—was beyond him. And then she'd had the nerve to call him grouchy, with a toss of her summer-blond hair. Grouchy as a wounded bear, if memory served correctly.

Ellison Marchuk would not have been his first choice, but she was a woman and she was next door, both qualifications that put her head and shoulders above anyone else he knew. Surely she would have some idea what to do with a baby. At this point, looking at the tiny face twisted in agony, *anyone* would know what to do better than he did. His nerves were fraying more by the minute. He just needed help quieting her crying. He'd take it from there.

Amidst the shrieking cries and against his better judgment, he wrapped the blanket around Darcy and headed for the door.

Elli rubbed her eyes and slid a bookmark into the textbook, pushing it to the side. If she read any more today about profit-and-loss statements she'd go cross-eyed by the end of the week. Taking the courses by correspondence had benefits and drawbacks. Still, they'd help her get back on her feet, something she needed to do sooner rather than later. Being laid off from the hospital was just the icing on the cake after the year from hell. It was time to take action. To find a purpose again.

Right now she just wanted a cup of hot chocolate and something to break up her day—make her stop thinking. She'd had way too much time to think lately. About all her failures, mostly.

She jumped as someone pounded on the front door, and she pressed a hand to her heart. She still wasn't used to the way things echoed around the vaulted ceilings of the Camerons' house, including the sound of her footsteps as she went to the foyer. The house was so different from the condo she'd shared with Tim in Calgary. It had been nice, in a good area of town, but this was...

She sighed. This was exactly what Tim had aspired to.

This was the sort of McMansion he'd mapped out for them. Maybe he'd get it yet. Just not with her.

The pounding sounded again. She peered through the judas hole and her mouth dropped open. It was the neighbor, the new rancher who lived next door. Her teeth clenched as she recalled their one and only meeting. Wyatt Black, he'd informed her in a tone that could only be considered brusque at best. He'd yelled at her and called her stupid. The remark had cut her deeply. Normally she would have brushed off the insult—she'd been called so many names as a clerk in the emergency room that she'd developed a thick skin. But in light of recent events, it had made her eyes burn with humiliation. She'd called him something, too, but she couldn't remember what. She vaguely remembered it had been more polite than the words going through her mind at the time. She'd stomped back to the house and hadn't seen him since.

Now here he was, all six brawny feet of him. Elli pressed her eye up to the peephole once more and bit down on her lip. Dark hair and stormy eyes and a mouth pulled tight in a scowl. And in his arms…

Dear Lord. A baby.

As he knocked on the door again, Elli jumped back. Now she could hear the thin cries threading through the solid oak. She reached out and turned the heavy knob, pulling the door inward, and stepped out into the afternoon sun.

"Oh, thank God."

Elli's eardrums received the full blast of the infant's cries mediated only by Wyatt's deep but stressed, voice.

"What on earth?"

Mr. Dark and Scowly stepped forward, enough that his body started to invade her space, and she stepped back in reflex.

"Please, just tell me what to do. She won't stop crying."

Whatever Elli's questions, they fled as she looked from his harried expression down into the scrunched, unhappy face. First things first. Her heart gave a painful twist at the sight of the baby. He clearly expected her to know what to do. She hated how her hands shook as she reached out for the soft bundle. The little girl was clearly in discomfort of some kind. And this rancher—Black—was certainly not calming her in the least.

Elli pushed the door open farther with her hip, inviting him in as she moved aside, trying to ignore her body's response to feeling the small, warm body in her arms. This baby was not William. She could do this. She pasted on an artificial smile. "What's her name?"

He swallowed thickly as he stepped over the threshold, his Adam's apple bobbing. Elli's gaze locked on it for a moment before looking up into his face. He had the most extraordinary lips, the bottom one deliciously full above a chin rough with a hint of stubble. The lips moved as she watched. "Darcy. Her name is Darcy."

Elli felt the warm little bundle in her arms, the weight foreign, painful, yet somehow very right. She pressed a hand to the tiny forehead, feeling for fever. "She's not warm. Do you think she's ill?"

Black came in, shutting the door behind him, and Elli felt nerves swim around in her stomach. He was not a pleasant man. And yet there was something in his eyes. It looked like worry, and it helped ameliorate her misgivings.

"I was hoping you could tell me. One minute she was asleep, the next she was screaming like a banshee." He raised his voice a bit to be heard over the screaming racket.

Her, tell him? She knew next to nothing about babies,

and the very reminder of the fact hurt, cutting deep into her bones. She scoured her mind for the things she'd learned about soothing babies from the books she'd bought and the prenatal classes she'd attended. Food seemed the most obvious. "Did you try feeding her?"

"She seemed to be fine after I gave her the bottle from the bag," he explained, rubbing a hand over his hair. "She drank the whole thing, sucked it right down."

Elli wrinkled her brow, trying to recall if Sarah Cameron had mentioned that their reticent neighbor had a child. She didn't think so. He certainly didn't act like a man who'd come into contact with babies before. He was staring at her and Darcy with his eyes full of concern—and panic.

A detail pierced her memory, a remnant of classes taken what seemed like a lifetime ago. "Did you heat the milk?"

The full lips dropped open slightly and his cheekbones flattened. "I was supposed to heat it?"

Elli's shoulders relaxed and she let out a small chuckle, relieved. Immediately she lifted the baby to her shoulder and began rubbing her back with firm circles. "She's probably got cramps," she said above the pitiful crying. It seemed the easiest solution at the moment. She began patting Darcy's back. Hungry, gas, cramps. Elementary. At least she could fake knowing what she was doing.

"I didn't know," he replied, a light blush infusing his cheeks beneath the stubble. "I don't know *anything* about babies."

"You might as well take off your boots and come in for a minute," Elli replied, not wanting to admit that she knew little more than he did and determined to bluff her way through it. She knew she'd made a mistake going into his bull pasture earlier this summer and she already knew what he thought of her common sense. She'd be damned if she'd let him see a weakness again.

They couldn't stand in the foyer forever. An enormous burp echoed straight up to the rafters and a laugh bubbled up and out of Elli's lips at the violence of the sound coming from such a tiny package. She was pleased at having discovered the cause and solution quite by accident. The expression on Black's face conveyed such abject surprise that she giggled again.

"I'm Ellison Marchuk," she introduced herself, her shoulder growing warm from the soft breath of the baby as she sighed against her sweater. "I don't think we met properly last time."

"I remember," he replied, and Elli felt the heat of a blush creep up her neck straight to her ears. "Wyatt Black, in case you forgot," he continued pointedly. "Thank you. My ears are still ringing. I was at my wit's end."

Elli ignored the subtle dig. Of course she remembered meeting him. It wasn't every day a perfect stranger yelled at her and called her names. She was more polite than that, and had been making an attempt to start fresh. She lifted her chin. "You're welcome, Wyatt Black."

Goodness, Elli thought as the name rolled off her tongue. The name matched him perfectly. She watched with her pulse drumming rapidly as he pushed off his boots with his toes. Even in his stocking feet, he topped her by a good four inches. His shoulders were inordinately broad in a worn flannel shirt. And his jeans were faded in all the right places.

She swallowed. She needed to get out more. Maybe she'd been hiding out in the Camerons' house a little too long, if she was reacting to the irascible next-door neighbor in such a way. Especially a neighbor with rotten manners.

Elli led the way through the foyer into the living room,

determined to be gracious. The room faced the backyard, then south over the wide pasture where Wyatt's herd now grazed—the very pasture where she'd indulged herself in picking late-summer wildflowers in an attempt to cheer herself up. The fields here were huge. She'd had no idea she was in the same pasture as one of his bulls.

"The Camerons have a nice place." His voice came from behind her. "I haven't been inside before."

"My father used to work for Cameron Energy," Elli remarked. "The Camerons are like second parents to me."

Wyatt remained silent behind her and Elli added lack of conversational skills to his repertoire of faults.

She took him straight to the conversation pit with its plush furniture. Windows filled the wall behind them, flooding the room with light, while French doors led out to a large deck. She gestured toward a chair, inviting him to sit. "Would you like her back now? She seems much more contented."

She held out her arms with Darcy now blinking innocently, her dark eyes focused on nothing in particular.

"She looks happy where she is," Wyatt replied, looking away.

Elli took a step back and went to the sofa. She sat down and put Darcy gently beside her. He couldn't know how caring for a child—even in such a minor way—hurt her. She worked hard to push away the bitterness. If things had gone right, she would have been in her own home cradling her own son right now. She blinked a couple of times and forced the thoughts aside. It could not be changed.

"Won't she fall off?" Wyatt's hard voice interrupted.

The rough question diverted her from overthinking. She didn't know. How old were babies when they could start rolling over? She didn't want him to see her indecision, and she adjusted the baby on the sofa so she was lying safely, perpendicular to the edge of the couch.

"How old is she?" Elli guessed at a month, maybe six weeks. She still held that newborn daintiness. A precious little bundle who had been through what appeared to be a rough day if the mottled, puffy cheeks were any indication. Could a day with Wyatt Black be described in any other way? Elli ran a finger down the middle of the sleepers, smiling softly as the little feet kicked with pleasure. At least she'd elicited a positive response rather than more crying.

When Wyatt didn't answer her question, though, she looked back at him again. He was watching her speculatively, his eyes slightly narrowed as if he were trying to read her thoughts. She was glad he couldn't. There were some things she didn't want anyone to know.

"What do you do, Ellison?"

Ah, he hadn't wanted to answer her question, and she didn't want to answer his either. It wasn't a simple question, not to her. Answering required a lengthy explanation, and it would only add fuel to his comment in the pasture that day, when he'd called her stupid. Maybe she was. A fool, certainly.

Maybe it was time he left. There was something not quite right in the way he'd avoided her question, something that didn't add up. He could mind his own business and she could mind hers and they'd both be happy.

"She seems fine now, but perhaps tired. You should take her home and put her to bed."

Wyatt looked away. Elli's misgivings grew. Her heart picked up a quick rhythm again. The only information he'd offered was that her name was Darcy, and it wasn't as if the baby could dispute it. He didn't answer how old she was, he didn't know to heat a bottle… What was this man doing with an infant? Was the child his? And if so, shouldn't he know *something* about caring for her?

She braved a look. As much as she didn't want to get involved, she could still smell the baby-powder scent on her shoulder, feel the warmth of the little body pressed against her like a wish come true. She took a breath. "She's not yours, is she?"

His eyes captured hers, honest but betraying no other emotion. "No."

"Then whose…"

"It's complicated."

She put her hands primly on her knees to keep from fidgeting. She briefly thought of all the news stories about noncustodial kidnappings. Sure, he was a crusty, grouchy thing, but was he capable of *that?* She didn't want to believe it. "I don't feel reassured, Mr. Black."

His steady gaze made her want to squirm, and she fought against the feeling. Should she be frightened? Perhaps. But she hadn't put herself in the middle of the situation. He had. A man with something to hide wouldn't have done that, would he? "You don't know what to do with babies," she remarked, screwing up her courage. "You don't even know how old she is."

"No, I don't. I've never held a baby in my life before today. Does that make you feel better?"

There was a little edge of danger to him that was exciting even as warning bells started clanging. "Not exactly."

She had to be crazy. Despite their first meeting, Wyatt Black was a stranger with a strange baby, in a situation she didn't understand and she was alone in the house in the middle of nowhere. Calling the police had crossed her mind more than once. But then she remembered the look on his face as he'd handed Darcy to her. It wasn't just panic. It was concern. And while he said little, there was something about him that she trusted. She couldn't explain why. It was just a feeling.

She'd learned to trust her gut feelings. Even when it hurt.

She picked Darcy up off the sofa cushion, swaddling her in the blanket. She simply had to know more to be sure. To know that the baby would be safe and cared for. "I need you to explain."

"Darcy is my niece. I think."

The ambiguous response made her wrinkle her nose in confusion. "Mr. Black…"

He stood up from his chair, his long, hard length taking a handful of steps until he paused before her, making her crane her neck to see his face. His jaw was set and his eyes glittered darkly, but there was a hint of something there that elicited her empathy. A glimmer of pain, perhaps, and vulnerability.

He reached behind him into his back pocket and withdrew an envelope.

He held it out to her.

"Read it," he commanded. "Then you'll know just as much as I do."

# CHAPTER TWO

ELLI STARED AT THE piece of paper, all the while aware of Wyatt standing before her, the faded denim of his jeans constantly in her line of vision. She read the letter aloud, her soft voice echoing through the empty room. Listening to the words made it more real somehow. Wyatt seemed to look everywhere but at the baby.

"'Dear Wyatt, I know right now you're probably wondering what on earth is going on. And believe me—if I had another choice…'"

Elli risked a glance up. Wyatt was staring at a spot past her shoulder, his jaw tightly clenched, his gaze revealing nothing. She looked back down at the plain piece of paper, torn from a notebook, with the edges rough and careless. Her stomach began an uneasy turning. This wasn't stationery chosen for such an important letter. This was hurried. Impulsive.

"I don't know if you were ever aware, Wyatt, but we share a father. I am your half sister. I tried to hate you for it, but you were never mean to me like the others. Maybe you knew back then. Either way… you're all the family I've got now. You and Darcy. And I'm not good for either one of you. If there were any other way…but I can't do this. Take good care of her for me."

The letter was signed simply "Barbara Paulsen."

If the letter were genuine—and she was inclined to think it was—then he was telling the truth. Darcy was his niece. More importantly, the words themselves disturbed her. Twice she had said she had no choice…why?

"Your sister…" she began quietly.

His boots did an about-face and she looked up from the paper. He was no longer directly in front of her. He had moved and stopped at the front window, looking out over the hedge and small garden. There was a stiffness in his posture that caused Elli a moment of pause. Surely a mother's care was better than this detachment. Faced with an infant, Wyatt showed the same cold, stubborn side as he had the afternoon they'd first met. Babies needed more than bottles and a place to sleep. They needed love. She wondered if Wyatt Black was even capable of tenderness.

She cleared her throat. "Your sister," she continued, her voice slightly stronger, "must trust you very much."

"My sister?" The words came out in a harsh laugh. "We have a biological relationship, if that. I went to school with her, that's all."

"You don't believe her?"

He turned slowly from the window. His dark eyes were shuttered, his expression utterly closed, and she couldn't begin to imagine what he was thinking. Nothing about his face gave her a clue. She wanted to go over and shake him, get some sense of what was going through his mind. It was clear to her that there was a plea in Barbara's note. She was asking for help. And he was standing here like some judgmental god doling out doubt and condemnation.

"There were rumors…I ignored them. It certainly makes

sense—most of it anyway. It's not much of a stretch to think that my father…"

There, there it was. The flash of vulnerability, in his eyes and flickering through his voice. Gone just as quickly as it had surfaced, but she'd caught it. What sort of life had he had as a boy? He wasn't shocked at the discovery of his father's betrayal, she realized. But he was bitter. She had to tread carefully. She folded up the letter neatly and handed it back to him.

"What if it's not true?"

His lips became a harsh, thin line. "It probably is," he admitted. "But I need to find out for sure. In the meantime…"

"Yes," she agreed quietly, knowing he had to see that Darcy was his first priority. "In the meantime, you have a more immediate problem. You have Darcy. What are you going to do?"

"I am hopeless with babies. I know nothing about them." His dark eyes met hers, looking as if he expected agreement.

"That goes without saying," she replied, crossing her arms. "But it doesn't change that Darcy has been left in your care."

"I don't know what to do. A few hours and I've already screwed up. I've never been around babies."

Elli offered a small indulgent smile. At least he seemed concerned about getting things right. Maybe she was judging him too harshly. "You were one, you know. A baby. Once."

"My memory is a bit dim," he reminded her, but she could see her light teasing had done its work. His facial muscles relaxed slightly and she thought there might actually be a hint of a smile just tugging at the corner of his lips. Just as soon as it came, it disappeared, so that she wondered if she had imagined it. The moment drew out and Elli's gaze remained riveted on his face. When he wasn't looking so severe, he was really quite…

Quite good-looking.

Darcy kicked on the sofa, a tiny sigh and gurgle breaking the silence. Elli looked away, wondering what on earth the child might be thinking, totally oblivious to the chaos around her. She thought briefly of Darcy's mother, Barbara, and felt a flash of animosity. How could a mother, any mother, simply drive away and leave this beautiful child on a stranger's doorstep? Did she not know how lucky she was? And yet…there was a sense of desperation between the lines of her letter. For some reason Barbara didn't think she could look after her own daughter. She was so afraid that she'd left her on the front porch of a man little more than a stranger.

Wyatt sat down on the sofa on the other side of Darcy, the cushions sinking beneath his weight. "I know," he said, as if replying to the question she hadn't asked. "I don't know how she could do it either. I haven't seen her in years. Maybe it is all made up. But maybe it's not. And I can't take that chance with Darcy."

"What do you mean?" Elli turned to face him, keeping her hands busy by playing with Darcy's feet, tapping them together lightly. She was already feeling the beginnings of resentment toward a woman she had never met. Darcy was so small, so precious. Elli had learned from years working in the emergency room that she shouldn't judge. But it was different when faced with an innocent, beautiful child. She *was* judging. It was impossible not to. She would give anything to be playing with her own child's feet at this moment. She knew in her heart that if William had lived, nothing could have pried her away from him.

Wyatt scowled slightly, resting his elbows on his knees.

"If she is my niece, I can't just call the police, can I? Because we both know what will happen to her then."

Elli nodded, pulled out of her dark thoughts. She had to look away from Wyatt's face. Was that tenderness she'd glimpsed in his eyes? The very emotion she'd doubted he possessed only moments ago? He might be inept, but he was trying to do the right thing.

"I can't just let her go into foster care. If I do, maybe there's a chance that her mother will never get her back. I can't let that happen. At least not until I know for sure. I need to find Barbara, talk to her."

Elli tried hard to fight away the surge of feeling expanding in her chest. She could already feel herself getting involved, getting sucked into a situation not of her making. Coming here, housesitting for the Camerons—that was supposed to be her way of taking a first step toward building a new life. Her chance to try again away from the drama and pitying looks. *Poor Elli. Bad luck comes in threes. Whatever will she do now?* She'd had enough of it.

A bachelor next-door neighbor with a baby wasn't exactly the type of special project she'd been looking for. She drew her attention back to the letter.

"This woman, this Barbara, even if she is your sister, Mr. Black, deliberately left a six-week-old baby on the doorstep of someone she barely knew with no guarantees that you would even be there." Elli fought to keep the anger, the frustration, the passion, for that matter, under control. This wasn't a subject she could be rational about. She knew it. It was the exact reason she should steer clear of the whole mess.

"Doesn't that tell you how desperate she is?"

Without warning, tears stung the backs of her eyes and she bit down on her lip. She got up from the sofa so that he couldn't see her face. So he couldn't see the grief that bubbled up.

She went to the kitchen, going instinctively for the kettle to give her hands something to do. Losing William had nearly destroyed her. It had certainly destroyed her marriage. And now that baby Darcy was quiet and content, the emergency was over. There was no way on God's green earth she was going to tell Wyatt Black—a man she'd just met—the sordid story of her disastrous pregnancy and resulting divorce.

She plugged in the kettle and took out a mug, hesitating with her hand on a second cup, trying to regain control. She should send him on his way. Remind him to warm up the bottles and wish him well.

He appeared in the doorway to the kitchen, filling the frame with his solid figure. She paused, the cup in her hand, looking up into his unsmiling face. He had Darcy on his arm in an awkward position.

Elli sighed, putting the mugs down on the counter. She'd taken the new-baby classes with Tim by her side. Back then it had been with dolls and smiles and laughter as the instructor showed them how to do even the simplest things. She'd blocked out those times from her mind deliberately, because they were so painful. But with Wyatt and Darcy only footsteps away, they came rushing back, bittersweet. She'd been excited to be pregnant, but also overwhelmed by the impending responsibility of caring for a baby. How must Wyatt be feeling, thrust into the situation with no preparation at all?

"Here. Let me show you." She went over to him and was careful to touch him as little as possible. Her fingers brushed the soft flannel of his shirt as she adjusted the pink bundle just the way she'd held the doll in classes. She forced the pain aside and focused on the task at hand.

Darcy looked up, eyes unfocused, seemingly unconcerned. Elli moved Wyatt's hand slightly. "You need to support her neck more," she said quietly, remembering what she'd read and heard. "Babies can't hold their heads up on their own at first. So when you pick her up or hold her, you need to make sure she has that support."

He cradled her close. "Maybe I should call someone. I really don't have a clue. She'd be better off with someone else, right? You said it yourself. I'm hopeless."

His eyes were dark and heavy with indecision, and shame crept through her. How could she have said such a thing, knowing how hurtful it could be? No matter how grumpy or grouchy he'd been, she could do better than throwing insults around. Elli could see that he was trying to do the right thing.

"No one was born knowing how to look after a baby, Mr. Black." She kept up the use of his formal name. The last thing she wanted was familiarity. It would be too easy to get involved. The instinct to protect herself fought with the need to help. "And if it's true, you're family. Doesn't that count for something?"

"More than you know," he replied, but there was no joy in the words. "Well, she's here now. I have a ranch to run. How can I possibly look after a child and do all that too?"

It did look as if he was beginning to think of the issue beyond *Could you get her to stop crying.* The kettle began to whistle and Elli swallowed thickly. "Do you want some tea?"

He shook his head. "No, thank you. I should get going, try to figure this out. First of all, I need to find Barbara."

"You seem to place a lot of importance on family, Mr. Black. That's to your credit."

His jaw tightened again, and Elli flushed slightly, not

knowing how what she'd intended as a compliment had managed to give offense.

"People tend to appreciate what's in short supply, Miss Marchuk."

He'd reverted to using Miss Marchuk now, too. The heat in her cheeks deepened and she turned away to pour the boiling water into her mug. His footsteps echoed away from the kitchen down to the foyer again, and she closed her eyes, breathing a sigh of relief.

She heard the door open and suddenly rushed from her spot, skidding down the hall in her sock feet, wanting to catch him before he left altogether. "Mr. Black!"

He paused at the door, Darcy now up on his shoulder and her blanket around her. A gust of wind came through the opening and ruffled his hair, leaving one piece standing up, giving her the urge to reach up and tuck it back into place.

"Yes?"

His one-word response brought her back to earth. She'd remembered something else, like a page torn from a book. "Heat the bottle in hot water. Then put a few drops of the formula on the underside of your wrist. When it's warm, but not hot, it's the right temperature."

For a few moments their gazes held, and something passed between them that was more than bottle-warming instructions. She didn't want to think about what it might be; even the internal suggestion of it hurt. She took a step back and lowered her gaze to the floor.

"Thank you," he murmured, and she didn't look up again until she heard the click of the door shutting her away from them both.

Elli struggled for the rest of the afternoon, all through her tea and while she made herself a grilled cheese and ham sandwich for supper. It was comfort food, and one she rarely allowed herself anymore. The months of criticism from Tim had caused her to burrow further into her grief. And like a nasty cycle, the further she withdrew, the more she had satisfied herself with food. His cutting remarks about her figure had been only one hurtful part of the disintegration of their marriage.

She put her plate into the dishwasher and cleaned the crumbs off the counter. The problem was, she couldn't get Wyatt and Darcy off her mind. Remembering how William had died made her want to run away from the situation as fast as her legs could carry her. And on the flip side was knowing that on the other side of the line of poplar trees, in a very modest bungalow, there was a rancher who knew even less than she did about babies. One who cared about what happened. At the same time she knew that Darcy would be the one to suffer while he tried to figure things out.

She swallowed, went to the windows overlooking the fields to the south. Wyatt's cattle roamed there, the red and white heads bobbing in the evening dusk, where she lost sight of them over a knoll. How was he managing now? Was Darcy crying, and was Wyatt trying to soothe her?

Elli wiped her fingertips over her cheeks, surprised and yet not surprised to find she was crying. She'd never even had the chance to hear William's cries. The absence of them had broken her heart cleanly in two. She got a tissue and dabbed the moisture away.

What would Wyatt do when he had to work? Had he managed to feed her properly? It wasn't fair to Darcy that Wyatt learned these things in trial by fire. And it was only Elli's stupid fear preventing her from helping. Shouldn't the welfare of the baby come before her own hang-ups?

She wiped her eyes once more, pity for the infant

swamping her. Shouldn't someone put that baby ahead of themselves?

Before she could reconsider, she grabbed her jacket from the coatrack and made the short trek across the grass to his house.

Wyatt paced the floor, Darcy on his shoulder, her damp lips pressed to his neck. His shoulders tensed as he thought about all he should have accomplished around the farm this afternoon. He'd managed to boot up the computer long enough to find Barbara in an Internet search, but when he called the number listed, there was no answer. He'd tried twice since, during moments when he'd thought Darcy was asleep.

She managed exactly seven minutes every time, before waking and crying. Crying that stopped the moment he put her on his shoulder and walked the floor. Which was great in the short term. But at some point he needed to eat. Sleep. Do chores.

More than once he'd felt his control slipping and wondered if he was more like his father than he'd thought. God, he didn't want to think so. From Wyatt's earliest memories, crying hadn't been tolerated. Mitch Black made sure of that. Wyatt wanted to think he had more self-control than his father. More compassion.

But baby Darcy was testing him.

He'd try Barbara's number once more. And then he'd call someone. He tried to ignore the end of the letter. The part where she apologized and said she trusted him. He'd given her no reason to. And yet…something about it made him feel as if he would be failing her if he didn't do this.

He sighed, turning back toward the kitchen, craning his neck at an odd angle to see if Darcy was asleep. It was almost as if he was operating on two levels—the one that needed information and planning, and the one with the immediate, pressing problem of keeping a baby's needs met.

Suddenly he had a new respect for mothers who seemed to juggle it all with aplomb.

A knock on the door broke the silence and Darcy's hands jerked out, startled. A quick check showed her tiny eyes open again. Wyatt pushed back annoyance and headed for the door, with a prayer that it was Barbara saying it had all been a mistake.

Instead he found Ellison Marchuk on his dilapidated porch.

"Oh," he said, and she frowned.

"Disappointed, I see." She pushed her hands into her jacket and he fought against the expansion in his chest at seeing her again.

This afternoon he'd been an idiot. He'd rushed over there thinking only of getting help, but he'd been inside all of thirty seconds when his priorities had shifted. He was supposed to have all his thoughts on his predicament, and instead he'd been noticing her hair, or the way her dark lashes brought out the blue in her eyes, or how her sweater accentuated her curves. He wasn't disappointed at all. Even though he should be.

"Not at all," he mumbled roughly. "I was just hoping it was Barbara, that's all."

"It would solve everything, wouldn't it?" She offered a small smile. His gaze dropped to her full mouth.

"Are you going to invite me in, Mr. Black?"

Of course. He was standing there like a dolt, thinking how pretty she looked in the puffy fleece jacket. Clearly she wasn't thinking along the same lines, as she persisted in calling him Mr. Black. Her body language this afternoon had spoken volumes. She couldn't even meet his gaze at the end, and she'd taken a step back.

And now here she was.

He moved aside and held the door open for her to enter.

Instantly his eyes saw his house the way hers must—in stark comparison to the pristine, high-class Cameron dwelling. They were from two different worlds. It couldn't be more plain from the look on her face.

"I haven't had time to pay much attention to the inside," he explained, then mentally kicked himself for apologizing. He didn't need to apologize, for Pete's sake! It was his house, purchased with his own money. He could do what he damned well pleased with it. He'd be a poor rancher if he put dressing up the inside ahead of his operation.

"I expect you've been busy," she replied softly.

"Something like that." He forced himself to look away, away from the brightness of her eyes that didn't dull even in the dim lamplight.

"I just wanted to see how you were making out with Darcy."

"I can put her down for exactly seven minutes. After that, she starts crying again." He shifted the slight weight on his arm once more. "So I keep picking her up."

Her gaze fell on his arms and desire kicked through his belly, unexpected and strong.

"Babies like to be snuggled," she murmured. "Think about it. If you had spent the first nine months of your life somewhere that was always warm and cozy, you'd want that on the outside, too."

Was it just him, or had her voice hitched a little at the end? He studied her face but saw nothing. He realized she was standing in front of the door with her coat and shoes on. He should invite her in. She'd helped once today. Perhaps she could again.

"I'm sorry, Miss Marchuk…" He paused, hearing how formal that sounded. "Ellison. Please…let me take your coat and come in. I managed to make coffee. I can offer you a cup."

She looked pleased then, and smiled. His heart gave a slight thump at the way it changed her face, erasing the seriousness and making her look almost girlish. She unzipped the fleece and put it in his free hand.

"Coffee sounds great," she replied. "And please…call me Elli. Ellison is what my mother calls me when she's unhappy with something I've done."

She looked so perfectly sweet with her blue eyes and shy smile that he answered without thinking. "You?"

She laughed, the sound light and more beautiful than anything he'd heard in a long time.

"Yes, me. Don't let the angelic looks fool you, Black."

He turned away, leading her to the kitchen while his lips hardened into a thin line. Angelic looks indeed. He'd been captivated by them twice today already. As he considered the bundle on his shoulder, he knew that one complication was enough. No good would come out of flirting with Elli Marchuk. He'd best remember that. His life was here, this house, this ranch. Anything else was transient, capable of moving in and out at a moment's notice. He'd built his life that way on purpose, one planned step at a time. The last thing he wanted was to be foolish and impulsive and end up as unhappy as his parents had been.

Being careful to support Darcy's head, he tried once more to put her into her seat. He'd only just retrieved mugs from the cupboard when she squawked again.

He sighed. There was a reason he'd never aspired to parenthood.

"Have you fed her?"

Elli's voice came from behind him. It sounded like a criticism and he bristled, knowing full well it was a legitimate question but feeling inept just the same.

"Yes, I fed her. She burped, too."

The squawking quieted as Elli picked her up, and Wyatt turned around, trying hard to ignore feelings of inadequacy as Darcy immediately stopped fussing.

"Maybe she's uncomfortable. What do you think, sweetheart?" Elli turned her conversation to the baby.

"What do you think is wrong?" Wyatt asked, putting the coffeepot back on the burner.

A strange look passed over Elli's face, one that looked like guilt and panic. But it was gone quickly. "I couldn't say," she replied.

"But you were so good with her this afternoon." Wyatt put his hands on his hips.

"Lucky, that's all. I just…remembered a few things." The same strange look flitted over her features once more.

Wyatt took the coffee to the table. "You fooled me. You looked like you knew exactly what you were doing." So much that Wyatt had felt completely inept. A feeling he despised. He was used to being the one in control.

Elli and Darcy walked the length of the kitchen and back. After a few moments she admitted, "I haven't really cared for a baby before. The things I thought of were simply things I'd heard about. Not from experience, Mr. Black."

Her chin jutted up, closing the subject but making him want to ask the questions now pulsing through his mind. But then he remembered the old saying, "Don't look a gift horse in the mouth." He'd benefit from whatever insight she had and be glad of it.

"I don't really know what babies need," he admitted. "I

fed her, patted her back like you did, walked her to sleep, but every time I put her down…"

Wyatt almost groaned. Of course. He'd forgotten one important thing. He'd been so focused on getting formula the right temperature that he'd forgotten to check her diaper. Not that he had any clue what to do there either.

Pulling calves and shoveling out stalls was far less intimidating than one tiny newborn.

"She's probably due for a diaper change, isn't she?" He tried to sound nonchalant. This was a perfect opportunity. Elli must know how to change a diaper. He could simply watch her so he'd know better for the next time.

Instead, Elli came around the corner of the counter and placed Darcy back in his arms. "Here you go, Uncle Wyatt," she said lightly. "You get diaper duty. I'll fix the coffee. Cream and sugar?"

*Oh, boy,* Wyatt thought, looking down into Darcy's pursed face, his smug plan blown to smithereens. He was in for it now.

# CHAPTER THREE

WYATT HELD DARCY straight out in front of him. There'd been many firsts for him over the past few months, but this was something completely out of his league. For the first time in his life Wyatt Black was going to change a dirty diaper.

He glanced over at Elli, who was spooning sugar into cups without so much as a concerned glance in his direction. The last thing he wanted to do was look like a fool in front of her twice in one day. He did have a level of pride, after all. And he was generally a competent sort of guy.

But people—babies—were different than cows and horses and machinery. He wasn't nearly as sure of himself when it came to human beings. And not just babies. Each time he met Ellison, his tongue seemed to tie up in knots and nothing seemed to come out the way it should.

He went to the diaper bag, retrieved a diaper and laid the baby on her blanket. He removed her sleepers and some sort of snapped-on undershirt and then the diaper. Good Lord. Wyatt paused, unsure, completely out of his element. Darcy, who'd been sucking on two fingers, took the digits from her mouth and began to squall again, protesting against the cold. He heard Elli go to the fridge and back to the counter. He refused to look up to check if she was watching.

"Hang on, hang on," he muttered, trying to remember

how he'd taken the wet diaper off so he could put the new one on the same way.

"Do babies always cry so much?" he grumbled as he cleaned up Darcy. He reached inside the bag for a new diaper.

Elli came to his side, laying a hand on his arm. "It's the only way they have of saying what's wrong," she said quietly. His arm warmed beneath the touch of her fingers. It felt reassuring and friendly, not the kind of caress he was used to. The touches he was accustomed to were more demanding. Wanting something, rather than giving.

"Do you know how to do this?" he asked, holding up the tiny diaper.

"I haven't done it before...on a baby," she replied, her gaze darting away from his.

"Meaning you've done it *not* on a baby?" he teased, wondering what had put the dark look on her face.

"A doll," she replied, her lips firm. "I've diapered a doll before."

There was something in her voice that reached inside him and grabbed his attention. A defiance, and a defensiveness he hadn't expected. But did he want to know? No, he decided, he didn't want to dig into whatever reasons Ellison did or didn't have for anything. But it didn't mean he was insensitive to her feelings, whatever they were.

"Can we figure it out together?"

Her gaze went back to him now, the irises of her eyes a glowing sapphire. "Wyatt..."

She'd dropped the Mr. Black and used his first name. His gaze dropped to her lips—he couldn't help it. They were pink and finely shaped and very soft looking.

He had to be careful here. Very, very careful.

"Which bit goes at the back?" He shook the white diaper gently.

She pulled back a few inches and looked away. "I think this way," she said, sliding the diaper underneath Darcy's bum, tabs at the back. "And diaper cream. There should be some of that, right?"

Elli watched as Wyatt dug in the bag and pulled out a tube. When he handed it to her, their fingers brushed and she pulled her hand back quickly. The contact seemed to spiral straight to her tummy and she held her breath for a tiny instant.

"It doesn't bite," Wyatt quipped, and Elli forced a smile. Maybe it didn't, but she wasn't so sure about him. Unsure how to respond, she hesitated and looked at the label—it said barrier cream. Logically, it provided a barrier for the baby's tender skin. She smoothed some on with her fingertips, ignoring the odd sensation of knowing Wyatt was watching her.

"You don't want her getting a rash, right? And then…" She pulled the front up and went to fasten the tab. Only, she folded it over so it stuck to itself.

"Heck, I could have done that," he said from behind her, and she heard humor in his tone as her cheeks flamed. Darcy was looking up at her with wide eyes, as if to say, *Come on, people. What's the holdup?*

Elli began to laugh. Lordy, the situation was comical when she stopped to think about it. She heard Wyatt's warm chuckle behind her and then felt his body—*oh, God,* his very hard, warm body—pressed against hers as he reached around her to retrieve another diaper from the bag. "I hope we get it right this time," he murmured, his lips so close to her ear that she could feel the warmth of his breath. She suppressed a delicious shiver.

"We'd better. Or else you're going to run out of diapers in a hurry."

Elli slid the diaper under once more and this time

fastened the tabs securely to the waistband. "Ta da!" She slid away, needing to get away from him and his sexy voice and body. She avoided his gaze, the one she suspected was leveled right at her. Self-conscious, she tugged her thick sweater down over her hips, smoothing it with her palms. "Now you just have to get her dressed again."

She left him there and went to toss away the diaper and wash her hands.

He took out a new undershirt and pajamas and carefully dressed Darcy. Then he placed her in the seat and sighed, moving to tidy up the mess before taking his place at the table. After only a few hours, things that were not usually there were cluttering countertops. Bottles and creams and rattles, where there were normally gloves and keys and perhaps the odd tool. "I haven't had two moments to take a breath. And now I have to say thank you again."

"It was nothing," she replied quietly.

Wyatt's eyes narrowed. She had let down her guard for a moment, but there was something in her voice, something in the way she refused to meet his gaze right now. It had happened several times today. Evasion that told him there was a whole lot to Ellison Marchuk he didn't know. Whatever it was, it was her business. He took a sip of hot coffee.

The immediate issue was solved, but he was beginning to see there would be more. He had no proper baby equipment, a handful of diapers, a few more bottles left. He still had chores around the ranch to look after tonight— and more repairs in the days ahead than he could possibly imagine. Barbara had been a fool to leave her daughter here. Darcy belonged with her mother, not with him.

Elli watched Wyatt over the rim of her cup. She could almost see the wheels turning in his head as he mulled over what to do. She wondered if all that stuff ever erupted. She guessed it did. She suspected it might have been the case the day he'd read her the riot act in his pasture.

She was glad now that she'd followed her instinct and come over. Wyatt was trying to do the right thing, she could see that, but he was totally out of his depth. And he was proud. Watching him try to change the diaper had shown her that. He didn't want to ask for help. Men never did. And who would be the one to suffer? Darcy. Darcy couldn't explain to Wyatt that she was hungry or wet or uncomfortable or tired. Elli wasn't much more qualified. Everything she'd done today had been because of her prenatal classes. She'd been so afraid of caring for William that she'd signed up for a baby-care course. Until today, she hadn't had a chance to put those classes to use.

Being with Darcy, feeling the tiny body in her arms, smelling the baby-powder scent of her was so bittersweet it cut deeply into her soul, but the alternative had been staying at home and wondering and worrying. What would Wyatt do with her during the day? There would be formula to mix, baths to give, diapers to change. How was he supposed to do that and maintain his ranch? He already looked exhausted.

Her gaze fell on the car seat, and the half-closed lids of the angel within it. Then back to Wyatt, his dark hair curling lightly over his forehead, his eyes dark with fatigue and worry.

"I can't thank you enough, Elli. Twice today I was at the end of my rope."

Elli knew that to get mixed up with the situation was a mistake. He just needed to focus on the good. "You're doing fine," she replied. "Not many men would have the patience to walk the floor with an infant."

"But that's just it." He ran his fingers through his hair.

"I'm not that patient. I...I don't want to lose patience with her."

He wouldn't, Elli was sure of it. Even this afternoon, when Darcy had been screaming incessantly, his expression had been one of utter concern and helplessness. She reached across the table and squeezed his arm. "I think you're just experiencing something every new parent does," she said. "You want to do everything right. I can see how you care for her already, Wyatt. You'll do what's best."

"I wish I had your confidence."

She smiled brightly, wanting to finish her coffee and get out of there. At the moment she didn't know which was more dangerous—Darcy and her baby-powder-scented sweetness or Wyatt's dark sexiness. "You'll be just fine."

She was just finishing the last swallow of coffee in her cup when Wyatt asked plainly, "What if you stayed to help?"

Her mug hit the table with a solid thunk. "What?"

"I know it's a huge imposition, but I need to find Barbara, and do chores, and I can't take her to the barn with me and I can't leave her alone in here. I'd like to hire you to help me."

Heat blossomed in her cheeks. Wyatt didn't strike her as the kind of man who liked admitting weakness. The very fact that he was asking meant he was admitting he was over his head. But she wasn't the solution. "I'm not sure I'm cut out to be a nanny for hire," she replied, hearing the strain behind her voice and knowing the source.

"Look, it'd only be temporary."

"I'm sure there must be services in town, or nearby. Someone more qualified." Caring for a baby full-time? Oh, she could just imagine what her friends and family would have to say about that. They might even be right.

"I can't run the place and watch her at the same time.

I need help. And if it's you…" He coughed. Looked over at the car seat. "The fewer people that know about this—at least for now—the better. I can't be sure someone else wouldn't make that phone call. I just want to keep her safe and do the right thing."

"You trust me, then?"

"Is there some reason I shouldn't?"

She shook her head. "No. I'm just surprised, that's all."

Wyatt took a sip of coffee. "At this point, you're in as much hot water as I am. You're an accessory."

The words came out as serious as a judge, but the tiny upward quirk of his lips was back. Was he teasing? He was, she was sure of it. Warmth seemed to spread through her as she realized it. Moreover, she *liked* it.

Elli didn't know if she should feel relieved or panic. Right now a little of both was running through her veins. This was all she'd ever wanted, in a sense. She'd never been keen on a career the way the other girls in school had been. She'd known all along she wanted to be a mother. To have a house full of children, a home.

She thought once more of her friends and family. They would remind her that this wasn't her home, and this wasn't her family. They would be right. But maybe it was high time she confronted all those hurts. And Wyatt…she could tell he was a proud man, but not too proud to put Darcy's needs ahead of his own. How could she say no to him when his motives were clearly honest?

She looked around her. Lord knew the house needed a feminine touch and it was a sad business, cooking for one. She should know.

"All right," she replied. Considering her unemployed status, she'd be foolish to turn him down. But only for a little while, until he could get things sorted out. She couldn't get attached. And it would be very easy to love the tiny pink slumbering bundle. Elli knew she could love Darcy without even trying. Yes, eyes wide open. That was how she had to look at it.

His breath came out in a rush. "Thank you," he said, his relief clear in each syllable. "You have no idea how grateful I am."

"We have two things to do, then," she said quietly. "First, Darcy needs things. Diapers, formula, clothing. Is this really all her mother left her with?"

Wyatt nodded.

Elli sighed. If she were going to tackle her fears head-on, she might as well tackle them all. Perhaps it was finally time to let go. There was a whole room in Calgary filled with unused baby items. Why was she keeping them? As a shrine to William? It made her sad thinking about it. If she lent them to Wyatt, at least they would be of practical use. She could make a quick trip to Calgary and pick them up, and simply tell him that she'd borrowed them from someone who didn't need them.

"If you're looking at short-term, I know where you could borrow some items. No need for you to buy things you may never use again. It does mean a trip to Calgary tomorrow..."

"I can watch Darcy while you go. I don't want to totally disrupt your life, Elli."

"Thank you, Wyatt." She was glad to be able to go alone. It saved a lot of explaining at both ends. If she didn't have Darcy with her, she could avoid the questions at her parents' house, the probing, motherly kind. And if Wyatt stayed here, she needn't explain why she was in possession of a complete layette.

"Perhaps you can get a lead on Barbara in the meantime."

"I agree," he said, rubbing his lower lip pensively with a finger. "I can't help feeling she's in some sort of trouble."

This wasn't quite as easily solved as baby amenities. Wyatt pushed away from the table and went to the sink, putting his cup within it and bracing his hands on the counter.

"I found her number, but she's not picking up. The address didn't have a street number. It appears to be a Red Deer number, though."

Red Deer. A spark of an idea lit, one that might be able to solve all their problems. Elli got up and retrieved the cordless phone from a dock. "May I? I might be able to find an address."

"By all means."

She dialed in a number, then pressed in more keys for an extension, hoping Joanne was working tonight.

She was, but the query came up empty. Elli hit the end key and thought for a moment.

"She didn't have the baby in Red Deer," Elli said, furrowing her brow. "If she had, there'd be a record of it at the hospital. Let's try Calgary."

"I thought they wouldn't give out patient information," Wyatt said, leaning back against the counter. He ran a hand through his hair, leaving the ends of the nearly black strands slightly mussed, and very, very sexy. Elli swallowed. She was tired, that was all, and the dark outside made the cozy kitchen seem more intimate than it truly was. She could still feel the shape of him pressed against her back earlier and tried to ignore her body's response at the memory.

"They're not supposed to." She hit the talk button on the cordless phone once more. "I used to work in the emergency department. I have friends who will do me a favor, that's all."

A smile creased his face and Elli's breath caught. It was a slow, devilish sort of smile that she hadn't seen up to this point. The kind of smile that could do strange and wonderful things to a woman's intentions.

"Are you breaking the rules, Ellison? Because I had you pegged as Miss Straight and Narrow."

The words stung even as she knew he was teasing. How often had she faced that criticism? His perusal of her sparked her self-conscious streak once more. Why couldn't she have hit the treadmill more often? She crossed an arm around her middle, attempting to hide the flaws he must see. "You wouldn't be far off," she murmured. "But that particular title isn't all it's cracked up to be."

"Your secret is safe with me."

The phone grew slippery in her hand as her nervousness went up a notch. She hadn't been this alone with a man since Tim. In fact, she'd gone to great lengths to avoid it. And now Wyatt was working some sort of spell around her.

She was here for Darcy, that was all. She was being neighborly. There were all sorts of reasons she should have accepted his offer, beyond her cash-flow problem. It was the right thing to do. She might not know exactly what she was doing, but so far she and Wyatt had stumbled their way through the day, hadn't they? Four hands were better than two, right?

"Do you want me to make the call or not?" A note of annoyance crept into her voice. Annoyance at him, and annoyance at herself for worrying so much what Wyatt Black thought. Her mother always said if there was a wounded bird around, Elli wanted to nurse it to health. It had always frustrated her, both the teasing and the criticism inherent in the words. Was it so very wrong? So many times she'd felt her choices were looked down upon simply because they didn't line up with others' expectations. "If you have a better idea…"

Wyatt's smile faded. "Make the call."

She dialed the number she knew by heart.

Five minutes later she hung up, the address jotted down on a notepad. "She had the baby in Calgary. I've got her address in Red Deer. Darcy is five weeks and three days old."

Wyatt's dark eyes met hers. "I think we should go by Barb's place before you go to Calgary, don't you?"

Elli nodded. "It doesn't make much sense to stock up on baby things if she's going to be going back home, right?"

But even as she said it, she got a heavy feeling in her stomach. Barbara wouldn't be there. Looking into Wyatt's face, she could see they both knew it. All tomorrow would be was confirming what they already guessed.

"There's something else," Elli said, putting the paper down on the counter. "She listed you as her next of kin."

Wyatt's mouth fell open and he pushed away from the cupboard. "She did?"

"Either she's telling the truth or she's planned this from the beginning. Somehow…"

"It doesn't make sense, right? If she weren't going to keep the baby, she would have come to me before. Or given it up for adoption."

His thinking was along the same line as hers. "I think so, too."

"Which means Darcy is, likely, truly my niece."

Elli fiddled with the pen. "How can you be so sure?"

Wyatt's brow wrinkled. "Without seeing Barbara, talking to her…I suppose I can't. We both know we're not expecting to find her tomorrow, are we? But Elli, I can't see her making all this up."

Elli couldn't either. Too many things fit together. "What

if she's simply gotten in over her head? She didn't mention the baby's father."

"I get the impression she's doing this alone," he replied, his voice sounding weary.

"Me, too."

"Then the best thing is to find her and talk to her, right?" Wyatt went to the fridge, avoiding her gaze. "Did you have dinner? I haven't eaten. I can make us a sandwich or..."

Wyatt stood, the fridge door open, a packet of roast beef in his hand. The whole conversation felt surreal to Elli. This morning she had been working on an accounting assignment. Tonight she was contemplating sandwiches with Wyatt Black and trying to help him figure out what to do with a baby.

He shut the door of the refrigerator, holding the meat, mustard, and a bag of lettuce. Elli eyed the roast beef, but declined once more as he held up his hand in invitation. She'd eaten already. And the last ten pounds she wanted to lose weren't going to fall off on their own.

"You haven't mentioned any other family."

"That's because there isn't any." He took a plate off a shelf and slapped two slices of bread on it.

"So if Barbara is your sister as she claims..." She let the thought hang.

"Then she's the only family I've got," Wyatt confirmed.

Elli thought about that for a moment. As much as her mother's meddling and worried phone calls drove her crazy, at least she wasn't alone. She knew she could go home and her mom would make her homemade cabbage rolls and perogies and her dad would convince her to stay to watch the hockey game. She couldn't imagine not having them there.

"Can I ask you a question, Elli?" Wyatt went about

building his sandwich, layering lettuce and meat on the bread.

"I guess." As long as it wasn't a question she didn't want to answer. There were lots of those.

"Why did you agree to help me?"

Ugh. She didn't want to answer, simply because there were so many possible responses. Granted, he'd barged into the Camerons' house today and demanded her help, but she'd come back tonight under her own power. It was a chance to feel as if it all hadn't been for nothing. All the hope and loss should have a purpose. Wouldn't this be a chance for something good to come out of all the bad?

And if they were going to care for Darcy, shouldn't she at least make an attempt at being friendly? Surely she could ignore the way her pulse seemed to leap when he was close and how her cheeks flushed when he touched her.

"Look," she said, "I'm going to be honest here. I'm housesitting for the Camerons because I'm at one of those places in my life. I lost my job in some recent streamlining and I…" She felt the words clog up her throat but forged on doggedly. "I got divorced not long ago as well, so I agreed to housesit to help make ends meet. I've been doing some courses online to upgrade my skill set. But for the most part I'm out here in the boonies with only myself for company and feeling fairly useless when all is said and done. When you came barging in today, I wanted to help. Because Darcy is innocent. And because at least I feel somewhat useful again. So you see, you're kind of getting me out of a jam, too."

Wyatt had stopped chewing and put down his sandwich during her speech. Now that it was over, he masked his surprise, finished chewing the bite that was in his mouth, and swallowed.

"I bet that felt good."

And his lips curved. His dark, scary scowls lost all their power when he smiled, replaced with something even more potent.

"It did. Maybe I danced around stuff far too long today. I don't make a habit of going around and spilling my life story." She found herself smiling hesitantly in return. As the seconds drew out she realized they were standing there grinning openly at each other, another notch in familiarity gained. She turned away, embarrassed, shoving her hands into her pockets. Wyatt Black could be darned alluring when he wanted to. And she'd bet he didn't even realize it.

"I'm sorry about your marriage."

His words were sincere, and she sighed. "Me, too. We shouldn't have married in the first place. We were very good at pretending we were what we wanted in each other. He's not a bad man, he just wasn't…the right man." Losing William had been the final blow to a marriage already failing. That was the true grief, the part she wouldn't share with Wyatt. Once William had died, there wasn't any point in keeping up the charade any longer.

"This isn't my usual method of meeting people either," Wyatt acknowledged. "In fact…I tend to keep to myself most of the time."

"I hadn't noticed," she returned, and then felt sorry she'd been sarcastic, even if it had been meant as teasing. It was a reaction to remembering their first meeting and the disapproval on his face as he had spoken so harshly to her. She hurried to cover the barb by turning the tables on him. "So…turnabout is fair play. Now it's your turn to tell me about yourself."

He considered for a moment. "I don't usually talk about myself."

"Me either, but I spilled. Now you owe me." She raised an eyebrow and let a teasing smile touch her lips.

The comfort level in the room rose. Now that Darcy was sleeping peacefully, some of the tension had dissolved and they were suddenly just a man and a woman. There were so many things she didn't know about him, like where he came from and why he'd bought this run-down farm in the first place. He was a big question mark. She'd spent these past weeks all alone. Despite their rocky beginning, he was turning out not to be a bad sort. It was nice to have someone to talk to who didn't know about her past, bringing her baggage to every single conversation. Someone who didn't think of her as *poor Elli*.

"The fact that I'm willing to believe that Barbara is my half sister tells you a bit about my home life, don't you think?"

"I take it your parents weren't divorced, then."

Wyatt shook his head. "Nope. If Barbara's my sister, then it's because my dad had an affair with her mother." As if he suddenly found the sandwich distasteful, he put the remainder on his plate and pushed it away. "I know Barbara's mother had a rough time making ends meet. You can bet that my dad didn't offer any support. If it's true he was her father, he left them high and dry. My dad—"

But then Wyatt broke off, took his plate to the garbage and dumped the sandwich into it.

"I'm sorry."

They were the only words Elli could think of to say. Anything else would sound trite and forced.

"Not your fault," he replied. "And none of it helps us now."

He moved as if to leave the room, but paused beside her, close enough that if he shifted another inch their sleeves would be touching. He smelled like coffee and fresh air and

leather—a manly combination that had her senses swimming. Her breath caught simply at the powerful nearness
of him.

"Nothing will change who my father was. He wasn't a
very good man. Even if he isn't Barbara's father, I know
he could have been."

Elli turned her head and looked at Darcy, sleeping so
peacefully, and felt her heart give a painful lurch. Her
mother and father had somehow found the magic formula.
They'd always had a good, strong marriage. It was another
reason her own failure cut so deeply. She turned her head
back again and found herself staring at Wyatt's shoulder.
Now here she was with Wyatt and his own dubious beginnings. Stuck in the middle of them both was Darcy.

"What about you, Wyatt?" She found she wanted to
know, for Darcy's sake and for her own. She put her hand
on his sleeve. "Are you a good man?"

His head tilted sharply downward as he looked at where
her fingers met his arm. Then his eyes, nearly black in the
dim kitchen light, rose again and captured hers. Her chest
thumped again, but for an entirely different reason. There
was something edgy and mysterious about him, all mixed
up with a sense of unsuitableness. And the package was
wrapped very nicely. Surly or smiling, Wyatt Black was
unlike any other man she'd ever known.

"I doubt it," he replied. "I suspected the rumors about
my father were true but never asked. I ignored it instead.
What does that say about me? I stuck my head in the sand,
just like my mother."

Her heart softened at his confession. "You're not like
him, though," she said gently. "You're too good for that."

He pulled away from her grasp. "I wish I could be as
sure of that as you."

# CHAPTER FOUR

DARK CIRCLES SHADOWED Wyatt's eyes when he answered the door the next morning. He looked less than stellar, in faded jeans and a T-shirt that had seen better days. A suspicious spot darkened one shoulder. His hair was mussed on one side, as if he'd crawled out of bed only moments before. The thought made Elli's blood run a little bit warmer.

Elli stepped inside, out of the frosty chill. The mornings this week had been cool enough that she could see her breath in clouds. Wyatt's home, despite the run-down condition, was warm and cozy, and smelled deliciously of fresh coffee.

"Rough night?"

Wyatt raised an eyebrow, let out a small sigh. "Kind of. How did you know?"

She smiled, pointing at his shirt. "Spit up."

He angled his head to stare at the fabric. "I'm just tired enough to not be amused." Even as he said it, he offered a wry grin. "I didn't get more than a few hours. You?"

Elli hadn't slept much either. She'd lain awake a long time, wondering how he was faring with Darcy and if she had settled at all. When Elli had finally drifted into a fitful sleep, it had been to a mixture of dreams of Wyatt and William all jumbled up together. Her head kept drumming out a warning that getting involved was a grave mistake.

But her heart told another story, one of an innocent child caught in an impossible situation.

Personal wounds or not, it just wasn't in her to walk away and forget that someone needed her. Despite what she'd told Wyatt, this had nothing to do with the money. It had been so long since she'd been needed for anything— even if it meant learning as she went along.

"I worried about the two of you a little. How is Darcy now?"

"Napping."

She couldn't help the relief that flooded through her, knowing that things were going smoothly and there was no emergency that needed her attention. As much as she wanted to help, she wasn't very sure of herself. Laughing as she practiced diapering a plastic doll in baby-care class wasn't the same as caring for a live, breathing infant, not knowing how to soothe upsets or interpret crying. Yesterday she'd done a decent job of faking it. But the whole time she'd doubted herself.

They needed to find Darcy's mother and make things right again. She was skeptical they'd find Barbara at her home today. Elli held on to a little strand of hope that her intuition was wrong.

"You look like hell, Wyatt." She followed him into the kitchen, careful to step quietly in her stocking feet. "Did you get any rest at all?"

He shrugged and went for the coffeepot. "A little. Here and there. It was harder than I anticipated."

Elli hadn't expected him to admit such a thing. He seemed so proud and determined. Even yesterday he'd sought her help, but only when it clearly became too much for him to deal with. "Why don't you go sleep now? I'll stay and look after Darcy." The words came out far more confidently than she felt.

He handed her a cup and she heard him sigh once more. The thought had crossed her mind last night that she could stay at his house and give him a hand, as Darcy was sure to wake during the night. That's what babies did, right? Between the two of them surely they would have figured out what to do. But that also would have meant staying there, in his house, *with him*. Her visceral reaction to him last night had been unexpected. It had been attraction: elemental, surprising and strong. Staying overnight would not have been a good idea, and so in the twilight she'd made her way back over the dry grass to her house.

"I'm fine. I've gone on less sleep before, Elli. As soon as I've had something to eat, we can get going to Barbara's. The sooner we talk to her, the better."

"You don't want to go alone?"

"I was thinking that having Darcy with us might be a good idea."

Maybe Barbara would realize she'd made a mistake and Darcy would go back to her mother. Either way, surely Barbara would want to see her daughter and make sure she was okay.

While Elli sipped her coffee, Wyatt fixed himself some toast and spread it liberally with jam. He offered her the plate, almost as an afterthought, but she'd grabbed some yogurt and fruit already and waved him off. The quiet of the morning held a certain amount of intimacy. The past few months she'd spent utterly alone. To share coffee with someone over a breakfast table was a level of familiarity that seemed foreign. But surprisingly, not unwelcome. Perhaps she'd licked her wounds in private long enough.

Darcy was still sleeping when Wyatt came in from his chores, so Elli carefully fastened the safety buckles, getting her ready for the car. "We should put a blanket over her, right?" Wyatt looked up at Elli, waiting for confirmation.

Her heart thumped nervously. How could she explain her own trepidation and lack of experience without delving into a topic she had no wish to discuss? She couldn't, so instead of specific knowledge she relied on simple common sense.

"It is chilly this morning. A blanket is a good idea."

She was thinking about fastening the seat inside the vehicle when she remembered something else, a hang-on from her baby classes. "Babies should be in the backseat, Wyatt. But you just have your pickup, don't you?"

"Do you mean I can't take her in the truck?" He paused, hanging on to the car seat handle. He ran his spare hand through his hair.

"It has something to do with the airbags."

"I am so not cut out for this," Wyatt muttered. "I can't imagine what Barbara was thinking, leaving Darcy here."

Elli said nothing.

"Well? How am I going to put her into the truck?"

Elli's mouth opened and closed. "I don't know." She clenched her teeth, hating to admit she really didn't know.

"I thought women knew about these things."

Feelings of loss bubbled so closely to the surface that Elli grabbed his comment and answered sharply simply to cover. "That's a sexist comment if I ever heard one. And not the first time you've brought it up, by the way. I hate to disillusion you, Wyatt, but just because I was born female doesn't mean I'm hardwired to know a baby's needs."

"All the girls I knew in school babysat."

"You didn't know me in school." Her heart had started tripping over itself. She should have kept her mouth shut. Would he start asking questions now?

Would she answer him if he did? She bit down on her

tongue. No, she would not. She barely knew him. He didn't deserve to know about William. That was a treasure she held locked up, close to her heart.

His face blanked, his eyes and cheeks flattened with surprise. "I'm sorry. I guess I assumed all women want children. I didn't mean to touch a nerve."

And oh, that stung. It had nothing to do with wanting. No baby had ever been wanted more than her own. She blinked rapidly and turned away, opening the front door. "Wait here, and I'll get my car," she replied, knowing her tone was less than cordial but caring little. "We can take it instead." They would go and find Barbara, Darcy would go back to where she belonged and she could go back to ignoring Wyatt just as she had before.

On the walk to the Camerons' house, she felt her temper fizzle out, to be replaced by bleak acceptance. There was no sense questioning why she was helping Wyatt when on a personal level she didn't like him very much. It didn't matter that he seemed to rub her the wrong way or that she felt inept when caring for Darcy. It was quite simply that William was gone and his death had left a vast emptiness within her. But Darcy was not William, and Elli knew it quite well. It didn't stop the need to help. Or to hope that this would ease some of the grief she still felt whenever she thought of her son.

Back at Wyatt's, she helped him fasten the seat in the back, and spread a blanket over Darcy to keep her warm. She looked like a china doll, all pink and white, with delicate lashes lying on her cheeks as she slept. Wyatt paused for a moment, looking at Darcy, and Elli saw the hard angles of his face soften as he gazed down at her. When he caught her watching him, he turned away and got out of the back, shutting the rear door behind him. Elli, on the other side, touched the soft dark hair, wondering at

the sheer circumstances that had landed her in the middle
of such a situation. Wyatt was trying so hard. He could be
irascible, but she also knew that he genuinely cared about
Darcy already. He acted as if he was positive Darcy was his
niece. And she'd seen the look in his eyes just now when
he'd let down his guard. He would do the right thing by
her.

The smart thing would be to resolve it as quickly as
possible. To make things right and move on.

She motioned toward the driver's side. "Do you want to
drive? You know where you're going."

At his brusque nod she handed him the keys. They'd
check out Barbara's house first. And if they had no luck,
they'd come back here and then she'd be off to Calgary. She
could stop at her parents' house while her mom and dad
were at work. She hadn't been able to bring herself to get
rid of William's things before, but now was a good time.
Someone should get some use out of them.

The drive to Red Deer was quiet, and when Wyatt pulled
up outside a small bungalow, he got an eerie feeling. There
was no car in the yard. The shades at the windows were
all closed. No summer flowers bloomed outside like the
surrounding yards.

Ellie stayed in the car while Wyatt got out, approached
the front door. He knocked, rang the doorbell. No answer.
Tried the doorknob; it was locked.

Getting back into the car, he sighed, then his lips formed
a grim line. "No one's there. And I don't think anyone has
been there for a while."

Ellie's face fell. "What about friends, other family?"

He shook his head. "None that I know of. I haven't been
in contact with Barb for years."

What should he do now? The address was the only clue

he'd had. He couldn't even begin to know where to look, and he was still uneasy about bringing any authorities into it. He might not know much about babies, but the more he looked at Darcy the more he believed she was his niece. How could he do that to the only family he had in the world?

He couldn't. So it was up to him to come up with an idea.

"Wyatt, look." Elli pointed to the house next door. An older lady, slightly stooped and with tightly curled gray hair, had come outside. She paused when she saw the car, then picked up a watering can and moved to a tap on the side of the house.

"It's worth a try," he admitted, and got out of the car again.

"Morning," he called out.

The lady looked up, turned off the tap as Wyatt approached. "Good morning." She watched him with curious eyes.

"I'm looking for Barbara Paulsen. She lives here, right?"

"And you'd be?"

Wyatt swallowed. The answer had to be true and it had to put this woman at ease. She was looking at Wyatt quite suspiciously now, and he noticed her fingers tighten on the watering can.

"Family, but I haven't seen her in years. This is the last address I have for her, but nobody's home."

The answer seemed to appease the woman. "She lives here. We don't see much of her, though. She keeps to herself. Hardly ever see that baby she brought home. It's been a beautiful summer and last year she planted a whole bunch of petunias and marigolds. This year, nothing."

A huge lump of unease settled in Wyatt's stomach.

Dropping off a kid to a stranger, changes in behavior…he wasn't getting a good feeling.

"You don't know where she might be, do you?"

"Sorry." The lady put down her watering can. "I saw her leave yesterday morning, but I haven't seen her since. I can let her know you stopped in…"

She left the words hanging in the autumn air.

"Tell her Wyatt was here and I'd like to catch up with her." He aimed a smile in the woman's direction. At this point he felt he could do with any ally he could find.

"I'll do that."

Wyatt thanked her and went back to the car. No further ahead than before, except he now knew that she hadn't been back home since dropping Darcy off at his doorstep yesterday morning.

There was nothing to be done right now except go back to the ranch and try to come up with a plan on the way. Darcy's needs came first. He didn't want to have to go to the police, but if he kept coming up with dead ends, he'd have to.

He got into the car and shut the door, taking a moment to look back at the baby. "Darcy's still sleeping. Let's head home."

Elli nodded. "I'd like to get on the road. There are several things I can bring back that will make caring for her so much easier. A stroller, for one, so I can take her for walks, and something better than a car seat for her to sleep in."

He nodded and backed out of the driveway as Ellie's cell phone rang.

Wyatt kept his eyes on the road as Elli spoke on the phone. Seeing Elli this morning had made the day seem sunnier. For a small moment. Then he'd realized how stupid that was and he'd locked it down.

He passed a car and stared resolutely ahead. She looked so cute and cheerful, so sunny and blonde and...free. Just as she had that afternoon he'd encountered her in his pasture. He'd bet anything she was a real Pollyanna. She'd surprised him with her harsh words this morning, but he supposed he'd deserved it. He'd made a rash assumption, and he hated it when people did the same thing to him.

At least she'd walked away, so he hadn't felt the need to apologize.

Truth be told, he was glad for her help. Any attraction he'd felt last night in the intimacy of his kitchen was easy to tamp down. He wasn't interested. Certainly not in her. She had complication written all over her, and he avoided complications like the plague.

And the bit about his father...there could be no more of that. He'd felt an odd little lift in his heart when she'd expressed such confidence in his temperament. But she didn't know. She had no idea where he came from.

A snuffle sounded from the backseat and he glanced back. Darcy was still sleeping, the tiny lips sucking in and out. She was exhausted from her long night, just as he was. He wished he could catch up on his sleep as easily as she seemed to be able to.

A sigh slid past his lips as Elli chatted on the phone in the background. Like it or not, Darcy was his responsibility for now. If he wanted uncomplicated, he was in the wrong situation.

Elli's voice registered through his thoughts. "He's right here," she said. "Oh. *Oh.* I see. We'll be there soon."

Elli clicked her phone shut. "Wyatt, I have good news and bad news."

He looked over at her, unsettled by the anxiety that darkened the deep blue of her eyes. She bit down on her lip as he scowled back at her. Her teeth caught the soft pink flesh, and he had the momentary urge to kiss away the worry he saw there, to bring back the light, unfettered smile he remembered.

He pulled his attention back to the road. "Hit me."

"I know where Barbara is."

The flash of relief was quickly replaced by the knowledge that this was the good news and the bad news was yet to come; that it was likely about where Barbara was and he wasn't going to like it. "So? Where is she?"

"She was just admitted to the hospital." Elli tucked the phone back into her purse and straightened. "That was my friend—the one I called yesterday. She tried your number first, since you're next of kin. When she couldn't reach you, she took a chance and tried me."

Heaviness settled around his heart. Hospital? Was she sick? Barbara had trusted him because she was ill? How sick exactly? Scenarios ran through his head, none of them good. He kept thinking about her note and how she'd said she couldn't do it. A rock of worry settled at the bottom of his stomach. "Is she okay?"

"She was admitted to the psych ward."

Wyatt swerved and nearly put them off the road. "What?" His hands began to shake on the wheel and he pulled off onto the shoulder, putting the car in Park. Now he knew what had nagged him about Barbara when he'd read the note, the uneasy feeling he hadn't been able to put his finger on. Her mother had passed away when he'd been working in Fort St. John. The next time he was home and out having a beer with a few buddies, he'd heard the gossip about her death.

At the time he'd barely paid attention; small-town rumblings were really not his thing. But now he remembered, and the memory only added to his dread.

"Is. She. Okay." He ground out the words, fearful of the

answer, his mind on the innocent child in the backseat and what a huge dilemma this all was.

"Physically, you mean?"

He nodded, blocking out images that threatened to flood his brain. Awful possibilities. Scary ones.

Her hand came to rest on his forearm, lightly but reassuring. "Wyatt, what is it? You're white as a sheet."

Wyatt's muscles tensed beneath the weight of her fingers. Admitting to a complete stranger that he had a half sister in the world was bad enough. How could he explain to her that he already felt guilty about keeping quiet all these years? When they were kids, it was understandable. It would have caused trouble, trouble he tried to avoid at home. But once he was grown, he could have gone to Barbara and...who knows. He would have been away from his father's censorious anger and his mother's fearful glances. He might have had *family*.

Maybe that hadn't meant anything to his father, but it had meant something to him. When Barbara's mother had died, he'd let shame and embarrassment rule his good sense.

If he hadn't been so weak, maybe she wouldn't have been driven to what he suspected right now.

And he couldn't tell Elli any of it. He clenched his teeth. After all this time, it still ate at him.

"I just...the *psych ward*," he said meaningfully. "That's not good."

"You are listed as next of kin, remember. At least we know where she is now. They'd be contacting you regardless."

"They would?" He turned and studied her profile. Something was troubling her, more than the situation. He'd glimpsed it several times in the past twenty-four hours. As if she was remembering something unpleasant, and it was weighing her down. Much as he was feeling the deeper in he got.

She nodded, but wouldn't look at him. "Oh, yes. A new mom, showing up at the emergency room, needing a psych evaluation?" Finally she turned toward him, and her earnest gaze hit him like a punch in the gut.

"Don't you see? You can't protect her now. The first thing they are going to want to know is where her baby is."

# CHAPTER FIVE

ELLI'S WORDS SANK IN, one heavy syllable at a time. Of course. He'd watched the news enough to know that a new mother coming into an emergency room without her baby would set off alarm bells. Added to that he really didn't know what sort of state Barb was in. All he could feel was the heavy weight of knowing that Darcy was relying on him completely.

"Then we have to go there, don't we." The situation had changed now and the weight of responsibility grew heavier on his shoulders. This was no longer a few days of child care—it was now complicated by bureaucracy. Everything would be recorded, noted, in some chart. He felt the walls closing in and hated it.

Elli nodded. "Yes. If we don't, like I said, you're listed as next of kin. You'll be the first place they look for Darcy anyway. And this way, Wyatt…well, it wouldn't hurt to have Darcy looked over, as well."

"Will they take her away?" He looked at Elli, needing her to say no. The very thought of losing Darcy now to complete strangers was incomprehensible. He might not have been prepared, but he was family. Surely that counted for something. He had Elli to help him. It disturbed him to realize how much he needed her.

Elli felt her heart leap at his question, not so much the

words but the way he said them—unsure, and slightly fearful. The man had been up most of the night; he had never looked after a baby before, by his own admission. But the concern, the fear she saw on his face now touched her, deep inside. She wished she could put her arms around him and tell him it would be fine. But what would he think of her if she did such a thing? He'd read more into it than she'd intend. And they had to keep their relationship—the completely platonic one—separate from Darcy.

There was more to Wyatt than she'd initially thought. He wanted to do right by this baby. How could she fault him for that?

She couldn't. She applauded him for it.

He checked his rearview mirror and then pulled a U-turn, heading back the way they'd just come, back to the highway. She had to answer him honestly. "I don't know, Wyatt. I'm not in social services, though I would think they would want her to stay with her family. Let's just take it a step at a time, okay?"

Wyatt nodded, but she saw the telltale tick in his jaw anyway. She reached over and patted his thigh, meaning to be friendly and supportive. Instead she was struck by the intimacy of the gesture, the warmth of his denim-clad leg beneath her fingers, the way the fabric wrinkled just so at the bend of his knee. The small touch made her feel a part of something, and that scared her. She pulled her hand away. "It'll all work out," she reassured him. It had to. If not for her, for them. She'd do whatever she could to make sure of it.

She was relieved they had found Barbara, but as they drove south Elli twisted her fingers. This wasn't how she'd planned on today playing out. The agenda hadn't included a visit to the hospital, faced with old coworkers and reminders. And now Wyatt would be with her when she went to pick up the baby things. How could she possibly explain why she had a roomful of newborn paraphernalia at her mother's? What if she broke down? She didn't want to cry in front of him.

She would get through it somehow, she promised herself as she stared out the window. She had come this far. She would fall apart later. After all, she'd spent months pretending and going through the motions in public. She only had to do it for one more day.

Once they were inside city limits it took just ten minutes to reach the hospital. They parked in the parkade and made their way through to the emergency department.

"I'll stay with Darcy," Elli suggested, taking the baby seat from his hand and adjusting the strap of the diaper bag on her shoulder. She needed space from him, space to think without him always so close by.

She wished that Barbara was anywhere but here, at the Peter Lougheed Hospital. Inside were her old coworkers, many who had been her friends but who had drifted away from her since William's death and her divorce from Tim. There had been so many awkward silences in recent months. But she lifted her chin. What did she have to hide? Nothing. Why shouldn't she face them? Their whispers didn't matter anymore. Steeling her spine, she gave the car seat a reassuring bounce, tightening her grip. It didn't matter, not anymore, and she was tired of running away.

"You go ahead and check with the triage nurse," she suggested to Wyatt. "I'll stay in the waiting room with Darcy. She's waking up and you need to find out what's going on."

Wyatt went to the triage line and spoke to a nurse while Elli sat in one of the padded vinyl seats. She undid the chest strap to Darcy's seat and lifted the baby out, cuddling her in the crook of her arm.

Oh, she felt so good and warm, smelling of powder and the scent that was distinctly *baby*. "Hello, sweetheart," she murmured softly, not wanting to be overheard by the others in the room. She fought away the insecurities that had plagued her on the drive and decided to enjoy whatever time she had with Darcy. Being with her made her feel better, not worse. "You were such a good girl in the car," she whispered, touching the tiny fingertips, looking into the dark blue eyes that stared back at her, slightly unfocused. The little fist moved and clasped her finger tightly.

And just like that, Elli lost her heart to the tiny girl in the pink blanket. She blinked several times and swallowed past the lump that had formed in her throat. "Your uncle Wyatt and I are going to do everything we can for you, little one. I promise."

It felt strange joining their names together that way, but Elli knew she meant it. She already cared about Darcy so much, and Wyatt couldn't do it alone. She just wouldn't deceive herself into thinking it was something more, no matter how much her senses kicked into overdrive when he was around. She wasn't interested in fairy tales. She was interested only in reclaiming her life.

Wyatt returned, his face looking pinched and his gaze dark with worry. "Her doctor wants to speak with us," he explained. "Both of us, and to see Darcy."

She nodded. "Yes, but she's going to be wanting a bottle soon."

Wyatt picked up the empty car seat. "Okay." His shoulders relaxed as he turned away. But then he turned back once more and reached down for her free hand.

His strong fingers gripped hers and her heart thumped in response.

"Thank you, Elli. For everything over the last twenty-four hours. It helps knowing that Darcy is being taken care of, that I…" He paused, and a slight tint of pink stained his cheeks. "That I don't have to do this alone. It means more than you know."

He spun back toward the sliding doors, which opened on his approach. Elli's jaw dropped a little as she followed him; he expressed more confidence in her than she had in herself. Taken care of? Elli was feeling her way through this as much as Wyatt. But she couldn't stop the glow that spread through her at his words. Her confidence had taken such a beating since William's death. There were times she felt she'd failed at everything—wife, mother, even her job. Wyatt Black—ornery, pigheaded cowboy—had offered more encouragement than anyone else had in the past months. Not just with Darcy, though that was part of it. When he looked at her, she almost felt pretty. Desirable. That was as much of a miracle as anything.

She gently touched Darcy's nose as she passed through the doors. "I'd better be careful, huh, little one?" she whispered. "Before long I'll start *liking* him, and then we'll really be in trouble."

They were shown not to a curtained exam room but a different room, one with four walls and a door that the nurse shut behind them. They waited only moments before the doctor came in and shut the door behind her.

"Mr. Black, I'm Dr. McKinnon." The young woman held out her hand and Wyatt shook it. "I'm the one who admitted Ms. Paulsen earlier this morning. We admitted her for postpartum depression, and we'll be meeting and assessing her over the next several days."

"I'm just glad she's all right," Wyatt replied, but Elli noticed his face was inscrutable. The emotion he'd shown her only moments ago was gone, and in its place a wariness she thought she might understand. This hospital had been her home away from home, yet she was no more looking forward to the questions she'd face today than Wyatt was. At least she had the choice not to answer. A month ago standing in this department would have filled her with dread. Today, with Wyatt beside her, it didn't matter quite as much.

Dr. McKinnon looked at Elli now, smiling easily. "And Elli. It's good to see you, but surprising under these circumstances."

"Thank you," she replied carefully.

"Mr. Black, I'm going to talk to you about your sister's condition, but as you can understand there was significant concern about her baby."

"Yes, she left Darcy with me yesterday," Wyatt offered. Elli noticed he didn't elaborate on how Barbara had left her. He was trying to protect his sister. Every time there was a development, Elli could see how Wyatt took on the responsibility himself. It was admirable, but she imagined it must be a very heavy load to carry at times.

"At what time?"

"Late morning," he replied without missing a beat. He met the doctor's eyes steadily. "I'm not used to babies, so Elli has been giving me a hand." He smiled at Elli now, but the smile had an edge to it. He was nervous, she realized, and seeking her support.

She smiled back at him, and then at Dr. McKinnon. "Between the two of us, we've muddled through."

"Darcy does need to be examined, though." Dr. McKinnon was firm. "Elli, I'm going to have Carrie show you to a curtain and we'll have the peds on call come down. In the meantime, I can speak to Mr. Black about his sister."

McKinnon's voice softened as she rose and stopped to touch the downy crown of Darcy's head. "Would that suit, young lady?"

Darcy's answer was to pop two fingers into her mouth and start sucking.

"I'm afraid she's hungry," Elli replied. "Could someone heat a bottle for me?" She no longer had access to the rest of the department, nor did she want it. Her presence had already been noted, she suspected. People here knew her. There would be questions and murmurings when she showed up with a baby in tow. She knew how it looked. Granted, it was awkward considering Tim was still on staff. But her job loss had been cutbacks, pure and simple.

She wondered if she'd stayed married to Tim if it would have made a difference when it came to the chopping block. Then she wondered if she would have wanted it to. She had just enough pride to know the answer right away. Despite the financial hardship, being made redundant was a blessing, freeing her to begin again.

She resolutely clipped Darcy back into her seat and picked up the bag of supplies. Well, let them talk. It wouldn't change anything. She didn't work here anymore, wouldn't have to see these people on a regular basis like before. She was starting over.

"I'm sure that can be arranged. I'll be right back, Mr. Black."

She opened the door and Wyatt stood. "Stay with her," he said to Elli. There was a fierceness in his voice. "I'll come find you."

Her heart thumped at his words, knowing he meant them. Even knowing he meant them for Darcy, the effect was the same. It made her feel warm, protected. Wyatt would do whatever was in his power to protect them both.

She'd never met a man quite like him before.

"I won't leave her side," Elli promised, wishing she could touch him somehow to reassure him. She was too shy to do such a thing beneath the gaze of an old colleague, so she offered a small smile instead and cast her gaze down, following Dr. McKinnon out the door.

At the desk her friend Carrie hung up the phone. "Ellison." She got up and came around the desk, giving her a quick hug. "Gosh, it's good to see you."

"Hello, Carrie." Elli couldn't help but smile at the warm reception. Of all the staff, Carrie had been the one who'd remained the most normal when it came to Elli's ordeal. "Interesting circumstances, huh?"

The clerk's face broke into a wide grin in response. "You know the E.R. Something needs to break up the boredom."

"Can you show Elli to a curtain, Carrie? And page Dr. Singh—we need to do a physical on the baby." Dr. McKinnon smiled at Elli. "It is good to see you again, Ellison."

She went back to continue her meeting with Wyatt while Elli and Carrie looked at each other.

"Let's find you a spot," Carrie suggested, and led the way through the twists and turns of the unit. She entered a curtained cubicle and put the car seat next to the bed.

"Thank you, Carrie. Could I trouble you to heat a bottle?"

"Of course you can. What a shock, though, seeing you here with a baby, when…"

But Carrie's voice drifted off and her cheeks colored. "I'm sorry, Elli. That was insensitive."

"You were going to say 'when it's so soon after William died.'"

"We were all so sad for you and Tim."

Funny, Elli realized—saying William's name had come more easily than she'd expected. And the mention of Tim didn't upset her as it might have. Maybe she had Wyatt to thank for that, too. If he hadn't asked for her help, she'd still be hiding away instead of facing things.

"It gets better," she said, trying a smile for Carrie's benefit. "I'm not sure I'll ever get over losing William completely, but at some point you have to start living again."

Elli stood rooted to the floor, dumbstruck. Had she actually said that? *Start living again?*

"Can't say as I blame you…your Mr. Black is pretty easy on the eyes."

Elli felt her body grow warm all over at the mention of Wyatt. "It's not like that…."

"What a shame."

She looked over and found Carrie watching her with an amused expression. "It's that obvious?"

"He's very good-looking. Tim would be jealous."

Elli shook her head. "I doubt it. It doesn't matter anymore anyway."

She realized she meant it. It didn't matter. How had all this happened since yesterday? Yesterday she'd merely been thinking about what to do next. Afraid of taking a wrong step.

"I'll go heat your bottle." Carrie tapped her arm lightly and scooted out of the cubicle.

Elli sat on the edge of the bed, covering her mouth in surprise. She thought of Wyatt's wild eyes as she'd opened her door and chuckled. "Well, I guess when you're thrown in the deep end, you have to swim," she murmured.

A few minutes later Carrie returned with the warmed bottle. "I wish I could stay and chat," she said, taking a quick moment to sit in the seat next to Elli. Elli picked Darcy up and cradled her in her elbow, then reached for the bottle. As Darcy began to suckle on the nipple, Carrie let out a sigh. "I've missed you. But I can only spare a minute. Forgive me, Elli, but…does it hurt? Just knowing?"

Elli didn't need help interpreting. Of course it hurt, knowing what she'd missed. She smiled wistfully at the young woman who had been her coworker for nearly two years. "A little. She's precious, isn't she?"

"A doll. And this Black, he's her uncle?"

Elli ignored the leap in her pulse at the thought of Wyatt. "Yes, and he lives next door to where I'm staying at the moment. Thank you for calling me today," she added. "We'd gone to Barbara's home to find her but came up with nothing."

"It was just a chance I took, after you called me last night. I'm glad it worked, though. That woman came in here all alone, poor soul. She needs someone in her corner."

And that someone was Wyatt. Elli could think of few better.

Darcy took in too much milk, coughed, spluttered and sent up a wail. At the same moment Carrie's pager went off.

"I've got to go."

"I'll be fine," Elli replied, settling down in the chair and giving Darcy the bottle once more.

Familiar sounds, hospital sounds, filtered through the curtains—the hushed footsteps of nurses and the quiet, confident tones of doctors. The odd moan or catch of breath of those in pain, and the sound of gurney wheels swishing on the polished floors. For a moment the memory of it was a bittersweet stab in her heart, a reminder of a past life that she'd once considered perfect. She was at home here, the sounds and smells so familiar they seemed a part of her. Once she'd waited out a particularly tense bout of Braxton Hicks contractions and Tim had checked on her every ten minutes.

With a free finger Elli stroked Darcy's hair. She had to stop thinking about what might have been. It never *would* be. She was so tired of feeling sorry for herself. It was exhausting. Nothing she could do could bring her own precious baby back. Being with Wyatt and Darcy had made her face it head-on, making her want to get on with simply missing him rather than the futility of wishing for what she could never have.

She looked down into Darcy's face—the closed eyes with the lids that were nearly transparent, the way one tiny hand rested on the side of the bottle as if to keep it from disappearing. "Who knew," she whispered, "how important you'd turn out to be?"

The curtain parted and Wyatt stepped through, with Dr. McKinnon behind him. "How's she doing?"

Wyatt's eyes were troubled, but the fear had subsided slightly. She smiled up at him. "We're right as rain. How about you? What's the news on Barb?"

"I'm going to see her," he replied. He reached out to tuck the blanket more securely around Darcy's feet and Elli noticed his hand was trembling.

"Wyatt?"

He finished fussing with the blanket and looked up. "They're letting me visit her, and then…" He cleared his throat. "And then I have to talk to a social worker."

The tone of his voice made it sound like the seven tortures of hell. Wyatt was a private man—Elli had sensed it from the beginning. He'd been reluctant to give her any sort of details at all, skirting around issues to give her just enough answers. Elli knew that speaking to social workers was going to be intrusive at best.

She tried to smile reassuringly. "All signs point to her trying to get help, Wyatt. This is a good thing. And it fits with the letter she left you, don't you think?"

"I hope so. I just…I don't want her going into foster care, Elli."

"I know that, and they will, too. Once Darcy's had her checkup, I'll meet you. How about—the cafeteria downstairs?"

"Okay."

Elli was aware of Dr. McKinnon waiting for Wyatt and wished for some privacy so they could talk without being overheard. "Unless you'd rather I went with you." Elli doubted Wyatt was prepared for what he'd see in the psychiatric ward. "It's good she's admitted, but it's not an easy place to visit, especially the first time."

"Knowing you're caring for Darcy is all I need," he responded, his gaze sliding away from her. "I'll find you once I've spoken to her."

He looked so uncomfortable her heart went out to him. She stood, Darcy resting along her shoulder, and went to stand in front of him. He was desperately trying to do the right thing, and he hadn't seen his half sister in years. These were hardly optimum circumstances for a reunion.

Damn the doctor and whatever scuttlebutt was filtering through the unit. Elli didn't care anymore. She lifted her free hand and touched his cheek lightly. "It will be fine," she murmured. "Darcy's safe and Barbara is in good hands."

He placed his hand over hers, sandwiching it between his palm and his cheek. It was warm there and soft, with only a slight prickle of stubble from his jaw. "Why are you being so helpful, Ellison? This is not your problem." He closed his eyes for a few moments as he inhaled and exhaled slowly.

"Because I can see you're trying to do the right thing and at great personal sacrifice."

Without saying another word, he turned her palm, pressed a quick kiss into it. His lips were warm and firm in contrast to the stubble on his chin. Emotions rushed through her at the tender gesture, so sweet and so unexpected.

He cleared his throat and squared his shoulders. "The cafeteria," he reminded her, and without another word left the curtained area.

Elli pressed her hand to her lips, shocked at the intimate touch, flustered, and...my word. She was pleased.

This wouldn't do. Wyatt was only reacting to the situation. He had said it himself. He was thanking her for helping, that was all. Everyone's emotions were running high. She couldn't read too much into it.

She struggled to remember that he'd never had any interest in getting to know her before Darcy had come on the scene. They'd been neighbors for two months and had crossed paths only once. And yes, maybe they were getting to know each other better, but she also knew that if they'd met elsewhere—on the street, in a shop—his head wouldn't have been turned. Heck, he'd shouted at her the first day they'd met. She was still carrying around an extra ten pounds she'd put on during her pregnancy, and her looks were what she'd consider strictly average. The caress meant little when she put it in perspective.

She took a moment to change Darcy's diaper, slightly more comfortable with the task than yesterday as she dealt with sticky tabs and squirming, pudgy legs. In less time than she might have imagined, Darcy was dressed and happy. Elli took out a rattle and smiled as the baby shook it in her tiny fist.

The curtain parted once more and Dr. Singh entered. He saw Elli and his face relaxed into a pleased expression. Then his gaze dropped to Darcy, kicking and cooing on the white sheets of the bed.

There was a flash of consternation on his face and Elli felt a sickening thud in the pit of her stomach. She'd conveniently forgotten why she'd avoided coming to the hospital over the past few months. Now she remembered. She hadn't wanted to have to deal with explanations and platitudes. Carrie was one thing; they'd been close friends. But every other person she knew in this hospital saw her as Elli who had married a doctor, carried his child, lost it, lost her marriage and finally her job. *Poor Elli.*

"I understand this is our missing Baby Paulsen." He covered the momentary awkwardness with a smile.

"Yes. Her name is Darcy."

"You brought her in?" He went to the bed and watched Darcy for a moment while Elli looked on anxiously.

"Yes and no. Darcy has been with Barbara Paulsen's brother, and he's a friend of mine. I've been giving him a hand."

"He must be a very good friend."

"A friend in need is a friend indeed," she quoted, trying to make light of it. She knew how it would look if she admitted they'd only truly become "friends" yesterday. But looking at the outside of a situation was rarely like looking at it from the inside, so she kept her mouth shut.

Elli waited while Dr. Singh gave Darcy a thorough check. He turned to her and smiled. "She's perfectly healthy," the doctor stated.

Elli stared into Dr. Singh's chocolate eyes, surprised at the concern she saw there. Was there something wrong with Darcy he hadn't wanted to say?

Dr. Singh sat on the edge of the bed and rested his hands on his white coat. "This isn't about Darcy," he said quietly. "It's about you, Elli. I want to know how you're doing since William's death."

His quiet concern ripped at her insides at the same time as it was comforting. People didn't know what to say to her—she got that. But no one asked how she was, or spoke

William's name. Even today—it was the first time she'd been able to say his name without her voice catching. To everyone else he was always called "the baby," as if he'd never been named. As if keeping him nameless would make it somehow easier. It wasn't.

"I'm doing okay. Better now." She was happy to realize it was true.

"How did you end up caring for Darcy?"

"Wyatt didn't know what to do," she said, trying to lighten things by giving a light laugh. "Of course, neither did I, really, but I was conveniently just next door." She smiled then, genuinely. "Tell me, Dr. Singh, how can a person resist an adorable face like that?" She motioned toward Darcy, who seemed intent on the rattle clenched in her tiny fist. The pieces clacked together as she shook her pudgy hand. Only, Elli knew it wasn't just Darcy's adorable face that counted. Wyatt's was becoming more of a pleasure each time they were together.

Dr. Singh smiled. "You can't. I just want to make sure you're okay with this. I know you must be grieving still."

Elli swallowed, but was surprised that the tears she expected were nowhere to be found. When was the last time before today that she'd thought of William without crying? She was getting stronger. "I am grieving, of course. But it's different now, and I think helping care for Darcy is good for me. I can't always wish for what will never be. I have to look forward rather than backward."

"Good." Dr. Singh put his hands on his knees and boosted himself up. "I am glad to hear it. It is good to see some roses in your cheeks, Ellison."

The roses bloomed pinker than before, because Elli knew it was Wyatt and his caress that had put them there. And she didn't want to start having feelings for him. She was finally just starting to get a handle on her emotions.

The last thing she needed was to get mixed up with some-one again. To rebound.

Maybe she should just look upon this time as a lovely gift. For the first time in months she felt alive.

"Thank you, Dr. Singh. Wyatt will be involved with social services because I know he wants to look after Darcy until Barbara can again. Would it be okay if he listed you as her pediatrician?"

"By all means."

Elli gathered her things. "It was good to see you, Doctor."

"And you." He smiled, then left the room with a flap of his white coat.

Now at loose ends, Elli realized she hadn't eaten all day. When there was no sign of Wyatt in the cafeteria, she hefted the car seat and made her way to the coffee chain near the west doors. A steamed milk and a muffin would do the trick, she thought. Carrying the paper bag and car seat while balancing a hot drink took more dexterity than she'd expected, and she went slowly back to the cafeteria, where she could at least sit down and wait.

When she returned to the entrance of the cafeteria, she came face-to-face with Wyatt. It took only two strides of his long legs before he caught up to her. "Where have you been?" He whispered it, but there was a hard edge to the words, so very different than the last time he'd spoken to her.

"I just went to buy a steamed milk," she explained, feeling the color drain from her face at his thunderous expression.

"Your timing stinks." He ground out the words.

"Is there a problem?" A woman's voice came from beyond Wyatt's shoulder and Elli closed her eyes. She'd disappeared with Darcy at the same time Wyatt had come to find her with…

"Ellison Marchuk, this is Gloria Hawkins from Child and Family Services."

Elli handed Wyatt the hot cup, her appetite lost. "Ms. Hawkins," she said quietly, adjusting Darcy's weight and holding out a hand.

## CHAPTER SIX

IT WAS PAST DARK BY the time they arrived home again, and on the drive Wyatt had taken the time to cool down. Now he stared around his house with new eyes. In the space of little more than a day his whole life had changed. This run-down bungalow and farm had been enough for him. He'd bought it seeing the potential, and he had lots of time to fix it up the way he wanted. Or so he'd thought.

But this was a bachelor's house, sparsely decorated and functional. He had to make it a home, somewhere welcoming and comfortable rather than a simple place to lay his head. There was more at stake. It needed to be a place for *family*. No matter what happened, he had family now.

Elli was in the kitchen, cooking some sort of chicken dish for dinner. Already he could see small changes in the house, and it put him off balance. His desk was tidy—pens in a can she'd unearthed from somewhere. She'd gone through and straightened what things he had, giving the house a sense of order that seemed foreign. He shouldn't feel as if Elli was taking over—he knew that. She was going above and beyond with helping. But somehow he did. As though the house wasn't his anymore.

Darcy was watching from her spot in the car seat, her dark eyes following Elli's every move from stovetop to counter. Wyatt stood at the doorway, nursing a beer, fighting the false sense of domesticity. It was all temporary, not real. Darcy was not his child, and Elli was not his wife. It was a short-term situation. Before long things would go back to normal.

He couldn't deny he'd had flashes of attraction over the past day and a half, but he wasn't truly interested in Elli. Elli didn't care for him either, he knew. Anything that had happened so far was because of the extraordinary position they were in. When everything settled, they'd each go back to their own lives. He got the feeling that she was too much of a city girl to want the isolated life in the country for long. He couldn't get used to seeing her here. Darcy, on the other hand, was his niece. As things played out, he knew he wanted to have a home where she and Barbara could come to visit as often as they liked.

His mom would have wanted that. She would have wanted him to accept Barbara and make her welcome. Despite her difficult life, he didn't know anyone with as generous a heart as his mother.

But for now, this was reality, until Barbara was well enough to look after her daughter. There was work to do to make this a family home. He'd promised it to the caseworker at the hospital. He'd been so nervous, afraid she would take Darcy away into foster care anyway. And he'd growled at Elli for not being there right away. She had done nothing wrong. Instead Elli had been calm, and she had been the one who had carried the meeting. She'd been composed and articulate and reassuring when Wyatt had been scared to death. He wouldn't let that happen again.

"Do you like squash?"

Elli's voice interrupted his thoughts and he straightened. "Yeah, I guess."

"You guess?" She finished wiping a spoon and put it down on the counter. Her blue eyes questioned him innocently, but he knew there was little of innocence in his thoughts. Lord, but she was beautiful. Not in a flashy way either. At first her looks seemed ordinary. But they grew on a man—the glowing complexion, the blond streaks in her hair. The way her clothes seemed to hug her curves and how those curves caught his eye. Most of all, it was her eyes. Elli wasn't his woman, but those eyes got him every time.

He'd looked into them earlier today and had forgotten himself. That caress in the E.R. had been a mistake, brought on by her understanding and the fact that she was simply there for him. He'd felt it again when he'd tried to explain to the caseworker why keeping Darcy was so important to him, while still protecting himself. He'd fumbled the words, but Elli had put her hand on his arm and smiled at him.

"My mom used to bake squash in the oven," he said, coming forward and putting his empty beer bottle beside the sink.

Elli smiled, her face a sea of peace and contentment. She looked so at home, so…happy. He wondered how it could be so when he'd dragged her into this situation, turning her life upside down as well as his.

"I can do that," she answered. "As soon as I find a baking dish."

He found her a proper pan and put it on the counter. "You like to cook," he stated, starting to relax. His version of cooking consisted of baked potatoes and frying a steak.

"I do," she answered, still smiling. She took a small squash and quartered it, scooped out the middle and slathered the orange surface with a paste of brown sugar and butter. She slid it into the oven beside the chicken in mere seconds. "My mom taught me how to cook when I was just a girl. It was one of the things we did together. I make a wicked cabbage roll. Though I've never quite mastered the technique of her perogies. She makes them from scratch and they're the best thing I've ever eaten."

Wyatt leaned back against the counter and nudged Darcy's hand with his finger. The baby grabbed it and batted her hand up and down while Wyatt smiled. He liked her—when she wasn't crying. A baby's needs were uncomplicated and he liked that. Food, a dry bottom and love, he supposed. A simple love, a warm place to cuddle into and feel safe.

At that moment he missed his mother with an intensity that shocked him. It had been five years, but now and again the grief seemed to come from nowhere. His finger stopped moving with Darcy's and he swallowed.

"Wyatt?"

Elli was watching him curiously. "Are you okay? You look funny all of a sudden."

He shook off the sadness. What had come over him? He never indulged in sentimentality. Maybe it was Elli. She reminded him of his mother, he supposed. His mom had been the one to make their house a home when he was growing up, and he realized Elli was doing the same thing now with him, and Darcy.

"I was just remembering my mom," he replied carefully. "You remind me of her, you know. She was always cooking and smiling. I didn't realize how much I missed it."

Her smile faded and a tiny wrinkle formed between her brows. "I remind you of your *mother?*"

Apparently that wasn't what she had expected to hear. Belatedly he realized that most women wouldn't find that an attractive comparison. He stumbled over trying to find the right words to explain. "Only in the very best ways, Elli. She was the one who made our house a home. You're doing the same thing for Darcy and me without even real-izing it."

Damn it, was that pain on her face? What had he said that was wrong? He was trying to pay her a compliment and it was coming out all wrong. "I'm sorry if I said something to upset you."

"You didn't," she murmured, but she wouldn't look him in the eye anymore.

"Do you want to talk about it?"

He couldn't believe he was asking. But he'd heard snatches of whispered conversations today. There was more to Elli, and he found himself curious. The people at the hospital where she'd worked knew. But she'd said nothing to him about why her marriage had failed. And the bits he'd heard left him with more questions than concrete information.

"There's nothing to talk about," she insisted, moving back to stir something on the stove. But he knew. She was covering. He'd done it a thousand times himself.

"How did Barbara seem to you? You never said." She still had her back turned to him, but there was a slight wobble on the word *said*. He *had* touched a nerve. A part of him wanted to pursue it and another part told him to leave it alone. If she'd wanted to talk, she wouldn't have changed the subject.

But he wasn't sure how to proceed. Talking about Barbara was a loaded topic, too. The moment he'd entered the hospital room Barbara had started crying and apologiz-ing. Her doctor had gone with him, and Wyatt had let her take the lead. Calm but compassionate. Problem was, Wyatt had never seen himself as a very compassionate man.

So Barbara had cried and he'd held her awkwardly. She'd apologized and he'd tried to say what he thought were the right words—that the most important thing right now was for her to get well. He'd insisted that Darcy was well taken care of.

"Seeing her was odd. She was like the Barbara I remembered, and yet she wasn't. There was an energy about her that wasn't quite right."

Elli nodded. "Her perspective is so skewed right now, and she's afraid. When I worked in the E.R.—"

She halted, but Wyatt wanted to know. She'd worked at the very desk where he'd checked in today. How had today affected Elli? It had been so hectic he hadn't asked.

"When you worked in the E.R.," he prodded.

"I was just going to say we saw lots of mentally ill patients. People who for one reason or another couldn't cope. That Barbara could recognize that in herself, that she checked herself in…" Elli met his gaze. "It was a brave thing to do. Certainly nothing to judge her for."

"Did I judge her?" He straightened in surprise. He hadn't, had he? Had he judged or simply been concerned?

"No, but I did. The moment I saw her note and saw Darcy. I'm sorry about that."

She turned back to the stove. Wyatt stared at her back for a few moments before stepping forward and simply putting a hand on her shoulder.

"So did I. I asked myself how a mother could do that to a child. Today I realized how much courage it took for her to do what she did."

"Thank you," Elli whispered.

He took his hand away, already missing the feeling of warmth that had radiated through his palm. He put his hand in his pocket instead. "Three times she asked where Darcy was. Eventually she got so agitated the doctor suggested I come back later. She reassured her that Darcy was getting the best of care. I felt a lot of pressure when he said that."

"You're doing the best you can, and she's got a clean bill of health. Don't be so hard on yourself."

But it was impossible not to be. It highlighted his failure as a brother, if nothing else. Maybe if he'd made an effort years ago, this would never have happened.

"She's going to be okay—that's the main thing. It was easier speaking to her doctor. She seemed very pleased that Barbara was asking about Darcy so much. That she'd taken steps to make sure the baby was looked after."

A memory flashed into his brain, of his mother when he'd graduated from high school. He'd been in a suit she'd bought on discount in Red Deer, and his father was nowhere to be found. *Don't think about your dad,* she'd said, taking his hand. *You remember this. Family is important. Don't let your dad teach you otherwise. Family is everything.*

She'd gotten tears in her eyes then. *You're everything, Wyatt.*

He realized now that she had to have known about Barbara all along. And still she'd stayed with his father. Why? He'd never know now.

"Asking for help is a positive sign," Elli agreed. She fiddled with a set of old pot holders.

"I should have been there," he replied, the confession taking a load off his shoulders. "I knew deep down she was my sister. I knew what had happened to her mother and I pretended she didn't exist. If only…"

"Don't." Elli's voice intruded, definitive and strong. "Do not blame yourself. You were a teenage boy. There is no before. There is only now." She blinked rapidly. "There is only now."

The words seemed to catch her up so completely his thoughts fled. "Are we still talking about Barbara? Or about you?"

His heart pounded as she turned her eyes up at him

once more. He couldn't resist her when she did that. Years of choosing to be alone hadn't made him immune to a beautiful woman. He could rationalize all he wanted, but the truth was he didn't want just any woman—he wanted her. He wanted a connection with another human being, something to anchor him so he didn't feel this was spinning out of control. Elli seemed to get to him without even trying.

He stepped forward, cupped her face in his hands and kissed her. All the self-recriminations vaporized; all the doubts fled in a puff of smoke. Nothing mattered for a few blissful seconds. There was only Elli, her soft skin, the moist taste of her lips, her body close to his. God, he'd needed this, badly. And when she made a soft sound in her throat, he deepened the kiss.

Surprise was Elli's first feeling, quickly chased away by the sensation of his lips on hers and his hands cradling her face like a chalice. Her emotions had been riding close to the surface all day, facing all the things she should have faced long before now. But she'd held herself together, through the hours at the hospital and even facing William's things at her mother's. Tonight, alone with him, the words had sat on her tongue burning to be said. And still she couldn't. But somehow he seemed to know anyway.

Oh, he smelled good. She could still smell the remnants of the aftershave he'd put on this morning, something simple and rugged. His lips were soft, the faint stubble on his chin was rough and the combination was electrifying. She heard a sound—coming from her own throat—and he deepened the contact in response.

She met him equally, nerves and excitement rushing in waves throughout her body as she slid her arms around his waist and put her hands on his back, pulling him closer.

The points where their bodies touched were alive and

she rejoiced, knowing it had been several long, lonely months since she'd felt such an intense connection with anyone. Elemental, raw and feminine.

He gentled the kiss, sliding his hands over her shoulders and down her arms as his lips parted from hers. His mouth hovered mere inches away from hers as their breath came rapidly, the sound echoing in the quiet kitchen.

"Why did you do that?" She whispered it, but the syllables sounded clearly in the silence. His kiss had made her feel like a woman again. But she wanted to hear him say it. She needed him to admit to the chemistry. She had despaired of ever feeling it again, of inspiring it again in a man.

"I don't know what came over me."

For once, Elli refused to let her inner voice speak. She knew what it would say—that he didn't find her attractive. The inner voice would make excuses. But she didn't want excuses. She wanted to believe in the power of the action itself. She wanted to believe in the attraction she'd felt humming between them.

She desperately needed to believe she'd been worth it. As long as he didn't apologize. She couldn't bear that.

"So it was because..." His hands rested on her arms and she kept hers about his waist. She wanted to keep touching him, just a few moments longer. He was so warm and strong.

"You keep looking at me and I—"

He broke off, pushed backward and dropped his hands.

"You?" she prompted. She wanted him to say the words. Her whole body begged him.

"I couldn't seem to help it."

The sweetness of it filled her. This was what she'd been missing. How long had it been since she'd felt desirable?

How long had she been picking apart things she'd done, words she'd spoken, how she looked? Her hair was too flat, her bottom too wide. She still carried weight around her middle from her pregnancy. But handsome Wyatt Black didn't seem to care about any of it.

His gaze probed hers. "But it was probably a mistake. We can't let this complicate things, Elli. We have to put Darcy first."

And just like that the bubble popped, taking the fizz out of the moment. Of course they needed to put Darcy first. He'd told the caseworker that she was a friend helping him care for his niece. He'd stressed how Darcy was the focus for both of them at this moment, and how having two people was vastly better than one. The baby was first priority. And that was as it should be. She was letting her vanity get in the way.

But it hurt. And she didn't know why. It shouldn't matter. Where would it lead? Nowhere. He was absolutely right.

"Of course we do." She gathered her wits and retrieved the pot holders, then went to the oven and took out the chicken. It *did* matter and she *did* know why. She was seeing a new side to Wyatt and she liked it. She was starting to care about him.

"Elli—I don't know how to thank you for all of this." He looked down at Darcy and Elli's heart wrenched at the tenderness in his face. Did he realize he was half in love with his niece already?

*She* should be thanking *him*. For pulling her out of her half existence and giving her a purpose again. For feeling, for the first time in months, like a woman. But she couldn't say any of that without explaining what came before, so she merely replied, "You're welcome."

Silence was awkward so she made herself busy, filling a

plate for each of them, and with Darcy napping, they took them to the table.

The light was low and so were their voices as they discussed what had happened at the hospital. It wasn't until Wyatt suggested she stay over that she had a moment of pause. A big moment.

"What do you mean, stay over?"

Wyatt put down his fork. "We told the caseworker that you were helping me, right?"

"Well, I know, but…"

"But I have livestock to look after as well, Elli. I know she is my responsibility, but I can't see how I can be up with her all night and work all day." He paused, looked down at his plate and back up again. "We should discuss your wage. I don't expect you to do this for nothing. You've done more than enough the last two days."

Elli's face flamed. That wasn't where she wanted this to go, a discussion of money. "We can talk about it later."

"But Elli…"

"There's no rush, Wyatt. Helping you with Darcy is not taking me away from anything more important, I promise."

"Then you'll stay?"

The idea was so seductive. She wouldn't admit it, but the Camerons' house was big, beautiful and incredibly lonely. Here at Wyatt's, despite the general frayed-around-the-edges look, there was life and conversation and purpose. But what would she be getting into? She had just admitted to herself that she was starting to care for Wyatt. *He'd kissed her.* Being here 24/7 was just setting herself up for hurt down the road.

"I'm right next door if you need me."

His gaze pinned her for several seconds before he picked up his knife and fork and started eating again. He'd taken exactly two bites before he put them down again, the clink of silverware against plate loud in the uncomfortable silence.

"Is this about me kissing you just now, Elli?"

She didn't want to look up, but she couldn't help it. His eyes were completely earnest—not angry, but probing, as if he was trying to understand. But of course, he couldn't.

"No, Wyatt, honestly it's not." It was only a partial lie.

"You can have the bed," he said, his voice low and rough. "I don't mind sleeping on the couch."

"Wyatt..." He was making it so difficult. How could she sleep in the bed, knowing he was just down the hall, folded up on the short sofa? The very thought of it made her heart beat a little faster. "I can help you, but you have to understand...I have assignments due. I'm taking some bookkeeping courses." It was a paltry excuse; she'd just got through telling him she had nothing pressing. She could easily do the assignments on her laptop and log in to the Camerons' wireless connection to send them in.

He was silent for several long moments. Elli looked up in surprise when he straightened his shoulders and squared his jaw. He looked like a man about to face his executioner, like one who was about to say something very unpleasant and the words were souring in his mouth. Butterflies swirled in her stomach.

"Elli, the one thing I cannot do is let that baby go into foster care. I promised. And I cannot do it alone. I barely got a few hours' sleep last night. I need you, Elli. I will not let that baby be taken away by child services. *I need you.*"

She tried to push away the rush of feeling that came upon hearing the words. She hadn't known him long, but she'd thought him too proud, too stubborn to admit such a thing.

He didn't need *her*—she understood that. He needed the help, but not her. She was, however, the one person who was here. And the assignments were an excuse. She'd been waiting for a chance to do something important, so what was holding her back? A crush? Didn't she trust herself enough to be smart?

Surely she could keep that in hand. Wasn't Darcy worth it? If it were William, wouldn't she want someone to do the same?

That was the clincher. Of course she would. She was in a unique position to help a child. To refuse for personal reasons was beyond selfish.

"What makes you think they would take her away?" Elli sipped on her water. Wyatt was more open now than he'd been. It could be a good opportunity to learn more about him. Why did the mere mention of a social worker tie him up in knots? Because even the way he said the words was as if they tasted bitter in his mouth.

"Look at this place." He pushed away his plate. "It is not the picture of a family home. I am not set up for a baby. I am a single man with no experience with infants. All that is working against me. I can't give them more ammunition. I need to make this place into a family home."

"You realize that they aim to keep children with families, right? That you're on the same side?"

But Wyatt shrugged it off. "Maybe so, but there are no guarantees. You don't know what it does to a kid to be taken away."

Her heart ached at the pain in his voice. "Darcy is only a few months old. She wouldn't remember, Wyatt."

"How do you know that? How do you know someone else will be kind? What happens with Barbara? Do you know what the doctor said? She said that Barbara had taken steps to make sure Darcy was safe. She removed herself from the situation. She put Darcy in the care of someone she trusted. Despite being ill she made decisions based on good mothering. I will not betray that faith she placed in me."

"Wyatt." Elli tried to contain her shock at his vehement words. She reached across the table and laid her hand over his wrist. His pulse hammered beneath her fingers as the bits clicked into place.

"When did it happen?" She asked it gently.

Wyatt turned his head to the left and looked out the window at the approaching darkness. "What are you talking about?"

She squeezed his wrist. "How old were you when you were taken away?"

He started to push back from the table, but she kept her hand firmly on his wrist. He paused halfway up, then sat back down. And this time when he met her gaze there was defiance, an I-dare-you edge in the dark eyes.

"I was nine."

"Oh, Wyatt."

"I was gone for a whole week. That's all. It was too long. I ran away twice trying to get back home. They let me go back when he promised."

"Promised what?" Elli felt slightly sick, afraid of what the answer was going to be, sad for the little boy he must have been.

"Promised he wouldn't hit me again."

Her mouth tasted like bile. "Did he?"

"No. Not with his fists, anyway. But he'd done enough. I always knew what he was capable of."

"Weren't you afraid to go home?"

He turned his hand over, studied her fingers, twined his with them. She wondered if he even realized he was doing it, twisting a connection between them as his jaw tightened.

"I couldn't leave my mother back there," he said simply. "I had to be with her. We only had each other, you see. Who does Barbara have if not me? Who does Darcy have?"

Elli's eyes smarted. Over in the baby seat Darcy started to snuffle and squirm, waking from her nap. Wyatt held hurts as deep as her own. So much made sense now, including his burning need to get it right. Did he think he was like his father?

"Wyatt, you could never be like him, you know that, right?"

His gaze was tortured as it plumbed the depths of her face. "How do I know that? When Darcy cries and I don't know how to make her stop..."

"You walk the floor with her. You came to me for help. Don't you see? You're doing a fine job with her. You're patient and loving. You're twice the man he ever was, Wyatt, I just know it."

His gaze brightened before he looked away.

"Okay. I'll move some things over. You won't have to worry about Darcy being taken away from you."

Relief softened the lines of his face. "Good. Because we still have to prove it at the social services home visit."

He rose and took his plate to the sink, then stopped at the seat and picked Darcy up, cradling her protectively against his chest.

How was Elli supposed to come through unscathed now?

# CHAPTER SEVEN

WHEN ELLI RETURNED from the Camerons' house with a bag, Wyatt was in the middle of the living-room floor, setting up the playpen they'd brought from her mother's. His dark head was bent in concentration, his wide hands working with the frame. Elli caught her breath and held it, pushing past the flare of attraction. She almost welcomed the stab of grief that came in its wake as she glimpsed the brightly colored pattern on the nylon. Darcy. The playpen had been meant for William, and she couldn't quite squelch the anger and pain, knowing he would never use it.

But why shouldn't Darcy have it now? Wasn't it better that it was going to be put to some use?

Wyatt fiddled with a corner and mumbled under his breath. Elli left her maudlin thoughts behind and smiled at his grumbling. "Having fun?"

Wyatt looked up, a wrinkle between his brows and a curl of hair out of place, lying negligently on his forehead. There it was again—the buzz of excitement. She bit down on her lip.

"There are way too many buttons and levers on baby things," he replied. He stood, gave the side of the playpen a quick jerk and the frame snapped into place. "There. It might not be a crib, but at least for tonight she won't have to sleep in her car seat."

Elli put down her overnight bag and went to his side. A plush pad lined the bottom of the playpen, decorated in farm animals. Darcy lay on the floor next to him on an activity mat, her attention riveted on a black-and-white zebra with tissue paper crinkling beneath the fabric.

"You're trying really hard." Elli knelt beside him and rested her hand on the nylon of the pen. In the short time she'd been gone she could see he'd tried to tidy up the living room. A lamp glowed warmly in the back corner and he'd put a soft blanket over the sofa cushions, covering the worn upholstery. The room was more homey than she'd thought, and the warm light highlighted a framed Robert Bateman print on one wall. It was a fine house, it was just…neglected. It wouldn't take much effort to bring it up to scratch.

"I never really had a reason before," he said quietly, getting to his feet. "I've been on my own a long time." A ghost of a smile tipped his lips. "And in case you haven't noticed, I'm pretty low maintenance."

She laughed lightly, drawn in by the cozy light and the easy way he spoke, but beneath it all warning herself she couldn't get used to it. "And babies aren't."

"Certainly not." He went to another box, one they'd just managed to slide inside the trunk of her car. "I should put this together next." As he opened the top flap, he carried on. "I can't thank you enough for arranging the loan. This stuff is brand-new! Where did you get it?"

She'd neglected to tell him that the house where they'd stopped belonged to her parents, and she'd determined ahead of time that should he ask she would simply answer that they belonged to someone who had lost a baby. The fewer details the better. She'd been spared explanations earlier, as on the drive home Darcy had been fussing.

The last thing she wanted was to tell him what had really

happened with William. But after his own revelation at dinner, she felt compelled to be honest with him. Maybe if she gave him just a bit of the truth, it would be enough to stop his questions. She had to talk about it sometime. Maybe then it would get easier.

"It was for me, for when I had a baby," she said, determined to keep her voice even. She didn't want to see the same pity on his face that she'd seen today at the hospital, facing her old coworkers again. The last thing she wanted from Wyatt was his pity. "I stored it at my mom's, that's all. You know mothers. You mention the word grandchild…"

He slid a flat board out of the box and put it to the side. "Wasn't that jumping the gun a little bit?" He said it easily, even teasing, but Elli was finding it hard to keep up the pretense. The logic of her decision to skim the surface made perfect sense, but she wasn't quite as successful at stifling the emotions that came into play. When she didn't answer, Wyatt looked up. His smile faded and those damnably dark eyes searched hers yet again.

"I've said something wrong."

He got up off the floor and went to her, not touching her, but she could see the wall of his chest and she blinked. She would not cry. Not again. She'd cried enough, and she'd done so well today. At some point she had to talk about it without falling apart. Wyatt didn't come with any preconceived notions about her, or her marriage to Tim. And once she left the Camerons' house, their paths would likely never cross again.

"It's all right," she said quietly. "You couldn't have known."

"What happened?"

"I was pregnant but…" She didn't want to go into too much detail. Concern was one thing, and it was already written all over his face. Full disclosure would bring the pity and sympathy. She'd decided to tell him, so why was it so difficult to say the words? "But I lost the baby," she finished on a whisper, unwilling to elaborate further. "All the things we'd bought we put at my mother's, thinking they'd still be there later."

"But there was no later," he guessed.

She kept staring at the buttons of his shirt, noticing oddly that their color matched the fabric precisely. "No, there wasn't," she answered softly. "Our marriage ended."

*And so did the dream,* she thought, but the idea wasn't as sad as it might have been. Tim had married her for the wrong reasons. He'd wanted a good wife, a home in a prestigious neighborhood and the picture-perfect family to go with it. In that, they'd been alike. She'd fancied herself in love with him when she'd been in love with her own dreams instead. It wasn't a mistake she planned to make again. She was stronger now. If she ever married again, it would be for nothing less than the real thing.

"I'm sorry," he said, and while Darcy stared intently at a blue elephant on the play mat, Wyatt took Elli into his arms.

It felt so good to be held there, nearly as good as his kiss had felt earlier. His chest was warm and solid, his arms gentle around her. It had been so long since she'd allowed herself to lean on anyone at all that she sighed, feeling a weight lift from her shoulders.

"Don't be sorry. It's not your fault," she murmured, knowing she should pull away but not quite ready to give him up so soon. She hoped that would be the end to the questions. He could go on thinking she'd had a miscarriage and that would be it. He didn't need to know how close to her due date she'd been, so close she could taste the sweetness of motherhood, only to have it ripped cruelly away.

His wide palm stroked her hair and a shiver went down

her spine, a feeling of pure pleasure. A gurgle sounded from the mat as Darcy discovered a new texture.

"The last two days and you didn't say anything. I saw your expression a few times as you tended to Darcy and knew there was something, but…" He pushed her away from him so he could look into her face. Not pity there, then. No, it was pure compassion, and she felt her determination to keep him at arm's length slip another notch. "If I had known…how callous of me," he finished, squeezing her hands.

"I could have said no." She smiled a little, squeezing back. "You and Darcy needed help. You couldn't have known."

Darcy grew tired of being ignored, and squawked. Wyatt let go of Elli's hands and went to the baby, picked her up in his wide hands and rested her in the crook of his arm.

"Yesterday I was terrified to touch her, and already she seems to settle when I hold her."

"You're a natural." Elli smiled, glad to leave the topic behind. She reached up to adjust Darcy's shirt.

"Hardly. But I want to do right by her. And if this is too much for you, I understand. I wouldn't have asked if I'd known how it would hurt you." Darcy's chubby hand grabbed at his lower lip. He removed her fingers gently and kissed them.

Elli was sure he hadn't consciously done it, but there was a tenderness to Wyatt that was utterly unexpected. It was in the way he'd put his arms around her, the way he held Darcy in his arms and vowed to fiercely protect her. She hardly knew him, but in some ways she already understood him better than she'd ever understood Tim. Tim had spoken to her as a doctor would, using technical terms and medical explanations. Wyatt didn't. He simply offered a genuine "sorry" and a hug.

"No, it's good for me. I should have stopped hiding away ages ago. I've put off moving on, and caring for Darcy is helping with that. It hurts, but you're not the only one benefiting from this arrangement."

"As long as you're sure…"

"I'm positive."

The atmosphere in the room seemed to lighten. "Okay, then, can you take her while I put this thing together?" Wyatt smiled, pushing the serious topics to the side and moving back to the present problem, and Elli was grateful. They'd learned something new about each other today and they were still standing. Her initial impression of him, the one where she'd labeled him a complete grump, wasn't bearing out. They were—to her surprise—becoming friends.

"Sure. She's due for a bottle anyway." Elli took Darcy in her arms, realizing she was getting used to her weight there, and liking it. As Wyatt organized hardware and parts, she went to the kitchen and heated a bottle, then came back to the living room, settling in the corner of the sofa. Darcy's warm weight relaxed in the crook of her elbow as she took the bottle, the blue eyes staring up at Elli with what felt like trust.

She sat quietly while Wyatt put together the change table. The silence was pleasant. Wyatt might think his home wasn't good enough, but it held something that many homes with better furniture and fresher paint didn't. It held comfort. A gurgling sound from the milk being pulled through the nipple made Elli smile.

How could it be that she felt more at home here than she had at her own condo with Tim? The thought disturbed her. How could she have been so wrong? How could she have fooled herself so well? Why had she settled when she'd really wanted something so much simpler?

"What do you think?"

Wyatt's voice pulled her out of her musings and she realized that he was standing proudly next to the change table. The maple-colored wood gleamed in the lamplight and a quilted pad fit on the top. No more changing Darcy on a sofa cushion or bed or whatever happened to be near. She had a place to sleep and now a table where they could organize her diapers and supplies. Darcy was settling in. And so was Elli. She wasn't yet sure if it was a good thing or not.

It felt right, which scared the daylights out of her. It would be fine as long as she kept up her guard. Then she'd find a new job, and an apartment somewhere. An apartment that she knew now would be more like Wyatt's home. Set up for comfort, not for style.

Darcy had fallen asleep and Elli put her down on the sofa. "It looks great," she said, going over to the table and running her fingers over the polished wood. "Where should we put it?"

Wyatt shifted his weight, suddenly awkward. "I suppose wherever she sleeps. The second bedroom still needs to be cleaned, and probably painted. I tried to get the rooms I needed livable first."

"And it doesn't feel right putting her in here."

"Well…"

"I still feel funny taking your room, Wyatt. I can sleep on the couch."

"No, I wouldn't feel right. You take the bed. I'm up at six for chores and I'd wake you."

"Then I can keep Darcy in with me."

"You're sure?"

"Yes, I'm sure. Isn't that why you wanted my help? So you can look after your livestock and I can look after Darcy?"

"Yes, but I…"

"Feel guilty."

A small smile played on his lips. "Something like that."

"I can take care of myself, Wyatt."

"Will you let me know if you need anything, then?"

"Do you always try to take care of everyone?"

His gaze slid back to hers and she remembered the way he'd drawn her into his arms, the way his lips had felt against hers. She was determined to make her own way this time, but there was something alluring about the thought of being looked after by Wyatt Black.

"Is that a fault?"

She couldn't help but smile, her heart tripping along a little faster than normal. "That's the standard 'answer a question with a question' technique. But I'll let you off the hook this time. We've got more important things at hand. There's a small matter of needing baby things," she said, taking a step away. Being close to Wyatt was becoming a habit and one she had to break. "We're on our last outfit, and nearly out of diapers. The can of formula I bought isn't going to last, either. If you start a list, I can run into town in the morning and do some shopping."

"That would be very helpful, but I don't want you to feel—"

Elli interrupted, laughing. "Stop it. You asked me to help and what, now you feel guilty about it?"

"You're teasing me." He said it with surprise, and Elli felt a frisson of pleasure skitter along her spine. It did wonders for her confidence to know she could put him off his balance.

"Maybe a little. You're so serious, Wyatt. You need to relax."

Wyatt fiddled with the screwdriver, finally putting it

back in a leather pouch. "I don't mean to be so serious," he confessed.

Elli recognized it not only in him but herself lately, as well. Maybe they both needed to lighten up. These little exchanges with him definitely made her feel better.

"You're concerned about the home visit, right? So let me do this, get the basics covered while you worry about work. A girlie shopping trip is just what Darcy and I need." She rubbed her hands together.

A quiet pause filled the room. She exhaled and continued in a calm, logical tone. "Isn't that why you asked me to stay?"

"I know you're right," he conceded. "About the necessities, anyway. And if it means I don't have to shop…" He strode off to the kitchen and Elli followed, stopping when she heard the tinny sound of a coffee can. Wyatt had relaxed for a few minutes, but now his jaw was set again in what she was beginning to recognize was his stubborn look. He took a wad of bills out of the can and started counting it off.

"How much do you think you'll need?"

Elli gaped. "You keep your money in a *coffee can?*"

"This is my emergency fund. It's easier to give you the cash than it is to sort out banking cards or credit cards." He held out several bills. "Take it and get what you need tomorrow. I don't dare take another day away from the stock, and you're right. It will be a huge help."

She reached out and took the money. "Okay, then."

He put the lid back on the can and returned it to a low cupboard. Elli frowned. Wyatt resorted to a can? It seemed so…old-fashioned. Just when she thought she was starting to puzzle him out, something else cropped up that made him a mystery. Maybe she should just stop trying.

"Come on," he said, turning back to face her, the earlier

stubbornness erased from his features and replaced with a smile. "Let's get the two of you settled."

Elli was following him down the hallway and his heart was beating a mile a minute. He didn't know what to do about Elli anymore. She was such a puzzle. Wounded and emotional one moment, teasing him the next. He couldn't forget the expression on her face when she'd told him about the miscarriage. It all made sense now. The odd looks that shadowed her face at times, the way she had first handled Darcy, as if she was afraid. And then…oh, God. The comment he'd made yesterday about all girls wanting babies. What an ass he was. He wanted her help, wanted her to feel at home and her confession made him feel like a heel.

Inside the bedroom he suffered another bout of embarrassment. The room was, at best, plain. A bed and a dresser, nothing on the walls, nothing inviting or cozy as he'd expect a woman's room to be. He'd never put much thought into decorations or felt the need to clutter things up with objects that held no meaning. He supposed that philosophy made his place look a bit spartan.

"I'm sorry it's not very fancy," he apologized, seeing the room through her eyes.

"It's fine," Elli replied. "I expect you've put your energies into the ranch and not the decor."

As she put down her overnight bag, Wyatt stripped the white sheets off the bed and tossed them into a plastic hamper along the wall. "That about sums it up," he agreed. He wondered what she was thinking. He knew how the house appeared. The petty cash he kept in the kitchen probably didn't help. It wasn't as if he didn't have the money to fix things up. He'd just put his priorities elsewhere.

"I'll get some fresh sheets," he murmured, going to the hall closet. The couch wasn't going to be comfortable, but

Darcy was his niece, not Elli's. She had no reason to stay, but she was doing it anyway. She was his guest. And yet the thought of her sleeping in here, in his bed, Darcy in the playpen beside her, did funny things to his insides.

He hadn't expected an instant family, no matter how temporary. After years of solitude, it was odd to have others sharing his space. In particular Elli, with her shy smiles and soft eyes. She seemed to take everything at face value and didn't judge because of it. And in a few short days she seemed to be everywhere.

It almost made him want to explain things to her. Things he had never explained to anyone.

He returned with the sheets. Elli had put Darcy in the middle of the bed and he heard her coming behind him, carrying the playpen. She brought it into the room and smiled. "If I put it beside the bed, I can get to her easily when she wakes," Elli explained. "A flannel sheet underneath her and the blanket should be enough. The nights aren't too chilly yet."

She put the sheet on the mattress pad and Wyatt picked up Darcy, placing her gently on the soft surface. She blinked up at him.

Then he looked at Elli and felt his heart turn over. She was looking at the baby with such tenderness it hurt him. Now he knew she'd lost her baby and her marriage and her job. And yet she greeted life with a smile. It was more than he'd managed for many years. He'd spent a long time drifting around, working, making enough money to settle somewhere, never getting too close to anyone. He'd lost his entire family and he'd spent his time nursing his wounds. Perhaps he'd nursed them too much. Buying this place—making it into something profitable—was his way of moving on.

But now it was different. He had a family, even if it

wasn't quite the one he'd expected. And Elli was a part of it whether it made sense or not. He was surprised that he wanted her to be.

He smoothed the sheet over the mattress and pulled up the comforter. "Are you sure you'll be warm enough?" Elli's cheeks flushed a little and he was charmed. "There are extra blankets in the hall closet."

"This will be fine," she murmured. "You're going to need the blankets anyway."

"And a pillow. I hope you don't mind if I take one."

"Of course not." She stared at the bed again and the nerves in his stomach started jumping, just as they had in the kitchen before he'd kissed her. The temptation was there. He wondered what it would be like to lie beside her. In his bed. To feel her body close to his, to kiss her in the dark, to hear her whisper his name.

He grabbed the pillow. After everything that had happened today, his libido had to stay out of it. He wanted to ask her what had happened. He wanted to know how her husband could have let her get away, if he'd been there for her or not. By the way she'd melted in his arms, he'd guess not. Not the way she deserved.

"The bathroom is down the hall. I'll bring the change table in and then say good-night."

Elli nodded dumbly and the temptation to kiss her reared up again. But he put it off. She was still a little jumpy from earlier, and it felt wrong to press.

When he delivered the change table, Elli was sitting cross-legged on the bed, a book and a small laptop open in front of her. Darcy was there, too, on top of the covers with a ring of plastic keys clutched in her chubby fist. As Elli turned a page in the book, she absently rubbed Darcy's foot with her free hand.

Wyatt swallowed.

Why did having her here feel so right? Why had he felt like such a miser counting out bills to give her? He wasn't rich, but he had this place and he could certainly afford to put food on the table and buy the necessities. Maybe it was time he put some effort into the inside, bringing the house up to scratch.

Why couldn't he get her off his mind?

He put down the table along the far wall and looked at the two of them, so comfortable and so right. Odd that he'd spent so many years roaming around looking for the right opportunity and here it was, dropped into his lap. Darcy's arrival had thrown a kink into things, but he understood the reason now. It wasn't about the ranch or cattle or making his mark.

It was about family. And it was about Elli.

His mother, even when things were at their worst, had cautioned him not to be bitter. She had begged him not to judge the world based on his parents' marriage. He had anyway, for a long time.

But when he looked at Elli, those jaded thoughts seemed far away. She had obviously been through a lot and she was still smiling. Maybe he could make things better for her in a way he never could for his mom.

She put her hand on Darcy's tummy, rubbing absently, and the bubble burst. How could he be thinking about being with her when Darcy was his first priority? He had to ensure that Darcy stayed with him until she could be reunited with her mother.

"You're staying up for a while, then?"

Elli looked up from her book and smiled. "Darcy's not ready for sleep yet. If I finish this assignment, I can send it tomorrow."

He nodded. "Elli, about the money…you know where

the can is. What I'm saying is, take more if you think you'll need it."

"I don't want to spend you out of house and home," she replied, but she focused on her book instead of on him.

So that was it. Did she think he was so poor a few things were going to strap him? "That's just petty cash, Elli," he explained, putting his hands into his pockets and smiling. "You're not going to break the bank. Besides, I trust you."

That got her attention and she looked up. "You do?"

"Is there any reason I shouldn't?"

Her cheeks blossomed and he thought once more how pretty she looked.

"I did think about picking up a few things to spruce up the house a little, but wasn't sure how to ask."

"Of course. I'm hopeless when it comes to decorating. I think it's a guy thing. I'd be happy for you to pick up some stuff. It might help make things look nicer for when family services does their assessment."

He went to the door and rested his hand on the frame, not wanting to leave but feeling silly staying.

"Wyatt?"

"Hmm?" He turned back around, fighting the strange urge to kiss her good-night. Maybe it would be best if he just got the hell out of there.

"I won't take it all, don't worry."

"Do I look worried?"

She smiled an angelic smile and he clamped down on the desire that rushed through him. "Actually, yes."

"Not about that," he replied, and before he could change his mind, he closed the door behind him and went to make up the lumpy couch.

It didn't matter. He wasn't going to sleep tonight anyway.

# CHAPTER EIGHT

ELLI DID A QUICK CHECK of the house to quell the nerves dancing around in her stomach. The phone call had come earlier than they'd expected. The social worker from Didsbury was coming in the afternoon.

She was glad she'd gone shopping early that morning. A cheery new tablecloth dressed up the kitchen and she had also bought matching tea towels and pot holders. Wyatt had finished the chores outside and just after lunch he'd brought in his toolbox and fixed the sagging front door so it opened and closed easily. Now he was taking a shower. Darcy was bathed and sweet smelling and dressed in a new pink two-piece outfit.

Elli now took a moment to brush her hair and twist it up, anchoring it in the back with a clip. The refrigerator was full and the house tidied. Darcy had enough formula for several days, diapers stacked neatly on the change table, and several cute, serviceable outfits. It had been a bitter-sweet pleasure shopping for them, picking them up and choosing the patterns and styles. It was something she'd never had the chance to do for William, and it had been fun. She would have enjoyed the day out, regardless, as she'd finally felt she had a purpose. She hadn't realized how much she'd missed it until she was needed again.

But all in all she was nervous. Both for Wyatt, who

had a lot riding on this meeting, and for herself. She had been with Wyatt at the hospital and now at the house. She knew that she would also have to answer questions. And without knowing what the questions would be, she couldn't anticipate the answers. It wasn't even so much talking to a complete stranger. There seemed to be some safety in that. It was airing everything in front of Wyatt. She shouldn't care what he thought, but she did. His opinion mattered.

She heard the dull thump of Wyatt's stocking feet coming down the hall and she took one last glance in the mirror, forcing the worry lines from her face and pasting on what should look like a pleasant smile. She'd taken extra care with herself, too, dressing in navy slacks rather than her usual jeans, and a soft raspberry-red sweater. When she turned he was standing behind her, and the curve of her lips faltered the slightest bit at his appearance.

He was so handsome. Even in neat jeans and a blue-and-white-striped shirt, he still exuded that little bit of rough danger, of excitement. It was in his deep-set eyes and the just-a-bit-too-long tips of his dark hair. An air of carelessness, when she knew in many ways that *careless* was one of the last words she could use to describe him.

It made for an intriguing package.

"Do I look okay?"

Worry clouded his enigmatic eyes, and she reached out, putting a hand on his arm. "Of course you do."

"Maybe I should have dressed up more."

Elli tried to picture him "dressed up" and it wouldn't quite gel. He belonged in well-fitting jeans and cotton shirts that emphasized his broad shoulders. "I don't think so. This is who you are. And today of all days, you need to be yourself. You can't pretend to be someone you're not."

A furrow appeared between his brows. "Not helping," he replied, and Elli laughed.

"Who would you trust more? Someone who looked great but was clearly uncomfortable? Or someone who looked calm, capable and comfortable in their own skin?"

He moved his arm so that his fingers could twine with hers. A thrill skittered down the length of her arm at the simple touch.

"That's how I appear? Wow. I didn't realize these clothes had special powers." Finally a smile broke through his tense features. "You look nice, too. The red brings out the roses in your cheeks."

When Wyatt smiled Elli felt as if a candle had been lit inside her. Maybe because he didn't bestow his smiles frivolously and they seemed to mean more because of it. "You're teasing me," she accused softly, pleased he'd noticed her extra effort. She resisted the nervous habit of straightening her clothing. She'd had the sweater for ages and had never worn it, thinking it too bold. After last night, and with the social worker coming, she'd wanted Wyatt to see her in something other than her normal exciting-as-a-mushroom colors.

He nodded. "You look as nervous as I feel. You even put your hair up." His gaze roamed over the twist, held with a clip so that a few ends cascaded artfully over the top. "I like it. It makes you look…sophisticated." He let go of her fingers. "Too sophisticated for a run-down ranch in the boondocks."

But Elli had noticed things in the past weeks, too, even if it had just been from a distance, on the deck of the Camerons' house. "This place isn't run-down. You have already made a lot of improvements. It takes time and hard work."

Wyatt's keen gaze caught her once more. "Of anything I expected today," he said quietly, "I didn't expect that. I didn't expect your unqualified support. Thank you, Elli."

The sincerity in his voice made her want to hug him, but she could not. Would not. Sure, she could see the differences and yes, she was attracted to Wyatt. But once this "situation" was resolved he would be back to being a full-time rancher and she would be...not at the Camerons'. This was meant to be a time to forge her own new life, not be sucked into someone else's again as she had been with Tim.

Wyatt's kiss last night was just an indulgence in fantasy. It had been lovely, but she couldn't let it be a life-changing event. She did not want life-changing events. What she wanted was to rebuild and begin again, this time much stronger.

"You're welcome. And try not to worry so much. Darcy should be with you. You're her uncle. It's not like this is forever, either."

She said the words to remind herself as much as him. It would be far too easy to get caught up in the situation and mistake it for reality.

Both of them heard the car turn up the drive, and in concert they turned their heads toward the front door. "This is it," Wyatt murmured, and the wrinkle reappeared in the middle of his brow as Elli straightened her sweater. There was no time to recheck her makeup. She would have to do as she was.

Wyatt opened the door and stepped out onto the veranda. Elli noticed that while the paint was still peeling, there were several pieces of yellowy fresh lumber where Wyatt had shored up the steps and floor. Sometimes it seemed he could do anything with his hands and a few supplies.

A young woman barely older than Elli got out of the car. She was tall and dark haired, the straight tresses pulled back in an elegant sweep. There was nothing about the woman that was ostentatious or over the top, but she was the kind of put-together female who always made Elli feel just a bit dowdy. Now, with only a sheer layer of foundation and some lipstick for makeup, Elli felt the difference keenly. It made her want to fade into the woodwork.

Come to think of it—perhaps that wasn't such a bad idea. The less she was in the spotlight today the better.

She slipped back inside as Wyatt greeted the woman. "Miss Beck, I'm Wyatt Black. I'm glad you could come today."

Oh, he was smooth, Elli thought, envying how he could cover up all that nervousness with charm. She heard the higher sounds of the woman's reply and bit down on her lip.

The door opened and Wyatt held it for Miss Beck to come through. She stepped inside and looked around briefly before moving to unbutton her coat.

"I appreciate you being so accommodating," she said as Wyatt stepped forward to take the coat from her. He hung it on a peg behind the door and rubbed his hands together. Elli watched it all from the living room, where she quietly folded a load of towels she'd taken from the dryer only minutes before. Anything to keep her hands busy and not twisting together as she was tempted to do.

"There was no reason to put it off. Of course you want to make sure Darcy is well looked after. We want the same things, Miss Beck. The best of care for my niece while her mother recovers."

That earned a smile from Miss Beck. "So we do," she agreed. "Please call me Angela. I can't quite get used to Miss Beck. It makes me feel like a schoolteacher."

Wyatt smiled back and Elli held her breath. Perhaps this wasn't anything to be so nervous about. Perhaps the caseworker at the hospital had been unusually stern.

"Like any government agency, there is paperwork that

needs doing, and procedure we need to go over. Might I see Darcy first, though?" Angela suddenly noticed Elli in the living room. "Oh, hello."

Elli swallowed and felt even shorter than her five feet three inches and every ounce of her despised extra pounds. She tried standing taller and held out a hand. "Hello. I'm Ellison Marchuk."

"Elli is helping me out with Darcy," Wyatt explained. Angela nodded, but Elli didn't feel any easier. How would it appear? Like a friend? Like a girlfriend? Which did she prefer? She wasn't sure.

"Darcy's sleeping right now, but I could get her up. Or you could peek at her. I'm sure she'll be up soon."

"That would be fine."

Elli led the caseworker down the hall to the bedroom. She had made the bed and besides the playpen and change table she'd added a few velvety throw pillows to Wyatt's bed and a cute mobile of puppies and kittens in primary colors, attached to the side of the playpen. They both peeked over the side. Darcy was sleeping, covered to her armpits with the pink blanket and with both hands resting on either side of her head in a classic baby pose. Elli's heart twisted as she looked down at the peaceful face. Darcy had no idea of the turmoil going on around her. If Elli could do one thing, it would be to make this as easy on Darcy as possible so she never need suffer any long-lasting effects from being separated from her mother.

They tiptoed out and Angela turned to Elli. "She's a beautiful baby."

Elli nodded. "And good, too. Well, as good as you'd expect a newborn to be." She smiled. This woman felt like an ally. It would be all right. It had to be.

Wyatt was waiting in the kitchen, sitting at the table staring at his hands. When they entered he stood up.

"Shall we get started?" Angela Beck was all business now and she picked up her briefcase, taking out a file folder. "We need to work through your application first, Mr. Black."

The volume of papers she laid out was staggering. Wyatt looked at Elli and she felt his hesitation clear across the room.

"Is this all really necessary? It's such a short-term thing, after all."

"Perhaps, but perhaps not. We don't really know when your sister will be able to resume care for Darcy or how long you will be temporary guardian. Does that present a problem?"

Wyatt's hands unfurled and he looked her dead in the eye. "Absolutely not. Darcy can stay here as long as it takes. I'm the only family they've got and it's only right that Darcy stay with me until Barbara is well."

"Then let's proceed."

Elli went through the motions of putting on coffee while Wyatt and Angela worked through the application. She gave a cup to Angela, then fixed another the way Wyatt liked it and put it by his elbow. His shoulders were so stiff. Despite his easy smiles, she could tell he was wound up tighter than a spring. She put her hand on his shoulder for just a moment and squeezed.

The hands of the clock ticked on as Wyatt went through his orientation. Elli fed Darcy when she woke, changed her diaper and put a load of laundry in the washing machine. Finally Angela Beck tamped the papers together and put them into her briefcase. "That was great coffee. Why don't we take a minute and you can show me around, Mr. Black?"

Elli put Darcy in the new windup swing, and the motion ticked out a rhythm as she tidied up the few dishes in the sink. Wyatt gave Angela a brief tour, outlining how long he'd lived there and what improvements he'd already made to the property as well as what he had planned in the days ahead. "I'd focused more on the livestock and ranch when I first moved in," he explained. "But Darcy changes things."

"How so?"

They paused at the end of the hall and Elli held a cup in her hand, the dishcloth dripping water back into the sink, waiting for his answer.

"Having a child under your care changes your priorities, wouldn't you agree?"

"I would."

Elli carefully placed the cup in the drying rack. Did Wyatt know how rare he was? He wasn't putting on a show for the social worker as some people might. He was answering honestly, sincerely. No one could dispute his dedication to his niece, surprise appearance or not. He was a man who would do what needed to be done, a man who would do the right thing. He'd do anything for someone he loved, she realized. At personal sacrifice to himself. She didn't know many men like that.

"And Miss Marchuk, is it?" Angela Beck's astute gaze pinned her in place. Elli felt awkward and plain next to Beck's efficiency. Lord, the woman was well put together. Not a hair out of place, while Elli could feel a few flyaway pieces fraying around the edges of her face.

"That's right." She curbed the urge to say *Yes, ma'am*. Angela Beck couldn't be any older than Elli was.

"How long have you and Wyatt been living together, then?"

Elli felt her control slipping by the sheer surprise of the question. "Living together," she repeated, somewhat stupidly, then looked to Wyatt for guidance.

Angela raised an eyebrow. "Our eligibility requirements state that if there is cohabitation the relationship must be a stable one for the good of the child. We require a twelve-month minimum."

Wyatt couldn't be disqualified as a temporary guardian simply because she was here. It was wrong. "We're not living together," she replied.

"Oh?" The tone of Beck's voice said she didn't quite believe it.

"Ellison is the nanny," Wyatt supplied. He sent Elli a dark look and gave his head a slight shake just before Angela turned and looked at him.

"Your nanny?"

"Of course. I do have a ranch to run, and I needed help. Elli has agreed to help out temporarily. It's a much better solution than a daycare. I cannot be in the house all the time, and I can't take Darcy with me to the fields and barns."

"Of course."

"This way Darcy isn't being shifted around to different people each day. She is here, with me, and with Elli. Isn't it good to have normalcy? I thought a nanny was a far better option."

Elli stood dumbly through the exchange. She knew why he'd said it and it made the best sense. But it stung. It stung a lot. Was being in a relationship such a bad thing? Not that they were, but the way he'd put it sounded so cold.

"A stable environment is definitely one of the things we look for," Angela replied. She gestured toward the table, inviting Elli to take a seat. "And Mr. Black is paying you, Ms. Marchuk?"

Elli swallowed, but schooled her features. If Wyatt could do this, so could she. "Yes, we've agreed on that arrangement."

"Ms. Marchuk, how do you know Mr. Black?"

Elli couldn't look at him. She knew if she did it would seem as though she were looking to him for answers. She sat at the end of the table, perching on the edge of the chair. "We're neighbors. I've lived next door to Wyatt for the last two months, ever since he moved in."

Angela Beck took the chair opposite, leaving Wyatt standing in the doorway. "And you're not romantically involved?"

Elli thought back to the kiss last night, and it was like being there again, feeling Wyatt's hands on her arms and the softness of his lips against her own. But did a kiss signify romantic involvement? On the surface, she supposed it did. But they had backed off and put Darcy first. And he had just called her the nanny in front of the social worker. The nanny. Not "a friend" or even a neighbor. The nanny. That told her quite clearly where Wyatt's feelings stood.

"No, we're not dating." That at least was truthful. Until Darcy's arrival, the sum total of their interaction had been a brief argument in the middle of a pasture. She still refused to look at him, instead seeing the dark blue denim of his jeans in her peripheral vision.

"And how long have you lived next door?"

Elli lifted her chin. "I'm housesitting for family friends at the moment. I was laid off from my job in Calgary and took the offer to stay at their place while I upgrade some courses and look for work."

She really hoped that didn't sound pathetic. Lord knew she wasn't alone. Lots of people had lost their jobs lately as the economy tanked. Surely she couldn't be judged just because she'd been a victim of budget cuts.

"And you're single?"

"Recently divorced."

She could feel Wyatt's gaze on her and she refused to

meet it. She knew if she did she would blush and that would betray her words. She hadn't lied. They weren't dating. But it didn't mean there wasn't an attraction on her part and she did not want to give that away. There was too much at stake.

"Children?"

She swallowed, held Beck's gaze. "No."

"What do you feel qualifies you for this position, then?"

And finally she couldn't help it. Her gaze rose to Wyatt's. His face was nearly unreadable, but she saw a softening around his eyes. He was thinking—as she was—of the baby she'd lost. And he would not say a word about it. She could tell by the compassion in his eyes. Her secret was safe.

She faced Angela again and offered a smile, bolstered by Wyatt's silent support across the room. "I'm available," she began, "and more than that, I have love to give. A baby's needs are simple—food, sleep, diaper changes. Anyone can provide that. What Darcy needs is love and attention and security. I can help Wyatt provide all of that. Most daycares won't even think of taking a newborn. With me here, Darcy is guaranteed to have the undivided attention of at least one of us at all times. She'll have some sort of consistency."

As she finished, a thin cry came from behind her. "And speaking of," Elli continued, trying very hard to smile while keeping a tight grip on her emotions, "I think someone would like her swing wound again. If you'll excuse me?"

"Of course. It is a perfect time for me to begin the interview with Mr. Black."

Darcy was sucking on her hands again, so Elli quickly warmed a bottle and took it with her to the bedroom. "I'll give you some privacy," she murmured to Wyatt as she passed him. "We'll be in the bedroom if you need me."

The softened look around his eyes was gone, replaced by a hard, distrusting edge. He was so afraid, she realized, and wondered why. Everything she'd seen him do the past three days—everything—had been for Darcy's well-being and at sacrifice to his own. Was he hiding something more that she should be concerned about?

"It'll be fine," she reassured him in a low voice. She wanted to reach out and touch him but held back. It wasn't the time or the place, not when she was simply the nanny. Remembering his choice of words made it slightly easier for her to walk away.

Once in the bedroom she arranged the spare pillows on the bed and got comfortable, Darcy cradled in her arms. "Okay, sweet pea," she said softly, adjusting her position and Darcy's weight until both were comfortable. Darcy eagerly took the bottle and Elli sighed. She could hear Wyatt's deep voice and Angela's feminine one from the kitchen. Her back stiffened against the headboard, and she sighed. The sofa would have been more comfortable, but Wyatt needed privacy. Elli thought briefly of the rocking chair she'd bought but Tim had returned to the store, insisting it didn't match their decor.

The solid wood and Quaker design would have fit in here perfectly.

It would have fit in, but she didn't. Even if she had been pretending she did, she realized. Today had shown her that. She was still on the outside, looking in through a dusty pane of glass. This wasn't about her. It was about Wyatt and Darcy and protecting his family. His explanation today that she was "just" the nanny had shown her that he would do what was necessary to keep Darcy with him. That he was sticking to their original arrangement. And of course he should.

But it was very clear that she was not Wyatt's priority despite their pretty little scenes together. If nothing else, the past few days had shown her that dissolving her marriage to Tim had been the right thing. For even if she didn't belong here, she was coming to understand what it was she wanted. And it had nothing to do with a fancy house and expensive car and having the right things.

She wouldn't settle for anything less than it all. Not ever again.

# CHAPTER NINE

WYATT COULDN'T AVOID the house any longer. Not the house in particular, but Elli. Darcy was too little to ask questions, of course, but Elli could. And would. She seemed to notice every little thing about him, reading him better than anyone he ever remembered.

It was incredibly disconcerting.

But dark was coming on and he'd relied on her for too long today. Darcy was his responsibility and Elli was here to help. He couldn't hide out in the barns any longer. Chores were long finished. It was time to regroup and move on.

He made it as far as the veranda, with his hand on the handle of the door, but he couldn't make himself go in. Not yet.

Instead he turned, rested his hands on the old wood railing. The veranda faced north, and he gazed out over the brown, empty field across the road. Next year it would provide hay for his herd, and he could almost see the welcoming green-brown grasses, waving in the prairie wind.

This was all he'd ever wanted. A place to call his own. To leave the past behind him. To find his own way, make his own living. He'd done it, too, relying on himself, putting money away until he'd found this place. His Realtor had looked at him skeptically when he'd said he wanted it. It had been neglected and had fallen into disrepair. His herd for this year was small. But the challenge of rebuilding, of growing it into something vital and important was exciting.

Until today, when he'd had to face his past all over again. All the prying, awful queries that he'd had to answer about his upbringing. He had come away from the meeting angry and resentful and afraid, and those were three emotions he'd worked very hard to overcome. He couldn't explain it all to Elli. He needed her on his side in this and if she knew the ugly truth she'd be gone like a shot. Elli was too good, too pure to get wrapped up in his baggage. He'd do well to remember it.

When he thought of her waiting inside, he tensed all over again. She'd looked so pretty today in her red sweater and makeup. He hadn't missed the little touches around the house either, the pillows and tablecloth and, for heaven's sake, matching dishcloths. He scowled. Before Miss Beck had come he'd recognized them as a good idea. But now… this was his house. Elli's presence was everywhere, in every corner. The past forty-eight hours had moved at warp speed and he was struggling to keep up mentally and physically. Coming in to a bunch of feminine touches was simply too much. Something had to give.

"Wyatt?"

He spun, his breath catching in surprise as she appeared as if she'd materialized from his thoughts. The porch light highlighted her pale hair, making her look soft and alluring. "I didn't hear you come out."

"No, you were in another world."

She was right, and it had been a world with her in it, so he didn't answer.

She stepped up beside him, mimicking his stance with her hands on the railing. Her voice was soft, so that it almost seemed part of the breeze. "Do you want to tell me where you were?"

He deliberately misunderstood her. "In the barns."

She laughed lightly, ending on a sigh. "That's not what I meant."

He expected her to go on, but she didn't. She just waited patiently, as if it didn't matter if he said anything more or not. She simply stood beside him, breathing deeply of the crisp autumn air. Her scent, something light and floral, drifted over to him and he felt his muscles tighten in response. This was why he'd stayed away. Because after Angela had departed, he'd wanted nothing more than to seek Elli out. To have her near, to bury his face in her sweet-smelling hair and feel that everything was right again. And that would have been a mistake.

"Where's Darcy?"

"Sleeping. She had a bath and her bottle. She's such a good baby, Wyatt. When you first showed up at my door, I had no idea what I was doing. But Darcy's shown me, bless her."

"You didn't seem unsure. Angela seemed pleased enough with you being Darcy's nanny." Wyatt turned away from the view and rested his hips against the railing so he could look into her face. It was calm, serene even, while he still felt in such turmoil. Again he fought against the urge to pull her into his arms. No, he was stronger than that. He had to keep the lines drawn.

"Nanny." Elli's voice sounded flat. "That certainly tells me where I stand, doesn't it?"

Was she angry with him? She crossed her arms over her chest, chafing them as if she was cold, but even Wyatt understood the defensive body language. "What was I supposed to say, Elli?"

That caused her to pause, and her gaze flew to his.

"What was I supposed to tell her?" he asked. "That I barely knew you? That we were friends?" He swallowed hard. "That I kissed you last night and it was a mistake?"

"Of course not," she whispered. Her eyes had widened as he'd spoken and he regretted the harsh way he'd said it.

"I had to present everything in a positive way for Darcy's sake. And thank God I did. I might lose her anyway now."

Elli's lips dropped open. He could see she was surprised by his last remark, and part of him wanted to confide in her but another part wanted to lock it all away as he'd done for the past fifteen years.

But Elli's response surprised him. "I'm not just a nanny to you, then?"

"Elli…"

"That was our agreement, but I really hated that part, you know. The part where you cozied up to her with your smiles and saying all the right things and passed me off as only the nanny, like some appendage to the situation that could be replaced at a moment's notice if it wasn't convenient."

She reminded him of a little girl who lifted her chin and accepted a dare while being scared to death on the inside. Defiant and terrified. He wondered why. Was she afraid of him? Of herself?

The air hummed between them while he fought for the right thing to say. "Why do we have to quantify our relationship at all? Elli, are you…" He paused, not believing it was true but wanting to know just the same. "Are you *jealous* of Miss Beck?"

A faint blush blossomed on her cheeks.

"You are." By all rights the knowledge should have made

him retreat, away from messy emotions that had no place in this situation. A solid reason to back away, his head was telling him. She'd managed to insinuate herself into nearly every aspect of his life in the past few days, and without even trying.

He should be backing off. But he found himself slightly flattered. Maybe she hadn't been as immune to his kiss last night as he'd thought.

He stepped forward, mysteriously charmed by the roses in her cheeks. He'd thought calling her the nanny was the clearest and best way of defining the situation, especially to someone who had a say in the matter. Angela Beck, for all her pretty looks and smiles, had more power than he was comfortable with. *He* didn't regret kissing *her,* not really. And it sure didn't stop him from wanting to do it again, despite his better judgment.

He was close enough that now she had to tilt her head to look up at him. It would take only the slightest shift and his lips could be on hers. The idea hovered there for a moment, and the way her breath was coming, in shallow, quiet gasps, he could tell she was thinking about it, too.

"It made me feel...pushed to the side," she finally admitted, lowering her chin and breaking the moment. "Marginalized. Like I was...somehow expendable."

That hurt, because making her feel that way was the last thing Wyatt wanted. Couldn't she see that he cared about her? That he was trying to protect her, too? But how could he do that and still protect himself?

"That certainly wasn't how it was meant," he consoled her. "Do you know what it meant to be able to say that today? To be able to point out that Darcy was cared for so well? And you were here, looking after her, and making coffee, and backing me up, showing her that I was right to trust you." He lifted his fingers to her face, touched the cool, soft skin of her cheek. "No one has ever done that for me before. No one. I never meant to make you feel like less because of it, Elli."

He understood her insecurity and refused to add to it by making her feel unimportant. He leaned forward, just enough that their bodies brushed and he lowered his head, his Stetson shadowing them from the light of the porch. Her lips were warm, pliant and just a little bit hesitant. The sweetness fired his blood more than any passionate embrace might have.

"It was just for show. You are more than a nanny, Elli," he murmured against her lips. "But I couldn't let the social worker see that."

Elli stepped out of his embrace. He could see her fingers tremble as she touched her lips and then dropped her hand.

"You trust me?"

"Of course I do. Why do you continue to doubt it? I would only leave Darcy with someone I trusted."

"But you hardly know me!"

His smile followed her as she went back to the railing, putting several feet between them.

"I know you better after two days than I know most people after two years, Ellison."

She shook her head, her face white now. "Don't. Don't say that."

"Why?"

"B-because it…it…" She kept stammering and his heart beat faster, not sure what her answer would be but knowing what he hoped. Nothing could have surprised him more, but there it was.

"Because it scares you?"

"Yes," she whispered.

The air began to hum again.

Elli blinked, swallowed. He watched each movement with great attention, trying to drink in every nuance of her. She had lost so much over the past months. Wyatt had overcome many of his demons through the years, but Elli's wounds were fresh. Surely, for this once, he could say what he felt if it meant giving her back some of her self-esteem.

"Angela Beck is no more beautiful than you, Elli."

"You're just trying to distract me." Her eyes narrowed. "My hair was a mess and any fool can see I am overweight and…well, she looked so put together and perfect!"

Was that what this was about? Perfection? He'd learned long ago that perfection was overrated and impossible. It was intimidating and unsustainable, as well. "What you are, Ellison Marchuk, is *real*."

He closed the distance between them once more, this time leaving her no escape as his body blocked her from the front and the railing from the back. He put his hands on her waist and drew her closer so that their bodies brushed. His fingers trailed over her ribs and down the curve of her hip. "I don't want you to be perfect. I want you to be just as you are. I like your curves, and the way your hair curls around your forehead, and just about everything about you."

"Oh, Wyatt," she whispered, and he could tell she was tempted to give in.

Elli heard the words and felt his hands slide over the pockets of her pants. She sighed, a sound of bliss and longing and fear. Did he really mean it? When was the last time someone had taken her as she was and it had actually been okay? Everyone always expected more of her.

She should be smarter, more ambitious, neater, prettier, thinner. And yet Wyatt didn't seem to care about any of that. At the same time she wanted to be more *for* him. He was a good man, she could tell. Strong and honorable and gorgeous without even trying.

His hand rested at her waist as his voice touched her, deep and sad. "Whoever told you otherwise isn't here now, Elli. Let it go."

Oh, the kindness was nearly too much to bear. If he kept on, she'd start crying and that would be a horrible mess. The only way to hold it together was to straighten her spine and dismiss his kindness. All of it, and keep only the sweet memory of his words locked inside like a treasure.

"Let it go like I suppose you have, Wyatt?"

She nearly cringed at how harsh her words sounded. Was she so wrapped up in protecting herself that she'd hurt him to do it? Shame burned within her. His hand stopped moving on her hip and she felt him straighten, the intimate moment lost.

"I don't know what you mean." He dismissed her comment, but she knew he was lying. She'd fought back simply to avoid being pulled down into more sadness, but his evasive answer somehow made her mad. She had been rude, but it had also been an honest question. He could see into her so easily—why shouldn't she know more about him? She wanted him to be straight with her. She needed it.

"You know exactly what I mean. You hightailed it out of here after Angela left and hid out in the barns ever since. That had nothing to do with me. What did you mean before, that you might lose her anyway?"

"It doesn't matter now," he replied, backing away. He turned and headed toward the veranda steps.

Elli watched him walk away, and anger warred with remorse for turning the tables on him. She'd thought she wanted to hear him confirm that yes, she was simply there to help Darcy. It would have made it much easier to fight her growing attraction, knowing it wasn't returned. But he hadn't. He'd brought up the kiss, the one she couldn't erase from her mind. And then he'd kissed her again, making her toes curl. Why had he done it? Because he meant it? Every cell in her body wanted to believe that, but a nagging voice in her head told her it was merely a method to distract her from the real issue—the reason he'd disappeared after Miss Beck had departed.

Now he was shutting her out and walking away when she was aching to understand why a mere mention of his interview made his face turn pale and his shoulders stiffen. What had happened to make him seek solitude for hours? Why was he hurting so much?

"Never took you for a runner, Black," she accused, heart in her throat. She deliberately provoked him, knowing that if she went the gentle route he'd simply dismiss her.

Her sharp words had the desired effect. He turned back and his eyes blazed at her. "You don't know what you're talking about."

"No, I don't. But I figure it's something big when it makes you leave the house and hide out in the barns. When you spend hours alone rather than face us in the house. When you miss dinner and bath time with Darcy and choose to spend the evening in an unheated barn. And it's got to be really something if you attempt to distract me by kissing me. I asked a simple question and you ran away."

"It's nothing." He started to turn away again, guilt written all over his face.

"No, it's not. It's a whole lot of something, and I know fear when I see it. If I'm staying here, if Darcy is staying here…" She paused, afraid to speak her mind, but wanting to be stronger than she'd ever been before. "If we're starting something, I think I deserve to know."

He spun on her so quickly she could react only by stepping backward. "I don't owe you anything," he growled.

"And if we want to talk about running, what exactly are you doing, Elli? I'm not blind. What are you doing at the Camerons' if not hiding away from life, huh? Running, hiding…we all have something, don't we?" He scoffed. "What are you doing here anyway? Playing at reality? You and your tablecloths and doilies and God knows what else."

Elli recoiled inside as the harsh words sliced into her, but she held her ground and lifted her chin. He would not intimidate her, even if he was one hundred percent right. She knew what pain looked like; she'd seen it in the mirror for months, and now she saw it in the hard planes of his face. They weren't so different in that way. Wyatt was simply afraid. Of what? What could be so bad that he'd fear Darcy was going to be taken away from him?

"I certainly didn't mean to overstep," she said stiffly. "I thought you wanted me to do those things. If you don't like them, I'll put them away and you can keep things just as you want them. And for the record, Wyatt Black, you don't owe me." She had taken Tim's insults, but those days were gone. She was stronger than that now. "Except not to play games." She slid her hands into her pockets, attempting to keep them warm. The evening suddenly seemed much colder. "If what happened just now between us was a game, it was very cruel of you, Wyatt."

His lips dropped open for a moment before he shut them again, forming a firm line. His hat shadowed his eyes, but she could feel the apology in his gaze.

"Oh God, I'm sorry. I don't play games, Elli. I never should have said that."

She knew in her heart he was being honest. Which meant what he'd said was true, and she tried to keep her pulse from spinning out of control. Lord, everything about him was so intense. What would it be like to be loved by a man like Wyatt Black?

"I know," she acquiesced.

His lips relaxed and his shoulders dropped. "I do owe you for all you've done. But not this. Please don't ask me this," he breathed.

Elli sighed, touched by the anguish in his voice. What was she doing? She could feel herself falling. Any plans and decisions she'd made about her future seemed to fly out of her head when he was around. Wyatt was *dangerous*. And it was *exciting*.

Sympathy and provocation hadn't worked. Maybe he had a right to his own secrets. "I'm going back inside, then. There's dinner in the fridge if you want to heat it up."

What an idiot she was, letting herself have feelings for Wyatt, giving in to the intense attraction that seemed to grow with each minute they spent together. He couldn't give her what she needed. He had too many things pulling at his time. Whatever else was between them was only muddying the waters.

Nothing surprised her more than the sound of the door as it creaked open, then clicked shut behind her.

She turned to see him standing in the doorway, his jaw set and his hair slightly messed as if he'd run his hands through it. His hat drooped negligently from his hand. "I am not a runner," he said firmly. "Not anymore."

"Then why did you take off? I came out from feeding Darcy and you were gone. I didn't know where until it got darker and I saw the lights in the barn."

He stepped forward, his eyes pleading with hers, as if they were begging her to understand. "Do you know the kinds of questions she asked, Elli? We're not talking generalities here. Every single last thing you'd rather not talk about? That's what they ask."

He tossed his hat onto a chair and covered his face with his hands.

The gesture was so sudden, so despairing, Elli was at a loss as to what to do. She felt his pain keenly, as piercing as a cold knife, the hopelessness of it. He exhaled slowly and pulled his hands away from his face. She almost wished he hadn't. His eyes were bleak, his cheekbones etched with agony. He looked the way she'd felt the morning she'd awakened and truly realized that William was not going to be in her arms ever again.

"Don't," she said, shaking her head. "I'm sorry I pushed. Don't say it, Wyatt, if it hurts too much. It doesn't matter."

But now he ignored her, as if he'd opened the door and couldn't help but walk through it. "She poked and prodded and pried for every detail you can imagine about any topic you can come up with. That interview invades every single aspect of your life. Perhaps now you can understand why I had to be alone."

"Did she ask about your relationship to Barbara?"

He snorted, a harsh, hurtful sound. "Top of the list. When did I find out she was my sister. Why did I want to look after her child when we barely knew each other. The fact that Barbara was the product of an affair started the probe into our family life."

Elli blanched. Of course. Digging around in painful events would make anyone want to turtle into themselves. "About being taken away? Your father's abuse?"

"Oh, yes." His hands fidgeted and he shoved them in the back pockets of his jeans. His eyes were wild now, like a cornered animal. "My father, that paragon of parenthood, and whether or not I'm cut from the same cloth. Do I solve things with physical violence. What are my thoughts on discipline."

"I'm so sorry, Wyatt."

He took several breaths before responding. "All the things I never wanted to talk about with another living soul. All the demons I've tried to outrun. That's what it was. So I could somehow prove myself worthy."

Elli felt tears sting the backs of her eyes. She understood that the last thing Wyatt would want was to be compared to his father. He was so gentle and caring with Darcy, so dedicated and determined to do the right thing. To insinuate otherwise would cut him to the bone. What if she'd been faced with the same interrogation? Would she have passed? Would she have been able to talk about all her mistakes?

Now she looked at him and saw him swipe at his eyes. Compassion overruled every bit of self-preservation she possessed and she rushed forward to take his hands. "Oh, Wyatt, I'm so sorry," she repeated, not knowing what else to say. "What can I do?"

He led her by the hand to an old battered wing chair. The light from the kitchen highlighted his sharp features as he sat, then tugged her down onto his lap. "Just let me hold you," he murmured, and she felt her heart quake as his arms came around her.

Mentally she'd been trying to push him away for hours. But it felt so good to be held. When William died Tim had pushed her away, pretending everything was all right, denying her the physical touches that might have given some comfort. She was beginning to see that Wyatt, with all his baggage and secrets and sometimes prickly exterior, was far more giving than Tim had ever been and yet he had more reason to hide. She curled into his embrace and tangled her fingers through the dark strands of his hair, wanting to give back to him just a little bit.

"I can do that," she whispered, and for long minutes they sat that way, absorbing strength from each other.

And somehow without meaning it to happen, Elli felt a corner of her heart start to heal.

"Do you know what the saving grace is in all of this?" Wyatt's soft, deep voice finally broke the silence.

"Hmm?" she asked, her eyes closed as she memorized the shape and feel of him, the scent, the way his chest rumbled when he spoke.

"My mother. When I think of Barbara, I think of my mother. Mom would not have turned Barbara away, even though she would have been a reminder of my father's infidelity," he said. His arms tightened ever so slightly. "My mother was kind and generous, and had every reason to be bitter. But she wasn't. The only way I've gotten through this at all is thinking about her. If I was cursed with one parent, I was blessed with the other. I've always tried to be more like her...even if I do look like him."

*Of course,* Elli realized. What must it be like for Wyatt to resemble someone who had betrayed the very nature of fatherhood? Of course he would want to emulate his mother. "What was she like?"

She felt his facial muscles move as he smiled. "She could do anything. Cook, sew, sing...not that my father gave her much to sing about. But she did it when he was away. She always tried to make things special for me, and she seemed to apologize when she couldn't."

"Why did she stay? Why didn't she take you and leave, Wyatt?"

His response was typical and sad. "Where would she have gone? She was afraid he would find her. Or that he would try to take me. Not that he really wanted me. It was about possession with my father."

She was starting to understand why all the prying questions had affected him so deeply today. "This all came out this afternoon?"

He nodded. "I will not be like my father, Elli."

"Of course not." She straightened and cupped his chin, tilting his face up so she could look him in the eyes. "And you're not. Looking after Darcy isn't about possession for you. I know that. It's about family, and acceptance, and responsibility."

"You see that. But I'm not sure Angela Beck did. It isn't so pretty when it's in black and white."

"What happened to your parents, Wyatt?"

His gaze was steady on hers. "I was working in Fort McMurray. They'd been traveling together and my father had been drinking. The crash killed them both instantly."

She let the news sink in, knowing there was nothing she could say that would be more than a useless platitude. And after today's interview Wyatt was afraid he was going to lose Darcy, too. Darcy and Barbara were the only family he had left. He was determined to look after them both, she could tell. What would happen to Wyatt if he failed?

He couldn't fail. She was here to help ensure it.

"They need to be sure, that's all. They are putting Darcy first, just like you are. They'll see that you're the right person to care for her until Barbara is well again."

"It doesn't make it easier," he replied, calmer now. "So now maybe you understand why I called you the nanny today. I can't let them all down. They're all the family I have left. That's why I can't jeopardize the situation by keeping on like we have been."

She slid off his lap, took the chair opposite him and put her hands on her knees. "What do you mean?"

Wyatt's gaze was apologetic as he leaned forward, resting his forearms on his knees and linking his hands. "I know I said that you were more than just the nanny, but do you think today's visit is the end of it? What if Beck comes back and finds us like we were tonight?"

"We were hardly doing anything wrong," she replied, feeling a sudden chill on her shoulders now that his arms were not about her anymore.

"Maybe not, but how would it look to her? I insisted you are the nanny. I made it clear we're not in a personal relationship. You heard what she said. People cohabiting need to be in a relationship for at least a year, and we've known each other only days. I told her there was nothing romantic between us. If we continue on this way it means I've *lied*. And I simply can't risk it. Darcy is too important to me."

A part of her ached as he said it. She had enjoyed being held by him so much. But Darcy had to come first, and they both knew it. Tonight, she had only fooled herself into thinking she was important to him. And perhaps she was, but she was way down on the list. The new life she wanted to build wasn't here. She'd left the old dreams behind. Wyatt and Darcy were sidetracking her, and at times most pleasantly. Tonight she'd forgotten all her self-promises the moment he'd put his lips on hers. But she had to keep her eye on the big picture.

"Elli...I'm sorry. Sorry I've dragged you into this."

Her heart tugged, hearing him say her name that way. But her resolve was stronger, especially now that he wasn't touching her. She wouldn't let him see he had the power to hurt her. "No, Wyatt. I'm here of my own choosing. You're right. If she got the wrong impression, you could lose Darcy, and I know how much that would eat away at you. You have to do what's best for Darcy."

He nodded. "She's the most important thing now. And lying about our involvement would be a mistake I don't want on my conscience." His eyes were sober, and she thought perhaps held a glint of resentment. "Lies have a way of coming out sooner or later."

She thought of his father denying his own daughter and leaving Barbara's mother to fend for herself. She thought about all that she hadn't told Wyatt about William and felt a niggle of guilt. She hadn't exactly lied, but she hadn't told him the whole truth either. She wasn't sure she ever could.

"You are not your father, Wyatt. You always do the right thing."

The truth was bittersweet. The right thing was costing her. Just when she was starting to feel alive again, she was cruelly reminded of her own unimportance.

A thin cry sounded from the bedroom; Darcy was awake once more.

"So we keep it simple," she said, pushing on her knees and rising from the chair.

"Simple," he echoed.

Elli left him sitting in the dark and went to get Darcy. As she picked her up, warm and nuzzly from sleep, she realized that nothing about their relationship would ever be simple. Not after tonight.

# CHAPTER TEN

THE DAYS THAT FOLLOWED set a pattern, and Wyatt was true to their agreement. He was always pleasant and friendly, but there was no more talk of pasts and fathers or any other hot-button topics. Elli cooked meals, cared for Darcy and finished up accounting assignments, e-mailing them to her supervisor. Wyatt asked her quietly to leave the things she'd bought, but there were no more shopping trips to the home décor shop. The fall air turned colder and the leaves scattered from the trees, leaving a golden carpet on the grass. Wyatt cared for his stock, spent hours outside making repairs and moving the herd to different pastures. When he came in his smiles and touches were for Darcy.

As Darcy watched from her swing, Elli washed up the breakfast dishes and put them away in the cozy kitchen. Elli wasn't jealous. It was impossible to be jealous of Darcy, who was an absolute darling. But she found herself wishing that Wyatt could spare a few soft words and gentle touches for her. She missed him. She'd had a taste and she wanted more. Seeing him work so hard and lavish his affection on his niece only made him more amazing in her eyes. She'd promised herself never to settle again, but as she got to know Wyatt even more, she saw so many qualities she admired, wished for in a partner. Stability. Tenderness. Patience. Love.

She was falling in love with him, sure as spring rain.

But the way he'd put on the brakes and then slipped into their daily and functional existence so easily told her that the feeling wasn't reciprocated. Her hands paused on the handle of a cupboard door. Those first days together had been so intense. Emotions had run high and things had been in flux. Now things had settled into a routine. Whatever her feelings for Wyatt, they weren't returned, she was sure of it.

She should be relieved, she supposed. Soon Barbara would be out of the hospital and the Camerons would be back. Elli had to start thinking about what she was going to do next. She told herself that because her feelings were one-sided, there would be fewer complications when it came time to move on.

As she passed Darcy, she reached out and gave the tiny cotton-covered toes a squeeze. It was going to be difficult to see Darcy leave, too, but she'd always known she would. Wyatt would not be a part of Elli's life after that happened and that wouldn't change even if she wished it to. No, she needed to start looking for a job and a place to live as soon as she finished her course.

She heard Wyatt's boots on the veranda and checked the clock on the microwave. Right on time. The past few days he'd come in at precisely ten o'clock for a cup of coffee and a sweet. He did have a sweet tooth and she was more than happy to oblige. She'd enjoyed the looking after Darcy, and Wyatt's house, and cooking meals for more than herself. As the screen door slapped against the frame, she cautioned herself not to get too accustomed to it. She was going to be hurt enough when this was over; forming habits would not help.

Wyatt stood in the doorway, grinning as if he was holding some sort of secret, looking unexpectedly youthful. The lines that had crinkled the corners of his eyes were gone, and there was an air of hopefulness about him.

She couldn't help the smile that curved her lips in return. He looked so pleased with himself, his dark eyes alight with some mischief and his hair even more windblown than usual. He held his hat in his hands, and she noticed he was crumpling the sides.

"What are you up to? And I know it's not my banana bread making you smile that way."

He made a show of sniffing the air. "You're right, although now that you mention it, it does smell good in here."

"It's just out of the oven and too hot to slice, so stay away from that cooling rack." She struggled to keep her lips stern as she brandished a mixing spoon, but felt the corner of her mouth quiver. What was it about him that made her smile so easily? He looked like a boy with a new toy.

He came across the kitchen and tipped a finger at Darcy's nose. "I have a surprise for you both."

"A surprise?" Elli folded the tea towel in her hands and draped it over the handle of the oven door. Curiosity got the better of her and she couldn't resist asking, "What kind of surprise?"

"Just something I've been working on the last week or so."

Elli's mind whirred. The past week—that would be ever since the night they'd agreed to keep things platonic and he'd started spending more time in the fields and barns. What could he possibly have to surprise them with?

"Stay here, okay? I've got to bring it in."

She wanted to refuse but couldn't, not at the hopeful look he sent her before he spun and disappeared out the door.

She heard an odd clunking as he came back. "Close your

eyes!" he called out from the porch, and she did, anticipation causing a quiver in her tummy. No one had surprised
her in a very long time.

"Are they closed?" More clunking and thunking came
from the entry.

Elli giggled. "Yes, they're closed. But hurry up!"

Some shuffling and scraping and then Wyatt came back
to the kitchen. "Bring Darcy," he said, and Elli could see
he was practically bouncing on the balls of his feet. His
Stetson was pushed back on his head, making him look
even more young and boyish and very, very attractive.

She picked Darcy up out of her swing and said, "Okay.
Lead on before you burst."

He led the way into the living room. "What do you
think?"

In the corner where the makeshift table had been now
sat the most beautiful rocking chair Elli had ever seen.
Stunningly simple, with a curved seat and perfect spindles
along the back, painstakingly sanded and stained a beautiful rich oak. On the seat was a flowered cushion in blues
and pinks.

A lump rose in her throat as she tried to think of the
words to say. "It's beautiful, Wyatt," she murmured, holding tight to Darcy.

"I found it in the back shed, of all places," Wyatt explained. He went to the chair and stood behind it, resting
his hands on the back. "It was dirty and scratched, but it
just needed some love. Some fine grit sanding and a few
coats of stain."

He had done this himself? With his hands? Somehow it
meant much more knowing he hadn't just gone to a store
and picked it out. It almost felt…like a lover's gift. But
that was silly, wasn't it? Who gave a lover a rocking chair?

There was also the small matter of things being strictly friendly between them lately.

It felt intimate just the same.

"You did this?" The words came through her lips tight and strained. She tried to smile encouragingly to cover.

"It was a bit of a shock at first, you know," he said, undaunted by her cool response. "When I came in and saw all the...well, the feminine touches around the place. I've been a bachelor a long time, Elli, but you didn't deserve the criticism I doled out. And you know, I've gotten used to it." His eyes danced at her. "Now I even like it. I wanted to make it up to you and didn't know how. Then there it was and I realized you need a proper chair. Come and sit in it with Darcy."

Elli's knees shook now as she walked across the room. She hadn't meant to make Wyatt uncomfortable in his own home, and his apology had made things right. He didn't need to do this. She was touched.

"I didn't mean to overstep," she whispered.

"You didn't. You just had the sense to do what I wouldn't do for myself. Come on," he cajoled, giving the chair a little rock. "I've tried it. It's stable, I promise."

For days she'd lamented a comfortable seating arrangement for feeding the baby or for soothing her as she fussed. She'd remembered the chair she'd bought and returned while expecting William, and wished she had something similar, especially when Darcy seemed particularly difficult to soothe and Elli's back ached from leaning against the headboard of Wyatt's bed. But her reaction now was immediate and frightening. Grief and longing hovered on the edge of her heart as she was faced with the actual object rather than the thought. She inhaled deeply, struggling for control. How could she refuse to sit in it when Wyatt was looking so pleased with himself? And he deserved to be.

She could do this. She could stay in control. She sat tentatively on the seat, the weight of Darcy in her arms awkward in a way it hadn't been since the very first day. Her shoulders tensed as she leaned against the back. "It's wonderful, Wyatt. Thank you."

But he'd gone quiet behind her, as if he'd sensed something wasn't quite right. "You're tense," he observed, and his hands settled on her shoulders. "What's wrong?" His fingers kneaded gently, trying to work out the knots that had formed. And as he moved his hands, the chair began to rock.

Elli looked down into Darcy's contented face, saw the blue eyes looking up at her, unfocused, the tiny, perfectly shaped lips, and in the breath of a moment her control slipped and everything blurred.

Once the tears started, Elli couldn't make them stop. The chair tipped forward and back but each movement pushed the tears closer to the edge of her lashes until the first ones slid down her cheeks. She caught her breath on a little hiccup, trying desperately to get a grip on her emotions.

But the memory was so utterly real that she lost the battle.

"Elli...my God, what is it?" Wyatt came around from behind the chair and knelt before her. He swept the Stetson from his head and put it on the couch beside them. Her heart gave a lurch at the action, gentle and gallant. His face loomed before hers, his eyes shadowed with concern. She did love him. There was no way she could have avoided it. Knowing it was one-sided, on top of the pain already slicing into her, only increased the despair cresting over her.

"It's just...just that..." She gasped for breath and felt another sob building. "The last time I rocked...it was..."

But she couldn't finish. Her mouth worked but no words

came out. Only an oddly high, keening sound as she sat in the chair he'd made for her and finally fully, grieved for the son she'd lost.

It had been William in her arms, her son, unbearably small but perfectly formed, painstakingly bathed by the nurses and swaddled in the white-and-blue flannel of the hospital. No breath passed his lips; his lashes lay in rest on his pale cheeks. But she had held him close and rocked him and said goodbye.

Wyatt reached for Darcy, but Elli held on unreasonably, turning her arm away from Wyatt's prying hands. "No! Don't take him yet. You can't take him yet."

Then her ears registered what she'd said and she broke down completely with shame and grief. Wyatt took Darcy gently from her now unresisting arms and laid her on the play mat on the floor.

When he returned, he simply bent and lifted Elli out of the chair, an arm around her back and the other beneath her knees, lifting her as if she weighed nothing. She clung to his hard, strong body, putting her arms around his neck and pressing her forehead against it. He went to the sofa and sat, holding her in his lap. "Let it out," he whispered against her hair, and she felt him kiss the top of her head. "For God's sake, Elli, let it out."

She did, all the while clinging to his neck as the pain and anger and grief finally let loose. This was what she'd held in for months, trying to keep up appearances, determined to show the world she could function. It had been building all this time, brought to the surface by loving Darcy as she cared for her, and now spilled over by loving Wyatt, by trusting him.

And she did trust him. Even if he never returned her love, she knew she trusted him completely. In all her life she'd never known a better man. Gradually her breaths slowed, grew regular, and exhaustion and relief made her limbs limp and relaxed. He felt good, solid. Tim had scoffed at her tears, turning her away. Perhaps that had been his way of handling the grief—by not showing it at all—and she'd been forced to hold it in, too. With Wyatt there was no pretending. She could be who she had to be.

"I didn't know," Wyatt said softly, once she was in firm control. His hand rubbed over her upper arm, soothing and warm. "How long have you been holding that in?"

Elli sighed, her eyes still closed so she could focus on the feel of him, warm and firm, the way his fingers felt through the fabric of her sweater. "Thirteen months."

Over a year. William had been gone over a year and she suddenly knew she was no closer to being over it than she'd been then. She'd only gone through the motions.

Darcy lay on the floor, looking up at the colors and shapes of the baby gym above her. Watching her caused a bittersweet ache to spread through Elli's chest. She missed the opportunities most. The opportunity to see her son grow, change, to be able to love him and see the light of recognition in his eyes at the sound of her voice or the touch of her hands.

"I had been waiting so long to have my baby," she confessed, finally giving words to the pain. "I never had the chance to learn with him. To feed him or change him or rock him to sleep. I imagined what it would be like for months, but theory is different than practice." She tried to smile, but it wobbled. "And then you showed up with Darcy...." Her voice trailed off, uncertain.

He lifted his head and looked at her face. Oh, she knew she looked dreadful. She rushed to wipe at her cheeks, to smooth her messed hair. But Wyatt didn't seem to care about her appearance. He never had. He raised his left hand and wiped away the moisture beneath her eyes with the pad of his thumb.

He touched her cheek softly, cupping her jaw lightly in his hand and applying gentle pressure so she would turn her face toward him. "It was a boy," he said, and she remembered what she'd blurted out in the chair.

For a moment it had been as if she was back in the hospital with William instead of there in the living room with Darcy.

Wyatt kept a firm hold on his emotions. There was more going on with Elli than he had ever dreamed and somehow the chair had set her off. He'd done the only thing he could—held her until the storm was over. She tried to turn away, but he kept his fingers firm on her face. "Elli?"

"Yes, he was a boy," she whispered, and he caught the glimmer of remnant tears in the corners of her eyes. Her teeth worried her lower lip.

And if she knew it was a boy, it meant she'd carried him long enough to know. How long? Months, certainly. He couldn't comprehend what that must be like, to carry a life and then just…not. He thought she'd told him that she had miscarried. But it didn't add up, not now. When a person thought of miscarriage, they thought of pregnancies ended in the early stages, the first few months. To know her baby was a boy, and the rocking chair today… It didn't take much effort to connect the dots.

"You were further along in your pregnancy than you let me believe, weren't you?" He said it gently, urging her to talk. She clearly needed to. And he wanted to listen. Not because he felt obligated in any way but because there was something about Elli that reached inside him. He couldn't explain it, or quantify what or why. He just wanted to. He wanted to help her the way she'd helped him.

"I was six weeks to term," she murmured, and the tears

that had been sitting in the corners of her eyes slid silently
down her cheeks. "My water broke and I knew it was too
early. It should have been okay. We just thought he'd be
small, and spend some time in the neonatal unit."

It took her a few seconds to collect herself. "There was
an additional problem with his lungs we hadn't known
about, a defect. I…"

She stopped, lowered her head.

"You don't have to say it," he said gently, feeling his
heart quake for her. He'd been hiding out in the barns and
thinking only of himself, first to escape the false domesticity she was providing and then thinking how proud he'd be
to present her with that stupid chair to make up for hurting
her feelings. He'd thought about making it easier for her to
care for Darcy, and a way to say thank-you, since she had
yet to cash the check he had written. It had hurt, brushing
her aside and insisting they keep things platonic. If circumstances were different, he would have pursued her.

She was the first person he'd willingly told about his
past, and it hadn't been easy. But his pain was nothing
compared to hers. His loss was nothing when held up to
the loss of a child.

She carried on, even though he could barely hear the
whispered words. "I never got to hear him cry."

There was a plaintive plea in her words and he tightened
his arms around her. "I'm so sorry."

"I thought I was over it more than this," she whispered.
She wasn't fighting his embrace, and he settled more deeply
into the cushions. Her weight felt good on his lap, holding
her the way he'd wanted to for days. Just being close to her,
connected, felt right.

"Sometimes it takes people years to really grieve." He
sighed, knowing how long it had taken him to accept that
his mother was truly gone. It had been just recently that

he'd made peace with it. And only then that he'd been able to sort out his life and know what he really wanted. This ranch was that resolution put into action. A testament to his mother's faith in him and finally his faith in himself.

"Back in Calgary, everyone kept asking how I was doing. I could never answer them honestly. I had to put on a smile and give them some stock response."

"And your husband?"

"Grief either brings you together or drives you apart. Our relationship didn't have the right foundation, and it didn't weather the stress of it. Tim buried himself in work and I…"

When she paused, Wyatt gave her hand a squeeze. She was being brave, though he doubted she knew it.

"I built myself a shell."

Wyatt smiled. "Oh, I can relate to that, all right."

And finally, a smile in return, with puffy lips and red-rimmed eyes. "I guess you probably can." Then the smile faded.

"Ain't life something?" Wyatt shrugged. "I realized a while back that it's not the disaster that defines a person, Elli. It's what you do afterward that counts."

"And I haven't done anything." Her eyebrows drew together. "I've just put it all off."

"There's always today. Today's a good day to make a new start."

Wyatt knew what he wanted her to say. That this platonic relationship was a waste of time. That she would make a new start with him once Darcy went home. Barbara's doctors reported she was doing well and soon Darcy would be going home. There wouldn't be a social worker standing in their way.

"I'm not sure I'm quite ready for that yet. I just…oh." Her voice caught again. "I miss him," she said simply.

"No one said you had to do it overnight," he replied, disappointed. "But making a start—and getting it all out, if that's what it takes—is good."

"You're a good man, Wyatt Black."

She cupped his face in her hands and he felt her blue gaze penetrate. Even with the evidence of crying marring her face, he could honestly say he wanted her, more than he'd ever wanted a woman. It was deeper than a simple physical need. His gaze dropped to her lips and back up again and he saw acknowledgment in her eyes. "Not as good as you think," he murmured. His resolution was forgotten when faced with her sweet vulnerability.

Her fingers still framed his face and he leaned forward, needing to touch her, taste her, wanting to somehow make things right for her in the only way he knew how.

He put his lips over hers and kissed her softly, wanting to convince her to open up to him that little bit more. For a few seconds she seemed to hold her breath, and the moment paused, like standing on a ledge of indecision.

But then she relaxed, melting into him, curling into his body as her mouth softened, warm and pliable beneath his. As his body responded, he wondered how in hell any man in his right mind could have let her go.

Elli heard the small sound of acquiescence that escaped her throat as Wyatt took control of the kiss. Oh, his body felt so hard, so reassuring. He knew everything now and he wasn't running, he wasn't changing the subject. He was a man in a million, and he was kissing her as if she was the most cherished woman on the planet.

She melted against him, letting him fold her in his arms as he shifted his weight on the sofa. Want, desire such as she hadn't felt in months slid seductively through her veins.

His body pressed her into the cushions and she welcomed

the weight, feeling at once wanted and protected. As his mouth left hers and pressed kisses to her cheeks, down the sweep of her jaw, she suddenly understood that she wasn't cold, or standoffish, or any of the things Tim had accused her of. She had simply been waiting. Waiting for the right person to come along and set her free.

And she was. As Wyatt's mouth returned to hers, she slid her hands over his hips and up beneath his shirt, feeling the warm skin beneath the cotton.

His hips pressed against her and her blood surged.

"Elli…"

"Shhh," she replied, touching her lips to his neck and feeling his pulse pounding there. She licked along the rough skin, tasting, feeling pleasure not only in what he was doing to her but from knowing what she was doing to him. After months of feeling powerless, it was liberating, affirming, and she craved more.

Wyatt pushed against the arm of the sofa with his hands so that he was looking down into her face. Elli noted with satisfaction that his breath came in ragged gasps and his lips were puffed from kissing.

"I definitely need a new couch," he murmured, his voice a soft growl. "Not here. My bed."

Taking it to the bedroom was a logical next step and one Elli thought she was ready for, but a thread of nervousness nagged. "But Darcy…"

"Has fallen asleep on her play mat."

He looked into her eyes, took one hand and slid it over the curve of her breast.

It was almost impossible to think when he was touching her like that, and thinking was starting to sound quite overrated.

She ran her hand over the back pocket of his jeans and offered the challenge with her eyes.

In a quick move Wyatt was off her, and she felt the lack of him immediately. It was quickly replaced by exhilaration as he scooped her off the sofa and carried her down the hall to the bedroom. Once inside, he laid her on the bed, sat beside her and began unbuttoning his shirt.

Elli's heart slammed against her ribs. A slice of well-muscled chest showed as his shirt gaped open, and she wanted to touch it. She wanted him, but modesty fought to be heard. What would he say when he saw her body? She fought against her insecurities, trying to ignore the hurtful comments in her memory. He hadn't turned away yet. She had to believe he wouldn't now.

She swallowed as she knelt on the mattress and pulled her sweater over her head.

Wyatt was there in the breath of a moment, kneeling before her, pulling her forward so her skin was pressed against his. She thrilled to touch it, to feel the heat and strength of it against her. She reached to push his shirt off his shoulders.

And then they both heard it—a knock on the front door.

For a split second they froze, then Wyatt jumped off the bed and went to the window.

"It's Angela Beck."

"Oh, my God!"

The seriousness of the situation hit them both and Elli scrambled for her sweater as the knock sounded again. "You've got to answer the door!" she whispered loudly. "Go, Wyatt!"

He was already buttoning his shirt. "You're already dressed."

"Yes, but look at me!" She tried to keep the panic out of her voice, but didn't succeed very well. What had they been thinking, getting carried away? "My eyes are blotchy and my hair's a disaster!"

"All right. Take a moment to collect yourself." He gave her arm a quick squeeze. "It'll be fine."

But the worried look in his eyes belied his reassurances.

This was her fault. He had been clear about keeping things platonic and why. She should have stopped him at the first kiss. He hadn't put her first, and so she had done it for him. And now what a mess they were in!

Elli scrambled to tuck her hair into a ponytail as she heard Wyatt answer the door. She should have stopped him, but she hadn't wanted to. If they hadn't been interrupted, she would have made love with him.

And now, with the faint sound of Angela Beck's voice coming from the other end of the house, the insanity of it grabbed her. She wasn't sure how she was going to walk out there and pretend everything was normal, not when she could still feel his body against hers and taste him on her lips.

And beneath it all was a nagging fear. Would he blame her if today's visit went wrong?

## CHAPTER ELEVEN

WHEN ELLI ENTERED the kitchen, Angela Beck was seated at the table with a cup of coffee and Wyatt was calmly slicing through the banana bread. She exhaled slowly, thankful he'd been able to collect himself so quickly, giving her time to regroup. Fixing her hair, a reviving splash of cold water on her face and a good foundation had done its work, she hoped.

"Ellison!" Angela turned in her chair as Elli stepped forward. "I'm glad you're here. I stopped by to check on Darcy, of course, and give Wyatt an update."

Elli stole a glance at Wyatt, wondering what he'd offered for an explanation and afraid to respond lest she contradict anything he may have said. "Darcy's doing well. She really is a good baby."

"Yes, I saw her sleeping on her mat."

Darcy at least was a safe topic. "We put her down to play, and she just drifted off."

Wyatt broke in to the exchange as he put a plate of banana bread on the table. "Did you get your assignment sent, Elli?"

Elli took her cue and hoped to heaven she wasn't blushing. "Yes, I did, thank you. Only two more to go."

Wyatt smiled easily at Angela. "Elli is taking accounting courses online."

The conversation went well for several minutes as they sat and had coffee and sweets and talked about Darcy. Angela's face turned serious, though, when she began to speak with them about Barbara.

"The good news is, Barbara is making excellent progress. Her doctors are very pleased, as I'm sure you're aware."

Wyatt nodded. Elli knew he'd spoken to his sister's physician a few days earlier and had been encouraged.

"We do want to place Darcy back with her mom as soon as we can. As a mother, she needs to spend time with her baby, to develop that important bond. From our side, we need to ensure that the baby is in a safe, secure and loving environment."

"What does this all mean?" Elli asked, the banana bread suddenly dry in her mouth. Would this go on longer than planned, or shorter? And which did she want? The idea of staying here with Wyatt, especially after this morning, was heady. But scary, too. They'd nearly been caught, and she knew Wyatt would blame himself if Darcy went into foster care even for a short time simply because he'd fudged the truth about their relationship. The other option was that he'd be even more determined to keep their relationship businesslike, an arrangement that didn't suit her at all. Then of course, there was the chance that Barbara would be out of hospital quickly and Elli wouldn't have a reason to stay.

"It means that your situation here is hopefully going to resolve very soon. It also means that Barbara is going to need a lot of support. Because she went to the hospital, she'll get the help she needs. Her doctor will be monitoring her health, as will child and family services. Really, going for help was the best thing Barbara could have done. She'll have access to many resources to help her through this, some mandated and some not, including support groups."

"And family," Wyatt replied, folding his hands on the table before him. "I'm her brother. I'll be there, as well."

Angela smiled. "You haven't known you were a brother for long, though."

His smile was grim. "I certainly haven't acknowledged it. But I am her brother, and I intend to help." His lips relaxed a little. "Besides, I've grown very attached to my niece. I hope to see a lot of Barbara and Darcy."

"That's very good news, Wyatt."

Angela pushed back her chair and stood. "I should be on my way. Thank you for the coffee and cake."

"Anytime," Elli responded, relieved that their guest was leaving. She felt as if she was playing a very bad game of charades, and that at any moment Angela Beck would see clear through both of them.

"Any idea how long Barbara will remain in hospital?" Wyatt retrieved her coat and followed her to the door, while Elli hung back at the doorway to the kitchen.

"My understanding is that the doctors are evaluating her every day. While I don't have a specific time line, I believe it will be soon." She smiled then, buttoning her coat. "Your life will be back to normal before you know it, Wyatt." She looked over his shoulder at Elli. "You, too, Ellison."

Wyatt walked her to her car while Elli went back to the kitchen to tidy the mess. Back to normal? The idea was not as grand as it might have been a week ago. Did she want her life to return to normal? Back to the Camerons', back to looking for a job and a place to live, back to a world without Wyatt in it?

She knew the answer already. A world without Wyatt was gray, rather than filled with dazzling color. Was it so wrong to hope that today meant something more? As much as she would miss Darcy, didn't an end to their foster care mean that they wouldn't have to pretend, too?

Wyatt came back inside, shutting the door quietly behind him. The nerves in Elli's tummy started twisting and turning, both in anticipation and a little afraid of what to say now that they were alone. The first private words since being seminaked with him on his bed.

"That was close."

She put down the sugar bowl and went to the arch dividing the living room and kitchen. "I'm sorry." She felt she needed to offer an apology. She should have thought more and felt less. She had let her need for him cloud her judgment and they'd nearly been caught.

"Don't be sorry. I shouldn't have taken advantage."

Her head whirled. "Advantage?"

Wyatt's jaw tightened. "You were vulnerable this morning. It wasn't fair of me to…" He swallowed, as though there were something big in his throat he was trying to get around. "To kiss you."

She wanted to say *Maybe I wanted you to,* but the words wouldn't come. Because he wasn't looking conflicted about it at all. If he had gazed at her now with some sort of longing, some sort of indication that restraint came at a cost, she might have pushed. But his back was ramrod straight, his expression closed where earlier it had been transparent. The shrinking feeling in her chest was the dwindling of hope. Hope that he'd feel about her the same way she did about him.

"I can take the chair back out," he suggested.

"No!" She straightened, took a step forward. "Please don't. It's a beautiful chair, Wyatt, and you did a lovely job refinishing it. I'll be fine now. Really."

"Are you sure?"

She nodded. "Yes, I'm sure. It was so thoughtful of you

and it will make things so comfortable. I didn't realize I'd react so strongly. But it's over now, right?" Emotional hurt became a physical pain as she lifted her chin. "Don't give this morning another thought."

"Only if you're sure, Elli."

"I'm sure."

"All right, then."

She fought against the shock rippling through her as he ended the topic of conversation. They weren't even going to talk about what had happened? What had almost happened? Did he regret it that much? The thought made her crumple inside.

He moved to the sofa and retrieved the hat he'd dropped there earlier. "I'll be out moving the herd to back pasture," he said, and without another word he left.

Elli woke, an uneasy feeling permeating her consciousness. Moonlight sent faded beams through the window blind of the bedroom, and it was utterly quiet. Too quiet, she realized. Blinking away the grit in her eyes, she slid out of bed and went to the playpen to check on Darcy.

She wasn't there.

But the bedroom door was half-open and Elli padded over to it. She opened it the rest of the way with only a small creak and tiptoed down the hall. The blanket on the sofa was crumpled in a heap and the pillow held the indentation of Wyatt's head. In the slight light of the moon, Elli saw them.

Darcy's hands peeped out from beneath her blanket and her lips were open, completely relaxed with the telltale shine of a dribble of milk trailing from the corner of her mouth to her chin. She lay ensconced in Wyatt's arms, the latter clad in only a T-shirt and navy boxer shorts. His jeans lay neatly folded across the arm of the sofa. Heat flooded her cheeks at the sight of his bare feet and long legs. His eyes were closed, but she knew he was not quite asleep. One foot flexed slightly, rocking the chair gently back and forth.

He would be such a wonderful father, she thought as she watched them. Not once in this whole ordeal had he ever put Darcy somewhere other than first. She couldn't think of one single man who would have stepped up in the same circumstances with equal dedication and without resentment. There had been moments at the beginning that they'd fumbled with knowing what to do, but he had taken it on and he'd done it out of not only obligation but love.

He had so much to give. She wondered if he realized it, or if what he'd told her about his past crippled him the way her grief had crippled her.

The toe stopped pushing against the floor and the chair stopped. Wyatt's eyes opened and met hers across the living room.

Elli struggled to breathe, suddenly feeling as if there wasn't enough air in the room to fill her lungs. She was drawn back in the flash of a moment to yesterday morning, and what it was like to be held and protected in his arms. They'd been stilted and polite since, but now with her feet bare and wearing nothing but a nightgown, she felt the awareness return, sharper and stronger than before.

In the gray light his eyes appeared darker than ever and her nerve endings seemed to stand on end. The soft curves of the rocking chair and the pink-blanketed baby were in contradiction to the ruggedness of Wyatt's body. In that moment, with his gaze locked with hers, she understood what people said about men with babies. Strength and frailty, shadow and light, toughness and tenderness. It was a combination Elli was helpless against.

"She woke up," Wyatt whispered in the dark, setting the chair in slow motion again.

Elli put one foot in front of the other and perched on the edge of the sofa, only inches from where his bare knee moved as the chair came forward. "I didn't hear her," she replied, as quietly as she could. Not only because of Darcy, but because she was afraid to break the tentative shell around them.

"You were sound asleep," Wyatt answered, and she saw the corners of his lips tip up slightly. "You never moved when I went in to get her."

Elli looked away, staring at her fingers as they rested on her knees. Wyatt had been in the bedroom, watching her sleep? It was intensely personal and she wondered what he'd thought as he'd seen her there in his bed.

She'd been exhausted tonight and had to admit that she'd had the deepest, most restful sleep in months. It didn't escape her notice that it followed the purging of her grief earlier.

"What time is it?"

"Nearly five."

Goodness, she'd gone to bed before nine. For the first time in weeks she'd had a solid eight hours of sleep.

"I'm sorry I didn't get up with her." Elli noted the empty bottle on the table. She'd slept through it all, including Wyatt heating a bottle.

"I enjoyed it," he replied, smiling. "It wasn't long ago I would have thought it crazy to say such a thing. But for someone so small, she sure has a way of making us come around, doesn't she?"

The way he said *us* sent another warm curl through Elli's insides. Right now, in the predawn hours, it could almost be easy to believe that they were a perfect little family. It felt that way—adorable child, tired mother, husband who got up instead with the baby so mom could rest.

But that wasn't reality. It was a fantasy, a life she'd wanted more than anything before having to trade in her dreams for new ones. They were only playacting. Darcy was not theirs, and Wyatt was not hers.

"Let me put her back to bed," Elli suggested. "You need your sleep. You can get a couple more hours before breakfast."

She and Wyatt stood at the same time, and Elli put her arms out for Darcy. But switching her from Wyatt's embrace to Elli's was awkward, the more so because they didn't want to wake her. Wyatt's arm brushed hers, firm and warm. As he placed Darcy in the crook of Elli's arm, his fingers brushed over her breast.

Both of them froze.

Elli bit down on her lip, realizing that she was braless and once more aware that she was clad only in a light cotton nightie that ended at her knees. And Wyatt…he was holding himself so stiffly, careful not to touch her in any way. Her teeth worried at the tender flesh of her bottom lip as she tried not to be hurt by that. He was so close she could feel the heat from his body, the soft fabric of his T-shirt. And oh, the scent of him. The faded woodsy notes of his body wash from his earlier shower, mingled with sleep.

What would happen if she moved an inch closer? Two? If she tipped up her head to ask for his kiss? Would he accept the invitation?

Or would he step back, as he had that night on the veranda, and as he had yesterday after Angela Beck's visit? She wanted to tell him how she felt, but needed some sign from him first, something to encourage her that she was not alone. And since the accidental touch, he was not moving any closer.

So she moved back, adjusting Darcy's weight. "Good night," she murmured, too late realizing how silly it sounded, since it was already nearly morning. She turned away and took Darcy to the bedroom, not looking back.

It didn't matter.

The sight of him there, standing in the dark, was already branded painfully on her brain and heart.

Exactly two weeks after Darcy had been deposited on Wyatt's veranda she went home to her mother.

Neither Elli nor Wyatt were prepared for the news; despite Angela Beck's visit they had expected temporary care to last longer as Barbara regained her feet. For Elli it was too soon and yet too long as well; she already loved Darcy and felt a bond between them. There was no question that Darcy belonged with Barbara, but it was equally true that Elli had become attached to the blue-eyed angel who had been dropped into her life unceremoniously and was now leaving it under much different circumstances.

She had her goodbye moment with Darcy as she put her down for her morning nap. She kissed the warm temple, her nostrils filled with the scent of baby lotion and sweetness. She was determined not to cry, but wiped below her eyes anyway at the bit of moisture that was there. She had a lot to thank Darcy for—she could feel in her heart that healing strides had been taken. Sadness for William now wasn't as piercing as before. Somehow between Darcy's innocence and Wyatt's gentleness she'd been able to let go of the grief that had stopped her from living.

But goodbyes of any sort hurt, and she knew she had to do it now and get it over with, so that later she could simply pick up her things and leave.

She was folding the freshly laundered sleeper sets she'd

bought and laying them in the bottom of the diaper bag when Wyatt came in.

He said nothing, just went to the change table, picked up a soft stuffed bunny and turned it over in his hands. Elli kept folding and packing until there was nothing left to fold.

She looked up at Wyatt, who was watching her with worried eyes.

"Are you okay with this?" She voiced the question that he would not.

"You mean her going back to Barbara?"

Elli nodded.

"I don't have a choice," he replied, but Elli knew he was avoiding the real answer.

"I didn't ask that. I asked how you felt about it."

It felt good, being direct with him, especially since they'd danced around any type of personal topic since Angela Beck's visit. Darcy would be leaving today. So would she. There was no more time to leave things for later.

He stopped worrying the bunny and put the toy down on the bed. "We were told it wasn't going to be long," he said. "But of course I'm worried. I'm happy Barbara's done so well and that the doctors think she's ready. But she has a long road ahead of her, especially as a single mom. It is so much for her to handle."

"Family services will still be involved."

"Yes, of course. And her doctor, too. I spoke to her doctor this morning, and there are support systems in place. It all sounds fine."

"Yet you don't sound convinced."

He looked up and met her gaze. "I worry, that's all. One thing I know for sure. Barbara will have me behind her.

I'm going to be there for her. As her brother and as Darcy's uncle. Lucky for her, now I have practice as a babysitter."

"More than a babysitter, Wyatt." Elli zipped up the bag. "A father. You have been a father to Darcy these last two weeks."

His expression was difficult to decipher. Elli saw pleasure, but also pain, and perhaps denial. Knowing what she did about him, she could understand where such emotions might come from. But he wouldn't talk to her, not anymore. Ever since that morning when Angela Beck had shown up, he'd been closed off. And any softening that had happened in the dark at 5:00 a.m. was gone now. Perhaps there had been a mutual attraction, and something more than friendship between them. But there wasn't the trust she thought. Not from Wyatt. He'd backed away and hadn't had any trouble keeping away.

She'd already been in a relationship where they hadn't talked about their true feelings, and it had been their downfall. She wouldn't do it again. So she tried to make this, the end, as amicable as possible. "You made everything right for Barbara and Darcy," she said.

"You were the one who made this work," he replied, refusing to accept her words. "You were with her day and night, caring for her, making this place a home. And you accepted nothing for it. You didn't even deposit the check I wrote you. I checked. Why?"

*Because I needed you.* She heard the answer inside her head, but it never reached her lips.

With that answer, she began to doubt. Were her feelings for him solely wrapped up in overcoming her own problems? The answer hadn't come to her as *I love you.* It had been about need, and grief, and moving forward. She didn't want to think she'd used him, and she certainly hadn't meant to, but there was no denying the possibility that her feelings had been influenced by her needs. And with that possibility, the seeds of doubt were planted.

"I did it because I wanted to."

Wyatt stepped forward and reached for her arm. "Not good enough."

His hand on her biceps was firm and she shook it off. "I'm sorry if you're not satisfied."

She reached for the bag she'd already packed. She couldn't wait around for Barbara to arrive, to see Darcy put in her car seat and to watch her leave, taking a piece of Elli's heart with her. She had to get out now. Just his hand on her arm created a maelstrom of emotion she didn't want to deal with. Not today. Not with everything else.

"Elli…" His voice had a strain on it she hadn't heard before. "You're leaving. Can't we be honest before you go?"

Her heart pounded, wanting to be. But over the course of the past few years, so many of the things she'd thought were true had been only illusions. Could she say for certain this wasn't the same thing?

The issue of propriety during Darcy's stay was ended as of today. And yet he hadn't once said, *Please don't go.* He'd said, *You're leaving.*

"What do you want me to say, Wyatt?" She turned around to face him, willing her voice not to quiver. "Our deal was that I would stay and help you as long as Darcy was here. But she's not going to be here any longer and I am no longer needed as your nanny. Because that's what I've been, right? Darcy's nanny."

Her fingers gripped the handle of her bag, while every pore of her wanted to hear him contradict her. Not long ago he'd said very clearly that she was more than a nanny. Had that changed? The other morning, in the dark, her invitation couldn't have been more clear, but he hadn't stepped forward and taken what was offered.

"You weren't a nanny that morning here on my bed, were you." He said it as a statement, not a question. And the snap in his voice put Elli's back up.

"You cooled off soon enough." Oh bravo, Elli, she thought, seeing Wyatt's shocked expression. He hadn't been expecting such a quick response, she could tell. He couldn't put this all on her. If she'd given mixed signals, she'd taken the lead from him.

"Angela Beck at the door put things in perspective quite quickly," he replied. His forehead seemed to flatten as if he were displeased. "Getting caught would have been a disaster. Like you said before—our relationship had to be platonic."

"I don't want to argue before I leave, Wyatt. Please, can't we just leave things on good terms? You got what you wanted all along. You got to keep Darcy and fulfill your responsibility to your family. You did the right thing. Let's just leave it at that."

"And did you get what you wanted?"

The words hurt, because he didn't know what she wanted and she was too afraid to tell him. She was too afraid to ask how he felt about her and get pushed away again. Twice had been more than enough. Every single time in her life that she'd tried to be open with her feelings she'd been shut down. And Wyatt wasn't offering her anything in return, any level of safety that if she did open up would make it worth it.

"What do you *want* out of life, Elli?"

As he said the harsh words, the planes of his face changed, more angled and taut. He ran a hand through his hair that even when messy looked as if it was that way deliberately. She wanted to throw off the cloak of all her misgivings and just tell him how she felt. But she couldn't. She could still hear Tim's words in her ears, the ones she'd passed off as coming from bitterness and pain. She understood now that there had been a kernel of truth in them just the same and that they had affected her even if she hadn't wanted them to. Words that had cut her to the quick. *Go ahead. Walk out on our marriage. You failed our baby and I'm just another casualty.*

The words came back with disturbing clarity now because she knew they were true.

She did blame herself for William's death, and she did walk out on their marriage.

# CHAPTER TWELVE

WYATT WATCHED THE COLOR drain from Elli's cheeks. Her eyes loomed large within the pale skin of her face. It was a fair question. What did she want, and why wouldn't she just say it? Now that Darcy was leaving, nothing stood in their way. Why wouldn't she come to him?

He had seen her face when she'd come into the kitchen the day Angela Beck had visited. Maybe they'd both been carried away in the moment, but he hadn't expected her cool response. They'd both known what could have happened if they'd been caught together, what else could he have done? And he'd tried to bridge the gap by offering to remove the chair, but she'd stared at him with those huge eyes and he'd felt the gap between them widen.

She was afraid, and he knew it. This morning he'd tried pushing to see if he could make her react with honesty, but if anything she was withdrawing further. And he couldn't do it anymore, not knowing how fragile she was. Maybe she needed more time. He would never push where he wasn't wanted; he'd seen his father muscle his way through relationships enough to know making demands and bullying didn't work. You couldn't force love. And he was pretty sure he was falling in love with Elli.

What would she do if he just came right out and said it? As they stared at each other, her chalk-white and him with tension cording every muscle, he knew exactly what she'd do. She'd run.

"I've got to go."

"Elli." He took a step forward, and in spite of his determination not to push he found himself gripping the tops of her arms, forcing her to look up at him, wanting to grab one last chance. "Don't run."

The color rushed back into her cheeks and her blue gaze snapped up at him. "What are you offering, Wyatt? What do *you* want out of life? Because knowing that would help me out a lot. I can't figure you out, I really can't. And the last week and a half, you've gone out of your way to stay out of *my* way."

His hands felt burned and he dropped them away from her arms. Is that what she thought? That he couldn't stand to be near her? "Me?"

"You were the one that set up boundaries!" she cried.

Their gazes clashed and his dropped to her lips briefly, watching them open as her breaths seemed to accelerate.

"To protect Darcy!" Frustration was suddenly added to the cocktail of feelings rushing through him.

"Only Darcy?"

She'd very effectively turned the tables on him and he felt a slide of guilt run up his spine. All right, so maybe he was being cautious. And maybe he'd used Darcy as a shield to keep from admitting how he really felt. But he kept quiet now because he wasn't sure of her. He'd been there when she'd fallen apart and he'd seen her withdraw into herself afterward. She wasn't ready. He knew she was afraid. What woman wouldn't be after what she'd been through? He couldn't force her to open up.

"Fine. You want to know what I want, Elli? I'll tell you. I want this ranch to prosper, I want this house a home, I want a wife to love and a couple of kids. I want the kind of marriage my mother and father never had and I want to provide my children with the childhood *I* never had. I want the past to stop defining me and I want to prove that a pattern doesn't have to be continued." It all came out in a rush and it felt damn good to say it.

"Now go ahead." He lowered his voice and looked down at her, knowing she hadn't expected such an outburst. "Run. I know that's what you want to do."

She hadn't moved a muscle, but it seemed suddenly as if an invisible wall rose between them. Her complete withdrawal was cool and palpable. This was why he'd resisted. Because he'd known exactly how she'd react.

"I have to go," she whispered.

Her response didn't surprise him, but he felt the dull ache of disappointment. He couldn't beg for someone to love him. He'd left that little boy behind him long ago and he had too much pride. He went to the end of the bed, picked up the bag she had dropped when he'd grabbed her arms. "I'll walk you out."

Silently they went to the front door and Wyatt opened it. The fall air had a bite to it; in the low places of the yard the grass was still silvery with frost. Sunlight glinted off the few golden leaves remaining on the border of aspens. It was a perfect fall day. And yet there was no joy in it for Wyatt. By tonight he would be alone in his house again, only this time he'd feel the solitude much more keenly.

They hesitated on the porch for only a moment. Wyatt held out her bag and Elli took it without meeting his eyes. "Thank you for everything," he said, knowing it sounded formal, but pride kept him from speaking more intimately. "If there's ever anything you need…"

"Don't," she commanded softly. "Please, not this cold politeness. Not after everything."

She walked down the steps and half turned, and he

thought he caught a glimpse of moisture in her eyes before she blinked and it was gone.

"Goodbye, Wyatt."

He waited on the porch, watching her walk away down the dirt drive, feeling his heart go with her. Wishing she'd turn around and come back, hoping she'd be as honest with him as he'd been with her. If she would only do that, they might stand a chance. He needed her to stop. To come back to him. To let him make everything right somehow.

But she didn't. She walked on, her strides never faltering.

And as she reached his mailbox, a car slowed and made the turn into his driveway.

Barbara was here.

Elli felt every pound of her bag as the strap dug into her shoulder. She wouldn't look back. She couldn't. If she did, her resolve would falter. No, she reminded herself, holding the strap for dear life, she had to be strong. This time she had to be strong. This time she had to see the reality, not the dream. And the reality was Wyatt didn't love her, not the way she needed him to. Not the way she loved him.

As she stepped onto the interlocking blocks of the Camerons' front walk, she couldn't help but look over toward the house. A woman—dark hair, tall, like Wyatt— got out of the car, and Elli paused. It was like watching an accident and being unable to turn away even though she knew she should. Wyatt went down the steps with Darcy bundled in her blanket. Across the two lawns she heard Barbara's exclamation and saw her take the baby from Wyatt's arms. The way she held her, close to her body and with her head dropped low, made Elli's eyes sting. Barbara rocked Darcy in her arms even though she was standing, and Elli saw her kiss the perfectly shaped forehead.

She couldn't watch anymore.

Numbly she unlocked the door and stepped inside. She'd once been awed by the foyer's perfection, its opulence. Now it felt cold and empty. The cavernous foyer echoed with the closing of the door. She trudged up the tile steps to the living room, stared out the huge windows at the prairie extended before her, so vast and unforgiving. She took her bag to the guest room, dropped it inside and waited. For a sound. For anything.

But nothing came.

Next door, Wyatt was reconnecting with his sister and reconciling his past. Darcy would be going home, but he would see her often. She imagined them sitting in his kitchen now, perhaps drinking coffee, laughing, talking. He hadn't had to say goodbye to Darcy, as well. But she had lost both of them. She was alone.

And the worst part of it was that she knew she'd brought it on herself.

She'd said yes to his plea for help. She'd gone and fallen for him despite all her self-warnings to stay detached. And in the end she'd been too afraid to tell him how she felt, and so here she was. Alone. Again.

She told herself it didn't matter, because her feelings weren't returned anyway. She told herself it was better this way, because it wouldn't be right to stay so attached to him, or to his niece. She couldn't leave Darcy out of this either; she loved her, too, and felt the loss of her deep inside. And in that moment Elli realized an important truth. She was a mother. Maybe she hadn't had the opportunity to watch William grow, but she had loved him. She had a mother's heart.

Bereft, she buried her face in the pillow and let out the tears she'd held in all morning.

* * *

With a broad smile Wyatt refilled their soup bowls and sat back down at the table. He wasn't much of a cook, not like Elli. He missed her smiles already. He pushed the thoughts aside, to bring out later when he was alone. Tonight marked a milestone, even if his best efforts managed only canned soup and a sandwich. Reuniting with his sister seemed to eclipse his lack of culinary expertise.

"Sorry it's not fancier."

"Don't be silly." Barbara picked up her spoon and smiled. "Thank you. One of the things I promised the doctor I'd do for myself was eat better. This is just what I needed."

"Are you really okay?" Wyatt halted the progress of his spoon and his smile faded a bit. "I mean, you're going to be back to caring for Darcy full-time again. You're sure you're ready?"

Barbara's smile faded as the mood turned sober. "I'd be a liar if I said I wasn't scared. But I'm learning coping skills and I have a number to call anytime, day or night. Don't worry, Wyatt. Everyone is following up on me."

"That day or night thing," he said, putting down his spoon and taking her hand. "That goes for me, too. I suspected about our father all along, but I was a coward and said nothing. But not anymore. I'd like to be your brother, if you want me to."

Tears filled Barbara's eyes and she squeezed his hand. "You always were a good kid, and you turned into a good man. Even when I wasn't thinking clearly, I know I wouldn't have trusted you with Darcy if I hadn't believed you'd do your best by her. You went home with a black eye because of me once, Wyatt. I haven't forgotten."

"It's good to have family again," he said simply.

"Yes, it is. And I know you had help. Where's Ellison?"

Wyatt suddenly became engrossed with his soup bowl,

feeling pain at even the mention of her name and not wanting to show it to Barbara. "She's gone home."

"I want to thank her for all she's done."

Of course she did, Wyatt realized. But not now. "Now is probably not a good time, Barb. I think it was very difficult for her to leave Darcy."

He felt Barb's eyes assessing and stood up, taking his bowl to the sink.

"Only Darcy?"

A heaviness settled in his heart. "I don't know." He braced his hands on the edge of the counter.

"Is there something between you two?"

Wyatt turned around. Maybe he and Barb had a lot of missing gaps, but she had known him a long time, since they were children and in school together.

"Even if there was, there isn't now."

"I'm sorry, Wyatt. Are you in love with her?"

He had known his father's cruelty, but she had known his neglect. Now she was dealing with the results of her own failed relationship and making her way as a single parent. The way she was looking at him now told him she understood a little of what he was fighting against.

"I am."

"So what's stopping you from fighting for her?"

"We're not the only ones damaged here, Barb. Elli's had her own troubles to deal with. I got to a point where I was ready to move past it and take the life I wanted. But she's not there yet. And I can't do it for her."

Darcy made happy-baby noises from her seat and Barbara smiled. "I should get her home."

She rose and went to the seat, buckling Darcy in and picking up a blanket to lay over her.

"You'll be okay?"

"I'll be fine."

"You'll call me tomorrow?"

Barbara smiled. "You getting all big brother on me now?"

Wyatt grinned. "Feels weird, huh? But yeah, I guess I am."

To his surprise, Barbara came to him and hugged him. "Thank you," she murmured, and backed off slightly. "Sometimes the worst part in all of this is feeling alone. I think I'll like having a big brother."

He walked her out, taking the bag of clothes while she carried the seat. As they secured Darcy in the backseat, he added, "I kept the playpen and change table. Any time you need a break, Darcy's welcome to come stay with Uncle Wyatt."

"Thank you."

As Barbara started the engine and backed out of the driveway, Wyatt stood and lifted his hand in farewell.

When she was gone he went back inside, but the house felt instantly different. Empty, and lifeless. For two weeks it had been filled with noise and discord, but also with happy moments and somehow, family. Darcy had gone home with her mother, but he would see her again. He was her uncle. But Elli—soon she'd be leaving and heading off to wher- ever life was going to take her. And he missed her most of all. The way she looked sitting across from him at the table, or the way she joked with him about his sweet tooth. How she looked cradling Darcy in her arms, giving her a bottle, and how sweet she tasted when he kissed her.

He stared out the kitchen window, looking over the dark fields. They undulated like inky-black curves as cloud covered the rising moon. Droplets of rain began to splash against the pane, suiting his mood. He had tried to tell her what he wanted earlier today and she had been too afraid to reach out and grab it. He knew he couldn't force her to change.

But he also knew he didn't want to give up.

She was still at the Camerons', and he was here. Both of them alone. It didn't make sense, not when he wanted to be with her so much.

Energized, he went to the door and pulled on his boots, followed by his oilskin. All the things he should have said this morning he'd say tonight. It didn't have to be too late. He opened the door and was flipping up his collar when he saw her.

Standing at the bottom of his steps, her hair in strings from the rain, her shoulders huddled in her jacket.

For a split second they both hesitated, stared. Then he took one step outside and held out his hand.

She came up the steps and took it, her fingers ice-cold as his wrapped around them. Without saying a word, he pulled her into the circle of his arms.

They stood that way a long time, with the rhythmic patter of the rain falling on the roof of the veranda and the door wide-open behind him. Finally he kissed the top of her head, the scent of vanilla and citrus filling his nostrils.

"Come inside," he murmured, and he drew her in out of the cold and damp.

Once inside he could see the evidence of hard crying in her pink face and puffy eyes. It gave him hope. She'd been so contained, so cold today he'd had moments wondering if maybe he had imagined their connection. And then there was Darcy to consider. He knew part of the reason she'd left first was so that she wouldn't have to watch Darcy go.

"Darcy's gone home with Barb," he said, watching, gauging her reaction.

"I know."

"The house seems empty without her."

"I know."

She said it so sadly he wondered if that was the cause of her distress, and not him at all.

"Where were you going just now?" She tilted up her face, droplets of rain clinging to her pink cheeks.

"I was coming for you."

The world opened up for Elli as he said it. Her heart, so withered and afraid, expanded, warm and beautiful. She had been coming for him, too. But hearing him say it, seeing the agony etched on his face, gave her a rush of hope.

Her bottom lip quivered with emotion and she reached out for him. Her hands spanned his ribs through the heavy jacket and he threaded his fingers through her hair. Firm hands tilted her face until she was forced to meet his gaze.

"I was coming for you," he repeated, and then he kissed her.

When he finally released her, she admitted, "I was coming for you, too."

Elli had spent hours crying and hurting, but at the end of it there had been no solution. The pain of letting go of Darcy was what she'd dreaded, but in the end it wasn't the loss of Darcy that cut deepest. It was Wyatt. She didn't want to be held prisoner by fear anymore. She'd known that even if it never worked out, she had to make the important step of telling the truth. She would never know unless she asked. His welcome was more than she had dared hope for.

"Wyatt, I…I want to answer what you asked me this morning."

They were still standing next to the front door, water dripping from their coats, but Elli didn't care.

"Okay."

"You asked me what I wanted," she began, tucking the

wet strands of her hair behind her ears. "And my answer is the same as yours. It's all I've ever wanted, my whole life. I was always a puzzle to my mom, and my friends, and then my coworkers. I didn't have lofty aspirations like they did. I didn't want to be a lawyer or a doctor or a model, or even rich. All I wanted was a home, with a husband to love and a couple of kids. I wanted the kind of marriage my mother and father had and I wanted to be a mother more than anything. And for a while I had all that, or very nearly. And it all went up in smoke. And now, finally, I know why."

"Elli, I'm so sorry about that—"

"No." Elli cut him off. "I want the past to stop defining me and I want to prove that a pattern doesn't have to be continued, just like you. I'm done with settling, Wyatt. I convinced myself I could have it all with Tim, and I was wrong. I know I was wrong because…"

The next part was the hardest. It was putting herself out there, being emotionally naked. But what was the alternative? What more did she have to lose? Nothing. This afternoon had shown her that. She had cried and felt a bleakness unlike anything she'd felt before, even in her grief about William. Today she had, for a moment, given up hope, and the emptiness was more than she could bear.

"I know I was wrong because I didn't really love him. I loved the idea of him, I loved the fantasy of the perfect life I could have with him. I thought we would have it all. But it turned out it was nothing. Because I know now what it is to really love someone. The way I've fallen in love with you."

Her voice faltered to a near whisper as she finished, trying desperately not to cry, trying to fight back the fear she felt in admitting such a thing. Wyatt was gaping at her, saying nothing, his face a mask of surprise. And well he should be surprised. After holding things so tightly in her heart, letting them out in such a rush was unexpected.

"I gave up last time without a fight. Maybe because it wasn't worth fighting for. But you are, Wyatt. I don't want to walk away from you. I want those things with you. Is there a chance you might want them with me, too?"

She stood back, chin quivering, waiting for his answer.

He exhaled, the sound an emotional choke as he stepped forward. "Look at you—you're soaked."

She let him unzip her jacket and slide it down her shoulders. It dropped to the floor in a damp puddle. He cupped her jaw in his hands and forced her to look into his eyes.

"I love you, Elli."

He dipped his head and kissed her, the sweetest thing she had ever known. "It took you long enough," he murmured against her lips, and then he wrapped his arms around her ribs and lifted her off her feet. "I told myself I had to wait for you to be ready. But tonight, alone…I just couldn't."

She nuzzled against the collar of his jacket, smelling the unique scent of leather and rain and man mixed together. Joy rushed through her, chasing away the fear. Wyatt wouldn't say it unless he meant it. He loved her. She closed her eyes. She could handle anything if he truly loved her.

A laugh bubbled past her lips. "Long enough? We've only known each other a few weeks."

He only squeezed tighter. "We spent more time together the last two weeks than most people do dating. We shared things, things I hadn't told another person. What does time matter, anyway? I knew the night on the porch when we kissed."

"Then? When you pushed me away and decreed our relationship had to be platonic?"

"Yes, back then."

She laughed again. "You were faster than me. I couldn't admit it to myself until I saw you in the rocking chair with Darcy." Tenderness overcame her. "Loving you meant facing a lot of things I was trying not to face, you know."

He finally eased his hold on her and drew back. "There's so much I want to tell you. I don't know where to start. About Barbara today, and about me, and my plans…"

His dark eyes glittered with excitement and Elli felt uplifted by the possibilities. "One thing at a time," she teased.

"Come here," he said. He shed his jacket, hung it on the hook and took her hand, leading her to the rocking chair. This silly chair, responsible for so many things, shaped and polished by his hands. Hands that were capable of so much. As he sat and pulled her onto his lap, she lifted his hands to her lips and kissed them.

"I was so scared to come here, afraid you didn't really feel the same."

"I'm glad you did," he replied, turning his hands over so he could grip hers and mimic her action. "I wasn't sure how I was going to manage without you."

"Me?" She looked at him, surprised. "Are you kidding? Look at this chair, the porch, the door. All the improvements you've made around here. Is there anything you can't do, Wyatt? That's one of the things I noticed right off. You're so very handy."

"I had to be, growing up. God knows my dad was never around. I looked after my mom."

"Like you're looking after Barbara?"

The easy expression on his face faltered a little. "I suppose. I felt like I let her down."

"Why?"

The hesitation lasted only a moment. "Because my parents only got married because my mom was pregnant with me. And my father never let me forget that he was stuck in that marriage because I'd been born. When things went badly, he made sure I knew it was all my fault."

"Oh, Wyatt, that's a horrible thing to say to a child!" Suddenly pieces began to fit. "So you take on responsibility for everyone?" Her stomach began to twist. "For me?"

He closed his eyes. "Maybe at first. Maybe I did, because I could see you were broken and I wanted to fix things for you. I tried for a long time to make things okay for my mom, even though she kept telling me it wasn't my responsibility. But this morning I knew I couldn't. I couldn't fix you. That's something you have to do for yourself. It killed me watching you walk away. But I kept thinking that if I pushed, if I didn't give you that chance, some day you'd blame me, too. And it would be too hard to truly have you and then watch you walk away."

Elli leaned back against his chest. "It wasn't until this afternoon when you weren't there anymore that I realized. Being without you made it very clear how much I love you. I couldn't picture going on without you. I knew I had to try."

"I was looking out the window thinking what a fool I'd been to let you get away. I was going over to ask you to give us a chance."

"I left because you said you wanted those things but you never said you wanted them with me."

He sighed, putting his chin on the top of her head. "And I didn't say it because I was afraid of scaring you away completely."

"We're idiots," she decreed, and felt him smile against her hair.

"No, we're not. Because we both came to our senses."

For several minutes they rocked in the chair, absorbing each other, forging a new bond, two parts of a bigger whole.

"What now?" Elli finally asked. She wanted him to ask her to come back so they could work on their relationship. What she didn't expect was what he said next.

"How do you feel about ranching, and this house?"

She sat up a bit so she could turn her head and look him square in the face. "It's very cozy here."

"Could you be a rancher's wife? I'm no doctor, and I know we had very different upbringings."

Could she! "What difference does that make? What does it matter what you do?" She touched his cheek. "I just need to be where you are. I love it here. I've felt more at home in this house than any place I can remember. It doesn't pretend to be something it's not."

"And children? I understand that's a touchy subject. Are you okay physically? God, I never even asked that before. And I get you must be scared…"

Having children *was* a scary idea, only because she knew what it was to love so deeply and lose. But the dream had just been traded in—it hadn't died. She still wanted to be a mother, more than anything. "Nothing comes without risk," she said quietly. "And the idea of babies…oh, Wyatt," she whispered, and the back of her nose stung. "Not just babies. Your babies."

She couldn't say any more. Instead, they let the idea flower, fragile and tender.

"Whatever happens, we'll weather it," he said in response.

"I know," she replied. And she did know. This was what the real deal felt like.

"I love you, Elli."

He looked up at her, his brown eyes so incredibly earnest

and that little piece of hair flopping over his forehead. She reached out and smoothed it away.

He grabbed her finger and kissed it. "Marry me?"

"In a heartbeat," she replied, and she knew what it was to be home at last.

# MILLIONAIRE DAD: WIFE NEEDED

## NATASHA OAKLEY

**Natasha Oakley** told everyone at her primary school she wanted to be an author when she grew up. Her plan was to stay at home and have her mum bring her coffee at regular intervals—a drink she didn't like then. The coffee addiction became reality, and the love of storytelling stayed with her. A professional actress, Natasha began writing when her fifth child started to sleep through the night. Born in London, she now lives in Bedfordshire with her husband and young family. When not writing, or needed for 'crowd control', she loves to escape to antiques fairs and auctions. Find out more about Natasha and her books on her website— www.natashaoakley.com.

# CHAPTER ONE

THERE was no one there.

Lydia Stanford set her heavy briefcase down and banged again on the dark blue front door of the cottage, stepping back to look at the top floor windows that peeked sleepily out of a roof of handmade tiles.

It was picturesque, but she wasn't here to admire the view and it all looked ominously quiet. There was no glint of movement in the upstairs rooms. No sound of radio or television in the background. Nothing.

Well, nothing except the half-open window above the ramshackle single brick addition at the back. She lifted the brass plate covering the letterbox and peered inside. 'Ms Bennington? Are you there?'

Total silence.

'Ms Bennington? It's Lydia Stanford. We have an appointment at ten.'

*Had* an appointment at ten, she corrected silently. It was now nearly twenty past. *Damn and blast the woman.* Where was she? Lydia straightened and shook back her hair. *What exactly was she supposed to do now?*

Was it possible Wendy Bennington had forgotten their

meeting? Lydia wrinkled her nose and stared at the closed door as though it held all the answers. It didn't seem likely she'd have forgotten. The woman was in her late seventies but had a mind so sharp she made politicians quake at the knees the minute she opened her mouth. She'd lay money on her not forgetting a thing. Ever.

Which was why she'd grabbed at the chance to write an authorised biography of Wendy Bennington. It was the kind of *once-in-a-lifetime* opportunity which meant she'd broken off her first holiday in five years. Why she'd got the first flight back to London and had immersed herself in re-searching the inveterate campaigner's astonishing life.

*So where was she?* Lydia peered round the empty garden as though she expected to see Wendy Bennington walk up the path. Just yesterday the older woman had sounded so en-thusiastic about the project; surely she wouldn't have gone out? And leaving a window open? No one did that any more.

Lydia sucked in her breath and considered her options. She could, of course, get back in her car and drive back up the motorway to London. Or she could go and get a cof-fee in Cambridge and come back in an hour or so. Either one would be an irritating waste of her time.

She pushed the bell and rattled the letterbox. Even though it didn't seem worth doing, she bent down and shouted loudly, 'Ms Bennington?' Through the narrow opening she could see the green swirly patterned carpet, but nothing else. The cottage seemed completely deserted.

She half closed the plate, her fingers still on the brass. It wasn't a voice or even a definite noise that made her pause. Perhaps it was a sixth sense that something was wrong. She called again, 'Ms Bennington, are you there?'

Silence. And then a soft thud. Almost.

'Hello? Hello, Ms Bennington?'

She couldn't be absolutely certain, but she thought she heard the sound again. Not a footstep or someone falling…nothing that obvious. But something. She was almost sure of it.

Lydia straightened and shifted her briefcase into her other hand. Of course it could be nothing more exciting than a cat knocking over a waste-paper basket, but…

But if that soft noise had been the elderly lady's attempt to attract attention she wouldn't thank her for walking away and leaving her. Would she? She'd expect her to use her initiative…and do something. Which meant…

*What?*

Lydia chewed gently at the side of her mouth. It had to be worth a try at getting into the cottage through the open window. If Wendy Bennington had been taken ill…

It *was* possible. She might have fallen. Accidents in the home were very common, after all. If anything like that *had* happened, trying to get into the cottage would be the right thing to do. She glanced down at her watch, now showing twenty-five minutes past the hour.

With sudden energy, Lydia quickly walked round to the back of the cottage and stared at the small upstairs window. It was tantalisingly open. If she could just climb on to the flat roof, reaching the window would be child's play. It didn't look that difficult.

She glanced over her shoulder. There was no one around. No one to ask if they'd seen Wendy Bennington that morning.

There was no choice…

Lydia carefully concealed her briefcase beneath a large rhododendron and stood back to consider her options. It really wasn't going to be difficult—as long as the flat roof was strong enough to take her weight.

She took a moment to pull a black velvet scrunchie from her jacket pocket and twist her long hair into an untidy topknot before pulling the dustbin up against the wall. Then, holding on to the drain pipe, she hoisted herself up the first few feet—just high enough to get a grip on the roof.

Easy. Well, perhaps, not easy…but easy enough. And if Wendy Bennington wasn't home it would be just as straightforward getting out again. No one need know.

With the dexterity of the county-level gymnast she'd once been, Lydia swung her leg up and pulled herself on to the roof. If nothing else she could tell the elderly woman her home was a security disaster. Anyone could break in. Where she lived in London no one would dream of doing anything as foolish as going out and leaving a window open. You didn't even leave your car unattended in Hammersmith for five minutes without careful thought.

'What the hell do you think you're doing?'

A man's voice shot through the silence. Lydia's hand paused on the open window, her heart somewhere in the vicinity of her throat.

'Get down! Now.'

Startled, she turned and looked at the man standing below on the crazy paving. Tall. Handsome…in a scruffy, rough kind of a way. Mid-thirties, maybe late. It was difficult to tell.

And angry. Definitely angry. No doubt about that at all.

'What the hell do you think you're doing?' he repeated.

Lydia moved away from the open window. 'Getting in. I thought I heard a noise.'

'Really?'

'Yes, really,' she fired back, irritated by the heavy sarcasm in his voice. How many burglars did he know who went out on a job dressed in a genuine Anastasia Wilson jacket? It was time he took a reality check. 'I had an appointment with Wendy Bennington at ten—'

'It didn't occur to you to wait until she answered the door?' he asked with dangerous politeness, his accent at odds with his very casual clothes. Lydia looked at him more carefully. Whoever he was, he certainly wasn't the farm labourer she'd thought he might be.

And he wasn't as handsome, either. He had a hard face and an arrogant stance that made her want to explain the principles of feminism—very slowly—because he'd probably never grasped the concept of equality.

'It occurred to me, yes—'

'So, what changed your mind?' he asked, still in that same supercilious tone of voice.

Lydia struggled to hang on to her temper. 'Forty minutes standing about in the garden is probably what did it. I'm going to climb in and see if she's hurt. If that's all right with you?' she added, turning her back on him.

'It isn't.'

She looked round. 'Pardon?'

'I said, it isn't.'

'Don't be so…stupid. I had a ten o'clock appointment. I'm sure Wendy wouldn't have forgotten, it was too important. She might be lying hurt inside. Have you thought of that?' Lydia turned and pushed the tiny window open.

'I'd rather you used the key.'

'What?' She swung round in time to see him open the back door. 'H-How did you do that? The door was locked. I checked—'

'She keeps a spare key under the pot.'

Lydia watched him disappear inside with a sense of disbelief. *Damn it!* This couldn't be happening to her. It had been a very long time since anyone had managed to make her feel so completely foolish.

Logically she knew there was no reason for her to have known Wendy Bennington kept a key hidden. The idea that a formidable campaigner of human rights would keep her back door key under a terracotta flowerpot seemed, frankly, incongruous. But clearly she did…and the local populace all knew about it.

At least this particular member of it did. Who in…blazes was he anyway? *Arrogant, sarcastic, supercilious…* The words flowed easily. It didn't help knowing she might have reacted in a very similar way herself if she'd discovered someone about to break into a neighbour's upstairs window. Presumably he *was* a neighbour?

Gingerly Lydia lowered herself down, careful not to scrape her jacket on the brickwork. She brushed herself down and picked up her briefcase from under the rhododendron.

'Tall, dark and sarcastic' had left the door open, no doubt expecting her to follow him. She wiped her feet on the worn doormat and let her eyes adjust to the gloom. The small cottage window ensured the kitchen would always be dark, but the situation was made so much worse by the heavy net curtain hung on plastic-coated wire.

Lydia let out a low whistle. Even though the outside of the cottage was looking frayed around the edges and the garden was hopelessly overgrown, she honestly hadn't believed anyone lived like this any more.

The kitchen looked like something out of a nineteen-forties movie. There were no fitted kitchen units at all. Just a freestanding gas cooker that looked as if it ought to be consigned to a museum and a thickly painted cupboard with bakelite handles. The orange and cream marmoleum floor tiles had begun to lift and the whole room was dominated by a floor-standing boiler.

It was, frankly, grim.

She hadn't been aware that she'd had any preconceptions about what she'd expected Wendy Bennington's home to be like—but, clearly, she'd had many. She stepped over the twin bowls of water and cat food respectively and tried to ignore the faint odour of animal and stale cigarettes.

*This had been a mistake.* She should have stayed in Vienna, marvelled at the Stephansdom, eaten *sachertorte* and enjoyed the opera like any other sensible person. What the heck was she doing here?

She'd given up her holiday…for this. Crazy. She was crazy.

And there was still no sign of Wendy Bennington. The house was completely quiet except for the ticking of a clock somewhere in the further recesses of the cottage. She placed her briefcase down by the rusting boiler and looked across at the man as he flicked through the mail on the kitchen table.

'I'm Lydia Stanford,' she said with pointed emphasis, waiting for him to look up and acknowledge she was there.

'I know.'

'You know?' He said nothing. 'And you are?'

'Nick.' His eyes were still on the sheaf of letters in his hand. 'Nick Regan.'

Which told her absolutely nothing.

'Do you live nearby?' If he'd looked up he'd have seen her head indicate the direction of the only other house within a mile or so of the cottage.

'No.'

*No?* 'You're not a neighbour?'

He looked up at that. Very briefly. The expression in his brown eyes made it absolutely clear he'd no intention of assuaging her curiosity. 'No.'

*Nick Regan.*

Had she read his name anywhere in connection to Wendy Bennington? She was fairly sure she hadn't. All those hours on the Internet? All those pages of notes? Was it possible she'd missed something vital?

His accent spoke of an expensive private school education and his assurance indicated he was very used to being in the cottage. Comfortable, even.

Her eyes took in the expensive watch on his wrist and the soft leather of his shoes. Her mother had always sworn you could tell everything about a man by looking at his shoes. If she was right, this one had a bank account to be proud of, despite the worn jeans and faded jumper.

So who was he?

Someone Wendy Bennington had hidden from the public spotlight for over thirty years? A secret son?

She half smiled and pushed the thought aside. It didn't seem likely—which was such a shame because it would have made a great story.

It didn't fit, though. From all she'd learnt of Wendy
Bennington so far, she'd have been more likely to announce it proudly. Her whole life had been characterised
by a complete disregard for social conventions, so the absence of the 'father' wouldn't have deterred her. She'd
have told the world that her son's father was an 'irrele-
vance' and no more than a biological necessity.

'Should your name mean something to me?'

He looked up and then back at the letters in his hand. 'No.'

Lydia frowned, irritated. What was the matter with the
man? This kind of information was hardly highly classi-
fied. His behaviour was bizarre, to say the least. And rude.

'How do you know Wendy Bennington?' she persisted,
moving closer.

He threw the pile of letters back on the kitchen table.
'I've known her all my life.'

'Really? How's that?'

His dark eyes flicked momentarily across to her and
then he walked out of the room.

Lydia let out her breath in one long stream and just
about managed to bite down on the expletive which was
on the tip of her tongue. Perhaps he hadn't fully understood
that *she* was the one with the appointment.

Pausing only to shut the back door, she followed him
out into the narrow hallway.

'Wendy?' Nick Regan opened the door immediately to
his left and glanced inside.

'Is she there?'

He brushed past her. 'I'll check upstairs.'

Lydia gave in to temptation and swore softly as he took
the stairs a couple of steps at a time. Even allowing for the

possibility that he was genuinely worried, there was really
no excuse for his attitude towards her. Much more of it and
he was going to get the sharp edge of her tongue.

Her hand was on the newel post as he shouted down to
her, 'Get an ambulance.'

*Ambulance?*

'Quickly.'

*Dear God. No.*

Despite everything, she hadn't really expected that. For
all her dramatic attempt at breaking and entering, she
hadn't anticipated anything other than the elderly woman
had popped out to get some milk.

Her mind played havoc as she pictured Wendy
Bennington lying bleeding…or dead, even… She reached
into her handbag and fumbled for her mobile phone while
she ran up the short flight of stairs. 'What's happened?'

In the doorway she saw a figure, instantly recognisable
despite the flamboyant caftan and grey flowing hair,
slumped in the doorway. It wasn't the way she'd imagined
she'd meet Wendy Bennington.

Every picture she'd ever seen had shown Ms
Bennington to be a highly capable and formidable woman.
Her energy and strength had radiated from each and every
image. This woman looked simply old. Her face was filled
with fear and complete bewilderment.

Lydia flicked open her mobile and glanced across at
Nick, for the first time grateful she hadn't made this discovery alone. Presumably he would know whether Wendy
Bennington was prone to bouts like this and whether she
was on any kind of medication.

'I think she may have had some kind of stroke,' he said

quietly, his long fingers smoothing back a lock of grey hair.
'Wendy?'

Lydia watched as the woman on the floor frowned and
struggled to articulate what she was feeling—but what
came out of her mouth was incomprehensible. Her words
were slurred and her frustration mounted as she realised
she was communicating nothing.

'Wendy, can you touch your nose for me?' Nick asked.

Again that frown, two deep indentations in the centre
of her forehead, and yet there was no discernible movement. Nick looked over his shoulder. 'Have you rung?'

Lydia tapped out the emergency number and waited for
the operator's voice. It was only a matter of seconds, but
it seemed an age before there was an answer. Her hand
gripped on to the mobile until her knuckles glowed white
and she forced her mind to stay in the present.

The last time she'd telephoned for an ambulance it had
been for Izzy. Lydia felt her eyes smart with the effort of
holding back the emotion those images unleashed. She'd
never been so frightened as she'd been then. Waiting for
the ambulance to arrive had been the longest fifteen minutes of her life.

It had seemed like every minute, every moment, had
been stretched out to maximum tension and it was etched
on her memory. The feeling of complete helplessness. The
guilt. The regret. The panic. And the mind-numbing fear.
A whole hotchpotch of feelings she hadn't even begun to
unpack yet. All there. All reaching out towards her like fog
in a nightmare.

But this was different, she reminded herself. The circumstances were completely different. She forced her

breathing to slow and tried to focus on the questions she was being asked.

Nick looked over his shoulder. 'Tell them to take the left hand fork at the top of the lane. It's a confusing junction. They could lose five minutes or more if they take the wrong turn.'

Lydia gave a nod of acknowledgement and reached into her jacket pocket for the piece of paper on which she'd written the directions to the cottage. Wendy had been very thorough.

She watched Nick disappear into one of the bedrooms and return with a pillow and satin eiderdown. He used the pillow as a cushion and wrapped the elderly woman gently in the apricot-coloured eiderdown.

'Yes, the last cottage on the right.' The voice on the other end was precise and calming. 'About half a mile out of the village. Yes. Thank you.' Lydia finished the call and clicked her mobile shut.

'Well?' Nick turned to look at her.

'An ambulance is on its way.'

'Is there anything I need to do while I wait?'

Lydia shook her head. 'You've already done it. She said not to move her and to wrap her in something warm as she might be in shock.'

He smiled grimly and settled himself back down on the floor, taking Wendy's hand between his own. 'It won't be long now.'

Lydia watched the shadow pass across the elderly woman's face as she struggled to speak. She seemed so confused. Frightened. So unlike anything she'd been expecting to find in such a formidable woman—and yet would anyone be otherwise?

Her knowledge of strokes was woefully scanty, but she knew the consequences of them could be devastating. It didn't seem right. A woman of Wendy's courage couldn't be struck down like this. It wasn't fair.

*But life wasn't fair, was it?* It wasn't fair that her parents had died when they were so young. Or that her sister Izzy had miscarried her baby. Life had a way of kicking up all kinds of unpleasant surprises. She ought to know that by now.

Lydia put her phone back in her handbag, taking more care than usual to fasten the stud. 'Do you want me to put together an overnight bag? Or s-something…?' Her voice faltered as he looked up, his expression conveying exactly what he thought of her suggestion.

'I'll do it later,' Nick said curtly, 'and take it when I go to the hospital.'

*What was his problem?* He looked as though she'd told him she'd ransack the entire room instead of offering to gather together a few toiletries and a nightdress. Her eyes shifted to Wendy's hugely swollen ankle, visible beneath the eiderdown. 'I'll get some ice.'

'Sorry?'

'For her ankle. Whether it's broken or just sprained, ice will help it.'

He followed the line of her gaze. 'Right.'

Lydia turned and started down the stairs before she thought to ask, 'Does she have a freezer?'

'In the old scullery. She keeps a chest freezer out there.'

Lydia continued down the stairs. As she reached the bottom she jumped as a warm furry shape twisted round her legs. 'Hello,' she said softly. The cat mewed loudly and pushed that little bit closer. Lydia stooped and ran her hand across the sleek black fur.

Stepping to one side, Lydia carried on to the kitchen. Two concrete steps led down to the old scullery, the ancient copper wash tub in one corner. The freezer stood, large and white, on the far wall. Spots of rust discoloured the surface and the lid seemed to have slightly bowed.

There was so much about Wendy Bennington's house that made her feel unutterably sad. It was as though the elderly woman did no more than camp here. She'd certainly made no effort to make the place feel comfortable...or even like a home.

The freezer was in desperate need of being defrosted and Lydia struggled to lift the lid. She chipped off huge chunks of ice and lifted out the top basket.

Inside there were countless boxes of pre-prepared meals for one, half-opened packets of stir-fry and frozen vegetables. Surely more than enough to feed a single person for several months? Lydia lifted out a small packet of peas and headed back upstairs.

Nick turned as soon as she got there. 'Have you found something? Her ankle seems to be bothering her now.'

'You'll need to wrap this in a towel. It's very cold.'

But even as she spoke he'd pulled out a pillow from its pillowcase and tucked the frozen packet inside. She watched as he carefully held it up against the swelling and heard Wendy's small moan of pain.

'Is there anything else I can do? I'd like to help.'

Nick glanced up. 'If you want to be useful you could take your car down to the village and point the ambulance in the right direction.'

'I'm sure there's no need for that. I found my way here without a problem.'

'But it's a single track road and if they miss the junction there's nowhere to turn for a couple of miles.'

Lydia frowned, uncertain what to do. What he was saying about the junction was true—but it was more than that. He so clearly wanted her to leave.

She heard the elderly woman mumble incomprehensibly and wondered whether he wished her to go because he knew how much Wendy would hate being seen this way. If the situation was reversed, if she were the woman lying on the floor, she would prefer there were no strangers to see it.

And there was no doubt that Wendy trusted Nick implicitly, not once had she glanced across in Lydia's direction. Her eyes searched out his as though they would be her salvation.

It felt intensely private. His strong hand calmly held Wendy's frail agitated one in his. Lydia didn't think she'd ever seen a man so gentle or so eminently capable of managing a situation alone.

'I'll wait in the village.'

Nick scarcely noticed she'd spoken; his mind and energy were focused entirely on Wendy Bennington.

*As it should be,* she reminded herself. Of course, he should be totally concerned about the sick woman.

Lydia reached inside an inner pocket of her handbag and pulled out a business card. 'Would you call me? I'd like to know how Ms Bennington is doing.'

He turned, his expression unreadable. If he wasn't a poker player, he ought to be. She couldn't tell whether he thought it reasonable that she wanted to know what happened to Wendy or whether he thought it an intrusion.

'Please?'

His face didn't change, but after a short pause he reached out and took her card. 'Make sure you leave the front door open,' he said, tucking it in the back pocket of his jeans.

Lydia supposed she had to take that as an agreement that he would call her. Whether he would remember to actually do it or not was a different matter.

Quietly she walked down the stairs and into the oppressively gloomy kitchen. Her briefcase was still by the rusting boiler where she'd left it. Lydia bent and picked it up, before taking a last opportunity to glance about her.

*Sad.* It was a truly sad place.

Slowly she walked along the hall and carefully put the front door on the latch. It was strange that Nick Regan let Wendy Bennington live in such a way. He so obviously loved her. It was in the way he'd brushed her hair off her forehead and held her hand.

So who was he? Why was he *so* concerned about Wendy Bennington? It surely went beyond being a mere friend, but his name hadn't appeared in her research. As far as she'd been able to ascertain, Wendy had no family at all. Not even a nephew. An only child of only children.

She walked down the narrow front path, mulling over the possibilities. At the gate she stopped, mouth open in disbelief. His car was parked immediately in front of her own—and her mother's wealth barometer had been spot on. Nick Regan drove a top of the range sports car. *So who the heck was he?*

Lydia opened her car door, feeling vaguely ashamed. There was something in her which made it impossible to switch off 'the journalist'. Why couldn't she merely be pleased that Wendy had someone who loved her? Wendy had lived her life entirely for other people; it was right that when she needed help herself there should be someone to give it. Someone who cared because they chose to, rather than doing so out of a sense of duty.

She tipped the front seat of her more modest car forward and slid in her briefcase. Perhaps she hadn't been so far adrift in thinking he was behaving like a son? *It had to be a possibility because what else was there?*

The engine purred into life and Lydia took a last glance back at the cottage through her rear-view mirror. He was the right kind of age. Thirty-four, maybe as much as thirty-eight. Certainly no more.

Perhaps he was the result of a passionate affair? She let her imagination soar. An affair with a married man? Or the husband of a friend? Or was he a sperm donor baby? Or…

She was getting ridiculous. If Wendy Bennington had ever been pregnant someone somewhere would have written about it. She glanced up again at her driver's mirror and groaned at the image she presented. Her hair was still bunched up in a childish topknot. Hardly the look of an award-winning journalist.

*Damn.*

She ripped out the scrunchie and let her hair fall softly around her shoulders. Nick bloody Regan probably thought she was some kind of tea girl rather than the woman his…friend…had chosen as her biographer.

It shouldn't matter. Lydia crunched her car into first gear. It *didn't* matter—at all. But…but this was not turning out to be a good day.

\* \* \*

Nick heard her leave. First her footsteps on the stairs and then the sound of her car pulling away. He let out his breath in a steady stream and tried to settle himself into a more comfortable position on the floor.

He hadn't expected Lydia Stanford would give up so easily. Her kind always stayed to the last. They circled overhead, waiting for the kill, like the scavengers they were. The wonder was that she hadn't whipped out her camera and taken some photographs as 'background colour'—or whatever she called it to salve her conscience.

Nick rested his head against the wall. There were other journalists, with far better credentials than Ms Stanford, who would have been more than anxious to write an authorised biography. Some he would have trusted to do a fair and balanced job of it.

But Lydia Stanford…

*No.* He wouldn't trust her as far as he could spit. What Wendy had been thinking of to insist on a woman capable of building her career by using her own sister's tragedy he couldn't imagine. You had to be an automaton to do what Lydia had done.

Any normal person would have been overcome by grief at her sister's attempted suicide. They'd have hung by her bedside, too traumatised to do anything else.

But not Lydia Stanford. Ms Stanford had launched an exhaustive vendetta against the man at the centre of the scandal. She'd meticulously collected information on his fraudulent business dealings, making sure she had enough to ruin him.

And in the process she'd made her own fortune. Not bad

going. *But what about the sister?* How did she feel about being a stepping stone in her sister's career?

Even his ex-wife, Ana, wouldn't have been so coldly calculating. He rubbed a hand across the spike of pain in his forehead. *Or just not as overt?* But that made precious little difference to the people around them. They still got hurt. Collateral damage in a game they didn't know they were playing.

One thing was certain; Wendy's decision to choose Lydia Stanford had nothing to do with the mane of honey-brown hair which she wore in that half up, half down sexy thing women did. Nor would Wendy have noticed the amber flecks in her brown eyes, or her long legs, or, he altered his position slightly, her unfortunate taste for his ex-wife's jacket design. Presumably Ms Stanford thought it worth selling her soul to be able to afford an Anastasia Wilson jacket. Now Ana would most certainly have approved of that.

Nick shifted uncomfortably on the floor, listening out for the sound of the ambulance. He stroked the hand in his lap. 'It can't be much longer, Wendy. Hang on in there for me.'

He watched the frown of concentration and heard the quietly determined, 'Apple.'

He leant closer. 'What about an apple?'

With total concentration she carefully repeated, 'Apple.'

It made no sense. Nick kept stroking her hand and tried to sound calm and reassuring. The minutes ticked by interminably slowly.

He tried to picture Lydia Stanford at that crucial junction making sure the ambulance crew didn't waste precious minutes. She'd do that, he decided. She might have ambition running through her veins where lesser mortals had blood, but he believed she'd take a few moments to help the woman whose biography she'd agreed to write.

Even Ana would have spared a few minutes from her hectic schedule. His smile twisted. Or perhaps not. Ana spared no thought for anyone but herself.

The garden gate banged and he sat a little straighter. *Thank God.* 'Up here,' he shouted.

He heard the mumble of voices as they came into the hall; seconds later a face appeared at the top of the stairs. 'Wendy Bennington, is it?' the woman said, taking in the slumped figure on the floor.

Nick nodded, standing up and brushing down his jeans.

'Your friend made sure we didn't miss the turning.' She knelt down and spoke to Wendy. 'I'm Sarah. We'll soon have you sorted, my love.'

# CHAPTER TWO

Izzy put a plate of spicy crab cakes and salad in front of her sister. 'So, tell me. What's the matter?' She sat down opposite Lydia and flicked back her softly waving hair. 'I might have overdone the chilli in the dipping sauce, so go careful.'

Lydia took a mouthful of the crab cake. 'This is fantastic.'

'I know. It's the Tobasco.'

'You're getting good.'

'I'm a genius,' Izzy said, smiling over the top of her glass of wine, 'but that's not why you're here, is it? What's happened?'

'You mean apart from Wendy Bennington having a stroke?'

Izzy nodded. 'Apart from that. Although it's horrible for her, of course. I don't mean it isn't, but…'

The silence hung between them.

'You've seen far worse things than an elderly woman having a stroke, Liddy.'

Which was true.

'So, what's bothering you?'

Lydia sighed and looked across at her younger sister, un-

certain as to what it was that was nagging at her. It seemed
to be a whole mixture of things twirling about in her head
making her feel discontented. Irritated. That wasn't the
right word either.

It was as though she'd been travelling happily in one direction only to have it violently blocked off. Like a train
being derailed, if you liked. Normally she'd have worked
out a way to make it an opportunity, but…

Lydia winced. It didn't feel like an opportunity. It felt—

She didn't know what it felt like. There was something
about seeing Wendy Bennington slumped in that doorway
that had affected her deeply—and in a way she found difficult to understand. Instead of driving back to Hammersmith
she'd rung Izzy and begged a bed for the night.

But why? Her sister was absolutely right when she said
she'd seen and experienced so much worse.

In her nine years as a journalist she'd witnessed many
terrible things. Not just death and injury, but mindless violence and examples of sadistic cruelty that defied description. Some days it was difficult to maintain any kind
of belief in the innate goodness of human nature, but she'd
trained herself to cope with it. She was inured against it all.

Almost.

Certainly detached. Lydia picked up her wineglass and
sipped. It was as if a steel screen came down and kept her
objective. It was the only way it was possible to do her job.
She imagined it was similar to the way a surgeon worked.
You could care, really deeply, but not so much that it pre-
vented you from thinking clearly.

She looked across at Izzy, patiently waiting, her hands
cradled around her wineglass. The only time in her life

when she'd felt completely out of control was when she'd found Izzy unconscious. There would never, could never, be any event more terrible than finding her sister had taken an overdose.

She hadn't felt detached then. That night she'd experienced emotions she hadn't known she was capable of feeling. She'd believed Izzy would die and fear had ripped through her like lightning in a night sky. There'd been the sense of being utterly alone and desperately frightened. Not even the unexpected death of her parents had inspired such an extreme reaction.

The only thing that had kept her functioning, on any level, was the passionate hatred she felt for Steven Daly—the man responsible. Bitter anger had uncurled like a serpent within her. It had driven her. Had demanded retribution.

Looking at Izzy now, little more than two years on, it could almost have been a dream. She looked so young—and hopeful. Time was a great healer.

'Well?' Izzy prompted.

Lydia forced a smile. 'I think it was the house,' she said at last, trying to put words on thoughts she couldn't quite catch hold of. 'You've never seen anything like it. She lives in a cottage that time's all but forgotten. All alone in the middle of nowhere.'

'Perhaps she likes solitude? Some people do.'

'It's not that… It's…' Lydia frowned. 'The cottage smells of damp and cat urine…and then there are all these frozen meals for one in the freezer. It's so incredibly…sad. There's no other word for it—' She broke off. 'Oh, no!'

'What?'

'I'd forgotten about the cat.' Lydia put down her wine-glass. 'She's got a cat.'

'It's not your problem, Liddy.'

'But who's going to feed it?'

'Probably the irritating Nick Regan. It really isn't your problem,' Izzy repeated, taking in her sister's expression. 'If not him, there'll be a neighbour.'

'You think?'

'There's bound to be.'

Lydia relaxed. *Of course there was.* Wendy Bennington went abroad for long stretches of time. There were bound to be structures in place to take care of her pet. Lydia picked up her knife and fork. 'You're right. I know you're right. It's just…'

Izzy smiled. 'You really like this Wendy Bennington, don't you?'

'I hardly know her.' Lydia cut a bite-sized piece off her crab cake. 'We've spoken on the phone half a dozen times, no more. I'd never met her face to face.' Until today—when she'd been confused and frightened. Nothing like the woman she'd been expecting. The image of her slumped in her bedroom doorway hovered at the front of Lydia's mind.

'But you like her. I can tell you do.'

Lydia paused, fork halfway to her mouth. *Did that explain it?* She certainly admired Wendy. Had been flattered and very excited at the prospect of writing her biography.

Izzy seemed to follow her thoughts. 'There's no reason to think you won't still write the biography. Give it a few days and see how serious her stroke was. You might be surprised.'

'I might,' she conceded.

'Perhaps that Nick Regan will phone you.'

Lydia pulled a face. 'I'd be surprised at that. He didn't like me at all.'

'Why?'

'No idea.' Lydia thought for a moment. 'It didn't help that he found me standing on a flat roof, trying to get into the cottage through an upstairs window, but—' she looked up as Izzy gave a sudden spurt of laughter '—I don't think it was that.'

'I can't think why. Most people would think it odd.'

Lydia shook her head, a reluctant twinkle in her eyes. 'It probably didn't help,' she conceded, cutting another mouthful off her crab cake, 'but he *really* didn't like me. At all. You know, eyes across a crowded room, instantaneous dislike. No mistaking it.'

'Is he handsome?' Izzy sat back.

'That's irrelevant.'

'It's never irrelevant.'

Lydia ignored her.

'Well, is he?'

'No.' Even without looking up she could feel Izzy smile. She put down her fork. 'Not exactly.'

'Which means he is.'

'It does not!'

And then Izzy laughed again. 'He is, though. I searched for his name on the Internet while you were having your shower. He's gorgeous. A bit like…what's the name of that actor in… Oh, stuff it, I can't remember. Regency thing. You used to have him as your screensaver.'

'The actor from *Pride and Prejudice?* Nick Regan looks nothing like him!' Lydia protested.

'Not exactly, but a bit. He's got the same brooding, intense expression. At least, this Nick Regan does. He's an inventor. I think.' She waved her hand as though it didn't matter in the slightest. 'Basically, he *is* Drakes, if you get what I mean. He owns the company and came up with the idea of the electrical component in the first place. Worth millions.'

Lydia frowned. 'He can't be. That's Nicolas…' *Regan-Phillips.* She closed her eyes. *Damn it!* It couldn't be.

Could it? And, if so, what *had* he got to do with Wendy Bennington?

'I've bookmarked it for you to see.'

'I'll look later.'

Could Nick Regan be Nicolas Regan-Phillips? Izzy must have made a mistake. A multimillionaire corporate businessman and a human rights campaigner—what could possibly link the two together?

The cottage had been securely locked up. Lydia moved the terracotta pot with very little expectation of finding the key beneath it—but there it was.

She clutched the small tin of cat food and bent to pick up the key. If the almighty Nicolas Regan-Phillips had anticipated she might return to the cottage he might not have put it back there. So much for his apparently awesome ability to read character, but at least the cat wouldn't starve.

The back door opened easily. Izzy had laughed at her for deciding on making the thirty minute detour, but it felt like the right thing to do. How could she return to London knowing she could have done something to help Wendy but had chosen not to? And this was little enough.

'Cat,' she called softly. She set her handbag on the stainless steel draining board. 'Cat, where are you? Breakfast time.'

The bowl of leftover cat food on the floor looked revolting. Lydia picked it up with two fingers and carried it across to a plastic swing-bin. 'Why do people keep pets?' she mumbled softly to herself, turning back to the sink and giving the bowl a swill out. 'This is disgusting.'

'To keep them company?'

Lydia gave a startled cry and whipped round.

'Because they love them?' Nicolas Regan-Phillips said, leaning against the kitchen doorway, looking much more like the photograph Izzy had found than he had the day before. He wore a sharp and very conventional pinstripe suit. Power dressing at its most effective.

And he *was* handsome. Her sister's words popped into her mind and she silently cursed her. The resemblance to her favorite actor was really very superficial, but it was there all the same.

'I—I came to feed the cat.' Lydia turned away and pulled back the loop on the tin, irritated at the slight nervous stutter. *Where had that come from?* And, more importantly, why?

'So did I.' He placed a brown paper bag down on the draining board.

'I hope you don't mind that I—' She stopped herself, swinging round to look up at him as a new thought occurred to her. 'How did you get in?'

He held up a key. 'Front door.'

'Oh.' Lydia cursed herself for the inanity of her reply. Of course he would have Wendy's key. He would have needed it to lock up the cottage. What was the matter with her?

She carefully scooped out the contents of the tin with a spoon, aware that Nick continued to watch her. He made her feel uncomfortable, as though, perhaps, she'd been caught out doing something he considered wrong rather than the good deed she'd intended. 'I suddenly remembered I'd seen a cat. I couldn't leave it to starve,' she said, glancing up.

He really did have the most inscrutable face. Normally she was good at picking up emotional nuances—but Nicholas Regan-Phillips seemed to short circuit some connection and she was left uncertain.

On balance he didn't seem as angry as he'd been yesterday. More suspicious. She looked away. It probably wasn't anything personal. He had a reputation for avoiding journalists and for protecting his privacy. Lydia swilled out the empty tin under the tap. 'Does Wendy have a recycling bin?'

'I imagine so.'

Lydia looked up in time to catch his swift frown. If she puzzled him she was glad. He certainly puzzled her. What had he to do with Wendy Bennington? She hadn't managed to discover any connection at all. It was a mystery—and mysteries really bugged her.

'Shall I leave this on the side then?'

'I'm sure that'll be fine.'

Lydia carefully placed the tin at the back of the draining board and rinsed the spoon. 'How's Wendy?'

There was a small beat of silence while, it seemed, he evaluated her right to ask the question. 'Better than she looked yesterday.'

Lydia glanced over her shoulder, a question in her eyes.

'She's had a TIA. A mini-stroke, if you like. She'll be fine.' His mouth quirked into a half-smile. It was a nice mouth, firm and sensual. 'No permanent damage, but she's been told to make some life changes.'

'That's…fantastic.'

His smile broadened and something inside her flickered in recognition. 'I'd love to hear you try and convince her of that.'

'When will she be home?'

'Well—' he stretched out the word '—that depends on who you speak to. She's broken her ankle. It's a fairly simple break, apparently, and doesn't need surgery, but…'

Lydia looked around her and then down at the uneven floor levels.

Nick followed her gaze. 'Exactly. She's not going to manage here for a few weeks, however much she'd rather be in her own home.'

'No,' Lydia agreed. She placed the clean bowl back on the floor and picked up the other one. 'So, who's won?'

'The cards are stacked in my favour. I'm here to pick up Nimrod. Hopefully lure him in with food.'

Lydia emptied the water into the sink and put in some fresh. 'That's the cat?'

'Nimrod, the mighty hunter,' Nick agreed, moving away into the hall, his voice slightly muffled. 'I gather his namesake was Noah's great-grandson.' He reappeared moments later, carrying a cat basket.

'Great name,' she said, smiling at the incongruous sight of a city gent with rustic cat basket.

'Certainly appropriate. He's something of a killer cat. Wendy picked him up as a stray a couple of years ago, only he turned out not to be so much a waif as a con artist. If it moves, Nimrod will hunt it. There never was a cat more suited to life in the wild.'

Lydia laughed. 'Good luck getting it into that thing then,' she said with a gesture at the cat basket.

'So Wendy's warned me,' he said, setting it down on the kitchen table.

She rinsed her hands under the tap. 'I'm glad it's all sorted. It suddenly occurred to me, after I'd left, that you might forget about…Nimrod. I was going to contact you today.'

'How?'

She looked up, surprised by the abrupt single word question. 'It wouldn't have been too difficult. A call to your company…'

His nod was almost imperceptible, but she could see his attitude towards her change. 'I thought you didn't know who I was.'

'I didn't, but you have an Internet presence—'

'And you checked.'

Lydia thought of Izzy and smiled, deciding that she wouldn't tell him that her description of him had inspired her sister with a burning fascination to discover who had managed to rile her so much. There'd been little enough information to find, nothing he could object to.

He was thirty-six and divorced. His only child, a daughter, lived with her mother and he was hugely successful at what he did. Nothing particularly unusual in any of that.

'Do you always pry into other people's business?'

'Pretty much.' She looked about her for a towel on which to dry her hands. 'It's an occupational hazard. But, this time, you've got to acknowledge I was invited to pry.'

'Not by me.'

'By Wendy.' She turned to face him. 'Though I dispute the use of the word pry.'

His eyes narrowed. 'Do you?'

'She's led an amazing life. Don't you think it's in the public interest to have that properly chronicled? What she's achieved, particularly for women, is amazing.'

'I think what's deemed to be "in the public interest" is stretched beyond belief,' he said dryly, 'but that's not to undermine what Wendy has achieved.'

'Can't argue with that, I suppose—but I'm not here as a representative of any tabloid paper. Wendy will have complete control over what I write about her and, as long as it's truthful, I've no problem with that.'

'No?'

'Absolutely not.'

She sounded aghast, but Nick knew better. Confronting Lydia Stanford was like coming up against a snake in the grass. You could never trust her. Never.

Very early in her career she'd worked undercover to highlight the ill treatment of the elderly in care homes and, while you couldn't question the validity of her findings…you had to be suspicious of her ability to lie. And lie convincingly enough for colleagues to trust her.

Wendy might be impressed by her ability to stick to her purpose, of owning a cause and staying with it, whatever the personal cost—but he suspected a different motivation lay at the heart of it. He suspected her only cause was herself—Lydia Stanford. And where was the virtue in that?

She carefully folded the towel and threaded it back through the loop. 'So how do you know Wendy?'

'You don't give up, do you?'

Lydia smiled, her eyes the colour of topaz. Warm and beguiling. 'It's usually easier to give in and tell me what I want to know.'

He turned away as though that would stop him being drawn in. 'She's my godmother.'

'Really?'

'I have the rattle to prove it.'

She laughed. It was the kind of laugh that made him wish she was a different woman—and they were in a different situation. He ran an irritated hand through his hair. *He'd been celibate for far too long.* That rich throaty chuckle was exactly what could make him forget who and what she was.

'Actually, that's a lie. She didn't give me a rattle. I received two engraved napkin rings and a boxed china bowl and plate set from the other two.'

'And from Wendy?'

'A copy of the Bible, the Koran and the complete works of William Shakespeare.'

He watched the way her eyes crinkled into laughter. She was dangerous. You could easily relax in her company, forget that she used anyone and everyone near her to further her career—even a vulnerable sister.

People often described him as ruthless, but he would never have taken something so intensely personal and used it to advance his career. Lydia Stanford might claim that her sister had made a complete recovery, but he doubted it.

Betrayal was painful—acutely painful—and when it came so close to home it was difficult to ever recover from it. He had personal experience of it and her Anastasia Wilson jacket was a visual reminder.

Better to remember how that betrayal had felt. Better to remember how much pain the woman who'd decreed that jacket should be in precisely that caramel colour had inflicted. It didn't matter that it exactly picked out a shade in Lydia Stanford's long hair. Or that it accentuated a narrow waist and visually lengthened her legs.

It was a warning. And only a fool would ignore it.

'Have you read them?'

'What?' He brought Lydia back into focus. Her lips parted into a smile, showing her even teeth. The woman was stunning. Like a sleek lioness. A mixture of sunshine and fire.

'Have you read them all yet? The Bible, the Koran and the complete works of Shakespeare?'

'By the age of thirty-two.'

'I'm impressed.'

'I've never used the napkin rings, though,' he returned and was rewarded by the same sexy laugh. Hell, it did something to his insides that didn't bear thinking about.

He closed his hand round the handle of the cat basket. 'Have you seen Nimrod?'

'Not yet, but I'm sure he'll come in for food some time. He can't have had anything to eat since yesterday morning.'

Nick glanced down at his wristwatch. 'He'll have to do it in the next twenty minutes or I'll be out of time.' He strode over to the back door and called.

'Do cats come when you call?'

He looked over his shoulder. 'No idea.' Lydia was smiling, bright eyes ready to laugh and, God help him, he wanted to laugh back.

'Look, why don't you let me try and catch Nimrod? I can stay until he comes in for food.'

'I couldn't ask you to do that. I—'

'Why ever not?' She shook back her hair. 'You're obviously busy and I'm on holiday.'

'On holiday?'

Her smile twisted. 'I should be in Vienna. I flew back when I heard Wendy wanted me to write her biography.'

'You broke off your holiday?' He couldn't quite believe it. What a pointless gesture. His godmother would have been more than happy to wait. There was nothing so important about the precise timing of this meeting which meant it couldn't have been postponed.

'Guilty as charged. Over-developed work ethic.' She smiled, but this time it didn't have the same effect. Nick could see a different face.

It was none of his business whether or not Lydia Stanford chose to curtail her holiday, but it reminded him of Ana. Still, four years after she'd left, he thought about her most days. There were reasons for that, of course. Good reasons.

In the three years they'd been married Ana had never taken a holiday. Had never turned off her cellphone. It was a price she'd been prepared to pay to achieve her goals. He couldn't deny she'd been totally honest about that from the very beginning, and at the start he'd admired her for it.

Presumably Lydia Stanford would agree that that kind of commitment was necessary. They were wrong.

'I've got the laptop in the car. I can work here and drive Nimrod over to you later.' She looked across at him. 'It's not a problem.'

Nick glanced down at his watch. It was tempting to accept her offer. He had back-to-back meetings scheduled for the morning and paperwork that really needed looking at after that, besides squeezing in a visit to the hospital. But to accept meant…

She seemed to read his mind. 'Don't worry. I shan't take it as an endorsement of your godmother's choice of biographer.' She met his eyes. 'By the way, what is your problem with me?'

'Have I said there's a problem?' he countered.

'You haven't needed to. It's obvious.'

He hesitated. 'Wendy is capable of making her own decisions. In fact, she would strongly resent my interference in what doesn't concern me.'

Even in his own head his reply sounded pompous and formal. Famed for his 'tell it like it is' approach to business, how had he become so verbally challenged when confronted by a beautiful…?

What was she? Not a blonde or a brunette. Richer than a blonde and lighter than a brunette.

'I don't believe that for a minute.'

He looked up.

'Oh, I believe Wendy doesn't like interference in her business. I'm like that myself, but—' her eyes met his '—but I don't believe you don't tell her what you think. I've seen you two together, remember.'

He felt a small muscle pulse in his cheek. 'I don't want her hurt.'

'I won't.'

And, strangely, he believed her. There was an innate honesty in those rich eyes that made him want to trust her. Was that how she worked? Was it a highly cultivated technique which persuaded the unsuspecting to share their innermost secrets?

'If you slander her in any way I'll sue you.'

She didn't flinch. 'An authorised biography is just that—authorised.' Then her face softened. 'You really love her, don't you?'

'She's a special lady.'

'So I gather.' Lydia slipped her arms out of her jacket and placed it over the chair by the table. 'You can trust me. Where do you want me to take Nimrod to? Do you have a housekeeper to receive him?'

*A housekeeper. A nanny. A daughter.*

He didn't trust her. Not with one atom of his body. If he left Lydia in the cottage she would, no doubt, look around. She'd open drawers and search through Wendy's possessions. But then, Wendy herself had argued that she'd nothing to hide.

Let her search.

'My housekeeper is Mrs Pearman. Christine Pearman.' It felt as if he'd lost some unspoken battle. 'Did your research on me extend to knowing where I live?'

As soon as the words left his mouth he regretted his phrasing of them. Lydia Stanford was doing him a favour. Even if she did have an unacknowledged agenda of her own.

'You weren't that much of an interest, but I'm sure I can find out with a couple of phone calls if you want to make it a game.'

He'd deserved that, Nick thought as he fished in his pocket and pulled out his card case. 'It's a ten, fifteen minute drive from here. No more.' He scribbled down the address. 'I'll ring Christine and let her know to expect you. You'll need to phone up to the house when you arrive and they'll open the gates.'

Lydia took the card and looked down at it.

'If you need to leave before Nimrod puts in an appearance, I'd be grateful if you'd leave a message with my secretary and I'll come back this evening. The number's on the front. It's a direct line through to her. I don't want you to feel you have to sit here for hours.'

She turned the card over. 'It's not a problem.'

'No, well…thank you.'

Her eyes flashed up. 'You're welcome.'

'I'll lock the front door. If you leave the key beneath the flowerpot…'

'No problem,' she said again.

There was nothing left to do. 'The cage is here.' He pointed at the cat basket.

'Yes.'

It was just leaving that was the problem. It was walking back down the hall and shutting the door.

*Trust.* This was about trust. About leaving her alone in Wendy's cottage.

*Or was it?* There was the suspicion that this was about more than that. There was something about her golden aura that touched him. He knew it—and he was almost certain she did.

Danger. Fire. And Lydia Stanford. Like the Holy Trinity they belonged together.

'Thank you.'

'Give Wendy my…' *Love.* She'd been about to say love. Hardly appropriate for a woman she didn't know. 'Best wishes.'

His hand went to his tie. 'I'll do that.'

Lydia made herself smile. She didn't know what was

going on here. There were undercurrents she didn't understand. 'Perhaps she'll ring me when she feels...ready?'

'I'm sure she will.'

And then he left. Awkwardly—and she had no idea why. Why was it she felt so uncomfortable round Nicholas Regan-Phillips? It wasn't as if she wasn't used to men with influence and money. She was.

She heard the front door click shut and gazed about Wendy Bennington's tired kitchen. *What the heck was she doing?* And, more importantly, *why* was she doing it?

It was true, what she'd told Nicholas Regan-Phillips, she did have the time. This was her holiday.

*Nicholas Regan-Phillips.* What a mouthful of a name. Nick Regan. *His* Nick Regan suited him far better.

Lydia filled the old limescale encrusted kettle and set it on the gas hob. It was just so out of character for her to have agreed to kick her heels in such a place.

*Why would she do that?* This wasn't her problem.

But Nick Regan was, that little voice that sat some way to the left of her shoulder whispered. He was arrogant, rude, supercilious...and sexy. Lydia searched around for a coffee mug. Bizarrely, Nick Regan was very, very sexy— and he was probably the reason she'd agreed to stay.

Now, if Izzy knew that...

# CHAPTER THREE

SOME decisions just weren't good ones. Lydia glanced over at the cat basket, ridiculously pleased to see that Nimrod was safely locked inside.

There was no man, or woman, on earth who warranted the kind of self-sacrifice she'd endured today. Wendy's cottage was an unpleasant place to kick your heels for the best part of a day and Nimrod was the kind of cat who should be certified—and she had the scratches to prove it.

Lydia changed gear to negotiate a particularly tight bend. She'd gone wrong at the moment when she'd said it would be no problem to stay. She should have cited a mountainous pile of laundry and the possibility of a phone call from her former editor as reasons she *had* to be back in London.

Instead, she'd endured hours sitting on an uncomfortable sofa with a laptop perched on a melamine tray before being…well, here…and on her way to Nicholas Regan-Phillips's domestic empire. Though that part didn't bother her. She had to admit she had a rabid curiosity to see what it would be like.

There'd been any number of Internet articles about Drakes but Nicholas Regan-Phillips 'the man' had emerged as something of a mystery. It was pure nosiness, of course, but when fate landed you an opportunity like this one she was not the woman to let it go to waste. She was just dying to see what kind of place he called home, considered it reparation for an otherwise completely wasted day.

Another four miles and an unexpected sharp bend and the gates of Fenton Hall loomed impressively out of a quiet country lane. Lydia pulled the car to a gentle stop. The house itself was completely hidden from view. The gates were well over six feet high, tightly shut and were edged by equally high stone walls. It was taking a desire for privacy to rather extreme lengths.

She reached into her jacket pocket for his business card and came out empty. *Where had she put the blasted thing?* She leant over to pull her handbag off the back seat and flipped open the soft leather. His card was tucked in the small front pocket.

Lydia keyed in the number he'd written on the reverse and within seconds she was answered. 'Hello. I…er…I need…' she searched for the name on the business card '…I need…Christine Pearman. I'm delivering Nimrod, Wendy Bennington's cat. Mr Regan-Phillips said he'd phone…?'

'Oh, yes. Yes, of course.' The voice on the other end sounded distracted and agitated. 'I'll let you in. Can you tell me when you are inside?'

'Okay.' Lydia tossed the mobile on to her lap as the wide gates started to swing open. 'Okay, I'm through,' she said moments later.

'You haven't seen anyone, have you? No one's gone out?'

'No.'

'No one at all?'

*Good grief!* This was getting rather ridiculous. Lydia looked doubtfully at the receiver. If the voice at the other end belonged to Christine Pearman it sounded as if the other woman ought to be more careful about the films she watched. 'There's no one here but me.'

'If you follow the drive up, I'll meet you at the front.'

Lydia shrugged. *How bizarre.* The drive meandered gently until she stopped in front of a spectacular house. It was the kind that had been designed along the established order of what was considered beautiful. There were just the right number of windows either side of an impressive entrance. Wide steps curved up to a front door that would have made Izzy's artistic heart drool.

Conservative estimate: upwards of two million pounds worth of 'Arts and Crafts' real estate. She leant across to speak softly to Nimrod. 'Not a bad holiday pad. Quite a contrast from home.'

Lydia unfastened her seat belt and climbed out, catching sight of a beautifully manicured lawn stretching out to the side of the house. It was a stunning place. Which made it strange, surely, for such a wealthy man to leave a godmother he loved with so little?

She lifted out the cat basket. Why not set her up with a little cottage in the grounds? There was bound to be one. Probably more than one.

'Lydia Stanford?'

Lydia spun round. 'Yes. I have… Nimrod.'

'Mr Regan-Phillips did telephone,' the other woman said with a nod. Her eyes looked past Lydia and seemed to scan the bushes behind her.

It was strange, preoccupied behaviour. She'd expected

to be asked in for a cup of tea or something—a chance to see inside the inner sanctum of Nicholas Regan-Phillips's impressive home. A chance to glean some snippet of information she could regale Izzy with.

Instead the housekeeper seemed completely distracted. Her face was agitated and her eyes were continually darting around as though she were searching for something.

'Are you all right?' Lydia asked abruptly.

'Yes, I…' the other woman broke off '…that is…'

There was the sound of tyres on gravel and the housekeeper looked round. 'Thank heaven!'

Lydia turned round in time to see Nicholas Regan-Phillips's dark green Jaguar twist up the drive. She watched as he climbed out of the driver's seat and slammed the door shut.

Actually, she thought dispassionately, he was sexier than she'd first thought—if that was possible. He was taller, sharper. He looked as though he was used to the world working exactly as he wished it would. And there was something incredibly attractive about that.

She watched as his housekeeper surged forward, stopping him, the hapless Nimrod still imprisoned in the cat basket. Lydia caught no more than snatches of their conversation, words carried back to her on the breeze. 'We thought she was sleeping—'

Nick looked past her and his eyes locked with Lydia's. He crossed towards her, his feet scrunching on the gravel. 'I'm sorry. It seems my daughter, Rosie, has gone missing,' he explained quietly.

Instantly Lydia's mind flew through possible options. Was it possible she'd been kidnapped?

Something of that must have shown on her face because he added, 'It's something she does quite frequently. The grounds are fully enclosed; I'm sure there's nothing to worry about.'

Lydia frowned, trying to remember what she'd read in that Internet article. She was sure his daughter had been very young, but his words seemed to suggest he was the father of a teenager. 'How old is she?'

'Five.'

*Five!* He was remarkably unconcerned for a man who had misplaced his *very* young child. And wasn't he divorced from her mother? No doubt she wouldn't be quite so laid back if she knew he *kept* losing their daughter.

'How long has she been missing?' he asked, turning back to the housekeeper.

Christine was considerably agitated. 'No more than forty minutes. Sophie went in and checked on her before she came down for a cup of tea. We've searched the house thoroughly—'

'And down by the lake?' he cut in abruptly.

'Arthur and Tom are there now.'

His nod was decisive, as though he approved. Lydia glanced from one to the other. He clearly didn't expect anything other than that his daughter had lost herself in the grounds—which, lake aside, was probably fine.

His housekeeper obviously disagreed. Her face was pinched with worry and she clasped and unclasped her hands. 'She packed a bag this time. She's even taken her toothbrush...' Christine broke off and searched up her sleeve for a handkerchief.

Which meant, of course, that five-year-old Rosie had

made a decision to run away. Which meant she was un-happy. And, she 'kept' doing it—so she was very unhappy.

Now *that* should worry a father. Lydia glanced up at him and saw very little sign of emotion. Not much more than a flash of irritation in those clever eyes—and whether the root cause was Christine or his errant daughter she couldn't be sure.

His eyes flicked across to her…and then she under-stood in a sudden blinding flash of comprehension. His problem was with *her*. Or, more specifically, with her over-hearing his private business.

*As if she'd write anything about his daughter…*

Unless, of course, she discovered he was a bad parent. That would be different, she conceded silently. Then she just might…

Or might not. She wouldn't write anything that hurt a child. And it irritated her that he didn't instinctively *know* that about her.

Lydia caught herself up on her thoughts. It didn't mat-ter what he thought of her—or her profession. What mat-tered was an unhappy little girl hiding out in her father's grounds. And he ought to be looking for her.

'I'm in the way. I'll leave you to it…'

She was certain she saw a glimmer of relief. He held out his hand. 'Thank you for bringing Nimrod.'

'It's no bother,' she lied, automatically stretching out her own hand.

He had a good handshake, firm and decided, and she had the oddest sense of regret that he didn't like her. For some reason it hurt that he didn't trust her. She'd had people spit venom at her, but this bothered her more because it was so

unwarranted. As far as she knew, she'd never met him before yesterday, had never met anyone who knew him well.
So why?

'I've… I've put the key back under the pot.' He released
her hand. Lydia reached inside her jacket pocket for her car
key. 'Do let me know if there's any change with Wendy…'

He nodded.

'And—' she forced a bright smile '—I hope you find
your daughter quickly.'

'Thank you. Ring to the house as before and Christine
will open the gates.'

She nodded and, with a swift smile at the distraught housekeeper, Lydia turned towards her car. It was disappointing not
to have seen inside his house. She'd have liked to have known
whether Nick Regan-Phillips's tastes leant towards minimal-
ism or whether he was a staunch traditionalist.

She started the engine. Probably the latter. She could
imagine his home would be filled with tasteful antiques
sourced by others. Dining chairs designed by Rennie
Macintosh perhaps? That would suit the age of his house.
He probably saw them as long-term investments rather
than objects of beauty. He struck her as someone who
wouldn't choose anything based on an emotional response.

Which was a shame, because he had real potential.
Lydia slipped the car into second gear and glanced in her
rear-view mirror in time to see him turn and walk slowly
up the steps. He was sexy. In that British, uptight, public
school kind of way.

*Why was that so attractive?* She smiled. There was something about a repressed male that made her want to roughen
him up. See what was bubbling beneath the surface.

And with Nick Regan-Phillips there must be something. Drakes wasn't the kind of success that happened by chance—or even because of the old boy network. It had happened because of passion. And drive. And brilliance. There was no denying that. Whatever else he was, Nicholas Regan-Phillips was a brilliantly clever man.

Out of the corner of her eye she caught sight of a flash of red. A single glimpse of it and then it vanished behind a lush camellia. Instinctively she slowed down, her eyes searching for confirmation of what she thought she'd seen.

*Rosie?*

Or someone searching for her? Lydia pulled the car to a gentle stop, uncertain what she should do. This was not her concern—but when had that ever stopped her?

With sudden energy she climbed out of the car and leant on the open door. 'Rosie?'

She waited, listening closely.

'Is that you?'

There was no answer. Which either meant there was no one there or that Rosie didn't want to be found. Lydia hesitated. This was not her business and she was almost certain Nick Regan-Phillips would prefer her to leave him to deal with his missing daughter. But if she asked for the gates to be opened and Rosie slipped out she'd never forgive herself.

She shut the door and moved off the gravel path. 'Rosie? Everyone is looking for you.'

Still nothing.

Slowly she walked round a large camellia, her eyes searching for another tell-tale scarlet flash among the shrubs. 'Rosie?'

In spring and early summer, when the rhododendrons were in flower, this would be the most incredible sight, exotic and beautiful—but there was no sign of a five-year-old girl anywhere. Lydia shrugged, disappointed. She must have been mistaken.

Lydia threaded her way back along the path, but as she stepped out on to the gravel drive she saw a second flash of red. This time she didn't call out, but quickened her pace. She wasn't familiar with children, particularly those as young as five, but if this one was purposely running away from home she wasn't going to want to be found.

Nipping through a narrow gap, Lydia was surprised to find…anything. She stopped abruptly, amazed to see a child standing quietly beside the grass verge. She hesitated, uncertain what to say to a five-year-old she'd never seen before and who had run away from home. 'Are you Rosie? Everyone is searching for you.'

The little girl stared back at her. Not frightened, more curious. Lydia risked moving closer. Rosie's dark curling hair was tied up in one high pony-tail and she was wearing a bright red dress and white lacy cardigan. She looked more like a doll than a real living breathing girl.

But that was clearly a deceptive impression. Rosie obviously had a will of iron and at her feet lay an overfilled lime-green backpack to prove it.

'My name is Lydia…' she began, tailing off when she caught sight of something tucked behind Rosie's right ear. It was almost imperceptible because of the hair, but…unmistakable. Rosie wore a hearing-aid. In fact, as she looked closer she could see that she wore two.

*Rosie was deaf.*

Lydia stood absolutely still. Her mind worked quickly. This explained why the housekeeper was so worried. Why she'd asked whether anyone had been near when the gates had opened.

If Rosie couldn't hear when she called… And no one knew where she'd gone…

It would be a nightmare and if the little girl was determined not to be found…The grounds were extensive. It would take hours to search them properly.

She looked directly at Rosie and placed two fingers to her ear in the sign for 'deaf'.

Slowly the little girl nodded, her brown eyes wide and curious. Her fingers moved against her own ear and then pointed at her chest.

It had been a long time since Lydia had signed. A very long time. She was probably going to be very rusty, but there had to be something remaining of her first language. Her mother had used it always. It was the first memory Lydia had. Speech had come through friends and playgroup, television and social workers.

Lydia smiled and sat down on the grass verge. Making sure Rosie could see her mouth, she carefully finger-spelt L-y-d-i-a—followed by her sign name. It had been picked by her father because he thought she had bright, wide eyes. It brought back so many memories. Memories of her childhood. Friday evenings, the first in every month, spent at the local deaf club, where she had seen her parents relaxed and happy as they rarely had been outside their home.

Rosie's fingers moved rapidly and Lydia struggled to follow. She was out of practice. She picked up something

about a row. At least she thought it was the sign for 'row'—
it might have been 'war', but that wasn't as likely.

*Why couldn't she remember?*

Hating the slowness with which she had to reply, Lydia
tried to tell Rosie that her father was back at the house and
it was time to go home. The little girl looked thoughtful
and then shook her head.

*Why?* Lydia made the sign on the right-hand side of
her chest.

Rosie signed again. The same quick movements, but this
time Lydia understood perfectly. Rosie didn't want to go
home unless Lydia would tell her father why she'd run away.

To Rosie it probably seemed quite simple for a complete
stranger to tell Nick Regan-Phillips why his child kept trying to escape. But Rosie was only five. She couldn't possibly understand that between adults things were much
more complicated.

Nick would probably consider it interfering. Lydia
thought for a moment. It couldn't matter. Even if he
thought she was stepping way over the line he'd be grateful she'd brought Rosie home safely.

Lydia looked Rosie straight in the eye and signed 'yes'.
Then she held out her hand and, with complete trust, Rosie
put her own inside it. *Could it really be that easy?*

She glanced across at her car, wondering whether it
would be right to persuade a child who didn't know her to
get in it. On balance, she thought not. Of course, encouraging her to walk off with a stranger wasn't a great idea
either, but what was the alternative? At least they were still
within the grounds of Fenton Hall and the important thing
was to get her home.

It was also important to keep her promise. She'd managed to understand Rosie enough to realise how important it was. Someone had shouted at her and Rosie was sad. The two little fingers moving rapidly across her open palm had been her running into the garden. She'd packed her bag and run away.

Slowly the long-forgotten signs were coming back.

Rosie let go of her hand and tapped her arm to draw her attention. Lydia stopped and looked down as the little girl's fingers moved more rapidly than she could hope to follow. From nowhere Lydia seemed to be able to pull the sign for 'quick'. *'Too quick,'* she told Rosie and squatted down in front of her.

And the sign for 'again'. Two bounces of the first two fingers held straight. *'Again, please.'*

Rosie's face broke into a gentle smile. Watching carefully to see she was understood, she told Lydia she didn't like Sophie. That Sophie was cross. Sophie shouted. And that she wanted to find her grandma.

Lydia nodded her understanding.

Then Rosie asked her to tell her father that she wanted Sophie to go. She didn't wait to see what Lydia would reply. She picked up her lime-green backpack and tucked her hand back inside Lydia's.

*Who the heck was Sophie?* And what had she done to make Rosie dislike her so much? Lydia glanced down at the tiny figure beside her. She didn't look particularly cowed by whatever Sophie had done. She looked more like a determined little thing who was very used to getting her own way.

Until she knew otherwise, she was inclined to give the unknown Sophie the benefit of the doubt, but she would tell Nick what his daughter had said. Clearly Rosie felt she needed an advocate. Now that was something she was good at.

Nick held up his hand to stop the two women talking at the same time, both more than anxious to justify why his daughter's running away hadn't been anything to do with them. *God help him.* What exactly did he pay them for if it wasn't to keep Rosie safe?

'Let's deal with all of this when we know where Rosie is. Has anyone thought to look in the summerhouse?'

Christine looked affronted. 'I looked there myself. And searched the house thoroughly. I will lay my life on it she's not inside.'

Nick nodded. He was in no mood to pander to his house-keeper's wounded pride. Sophie looked belligerent beside her. As a nanny she clearly left a great deal to be desired. She might have had the most amazing references but she was lazy. If he'd known more about Rosie's needs he wouldn't have accepted Sophie into his home in the first place. She might have all the latest theories but she didn't seem to like children very much—or maybe it was just Rosie she didn't like?

Rosie certainly didn't like her. Perhaps they were simply incompatible and it was a mutual thing. As soon as he had a moment, he'd have to look into finding a more suitable replacement. Preferably someone who was specifically used to looking after a deaf child.

Ana had said it was difficult enough finding someone who was used to respecting the privacy of the family she was employed by without adding the impossible criterion of sign language. Clearly he had to try.

He sighed. 'Let's get this straight. You put Rosie to bed early—'

'For spitting,' Sophie cut in. 'I told her that the only excuse for that kind of behaviour was that she was tired.'

Nick drew a weary hand through his hair. 'And went down for a cup of tea?'

'I left her to think about what she'd done. I—'

'And neither of you heard her come back downstairs?' They looked at each other. 'Or go out through the front door?'

'I can't understand how it had been left open. I'm sure—'

Nick held up his hand again and Christine fell into silence. 'I'm sure you can't,' he said dryly, breaking off as there was a knock at the door. 'What is it?'

A second knock and he strode over and flung open the door, his voice freezing as he saw Rosie and Lydia standing in the doorway.

Lydia smiled, her hand poised to knock again. 'I caught sight of her as I was leaving and I—'

'You've found her!' Christine let out a cry of relief and ran forward to try and hug the little girl. 'I was so worried about you.'

Rosie stood stiffly, her little face stony and totally unreceptive to the embrace. But what amazed Lydia was that Christine hadn't made sure her mouth could be lip-read. In fact she hugged the little girl so closely that her words were completely lost in Rosie's hair, regardless of how much she might have caught with the help of her hearing-aids.

Lydia looked up at Nick. 'I saw a flash of red behind a camellia bush and went to investigate.'

'Thank you. Very much.'

And it sounded as if he meant it. Having braced herself to meet with his seemingly habitual reserve, she was stunned to see the hint of moisture in his dark eyes. *He really cared.* She caught herself up on the thought. *Of course* he cared. Rosie was his daughter. What had she expected?

He drew the little girl into the sitting room and knelt down in front of her. His mouth moved clearly so Rosie could lip-read. 'We were worried about you. You mustn't go outside on your own.'

But he didn't hug her. He didn't wrap his arms about her and tell her how much he loved her. He was stiff and awkward. Lydia wanted to thump him and tell him he was handling this all wrong. That it would take considerably more life experience than a five-year-old possessed to understand what the shimmer in his eyes meant.

And what did she know? She avoided relationships. Didn't want to become a mother because she couldn't contemplate bringing children into a world like this one. What had suddenly made her such an expert on human relationships?

She saw Rosie look away and realised that he'd lost her. She was one angry little girl and Nick had missed an opportunity to build a bridge. And he didn't even know it.

*What was it about rich people's children?* On the surface they had every advantage, but so often their parents didn't seem to have any real kind of relationship with them. They were put into the care of nannies and other 'professionals' before they could talk and dispatched to boarding school at the first opportunity.

She walked forward and took hold of Rosie's hand, feeling incredibly protective. For Rosie it was even worse than for most children of wealthy parents. Her mother had told her enough of her own childhood experiences for Lydia to be acutely aware of how difficult it could be to be born deaf in a hearing family.

Rosie had asked her to speak for her—and she would. She would make sure Nick Regan-Phillips listened. More than that; as far as it was in her power she would make sure things changed.

'Rosie asked me to tell you she's been very unhappy.'

Nick looked up at her words, stunned by them. Around them there seemed to be a pool of silence.

Lydia hesitated and glanced down at Rosie. She only hoped she'd judged this right. Had judged Nick right. If Sophie was the sulky-looking twenty-something in the corner she might be about to make Rosie's life much worse.

'I gather there was some kind of argument—'

'Yes, there was.' All eyes turned to the woman she'd assumed was Sophie as she forcefully interrupted. 'I will not have defiance and—'

'Sophie—' Nick glanced over his shoulder, his voice brooking no disagreement '—the important thing is that Rosie is safe. I think we can leave everything else to the morning.'

She looked as if she might have protested, but thought better of it. 'As you wish.' Her chin became just that little bit squarer. 'It's late. I'll put her to bed.'

Sophie held out her hand, but Nick forestalled her with a decided, 'No.' His hand reached out and stroked the top of his daughter's head. It was the first real sign of affection Lydia had seen between the two—and it reminded her of how he'd been with Wendy.

He'd been gentle. Kind.

Rosie curved towards her father and Lydia knew she hadn't misjudged him. There was a good man inside that city suit…and if he just let himself go…

'I'll put Rosie to bed myself.'

Lydia heard Sophie's sharp intake of breath and judged his announcement to be unprecedented, but she waited confidently for Sophie to be sent from the room.

She had little doubt he'd do that. She'd seen the way he cared and, whatever was really going on here, she didn't believe he'd want his daughter to be shouted at and bullied by a twenty-year-old something who thought she was God's gift to childcare.

Christine Pearman might be a nice woman who could be educated to care, but Sophie…no, Sophie was not that kind of woman.

Sophie was the kind of woman who knew best—always. She'd read the book and knew all the answers. It might be the kind of snap judgement Izzy deplored, but Lydia was quite happy to keep hold of Rosie's hand in hers and wait for Nick to justify her faith in him.

She wasn't disappointed. He stood up and looked directly at Sophie as he said, 'I'm sure you've found the whole experience very stressful, so I'll take care of Rosie now. Thank you.' Then he looked across at his housekeeper. 'That will be all for now, Christine.'

'D-dinner?'

'Will need to wait until Rosie is asleep.'

Both women left the room, cowed—and he'd not raised his voice. His words had been spoken with a quiet authority, expecting people to comply with his wishes.

Lydia, used as she was to a newsroom environment and the way the air frequently turned blue, found it impressive stuff.

It was strange he didn't inspire her with that kind of awe. All she saw was a man, albeit a sexy one, who needed a great deal of help with his daughter. Or perhaps it would be more accurate to phrase it as the daughter who needed help with her father?

She saw him glance down at their still-joined hands and felt a momentary pang of pity for him. He was out of his depth and floundering.

And he looked unbearably weary. He'd had a hell of a couple of days and what she was about to say wasn't going to make his life any better—at least, not in the short-term.

'Rosie has asked me to tell you she doesn't like Sophie.'

Her words acted like a slap. She saw the effect of them on Nick as though she'd taken a whip to him.

'She told you?' His voice sounded hollow.

'Yes.'

'You sign?'

Her eyes flew to his. 'You don't?'

His eyes didn't leave her face and she saw his effort to swallow.

*He didn't sign.* How could the father of a deaf five-year-old not have learnt something of the method she used to communicate? It was unbelievable. Criminal.

'Well, you should. How do you expect her to talk to you?'

# CHAPTER FOUR

NICK felt as if he'd been flayed on the raw. It spoke to the guilt within him. He didn't sign—and he knew he should be able to. Rosie was five years old. Since he'd been told his daughter was profoundly deaf he'd had over four years to learn.

There were reasons, of course, why he hadn't done. Good reasons. Or at least they'd seemed good until Rosie had suddenly come to live with him. And somehow, looking at Lydia's incredible amber-flecked eyes, he knew she wouldn't think his excuses good enough.

Which they weren't. He'd let his daughter down. When she'd needed him to comfort her he'd not even been able to ask what she liked to eat for breakfast. He'd been forced to pull cereal packets out of the cupboard and wait for her to either nod or shake her head. It was a form of communication, but it was limited.

Rosie had been given no alternative but to tell a complete stranger that she didn't like her nanny. What made it even worse was that he'd known that. Deep down. Or even not so deep. It had been obvious. He'd simply chosen to ignore it because it made his life simpler.

He'd argued that it gave Rosie some stability to have the same nanny she'd had when she'd lived with her mother. And Sophie was very highly qualified, with good references…

All excuses—and he knew it. Faced with his daughter's guileless brown eyes looking up at him, how could he not? And Lydia…

Her eyes told him exactly what she was thinking of him. She was looking at him with incredulity. She tossed back that incredible mane of hair, which framed a face that was more intelligent than conventionally beautiful, and her words stung him again. 'Rosie signs wonderfully. It's clearly her first language.'

'She's also able to lip-read very well,' he said defensively.

'That's not the point, though, is it? That's her understanding you, not *you* understanding her. You have a responsibility to Rosie and—'

'I'm completely aware of my responsibilities.' His voice sliced across hers, much harder than he'd intended. He resisted the impulse to apologise.

For one moment there was complete silence, during which Lydia's eyes didn't so much as flicker away from his. 'You're right,' she said at last. 'It's absolutely not my business to tell you how to raise your child, but—'

'No, it isn't.'

'But,' she continued as though he hadn't spoken, 'I made a promise to Rosie. I told her I would tell you how she feels and I fully intend to keep my promise.'

Then Lydia broke eye-contact, calmly kneeling in front of Rosie. She gently tapped his daughter on the arm and Rosie looked at her confidently, her brown eyes wide and trusting.

*And it hurt.*

Nick swallowed painfully. It hurt so much to see his daughter looking to someone else to tell him what she felt. Trusting them to do it.

He felt the whip of guilt. He should have made more time. He shouldn't have left her with a nanny like Sophie. He should have fought for her when Ana had left him. *Damn it!* He should have learnt to sign and made sure he'd forged a real connection with Rosie. The regrets pounded in his head like wave after wave on a cliff face.

He scarcely knew his child. *God forgive him.* And now he needed someone to help him communicate with his own daughter.

And for that someone to be Lydia Stanford…

*It hurt.* So much. It was difficult to have to be grateful to a woman like Lydia. He wasn't even quite sure what kind of woman she was. How did you meld together what he'd seen of her with what he knew about her?

It was incontrovertible fact that Lydia had used every skill she possessed to ensure Steven Daly and his associates were put behind bars. Her sister's miscarriage and suicide attempt had been made public knowledge during a long and complicated court case. All manner of private details about Isabel Stanford's life had been open to public scrutiny and cross-examination—for weeks on end.

It was easy to imagine how deeply humiliating it must have been for a shy twenty-three-year-old to have her life dissected and discussed over other people's breakfast.

Day after day there'd been photographs of the sisters. Lydia had looked strong, confident and utterly determined—her sister…had looked broken.

True enough, Steven Daly was a Machiavellian character who deserved to be in prison, but…how could Lydia sleep at night knowing what she'd exposed her vulnerable sister to?

One particular image, taken outside the courtroom on the final day, stayed with him. In that photograph Lydia's sister had been completely surrounded by reporters, dwarfed by them. She'd stood with one solitary tear resting halfway down her cheek. A moment frozen in time. She'd looked emotionally battered, alone and utterly heartbroken.

Lydia might argue she'd done it all for her sister, but he knew that wasn't true. There was no way the young, emotionally traumatised Isabel had been thinking of vengeance. She'd merely been concentrating on finding the will to stay alive.

When Wendy had told him she'd insisted Lydia Stanford was her biographer or she wouldn't co-operate, he'd been horrified. Everything he'd discovered about Lydia since then had only confirmed how single-minded she was. A woman totally focused on achieving her goals whatever the cost.

But when he'd met her…

Lydia hadn't been quite the woman he'd been expecting. She exuded a warmth he hadn't anticipated. A kindness.

If he'd simply met her…at a party perhaps? If he hadn't seen her give that interview after the jury had passed a unanimous 'guilty' verdict…

Then it would have been a very different story.

He knew he'd have been mesmerised by those incredible eyes and bewitched by the rich colours in her hair. He would have asked for her telephone number and he wouldn't have waited more than twenty-four hours before inviting her to dinner.

But beneath the attractive veneer Lydia Stanford was still a woman who passionately craved success in her chosen career—and he knew exactly what that kind of ambition was like to live with. He knew how cruel it could be—and how painful.

He watched as Lydia asked his daughter what she wanted to say. Her hands moved gracefully. She had beautiful hands with long tapering fingers and nails that were perfectly manicured. She also had a vivid scratch across the back of her right hand—no doubt a parting gift from Nimrod.

And then he had to watch as Rosie told Lydia what she *did* want to say. *Dear God.* His heart ached as he watched her tiny hands move in rapid jerky movements. Her face was full of expression as finally *his* daughter got the chance to tell him what she'd held locked inside her for all the weeks she'd lived in his home.

Rosie's little face began to crumple and he found that his feet moved and his arms locked tightly around her, his hand stroking the top of his daughter's head. Lightly kissing her curls, he rested his chin on the top of her head and looked across at Lydia. 'What did she say?'

Lydia's voice was husky as though she'd been affected by what she'd been told. Her beautiful eyes, still with the same flecks of fire in them, looked softer than he'd seen them before. 'It's complicated.'

'I imagine it is.' And suddenly it didn't matter whether Lydia Stanford was here only because she wanted a story. What really mattered, more than life itself, was Rosie.

And if Lydia was the means by which he could establish a relationship with his daughter, then he was going to welcome it—whatever the personal cost.

Rosie turned within his arms and he held her tightly, every muscle in his body striving to convey how much he loved her. As her sobs quietened, he held her away from his body and stared into her eyes, willing her to understand him.

Her eyes were so like his own. 'I'm sorry,' he said carefully. 'Rosie…I…' And then he looked across at Lydia. 'What did she say? Why is she so unhappy? Tell me,' he prompted when she seemed to hesitate.

Lydia stood up slowly and went to sit on a nearby sofa. She usually found words easy to find. From the school notebooks she'd filled with stories of sword-wielding heroines, to her career as a journalist, she'd always found it easy to say what she meant. Communication was what she did best.

But not this time. What she had to tell Nick Regan-Phillips was going to hurt him—and she didn't want that. In the space of fifteen minutes she'd gone from thinking him a poor parent to thinking him a flawed one.

She didn't understand why a parent of a deaf child who signed would refuse to learn it, but she had no doubt that he loved his daughter. Seeing him hold Rosie was probably going to be one of those images that would stay with her all her life. Even having seen Nick with his godmother she hadn't believed him capable of such honest emotion.

Lydia cleared her voice carefully. She had to tell him the truth—exactly as Rosie had told her. 'She… She understands why she was sent here. Or thinks she does.'

Pushing back her long hair from her face, Lydia tried

again. 'Rosie says she was sent here because her mother doesn't like her because she's deaf and she thinks you're too busy to have her live with you.'

A flicker of acute pain passed across Nick's face and Lydia didn't dare stop in case she lost her nerve. She'd promised Rosie. She *would* keep her promise.

'She says Sophie shouts at her because she can't hear and gets cross when she doesn't understand. She wants to go back to her grandma's house and live with her.' Lydia looked away, hating the raw look of pain on his face. 'I'm sorry. Really.'

Nick shook his head as though to absolve her from any part in his agony and then he kissed Rosie's head. His hand lightly stroked the top of her head and down the side of her cheek. 'I'm sorry.'

Then he looked at Lydia. 'How do I sign "sorry"?'

Lydia swallowed down the lump in her throat. 'You use your little finger for things that are bad.' She extended her own small finger and with the rest of her hand in a ball made small circles against her chest. '"Sorry". It's like this.'

He moved his own hand. It wasn't perfect—but Rosie understood. She reached out and stopped him moving his hand and then tucked in for a cuddle.

It was a beginning. Perhaps more than a beginning? Perhaps it was a breakthrough?

'She understood me.' His deep voice was incredulous.

Lydia smiled, her eyes shimmering with emotion.

'Will you tell her I won't leave her with Sophie again? I can't do much about her mother or grandmother, but I will stay with her myself.'

'Don't promise her what you can't give—'

'I won't leave her with anyone she doesn't want to be with.'

If almost anyone else had made that statement Lydia wouldn't have believed them, but Nick said it in a way that made her believe he would do exactly what he said he would. Goodness only knew what upheavals it would cause in his professional life.

Nevertheless it was the right decision. Unquestionably. Rosie needed him. It was what being a parent was all about. Selfless love.

As an onlooker Lydia could see it clearly. It was why she never wanted children of her own. She wasn't capable of selfless love. She never wanted to be in a position where she'd have to choose between what she wanted to do and what other people needed her to do.

Who was it who said it was a wise man who knew his limitations? Well, that applied equally well to women. She knew she could never subjugate her desires to the needs of another. She was too selfish. She hadn't been able to do it at eighteen and there was no reason to suppose she could ever do it in the future.

Lydia tapped Rosie on the shoulder. The little girl turned round. She could see from her hopeful expression that she trusted her father. Carefully she signed out what Nick had said. Rosie glanced at him and Nick nodded in confirmation.

Then Rosie smiled, her tiny heart-shaped face lit up with a beauty that defied the tear-stains. Seeing it, Lydia felt her own heart contract. If that expression didn't reward Nick for doing the right thing, then nothing would.

For the second time in as many days Lydia felt an outsider. She was a bystander to an emotional connection she wasn't part of. An onlooker. Not really needed.

It wasn't as if she really knew Nick Regan-Phillips and his daughter. She was here purely because of a series of circumstances and the sooner she left the better. Witnessing this kind of connection made her aware of an ache within herself. The emptiness and a longing for something more in her life. Something career success didn't give her.

Lydia stood up and, the minute she did so, Rosie turned. She stretched out her hand. Lydia took it in her own, but with her one free hand signed that she must go home.

The little girl vehemently shook her head.

Nick stood up a little shakily. 'I don't think she's ready to lose you.'

'I—'

'Have you eaten?'

It was such an abrupt change of subject that Lydia frowned in an effort to make sense of it.

'Eaten. I asked if you'd eaten yet?' he repeated slowly. 'After everything you've done for me today the least I can do is offer you dinner.'

'No, I haven't.' In fact, since Izzy's spectacular and totally sinful fried breakfast, she'd not eaten anything but the half packet of chocolate biscuits she'd tucked in the glove compartment of her car.

'Then stay for dinner.'

'But Christine Pearman won't be expecting another mouth to feed…'

'Christine is paid to expect the unexpected,' he said with all the old arrogance she disliked. How could he make a statement like that? Didn't he know that meals couldn't conjure themselves out of thin air? That they required planning and preparation before they appeared on the table?

But then Lydia thought of her empty flat. Her two close friends exploring Vienna without her. What was there to rush back to London for?

It was tempting to stay. Rosie tugged on her hand and Lydia felt herself weaken. 'Are you sure?'

'Yes.'

She looked up into Nick's dark brown eyes and thought what a staggeringly complicated man he was. He was also fascinating. It was at that moment that she knew she'd stay.

'I'll need to stay with Rosie until she's asleep, but then we could…talk.'

Her eyes moved to his mouth. *Talk*. Hmm, yes. They *could* talk. Did he know he had the sexiest mouth? Or that his lips would be described as firm and sensual in a romance novel? And then there was that slight indentation in the centre of his chin. She'd read somewhere that it was indicative of a sensual personality.

Who knew whether that was true, but looking at Nick Regan-Phillips you kind of suspected it might be. Lydia pulled her eyes away from his face, horrified at where her thoughts had taken her.

'You've obviously got some experience of being in contact with deaf people. I'd like to hear your suggestions for what would help Rosie.'

'Of course.' Put like that, how could she refuse?

'I'll ask Christine to bring you a drink through to the sunroom. Or even on the terrace, since it's been a lovely day.'

Lydia looked down at Rosie, who was staring up at her with wide eyes. *She must have been so lonely.* As the thought popped into her mind she realised that anything she could do to help Rosie she would do. It had been a long time since anyone had looked at her with such blatant adoration. Even if it was only the hero-worship of a five-year-old—it felt really good.

'Actually,' Lydia said, looking round for where she'd dropped her handbag, 'I've left my car halfway down your drive. I think I'll walk down and fetch it.'

'Okay. I'll ask Christine to watch for you and I'll meet you on the terrace in…' He glanced down at his watch.

'When Rosie is asleep.'

Nick's smile was swift. 'When Rosie is asleep,' he agreed.

She watched the two of them leave the room. They looked like one of those arty photographs of a dad walking along with his little girl. Certainly Rosie was pretty enough to be a child model. She had one of those symmetrical faces and huge speaking eyes.

Her mother must be a very beautiful woman. Lydia glanced around the room. There were no photographs—although that was to be expected. They were divorced, after all. It would be very unusual if there had been any.

But she was curious to know who the enigmatic Nick would have married. If she'd anticipated any part of the events of today she'd have spent longer on the Internet and discovered who it had been.

Lydia spotted her handbag tucked next to a red cushion and went to pick it up, just as Rosie burst back into the room. The question on her lips died the minute she saw the little girl's face. Lydia crouched down and received a resounding kiss on the cheek. Slightly moist, but completely perfect.

For the first time in her life Lydia thought it might be nice to have a child of her own one day. Someone who would love her unconditionally—and then she brought herself up short. She totally disapproved of people who had children for reasons like that. If she wanted unconditional love it would be better to get a dog. And she hadn't even got space in her life for one of those.

Standing up, Lydia signed 'goodnight'. That brought back memories too. Her mother had always signed the same thing every night. *'Goodnight. Sleep tight. Don't let the bedbugs bite.'* It was almost painful to remember. It was as though she'd blocked so many of those happy memories because of the ache they brought with them.

Rosie smiled shyly and then bounced from the room. The child's whole body language had altered in the short time she'd known her. The truly astounding thing was how little it had actually taken to have wrought such a change.

Nick had to be able to see that for himself. His daughter had simply needed to be listened to. Nothing earth-shattering about that. Everybody needed to be listened to. Lydia picked up her handbag. And then she wondered a little more about the former Mrs Regan-Phillips. What kind of woman was she? Would she object to the summary removal of the nanny she'd presumably chosen?

*It wasn't her problem.* She had to remember that. It was time she started to let other people fight their own battles. Izzy had said that yesterday.

*Izzy.*

Why hadn't she thought of that before? She needed to telephone her sister. Izzy was a teacher for special needs children. She might even know of someone who would be a perfect nanny for Rosie. Lydia started to fumble in her hand-bag for the cellphone as Christine came back into the room.

'Do you want me to show you out? Mr Regan-Phillips says you are bringing your car back up to the house.'

Lydia's hand, still in her handbag, closed around her mobile. 'Yes. Yes, I am.'

The older woman seemed to be a picture of cool control. If she hadn't seen her so flustered she wouldn't have believed it possible for this woman ever to be ruffled. 'I'll watch for your car and will take you through to the terrace as soon as you return.'

'Thank you.'

Together they walked along the hallway with its beautifully nourished oak floor. Lydia couldn't help but think how many hours it must take to keep it looking like this. Christine opened the heavy front door and held it wide.

Lydia paused on the top step as a thought occurred to her. She turned back. 'I hope my staying isn't too inconvenient for you.'

The housekeeper's mouth almost stretched to a smile but stopped short. 'It's not a problem.'

'Good.' Lydia skipped down the steps and started down the path towards her car. Glancing quickly over her shoulder to make sure Christine Pearman had returned inside, she pulled her mobile from her handbag and dialled her sister's number.

'Izzy?'

Her sister's voice sounded happy. 'Where are you? I've been trying to reach you for the last hour—'

'I know—' Lydia cut her off '—I've had my mobile turned off.'

'Why?'

'That's not important. Just listen to what's happened to me.'

Nick sat on the edge of Rosie's bed, watching her eyes close. Every so often she would force them open to check he was still there. Each time he smiled and gently closed her eyelids with his hand.

She was so lovely. *His* little girl. He'd hoped she'd been too young to fully appreciate what had gone on with her mother. It seemed she knew too much of some things and not enough of others.

Ana wasn't a bad person, just selfish. She wouldn't have actively wanted her daughter to be hurt. Perhaps that was why she'd not told Rosie that her grandma had died. She probably thought Rosie was too young to understand what was going on around her. How wrong Ana had been.

Rosie might not have picked up on everything, but she was in no doubt that her father was too busy for her and her mother didn't like her being deaf. Nick shook his head as though to rid himself of the thought and watched as his daughter fell into sleep. What kind of long-term damage did that do to a child?

He didn't know. *Damn it!* Nick reached out and stroked back Rosie's soft curls. It didn't matter any more. Whatever happened now, things were going to change.

Nick stood up quietly and turned off the main light, leaving the soft night-light on. He hadn't thought before how terrifying it must be for a deaf person to be left entirely in the dark. There was so much he hadn't considered.

Rosie's world was completely different from his. Her experiences, now and as an adult, would be different.

He ran a hand across his neck tiredly. It was the first time in his life when he wasn't sure he had what it took. Could he learn to be a good father? He smiled. Wendy would be amazed if she ever heard him say that. Knowing her, she'd probably think it was the beginning of wisdom.

'Is the little girl asleep?' Christine Pearman asked, coming up the stairs, towels in her hand.

'Rosie is, yes.' It was time they stopped thinking of her as a 'little girl' and started thinking of her as a fully formed human being, with needs and deep-seated worries of her own.

'Would you like me to listen out in case she wakes? Sophie has gone out to a movie. I think she assumed you'd given her the evening off…'

Nick stopped with his hand on the banister rail. 'That would be excellent. Thank you. Has Ms Stanford returned to the house yet?'

'No.' The housekeeper hesitated. 'I think she had a phone call to make. Sir, do you think this is a good idea? Ms Stanford is a journalist and you've always resisted—'

'Lydia Stanford is Wendy's choice of biographer. And since Wendy is coming to stay, I think you and I ought to get used to the idea of having Ms Stanford around.'

'Yes, sir.'

'And, considering everything she's done for me today, I think the least I can do is offer her a meal.'

Christine shifted the towels in her arms. 'Of course, sir.'

She walked down the landing, leaving Nick alone to wonder why Lydia Stanford had needed to make a call. Why she'd waited until she was out of the house.

Nick turned back to his bedroom and went through to his dressing room. He needed to get out of this suit. He tore off his rich burgundy silk tie and then hung it neatly in between red and purple ones on his colour-coded tie rack.

*Was this a good idea?* His fingers paused on the top button of his shirt.

Almost certainly this was not a good idea. Lydia Stanford was an ambitious woman. But, he argued, this was a thank you meal. A chance to learn more about the deaf world his daughter would inhabit. It was not a chance to get to know a woman who made him want to slowly undress her and throw her blasted Anastasia Wilson jacket out of a top floor window.

He swore softly. As long as he remembered that nothing was sacred to Lydia Stanford, he'd be all right.

# CHAPTER FIVE

LYDIA stood on the terrace, but given the choice she would have preferred to wait for Nick inside. It had been a pleasantly warm day rather than hot and now it was beginning to cool down still further.

The view, though, was spectacular. Everything about this house was spectacular. The lawn reached out in a gentle swathe to a wooded area below and continued on to what looked like a walled garden. In between there were huge specimen trees that had been allowed to grow to full maturity. Plenty of places for Rosie to hide from a nanny she disliked.

'She's asleep.'

Lydia turned at the sound of Nick's voice. Her first thought was that he'd changed out of his suit and into more casual clothes. Her second was that it was totally unfair.

He wore black jeans which hugged thighs that belonged on a professional sportsman, a white T-shirt and a thick charcoal-coloured over-shirt. The effect was electric. She, by contrast, was still in the clothes she'd left London i n yesterday.

'Has Christine given you a drink?'

Lydia shook her head. 'I didn't want one. I have to drive back to London tonight.'

'It's getting cold out here. Shall we go back inside?'

Gratefully she moved towards the house. 'The end of summer already. It's sad, isn't it?'

'Doesn't last long,' he agreed.

Their conversation seemed formal and awkward, as though neither of them knew quite what they were allowed to talk about. They were not friends, Lydia reminded herself. Their relationship could only be described, at best, as uneasy.

'It's a fabulous garden,' she observed, stepping through fully open glass doors that folded back to completely merge inside and outside spaces.

'It's my passion and why I bought this house. There's a little over six acres here and yet I can be in the centre of London within an hour.'

'It's very convenient,' she agreed as he led her through the reception room and across the hallway to a formal dining room.

It was exquisitely decorated although in slightly too heavy a style for her taste. The walls were papered in what she recognised to be an original William Morris design. The dining table was a rich oak and surrounded by the Rennie Macintosh chairs she'd imagined he'd own.

A traditional man in a traditional home. She loved it when people met her expectations. There was something so comforting about it.

'So,' she said brightly, 'how long have you lived here? And have you done much to the garden?'

'A little over two years. And—' he smiled '—not as much as I would like.'

'Spoken like a true gardener.' Lydia slipped off her jacket and laid it across the back of one of the chairs.

'Would you like to hang that up?' Nick asked, pulling out one of the chairs so that she could sit down. An old-fashioned gesture which suited the image she was building of him.

'I'm sure it'll be fine there. I might as well hang on to it in case I want to go out later and inspect what you've done.'

His mouth quirked into a smile. Her stomach did a little flip in recognition. It was a sexy smile and its power was increased by the fact that it came almost without any warning. She could imagine it could easily become something of an obsession to see how often she could make them happen.

Nick took the seat at the head of the table, immediately to the left of her. It was already laid for two, with fresh rolls and small curls of cold butter in tiny round dishes. 'I believe we're to have Celeriac Soup followed by Haddock Fillets with Coriander and Lemon Pesto.'

'Don't you know? I imagined you'd give your orders in the morning and the staff would...'

'It's too big a house to manage alone,' he replied neutrally. She had to admire him for refusing to rise to her bait.

'How disappointing! I was hoping for something much more "lord of the manor".'

Nick laughed. His face relaxed and Lydia felt her stomach clench. Sexy. The man was just sexy. Maybe breaking into Wendy Bennington's house had been a very good idea.

'It's difficult to get abject obedience past the unions these days.'

Christine walked in with a large tray, setting it down on an oak sideboard.

'Ms Stanford—' Nick began.

'Lydia, please.'

'And I'm Nick.'

It seemed a little late in the day to be deciding on using first name terms, but then she realised it was because she'd been thinking of him as Nick for a while. Yet neither of them had used the other's name in conversation. *How strange.*

'Lydia,' he continued smoothly, 'was wondering how much say I have over what I eat.'

Christine set the bowls in front of them. 'It would be lovely if he took an interest. He only cares about his garden. I think I could serve the same meal every night and he wouldn't notice.'

Nick raised an eyebrow as his housekeeper left. 'Well, there you have it.'

'I think you've offended her. You must make a mental note to show more appreciation,' Lydia teased. She picked up her soup spoon. 'What do you plan to do here? With the garden?'

'Actually I'm still undecided.' Nick picked up the bottle of wine which sat in an elegantly twisting silver coaster. 'Wine?'

'A very little.'

'You're driving,' he said with a smile. 'I remember.'

He made even that seem sexy. This was beginning to feel like a date. It was so strange. Yesterday she'd have said he wouldn't have given her the time of day. *Well, he hadn't.*

He'd been rude, arrogant and supercilious. She was almost beginning to forget that.

'Currently I'm working on creating a traditional kitchen garden inspired by the one at Audley End. In Essex.'

Lydia nodded. 'I know it.'

'I've put in some espalier trees and I'm currently building some raised beds.'

'You are?' she said, surprised. 'You're doing the work yourself?'

He smiled again. 'No enjoyment if you don't. That's what I'd intended doing yesterday, only I spent most of it at the hospital with Wendy.'

Lydia looked at him. That explained the scruffy clothes when she'd first met him. She would never have suspected he'd be a gardener. Somehow that didn't quite fit with a man who'd made millions from electrical components.

But then nothing about him really fitted with her idea of a man who'd devoted his life to electrical components. Nick had the kind of voice you'd listen to even if he was reading you the telephone directory and a body…that a nicely brought-up girl would do better not to think about.

And he was a gardener. She smiled. As far as her father had been concerned, that automatically put someone on the side of good, whatever indications there might be to the contrary.

'Actually, I agree.' Her dad had never been able to understand why anyone would spend a fortune on having a garden designed for them when the whole pleasure was in getting involved, actually getting your hands dirty.

She saw Nick's gaze move to her manicured nails and laughed. 'Not that I've done much gardening recently, I admit.'

His smile broadened and Lydia looked away quickly.

*She had to stop this.* The slightly uneven tilt of his mouth and the glint in his eyes had really started to do something to her. Izzy had said he was 'her type' and, despite all her protestations to the contrary, Lydia was beginning to wonder whether that was true.

Only physically, of course. She liked successful men, but she preferred them to be entirely self-made success stories. There was a hint of the silver spoon about Nicholas Regan-Phillips which meant she could have nothing in common with him. No one in her state comprehensive had had a double-barrelled name and, if they had, they'd quickly have pretended they didn't.

Which reminded her. Nick had done just that. 'Do you mind if I ask you a question?'

She fancied his eyes narrowed slightly. 'Not if I can reserve the right not to answer.'

'Deal.' Lydia picked up her soup spoon. 'Why did you tell me your name was Nick Regan?'

'Because it is.'

'Evasive. Why did you drop the Phillips part?'

His eyes crinkled in an acknowledgement of a hit. 'Your reputation went before you. I didn't want you to do what you did.'

'What did I do?' she asked, bemused.

'Find out who I was. Search me out on the Internet.'

Lydia sipped her soup. 'You were unlucky. There wasn't another Nick Regan so you were the closest match I could find. There was nothing much there, though. I'd have to go to much greater trouble to unearth any really interesting information. So far I've not found a skeleton in the closet.'

There was a small beat of silence and Lydia wondered whether she'd offended him. As ever it was difficult to tell. His face gave so little away as to what he was thinking. She'd meant the 'skeleton in the closet' bit to be a harmless quip, but perhaps it hadn't been the most sensitive thing to say. Particularly since one of the few things she did know about him was that he valued his privacy.

She took another sip of soup and was relieved when he said mildly, 'My turn to ask a question.'

'Fair enough.'

'What stopped you gardening?'

Lydia put down her spoon and picked up her wineglass. It was a simple enough question, but there were so many ways of answering it. The completely honest answer would be that her parents had died and the family house had been sold. She'd driven past it a year ago and her father's lovingly cultivated flower garden had all but vanished.

'Well…' her fingers moved along the stem of her wineglass '…I suppose university. Then work.'

'You don't have a garden in London?'

'I have a balcony.' Lydia smiled. 'And I'm the proud owner of two hanging baskets. You can't judge me by that, though. I assure you I do know my *Choisya ternata* from my *Campanula lactiflora.*'

'I'm impressed.'

He seemed to watch her from behind his wineglass. It was actually quite unnerving to be so unsure of what someone was thinking of you. And he was thinking something. Lydia returned to her soup and let the mild celery flavour of the celeriac swirl about her mouth for a moment, then looked up. 'I had a gardening childhood.'

Nick said nothing. It had the effect of making her want to fill the silence. Lydia pulled off a piece of the bread roll and carefully smeared on some butter. 'My father was a gardener. Professionally, I mean. He loved it. Some of my earliest memories are of helping him prick out seedlings.'

Lydia looked back fondly through the years. She'd loved being with him. Had loved the magic way he'd taught her to watch for the seasons. The Saturdays spent at his allotment and the joy of bringing home freshly dug new potatoes. One day, she promised herself, one day she'd move out of London, have a garden again.

'Loved? As in past tense?'

'He…died when I was eighteen.'

'I'm sorry.'

Lydia shrugged, trying to appear nonchalant. 'It was a long time ago.' But it still hurt. The suddenness of it. 'My parents were hit by a lorry while crossing the road. My father died instantly, my mother a week later in hospital from internal injuries.'

*Why was she saying this?* She never told people this. Never tried to describe what it had felt like to be eighteen and have the police tell you your parents had been involved in a fatal accident. Or how responsible she'd felt taking her twelve-year-old sister to the hospital, the days of waiting for their mother to die.

She never spoke of how much she'd resented missing her school leavers' ball and how ashamed she was of that feeling. Or of her decision to go to university and break up what was left of her family unit. No amount of success, it seemed, could ever assuage the guilt of that.

Nick tore a mouthful off his own roll and said nothing.

Why didn't he say something? He *should* say something, if only to be polite.

'They were deaf,' she stated baldly, filling the void. Wanting to provoke some kind of real reaction. 'The road markings had changed and they were looking the wrong way…and, of course, they didn't hear the lorry approaching.'

'And you're still angry?'

His question brought her up short. *Angry? Was she?* 'I don't blame the lorry driver…I just think it was a meaningless waste.' She sat back in her chair. 'My mum wasn't even forty when she died.'

'That's young.'

'Too young.'

Nick watched the colour of her eyes change, almost as if they really did have fire in their depths. There was anger there, he was sure of it. His own mother had died at twenty-three. But from illness. Did that make it better or worse? He wasn't sure.

He didn't have a single memory of his mother. Not one. It would have been nice to have remembered something. Nice, too, to have felt he'd known his father.

Nick watched as Lydia brushed her hair off her neck. She often did that, it seemed, but it was completely unconscious—and that made it so much harder to resist. It drew his eyes to the soft skin of her neck before her hair fell back in a soft cascade of rich honey-coloured silk.

He looked away and was grateful when Christine returned to take away the empty soup bowls. 'Has Rosie woken at all?'

The housekeeper's face almost stretched into a smile.

'There's not been a peep out of the little mite. It looks like she might have settled for the night.'

'Does she normally wake up?' Lydia asked, the haunted look in her eyes vanishing like morning mist.

It was Nick's turn to shrug. It was the kind of question he'd no intention of answering because of where it might lead. 'She's not used to the house.'

'Doesn't she stay with you often?'

Nick looked up and met her eyes. He could read the criticism in hers easily enough, but he wasn't prepared to bare his soul to this woman. This was touching on very personal ground and he'd no intention of being newspaper fodder again.

He moved to top up her wineglass, but Lydia forestalled him. 'No more, or I'll be over the limit.'

Nick filled up his own glass as Christine put plates of fish in front of them and a serving dish of lightly cooked vegetables in the centre. 'Thank you.'

'Yes, thank you. This looks completely wonderful, Christine.'

Lydia reached out and spooned a selection of vegetables, the long scratch on her hand very noticeable.

'That looks nasty,' Nick observed.

She pulled her hand back and looked at her injury. 'Wendy was quite right when she told you Nimrod didn't like going in his cat basket. He fought like a mighty hunter.' Nick watched her run her finger along the length of the scratch and then she looked up and smiled. 'I haven't seen him since I delivered him. I hope you haven't lost him.'

He forced an answering smile. 'He'll be around.'

She was completely beguiling. The way she moved,

spoke, laughed… Hell, her laugh ripped through him so he didn't know whether it was morning or evening.

What was it about him that made him fall for completely the wrong woman—always? He'd built a multi-million-pound business on recognising talent and building a team. His contemporaries rated his judgement, but when it came to women…

'How is Wendy?' she asked suddenly, giving him something concrete to focus on.

He watched the way she pulled her hand through her shining hair and saw it splay out on the black cotton of her blouse. He had read something about what it meant when a woman touched her hair. The trouble was he couldn't remember whether it meant she was or wasn't attracted to the person she was talking to.

Of course, it could just mean she didn't like her hair across her face. When he'd first seen her she'd had it tied up in that sexy waterfall-type thing. On balance, he thought he preferred it loose.

'I don't suppose you've had a chance to visit her in hospital today,' Lydia continued. 'Do you know when she'll be out?'

'Actually, I'd been to visit her before I came home tonight.' Nick picked up his wineglass and sipped, trying to concentrate on what she was saying rather than the way her mouth moved. *He had to stop this.* Concentrate on the facts. Focus on something entirely matter-of-fact.

'So, how was she?'

'She's made a complete recovery from the TIA. Scans show nothing to be concerned about.'

'That's good.'

Nick let himself smile. 'But she's to consider it a warning. They want her to cut down on her unhealthy fats and…give up smoking.'

He loved the way her smile broadened, the sexy glint that coloured her brown eyes. 'Does Wendy have a bad habit?'

'Again—' he paused to cut into his fish '—it depends on who you're speaking to. Wendy says not. She says she smokes for relaxation and it's not an addiction. Her doctor, on the other hand, considers twenty cigarettes a day something to be concerned about.'

Lydia's nose wrinkled in an attractive look of concentration. 'That's quite a lot.'

'Most worrying of all, she'll be staying here while she's trying to give up.'

And then Lydia laughed her low, husky chuckle. 'I gather she's a determined woman.'

'Like steel, though in this case it could work either way. Currently, I'm not convinced she thinks it's something she needs to do.'

'And her ankle?' Lydia speared a softly glazed baby carrot with her fork before looking up at him.

'They managed to persuade Wendy that the risk of arthritis if it didn't heal properly was significant enough to warrant surgery. Someone there must have a silver tongue because she was adamant she didn't want that.'

'Is it painful?' Her eyes clouded with sudden sympathy.

'It's a fairly standard practice, though I imagine it's not comfortable for the patient. They've made an incision on one side of her ankle and held the bone together with screws and plates.'

'Is she in plaster?'

He nodded. 'She's in a cast up to her knee.'

'How long for?'

'Approximately six weeks. But, obviously, she'll be able to go home before then. She's agreed to spend two weeks here and after that it's negotiable.'

Lydia smiled, gave another flick of her incredibly rich hair. 'This topping on the haddock is amazing. I've never thought of making a pesto with anything other than basil, but coriander works fantastically well.'

'Are you a keen cook?'

She pulled a face. 'Yes and no. I dabble, but I don't usually have much time for it. The genius in my family is Izzy. She's as passionate about cooking as you are about your garden.'

Izzy must be Isabel. Nick felt his muscles tense at the mention of her sister's name. He hadn't expected that Lydia would mention her. Certainly not with a voice that rang with affection.

Lydia looked up, blithely unaware. 'She's my sister. You know how some people can make pastry and it's just lighter than anybody else's? Well, that's Izzy. I gave up competing.'

'Are you close to your sister?'

'Very.' Lydia stretched out her hand for the jug and poured herself some water into an empty tumbler. 'We weren't always. There's six years between us, which was too big a gap when we were children, but when Izzy was…oh, I don't know…about seventeen, the age-gap ceased to matter.' She sipped her water. 'How about you? Do you have any brothers or sisters?'

'No.'

Lydia looked up over the rim of her glass. *That didn't surprise her.* If anyone had had 'only child' stamped on his forehead it had to be Nicholas Regan-Phillips. 'Did you want any?'

'It was never an option.' His hand clenched slightly on the stem of his wineglass, an outward sign that he hadn't liked her question.

When it came to Wendy or, more specifically, Wendy's *physical condition*, Nick spoke freely—but touch on anything remotely personal and he clammed up. She looked at him speculatively. There were so many things she wanted to know about him, but it didn't seem worth upsetting him. Not when she still hoped to talk to his godmother about her life.

'Well,' she said brightly, bringing her knife and fork together in the centre of her plate and sitting back, 'I'm very glad to have my sister. Particularly since she gave me a bed for the night yesterday.'

'She lives near here?'

Lydia nodded. 'Reasonably. After I'd pointed the ambulance in the direction of Wendy's cottage, I decided to drive over and see her.'

His fingers moved ceaselessly on his wineglass. It was quite distracting. 'Doesn't she work?'

She forced her eyes to look up. 'Pardon?'

'Your sister? I asked if she worked. It's mid-week…'

Lydia suddenly clicked. 'Not during the school holidays. She's a teacher. I don't know what she'd planned for yesterday, but she took me in with good grace and we had a chance to gossip.'

*Mostly about him.* Lydia let her smile broaden. It was tempting to tell him that Izzy thought he bore a strong resemblance to the actor who'd played Fitzwilliam Darcy in the recent film. It would have been fun to have seen his reaction.

Mentioning Izzy, though, had reminded her why she'd been invited to stay for dinner. *Rosie.* She mustn't waste this opportunity to do something useful.

'How often does Rosie stay with you?' she asked him as Christine came in the room with an empty tray to clear the table. Lydia saw the glance that passed between the housekeeper and her employer, but couldn't fathom why.

'This is her permanent home.'

'With you?'

'Yes.'

His answer came as a complete surprise. She'd read that his daughter lived with her mother. There was some excuse for his inability to communicate with Rosie if she only made bi-weekly visits. But if this was her permanent home…there was no excuse at all.

Lydia waited while Christine brought in apple and pear tart as dessert and placed a jug of double cream on the table. Nick reached out and touched his housekeeper's arm. 'Thank you for keeping an ear out for Rosie. I'm grateful.'

'It's my pleasure.'

'But you're off duty now. I'll check on her from now on so you can watch your Agatha Christie programme in peace.'

Christine smiled. 'I'll see you in the morning, sir.'

Lydia toyed with her spoon, waiting for the moment when Christine shut the dining room door behind her. 'Then why don't you sign?' she asked quietly.

She watched the muscle in the side of his jaw pulse, but he didn't answer. 'It isn't difficult to learn,' she offered, thinking perhaps he was nervous for some reason.

Nick glanced across at her briefly and then looked away. Clearly he was searching for the words he wanted to say. 'Her living with me is…a recent development.'

That fitted in with what she'd read, but she needed more information before she could understand what Rosie's needs were. 'Where did she live before?' It was like chipping away at granite. 'Nick?'

'With her mother.'

She willed him to say more. 'Who taught her to sign?'

Nick reached out for his wineglass, his natural scepticism returning. 'Is this relevant?'

Lydia put down her spoon and sat back in her chair. 'It is to Rosie. She's not some kind of package you can pass between you. She's deaf. She appears to sign very well and it's cruel to leave her with no one she can talk to in her own language.'

'I know.' His voice was quiet, but it demanded to be heard. 'I will organise something.'

'When?' Lydia waited, but he clearly had no intention of answering her. 'Nick, you asked me to stay. You said you wanted to talk about ways to help Rosie, so I stayed. But every question I ask you blank. Or you give me a monosyllabic answer which, to be frank, is really irritating me.'

The muscle pulsed once more in the side of his face. It was the only indication that he'd heard her. 'Would you like some more wine?'

'No.'

Nick put the wine bottle down carefully in the centre of the coaster. 'I never talk about my personal life.'

She blinked at the unexpectedness of his reply. She knew, of course, that he hadn't this evening. He'd been the one to ask the questions and, very unusually, she'd told him some of the most painful things about her life. Things she rarely told anyone.

'Why?'

'I consider it private.'

Lydia frowned. 'If we're not going to talk about Rosie, then why am I still here?'

She watched as he poured cream liberally over his tart and then offered her the jug. Lydia shook her head. It all looked completely delicious, but she didn't feel like eating any more.

It had been a long and very uncomfortable day and the truth was she'd really had enough of it. Now she wasn't quite so hungry and the commuter traffic was off the road, she was ready to go home. A little bit of solitude, a power shower and her own bed seemed a better option than continuing with this pointless conversation.

'I'm quite happy to discuss the merits of British Sign Language over Sign Supported English and residential deaf schools versus semi-integrated deaf units. What I'm not prepared to do is talk to you about the custody arrangements Ana and I have made.'

*Now that was why he was so successful in business.* Clear, concise and sparing no one. Lydia felt her hands clamp tightly together in her lap. Few men had ever made her so mad. Christopher Granger, her first editor, was one exception, but this came a really close second—and she was being irritated in her own time.

'It's a pity Rosie isn't able to compartmentalise her life as easily. Whether or not you want to discuss "custody arrangements" with me doesn't change the huge impact they have on your daughter's life.'

'I understand that.'

'Do you?' Lydia asked, warming to her task. 'You've got a daughter asleep upstairs whose observation is that her mother doesn't like her and her father is too busy for her. Perhaps you ought to consider letting her live with the grandma she loves so much.'

As soon as the words left her mouth she wondered whether she'd hit a bit below the belt. She couldn't help but see the flicker of pain pass across his eyes. Sometimes she didn't think before she engaged her mouth. 'I'm sorry. I shouldn't have said that…'

Nick sat back in his chair. 'She's dead.'

Lydia's startled eyes flew to his face.

'She died this summer.'

'Rosie doesn't know?'

Nick shook his head. 'To be honest, I didn't know she didn't until today. I would have thought Ana would have told her.'

'Clearly not,' Lydia replied bluntly. 'Maybe she found it too painful. You're going to have to tell Rosie yourself.'

He met her eyes.

'Try imagining what's going through Rosie's head right now. No wonder she keeps trying to run away. She must be so confused. Did her grandma sign?'

'I imagine so.'

'You don't know?' Lydia asked, mystified why he wouldn't know the answer to a simple question like that.

She was beginning to wonder what kind of 'custody arrangements' Nick and his ex-wife had for Rosie.

His face seemed completely shuttered. It seemed to her he was morbidly afraid of sharing any part of himself with anyone. Maybe he was uncomfortable talking to her and would be better with a professional carer.

'Doesn't Rosie have a social worker you could discuss this with? I know my parents worked with several very good ones who helped them enormously,' she said, thinking out loud.

Still nothing.

Or maybe his problem was specifically with her? Yesterday she'd been convinced he didn't like her at all. She'd been so concerned for Rosie she'd forgotten his earlier assumption that she might write something that would hurt his godmother. Perhaps this was all about that?

She finally lost patience. Lydia leant over the side of her chair and picked her handbag off the floor. 'Look, I don't think there's much point to this—'

'Please, finish your meal.'

She put her linen napkin beside her untouched plate and stood up.

Nick was on his feet. 'Would you like a coffee?'

'I don't think so.' Lydia draped her jacket over her arm. 'For the record, I'm not nearly as interested in your personal life as you think I am.'

She wondered for a moment whether he was going to protest, but she ploughed on regardless. 'You're clearly fixated by the fact that I'm a journalist, but the only information I've read about you told me your name and that you invented an electrical component which, frankly, I thought made dull reading. You've got an interesting godmother and a delightful daughter. Let's leave it at that, shall we?'

Lydia turned to leave and Nick reached out to stop her, his hand resting on her arm. She looked down pointedly and he removed it. 'I'm sorry.'

'It's not important.' And then, 'Oh, I forgot.' She reached round for her handbag and opened the flap. 'I spoke to my sister about Rosie. I hope you don't mind.' Lydia pulled out a small notebook and ripped the front page out. 'I told you she's a teacher?'

Nick nodded.

'She's a specialist teacher, so I rang her. I thought she might know of some useful contacts. Anyway,' she said, handing over the piece of paper, 'I jotted down the numbers she gave me.'

'Thank you.' His voice sounded tight and constrained.

'She also said she might know of a nanny who might suit your daughter—if, of course, you and…Ana decide on replacing Sophie. Izzy's happy to speak to you if you want to ring her. Her telephone number is on the back.'

She saw him look down at the piece of paper as though he wasn't quite sure what to make of it. *Well, that was his problem now.* She'd done everything she could do to help Rosie.

Lydia tucked the notepad back inside her handbag and flicked it shut. Turning abruptly, she walked confidently from the dining room, aware that Nick was close behind her. At the front entrance she stopped and waited while he opened the door.

'Lydia—'

She held out her hand. 'Goodbye. Please thank Mrs

Pearman for cooking such a delicious supper. I appreciated it.'

Nick took her hand and held it firmly. 'Lydia, I'm sorry if I've offended you—'

'Not at all.'

'It wasn't intentional. And thank you for everything you've done today. For bringing the cat here. And for Rosie…'

'You're welcome.'

Lydia shivered in the night air and slipped her arms into her jacket. She adjusted the collar and set her handbag back on her shoulder. Halfway down the steps she turned and looked back up at him. 'You know, you could have trusted me.'

'I don't trust anyone.'

Which just about said it all. Lydia turned and walked towards her car. If it was true that he trusted no one then it was one of the saddest things she'd ever heard—and such a waste.

Was it money that had done that to him?

Or life? Perhaps a combination of both.

She climbed into her car and started the engine before fastening her seat belt.

Looking over her shoulder, she gave a brief wave and started down the drive before remembering the gates. Then she shrugged. Nick would remember she needed them to be opened.

*It had been a peculiar day.* And one she wouldn't be at all sorry to leave behind. She only hoped, for Rosie's sake, that Nick would take the initiative and call Izzy. She couldn't bear to think he'd leave his daughter so lonely and isolated.

# CHAPTER SIX

WENDY BENNINGTON sat ensconced in a high-backed chair positioned so she had a view of the sweeping lawn on the west side of Fenton Hall, her injured ankle elevated on a high footstool. 'I like that girl,' she said decidedly, watching Isabel Stanford's battered car disappear down the drive. 'Talks a lot of sense. Wouldn't believe she'd ever taken an overdose, would you?'

Nick certainly wouldn't have believed it.

'She seems tougher than that,' Wendy added, accepting the cup of tea her godson handed her.

Nick absent-mindedly picked up his own teacup. It would seem that his much vaunted ability to judge character had been at fault—once again. Isabel Stanford certainly didn't blame her sister in any way. He'd misread the situation entirely.

'Pass me a digestive biscuit,' Wendy said, pointing at the plate.

Nick picked it up and held it out to her.

'Thank you,' she said, proceeding to dip the chocolate-coated biscuit in the hot liquid. 'You know, this is one of the greatest pleasures of being my age. I no longer care whether anyone thinks this is good manners or not.'

'Did you ever?' Nick was rewarded with a sniff that he knew meant that his godmother agreed.

She fixed her eyes on him. 'You're very quiet. What did you make of what Isabel had to say?'

Nick stretched out his legs. 'I think she's right in thinking a deaf unit will suit Rosie.'

'What about the girl she mentioned? Rachel? Very young, of course, but if she signs it might make Rosie feel more settled here.'

Nick didn't answer.

'You do need to do something, Nick. Rosie's devastated by her grandma's death. It might help to have someone to sign with. She certainly liked talking to Isabel.' Wendy's face grew hard. 'Ana should be horse-whipped for not having dealt with it better.'

*He didn't disagree.* When Rosie had finally believed what he'd told her about her grandma she'd sobbed as though her world had ended. It had ripped him in two to think that, as far as she was concerned, it probably had. She'd lost the one person she seemed to have loved, had been uprooted from the only home she'd ever known and dumped with a father she barely knew.

Nick picked up a biscuit. 'It's certainly worth meeting Rachel, particularly if she'd be prepared to act as Rosie's communicator at school.'

Wendy watched him for a moment and then sipped her tea. 'I don't think I've ever been told before that children who have cochlear implants have to learn how to interpret what they're hearing. It's fascinating.'

'That's never been an option for Rosie.'

'No,' Wendy agreed, adding, 'but it made me wonder, if Rosie had been a suitable candidate for one, how Ana would have coped with the discovery that it wasn't a cure-all.'

Nick frowned. His imagination hadn't taken him that far, but Wendy was right. Ana thought hearing aids, in whatever colour, were simply ugly. In her mind a cochlear implant would have returned Rosie to normal.

'Can't see her liking a plastic disc stuck on her daughter's head any more than she likes things attached to her ears.'

'No,' Nick agreed. She wouldn't have liked it and it would have been impossible for Rosie not to have known.

His ex-wife lived her life in a way that placed beauty beyond anything else in importance. She hated poverty and illness in equal measure. Anything Ana perceived as ugly almost caused her physical pain. It had taken him a while to see that. Even longer to realise it extended as far as their child.

He might never be able to quite forgive himself for having not fought harder to keep a relationship going with his daughter, but now, given this second chance, he wouldn't fail her.

There was so much to absorb in what Isabel had said. The idea that there was an established deaf culture was completely new to him. He hadn't known that many deaf people didn't consider themselves disabled, but described themselves as a minority group. Isabel had said that her father had passionately believed that.

*He was Lydia's father too.* No wonder she'd been so angry that Rosie was being denied access to her first language. He wished he'd taken the opportunity to ask more questions, had tried to understand more.

If he'd known then that Isabel had really supported her sister's actions he might have listened.

*He might even have kissed her,* a quiet voice whispered inside his head. There'd been moments during that dinner when he'd wanted to. He'd hated the way his body responded to her laugh and the movement of her hand through her hair. He'd not understood how he could be so attracted to a woman whose value system he completely disagreed with. After Ana, he'd vowed he would never let that happen again. And it had been easy…until Lydia.

It didn't matter. Whatever Lydia Stanford was or wasn't, Rosie had to be his priority now. But he couldn't help but wish he'd handled dinner with Lydia differently. He'd been rude—and there never was an excuse for that.

Lydia approached Fenton Hall with a sense of *déjà vu.* Almost two weeks and she hadn't given the place a thought other than to wonder how Rosie might be faring.

Actually, that was completely untrue. She'd been itching to know whether Rosie had tried to run away again, whether Sophie was still there, whether Nick had taken on board anything she'd said to him over that disastrous dinner.

Not that she'd thought it remotely likely when she'd left, although there'd been a glimmer of hope that something she'd said might have made a difference when Izzy had rung to say that Nick had called her.

Lydia rounded the final bend. The flowers he'd sent her were a nice touch too. Twenty-four long-stemmed red roses with a white card attached saying simply 'Thank you. Nick'. It was difficult not to be impressed.

She'd told herself red roses were a predictable choice

of flower and that twenty-four was an obscene number to send anyone. But then she'd already ascertained that he was a traditional sort of man and they habitually lacked imagination. Besides, he had plenty of money and she had given up a whole day waiting for a cat.

The heady scent of roses had filled her flat for all of last week and every time she'd looked at them she'd thought of him. Had wondered how he was getting on with Rosie. Whether his daughter was happy.

And she should have rung to say thank you for them. She'd almost done it—twice—but, for some reason, hadn't. That part annoyed her. She'd been struck down by a kind of adolescent nervousness she thought she'd long since outgrown.

Lydia pulled into the lay-by and reached over for her mobile. It was easier to phone to get the gates opened than to get out of the car and use the intercom. She always hated those things anyway. She felt so foolish talking to a crackling voice through a metal box.

Nick's card was still tucked in the front of her handbag. Her fingers hesitated before keying in the number.

*She was nervous.* How ridiculous.

It was probably because she'd not contacted him about the roses. She should have done that. If she saw Nick today—and she probably wouldn't—she only had to thank him for the flowers and move on. She was here to see Wendy. This was really no big deal. There was no need to feel embarrassed or remotely uncomfortable, she reminded herself sternly.

Besides, he was very unlikely to mention her leaving their dinner so precipitately because…well, why would he?

Lydia bit down on her lip. The trouble was she'd been so affected by meeting Rosie that she'd forgotten there was no reason on earth why Nick should confide in her. And, if she was honest, it had hurt her that he hadn't chosen to.

'Just phone,' she said out loud. 'Get it over with. This is work.'

Obediently her fingers tapped out the number. She didn't realise how tensely she was holding herself until Christine Pearman's contained voice answered.

Her initial relief was immediately followed by a wave of disappointment that it hadn't been Nick. Lydia stamped down hard on it. *What was the matter with her?*

'Is that Christine Pearman?' she asked, trying to inject her voice with professional confidence.

'Yes.'

'Hello. It's Lydia Stanford. Can you open the gates for me? I'm a little early, but I've got an appointment to see Wendy Bennington.'

'Yes, of course, Ms Stanford.'

Lydia tossed the mobile back onto the passenger seat and the gates started to swing open. She was almost at the house before she remembered she hadn't called back to tell Christine she was safely through. Presumably the housekeeper would have shut them anyway. She'd have to check, though. *How embarrassing.*

One glance up at the house made her feel infinitely worse. It seemed she was going to have to confront Nick after all. He was walking down the wide steps towards her. One glimpse of his athletic physique and she felt distinctly more flustered than before.

*Which was illogical.* Completely, utterly, irritatingly illogical. She absolutely wasn't interested in a man who hadn't been bothered to learn to sign for his daughter—even if he did fill a pair of jeans better than most.

She pulled the car to a stop and Nick was there to open the door before she'd even taken the key out of the ignition. Her voice sounded pitifully breathless as she looked up at him. 'I forgot to ring back and say I was through the gates.'

For a moment he looked confused and then he said slowly, 'They're on a timer.'

His reply left her feeling as foolish as she had when he'd calmly opened Wendy Bennington's cottage door. Of course, then she'd been standing on his godmother's roof, which had put her at a distinct disadvantage. 'Last time I was here I had to let Christine know when I was through.'

'Did you?' he asked, as though he hadn't the faintest idea why that had happened.

Lydia could feel the start of a blush. 'I suppose that might have been because Rosie had run away.' She forced herself to stop rambling and hid her face by reaching for her briefcase. 'How is she?'

'Judge for yourself,' he said, looking over his shoulder.

Behind him, Rosie was running down the steps towards her. Lydia let her briefcase fall back on the passenger seat and climbed out of the car to meet her.

Rosie's brown eyes were sparkling as she waved her hello, but what really touched Lydia was the confident way she tucked her hand inside her father's. She was so different from the stiff and awkward little girl Lydia had coaxed back to the house barely two weeks earlier.

The little girl tugged at Lydia's soft cotton skirt, waiting until she had her full attention before she signed excitedly that she had a surprise. Her young face was happy and her hands moved rapidly.

Lydia looked to Nick for confirmation that she'd properly understood what his daughter was saying. It seemed impossible that anything could have happened so quickly. 'She's got a new nanny?'

He looked at his daughter and then at Lydia. 'How can you possibly know she said that? What's the sign for nanny?'

Lydia smiled. 'Literally she signed "new person keep safe me".' Her hands moved so that Rosie was included.

Nick stroked his daughter's hair. 'I'm never going to get this.'

It was incredible—and very wonderful—to hear that he wanted to. Before Lydia could think of anything to say, she saw someone she vaguely recognised coming down the stairs.

*Rachel.* She pulled the name out of the recesses of her memory.

'Rachel?' *It couldn't be.* 'What are you doing here?' Lydia moved forward and lightly kissed Rachel on the cheek, standing back to look at her. The last time she'd seen her she'd had braces on her teeth.

'I'm here to support Rosie,' Rachel said, her hands moving smoothly in perfect sign language.

Everything started to fall into place. Izzy had said she knew someone who might be perfect if Nick needed someone for sign support who liked children, rather than a trained nanny.

'I'm studying for my interpreters' qualification at the moment,' Rachel said, with a swift smile at Rosie, 'and Rosie is helping me practise.'

'That's...so good.'

Rosie nodded vigorously and signed that Rachel was also teaching Daddy.

Lydia turned to look at him, her eyes wide with amazement. 'You're learning sign language?'

Nick made a really good attempt at the sign for 'try'. Rosie laughed and Rachel smiled and signed that he'd done well. Lydia felt like she'd stepped into an alternative universe. Completely different...but truly wonderful.

Tapping Rosie on the shoulder, Rachel said, 'We need to go. Rosie has a swimming lesson in half an hour.' Rosie followed the signs and flung her arms about Nick before waving goodbye to Lydia.

Lydia watched them walk round to the garages at the side of the house, her embarrassment gone. She felt a sense of satisfaction which was completely out of proportion to her contribution. 'They look like firm friends.'

'And Rachel's only been with us for a couple of days.'

'That's fantastic!'

'It couldn't have worked out better,' Nick agreed. He glanced down at his watch. 'I know you've got an appointment with Wendy, but I'm afraid she's asleep. I could wake her, but she had a bad night and you'll probably find your time is more productive if she's rested.'

'Of course.' Lydia flicked back her hair. 'Look, I could go and have a look round the shops and come back in...an hour or so. It's not a problem.'

Nick shook his head. 'Bring your briefcase inside and have a drink. Unless you need to go somewhere?' he added as an afterthought.

'A drink would be nice. It's been a long drive.' And she

smiled, flicking back her hair again as it blew over her face. He was making this very easy. It was almost as though they'd parted friends and she was determined to meet him halfway. 'The traffic out of London was horrendous. I don't know where the world has decided to go today, but they're all on the motorway.'

She pulled her briefcase from the car and picked up her jacket. 'If you're busy, don't feel you have to entertain me. You can sit me somewhere and I'll work quietly on my laptop.'

Nick didn't answer straight away. He waited while she slammed the car door shut and then led the way up the steps. 'Wendy says you've made a start on the biography.'

'The publisher gave me an outline of what they particularly wanted to include and I've added some of my own ideas and roughly planned it out. It's early stages. I thought I'd talk to Wendy and see whether she feels there's anything I've missed or, conversely, something she'd prefer I left out.'

*She was babbling.* Lydia took a deep breath and made a mental promise that she wouldn't speak again until she'd counted to at least twenty.

'Hot or cold?'

'I beg your pardon?' Lydia said, following behind him.

'Would you prefer a hot or cold drink?'

Lydia mentally caught up. 'Cold, I think. Thank you.' And then she remembered. 'I'd meant to say earlier, but…thank you for the flowers. I should have phoned—'

'You're welcome.'

'You didn't have to do that. I wasn't expecting…' She broke off and started again, saying simply, 'They're beautiful. Thank you.' Lydia groaned inwardly. That 'thank you' had sounded much better when she'd rehearsed it in the car. She was supposed to be back in professional mode. Cool, calm, collected and only interested in the biography she was writing.

'Wednesday is Christine's day off,' Nick remarked, pushing open the door to the kitchen.

Lydia followed. 'So you're in charge?'

'Still pampered,' he returned, with a glint of humour in his dark eyes. 'Food is left in the fridge with a stick-it note on the door telling me how long to cook it for.'

Nick opened the fridge door and Lydia caught the fluorescent yellow paper as it blew off. 'Better not lose this then,' she said, handing it back, 'or you'll be going hungry.'

He stuck it back on the front. 'You wouldn't believe that I managed to feed myself perfectly well when I was at university.'

Lydia tucked her briefcase down beside the wall. 'I bet the quality was slightly different.'

She was surprised by that sudden smile. It had the same kick as a neat Scotch. 'I was famed for my unusual combinations.'

'Such as?'

'Have you ever tried spaghetti and cold pilchards?'

Lydia laughed. 'Fortunately not.'

'You don't know what you're missing.' Nick turned back to look at her. 'I have fresh orange. Water, obviously. Homemade lemonade...'

'Homemade lemonade would be lovely. I don't think I've ever had that before.' Lydia shifted her weight from one leg to the other. She'd forgotten quite how sexy he was.

Or had she? It explained her almost breathless excitement about coming here today. Nor was she quite sure how he could make a simple T-shirt look quite so…

Well, so.

She blew her hair out of her eyes. Every movement he made stretched the fabric over a taut male body.

'I can't take the credit for it. Christine makes it from her grandmother's recipe. The exact combination of lemons to sugar is a closely guarded secret.' He poured it into a glass and handed it to her. 'What do you think?'

Lydia took a sip. 'It's lovely.'

Nick smiled and poured himself a glass. Lydia was as beautiful as he remembered, but softer looking. Her white floating skirt finished just above her ankles and a wide belt wrapped low around her waist. The colours in the plaited leather picked out the tawny gold and rich copper threads in her hair and the warm caramel of her jacket.

He glanced down at the Anastasia Wilson jacket she held protectively in front of her. She seemed surgically attached to the blasted thing. Presumably it was this season's must-buy. 'Shall I hang that up for you?'

'Thank you.' She passed it across.

Nick carried the visual reminder of his ex-wife out into the hall and realised that, for perhaps the first time since Ana had left, he could be reminded of her and feel absolutely nothing. It was as though the angst he'd carried with him for the past four years had evaporated.

Standing there, in his hallway, he knew with complete certainty that he'd come away with the best part of their marriage—Rosie.

He slipped Lydia's jacket on to a hanger feeling euphoric. He had Rosie. What else mattered? And then he re-alised something else. Women didn't wear Anastasia Wilson if they knew there was a possibility of meeting him. It might mean nothing, but…

He frowned. In his experience they just didn't do that. Ana's designs were so completely distinctive. They were instantly recognisable and, since he was feeling charitable, he'd admit they were beautiful. She'd a flare for cutting fabric that sent women flocking to her when they wanted something understated yet memorable.

But women didn't wear them round him. Not if they knew she was his ex-wife. It seemed to be some unwritten code. As though to do so would be rubbing salt into a wound. Which meant that Lydia still didn't know…

And that meant she hadn't gone home looking for the 'skeleton in the closet'. A concentrated search would have found considerably more information on him than she'd brought up by typing in 'Nick Regan'. She'd have been able to read about the man Ana had left him for. Handsome, French, well-connected and one of his oldest friends.

She'd have known that their affair hadn't lasted long. Ana had made the contacts she'd needed, became bored and returned to London. By the time their divorce was final she'd moved back to Hampstead Heath and billion-aire Simon Cameron had taken up residence in the former marital home.

*Was it really possible she still didn't know?*

# CHAPTER SEVEN

NICK walked slowly back into the kitchen. He felt as if the ground had started shifting beneath his feet, so much so that he wasn't sure what he believed about anything any more.

Lydia hadn't moved. Her back rested on the central island unit and she was sipping her lemonade. Was it really possible that her interest was focused exactly where she said it was—exclusively on Wendy Bennington?

If so, the irony was that he probably knew more about her than she did about him.

He knew Lydia had never been married, but had been romantically linked to at least two high profile men. That she'd graduated from Cambridge six years after he'd left there himself and that her career trajectory had had the forward motion of an arrow in flight. In fact, every indication was that she was a serious-minded journalist who took what she did very seriously indeed.

Which was why his godmother had wanted her as her biographer, that small inner voice reminded him. More specifically, Wendy had wanted her because of an article Lydia had written on Third World famine. She'd described it as 'insightful' and a 'bloody sight more interesting than many things I've read on the subject'.

Nick felt like a fool.

He'd been adamant that journalists were the scum of the earth on the grounds that he had the emotional scarring to prove it. Wendy had argued that, as in all professions, there were good and bad. Bad journalists chased a 'story' in the hope of building their own reputations; good journalists wanted to change the world.

He hadn't listened. Hadn't been prepared to. He'd been so convinced that Lydia had orchestrated the Steven Daly trial for her own benefit that he'd filtered everything so it supported that belief. He couldn't deny she'd written some life changing stories, but each one had systematically built her career. Her piece on Third World famine had won her a prestigious award. He'd never questioned her ability, only her motivation.

He'd argued that if Lydia was the kind of journalist who would use her own sister's private grief, what would stop her from using his? If her primary aim was to find things out that no one knew and publish them before anyone else, then Ana's rejection of Rosie would make interesting copy. It would even be possible to make it sound as though she was championing people whom society considered outside the 'norm'.

*But Lydia hadn't done any kind of search on him.*

'Shall we take our drinks outside?'

Lydia hesitated. 'Don't you have things you need to be doing? I really don't want to get in the way.'

'I'm ready for a break and it's a beautiful temperature now. I suspect it's going to be too hot to be out there later.'

'You're sure you've got the time?'

Nick nodded and ushered her through the sunroom and on to the terrace. As the sunshine hit her face Nick heard Lydia's small purr of pleasure and he felt something inside him splinter.

Whatever it was that had kept him cocooned and protected had shattered. It left him feeling vulnerable, like an old-time knight without his armour.

And he wasn't sorry. There was danger in this—and excitement. It was like starting out on an adventure without having any idea what the outcome would be. He couldn't remember the last time he'd been reckless in his private life.

Nick led her across to the comfortable Lloyd Loom chairs with their white calico cushions and watched her settle into one.

'It's beautiful here,' she said softly and glanced across at him.

He didn't quite have time to look away and her eyebrows rose in a mute question. Nick shook his head, uncertain what to say. Or even where to begin.

'What happened to Sophie in the end?' Lydia asked, her hands cradled around the coldness of her tumbler.

'She decided she didn't like working outside London, so we mutually decided to waive the notice period.'

Lydia laughed. 'How…convenient.'

'Wasn't it?' he agreed easily. It was a miracle his voice sounded so steady. He felt as if the world had started spinning on a different axis.

Lydia took a sip of her lemonade. 'Did Rosie's mother mind you arbitrarily removing her choice of nanny?' And then she slapped a hand over her mouth and shook her head. 'I'm sorry. I was so determined I wouldn't ask those kinds of questions.'

'It doesn't matter.'

'I—'

Nick interrupted her. 'Lydia, I owe you an apology for the other night.' He needed to give more. 'I was very rude to you—and you didn't deserve that. I…appreciate your concern for Rosie.'

Her eyes widened slightly and then she half shook her head. 'You would probably have got there without my meddling. I shouldn't be so quick to give my opinions. It really wasn't my business to—'

'And, in answer to your question, I haven't asked her.' His index finger swept a clear line through the condensation on his glass. 'Ana is…more than happy to delegate.'

Lydia turned to look at him and he was almost certain she'd understood exactly what he'd wanted to convey. There was a momentary flash of sympathy, for him or Rosie he didn't know, and then she made a determined effort to lighten the atmosphere.

She set her empty glass down on the low table. 'Rachel is lovely. I used to be her babysitter. Did she tell you?'

Nick nodded. 'And that her parents are profoundly deaf.'

'They were close friends of my parents.' Lydia twisted one strand of hair in a small corkscrew on her finger. 'We used to go on holidays together. Once we hired a narrowboat and went up the Grand Union Canal…' She smiled. 'They live a couple of streets away from my aunt and uncle, so even after Mum and Dad died they kept a close eye on Izzy. Made sure she was doing all right.'

'Whereas you went to university?'

Lydia looked up. 'Yes. Yes, I did.'

It took a moment before she realised that he probably hadn't meant that the way it had sounded to her. He'd stated simple fact. Izzy had gone to live with relatives and she'd gone to university. It was the truth.

Lydia wiggled her left foot out of her sandal and watched the sunlight glint on the intricate gold toe ring. Nick couldn't know the guilt she still felt over that decision. No one knew. It was something she carried deep within herself.

It was her own private burden to know that if she'd made a different choice then it was possible she'd have been able to prevent Steven Daly ever becoming important in her sister's life. She had to live with the knowledge that she'd selfishly ploughed on with her original plans.

In the beginning it had been easy. She'd told herself her parents wouldn't have wanted her to do anything else. That she'd worked hard for her place at Cambridge, the only person from her state school to be offered one, and they wouldn't have wanted her to give it up. She'd consoled herself with the thought that Izzy would be fine with Auntie Margaret.

But Izzy had cried. Had begged her. Twelve years old and she'd wanted to stay in her home. And it would have been possible—if Lydia had assumed the responsibility of being her legal guardian.

Everyone had made it very easy. Auntie Margaret and her family were only too happy to take Izzy in. They'd decorated a bedroom especially for her and had carefully transferred all her sister's posters so she would feel at home.

Only Lydia knew that she was too selfish ever to have given up her dream. She'd consoled herself with the thought that her future success would justify that decision. The need to prove her decision had been the right one had been the driving force of her life.

'What made you decide on being a journalist?' His voice startled her.

Lydia glanced up, glad to be pulled away from memories that hurt. She chewed gently on the side of her mouth as she considered her answer. 'Does it sound too pretentious to say I wanted to make a difference?'

Her smile was almost shy. Nick watched as she pleated the soft cotton of her skirt. 'No.' His answer surprised him. *Amazingly, no.*

'I decided I didn't have the temperament of a saint,' she continued, her smile self-derisory, 'so I had to find a different route. I was hopelessly naïve.'

He waited for her to say more, and when she didn't he prompted, 'Journalism isn't what you hoped for?'

'Human nature isn't.' She gave him a swift smile. 'It's painful sometimes to stand dispassionately on the sidelines reporting what you're seeing, but doing nothing to actually stop it. I have a natural tendency to want to fix everything and it's not always possible.'

'Not always,' Nick murmured in agreement.

An expression of sadness moved over her face like ripples in a puddle. If he'd been Wendy it would have prompted him to ask Lydia about Izzy's overdose and everything surrounding it—but he couldn't bring himself to intrude into what must be a deeply private place.

Or perhaps he wasn't that noble, merely scared of Lydia's reaction. Trust was something that was earned and he'd offered little by way of fair exchange.

'Have you ever regretted it?'

She smiled. 'Many times. When you say you want to be a journalist everyone warns you you'll start by doing the obituaries.' Her smile widened and the result was infectious. 'That's not far from the truth, although in my case I wrote the "What's On" pages for the local *Herald*. Equally dull and certainly not what I'd planned to be writing about.'

'But you didn't have to wait long for your big break.'

'No.'

'You must have been very young when you went to work undercover in a care home,' he prompted, wanting to know more about her.

'They wanted someone who wouldn't be suspected, so I posed as a student needing holiday work. What I saw was shocking…' She broke off. 'How do you know about that?'

He'd spoken without thinking. Nick felt as though the world had stilled around him and only the two of them were left moving. He decided on honesty. 'I looked you up.'

'You looked me up?' she echoed.

He shrugged, half nonchalant, half apologetic. 'I know you've a first in English and Politics from Cambridge, that your first job was on a local paper in Manchester, that your professed hobbies include hang-gliding and the theatre.'

There was silence while she assimilated what he'd told her.

'Actually,' she said slowly, 'I don't like hang-gliding.'

He hadn't expected that reaction. 'You don't?'

Lydia smiled. 'You can't believe everything you read.' Her lips twitched with suppressed laughter. 'I was asked to do an on camera report about hang-gliding and I couldn't do it. First time ever I'd bottled out of a job, but I'm totally scared of heights. It didn't matter how safe they tried to convince me it was.' Then she looked across at him, her incredible eyes full of mischief. 'So you looked me up?'

'Yes.'

'Did you find the bit about the award I won?'

'On the issues surrounding Third World famine? Yes.'

And then she laughed. She turned her sparkling eyes on him to ask, 'Was it just idle curiosity or were you looking for something specific?'

Nick knew he'd been right not to relax. 'Honestly?'

'Of course.'

He hadn't really expected any other answer from her. Not now. 'I was looking for something that would convince Wendy to reject you as her biographer.'

The laughter disappeared from those amber depths and he almost wished the words unsaid. 'Why?'

He looked down at his hands and then back at her expectant face. Honesty deserved honesty. 'I remembered your name from the Steven Daly court case.'

'Many people do,' she said quietly.

'I believed you were driven by ambition rather than...a sense of justice and...'

'Go on.' Her voice had a steely edge to it.

'And there's not much more to say. I thought you'd seen an opportunity and gone for it.'

Lydia sat back in her seat. His words had shocked her but, strangely, they hadn't surprised her. They explained so much. 'You thought I'd put Izzy through that...for me.'

'Yes.' He met her gaze unflinchingly. She had to admire him for that.

She let out her breath on a hiss. She'd wondered why

he'd been so antagonistic towards her. Now she knew. His attitude towards her had seemed so unreasonable—but if he'd seriously believed she'd been capable of using her sister's situation to build her career it made complete sense.

Lydia shook her head. 'I would never do that.' She was guilty of many things, but not that. 'Why did you think I'd do that?'

Nick leant forward in his chair, his elbows resting on his knees. 'It was the way Isabel looked during the trial.'

She nodded. She could understand that. Izzy had been frightened and intimidated by the whole experience.

'And then she disappeared from view.'

'She was exhausted,' Lydia said quietly.

'Not surprisingly, now I think about it objectively.' Nick pulled a hand through his hair. 'But at the time… *Hell!* I don't know what I was thinking exactly. I suppose I thought that, although Steven Daly was convicted on all counts of embezzlement and fraud, the only real winner seemed to be you.'

Lydia felt as if she'd been doused in ice-cold water. She'd never thought it could be seen from that perspective. She wanted to cry out that it was unfair, palpably untrue—and then she thought of the opportunities that had come her way because the case had been given such a high profile.

Steven Daly had been a tiny cog in a much larger machine. As she'd picked away at why he'd needed a quick injection of cash she'd uncovered a trail of deceit and fraudulent business practices. Lydia had followed every lead tenaciously, she'd called in favours from friends and used every skill she possessed to bring down an insurance scam far bigger than anything she'd dreamed of.

*And what had Izzy got out of it?* Nothing but the intrusive sympathy of strangers.

Whereas she…

Nick's voice was low. 'When I met her last week it was immediately obvious I'd misread the situation completely. I'm very sorry.'

*Which explained the roses.*

Lydia looked across at him earnestly leaning forward, his elbows resting on his knees. He might have misread the situation in thinking she'd forced Izzy through the court case to further her career, but he was right in thinking that she hadn't acted on her sister's behalf.

The truth of that had been nagging at the back of her mind for the past couple of years. She forced her foot back into her sandal. 'No, you're right. I did it for me.'

His head snapped up. She hated the look of surprise on his face. It would be easier to accept his apology and move on, but that wouldn't be fair—either to him or Izzy—and it wouldn't be the truth.

'I don't think I fully realised it at the time, but it was my revenge, not hers. When I began, Izzy wasn't in any condition to give an opinion on it and, if I'm honest—' she looked out across the lawn '—I'm not sure I'd have asked her anyway. I hated Steven Daly and I didn't even know one tenth of what he was guilty of. I'd no idea he'd stolen from anyone but Izzy.'

Nick sat silent and she appreciated that. Few people, if any, had ever allowed her to express how much she'd hated Izzy's ex-boyfriend for what he'd done to her sister.

Hate was ugly. Hate gnawed away at you and destroyed you. She knew that, but hate had been her motivation. The charitable would say it was love for her sister, but she hadn't acted out of love. It had been a desire for vengeance, and vengeance hadn't healed Izzy.

Time had. Time and the self-worth her parents had instilled within her with years of loving. That had been the panacea. It had nothing to do with Lydia's meticulously researched investigation into her ex-boyfriend's business practices.

Slowly, painfully slowly, Izzy had rebuilt her life because she'd found the inner strength to do it. It had all taken so long. Nothing had happened with the speed Lydia had wanted and she'd been glad she'd had another focus for her energy.

Izzy had made great strides forward only to slip back. It had been excruciating to watch but, over time, there'd gradually been more good days than bad. The loss of the man who'd lied and stolen from her was separated out from the miscarriage of her baby. With counselling she'd come to see them as different issues.

Izzy had needed time and space to grieve for the loss of her baby. Knowing she was carrying a new life had been the only thing she'd had to console her when her world had crashed around her ears—and it had been the final loss, the one she'd been unable to cope with.

'She certainly doesn't blame you.'

Lydia looked up, wanting him to understand. 'I find that quite difficult to deal with because you're right. She did hate the court case and I made her do it because Steven Daly was—is—' she corrected herself '—a truly foul man.'

'Many hundreds of people lost their life savings because of him,' Nick said quietly.

'I'm not sure Izzy was in any place to really care.' Lydia twisted the fronds of her belt into a tight screw and watched them slowly unravel. 'The thing she found most difficult was having to stand up in court and face him. I'm certain she wouldn't have done it…' *Without me*, she finished silently, aware that if she tried to say those words out loud her voice would have cracked.

She knew that Izzy would have buckled under the pressure if she hadn't been there to propel her through the whole experience by the full force of her personality. *Her* sense of justice. *Her* need to see him suffer.

At eighteen she hadn't been prepared to stay and look after Izzy. She'd felt she'd failed her and was determined not to fail her again. She hadn't stopped to think whether it was what Izzy wanted.

She looked up. 'I couldn't bear it that he should get away with everything. So you were right…in a way. It was about me. Izzy is too gentle a person to think about revenge or punishment.'

Nick felt the slow burning of an almost incandescent anger towards the man who had hurt these women so much. If Steven Daly hadn't already been safely behind bars he might have been tempted to see what he could do.

How could he have misjudged Lydia so much? Nick watched the pain pass across her face and wished he could do something to make it all go away. There was nothing. She'd said it herself—time was the only thing that could heal hurt like that.

Perhaps the only thing he could do for her was not offer platitudes and spurious comments of sympathy.

Nick cleared his throat. 'Do you want to walk?' As she

looked up, her face unusually vulnerable, he felt his smile twist. 'Wendy will wonder what I've done to you.'

She gave a half laugh and swiped at her eyes. 'Do I look a mess?'

'You look beautiful.'

He'd spoken without thinking and his voice resonated with honesty. He saw her eyes widen and then she said quietly, 'A walk would be nice.'

'I'll take you to inspect my kitchen garden.' Nick stood up and held out his hand. In the heartbeat before she allowed him to pull her up from the chair he wondered whether he should have done it.

As his fingers closed around hers he wondered what would happen if he pulled her in close and held her…for comfort. Only for comfort. She was so close he could smell the soft scent of her perfume.

Instead he let go of her hand and turned to face the sweeping west lawn. Lydia walked beside him. Every so often he felt the soft flick of her hair as it was blown against his bare arm. Once he glanced down to see if she'd noticed, but her eyes were fixed on a weeping willow in the distance. She was staring at the cascade of delicate lance-shaped leaves as though she'd never seen anything so fascinating.

Nick wanted to say something that would help her, something that would soften that hard edge of guilt. He settled on a quiet, 'Knowing Steven Daly is in prison must have helped your sister's recovery.'

Lydia turned to look at him, the soft breeze catching her hair and blowing it across her face. She raised a shaking hand and pushed it back. 'I'm not sure it makes any difference to Izzy.' And then she thought and added, 'Perhaps. A little. Maybe knowing she isn't about to turn a corner and walk into him has allowed her to heal, but...' she shook her head '...he isn't in prison because of anything he did to her.'

Lydia didn't dare blink. Tears pricked hard behind her eyes and she felt as though a hard lump had settled in her throat. 'I just can't get my head round that. Where is the justice in someone being able to deliberately wreck another person's life and there be no redress?'

'There isn't any.'

Lydia took a deep shaking breath. 'Izzy voluntarily transferred the money from the sale of our parents' house into a joint bank account. So if he hadn't used the money to shield his illegal activities from detection I wouldn't have been able to touch him. It made no difference to anyone that Steven is a vicious bully.'

'Physically?'

Lydia smiled, but it was entirely without humour. 'If he'd touched her physically I would have got to him long before I did. Domestic violence is a crime. There are laws in place to protect women from that.'

'But nothing to stop him stealing an inheritance.'

'His legal representatives argued very convincingly that there was no theft involved.' Even now, after two years, that hurt. 'It made no difference that he'd systematically set about breaking Izzy until she would do practically anything he asked her to do. We didn't have any proof, so that was that.'

'Did you know what was happening at the time?' he asked quietly.

Lydia nodded. 'Living away in London, it meant I saw the changes in her quite clearly. Over time she lost her sparkle. She began to change the way she dressed, stopped meeting her friends… Hundreds of little things that in themselves didn't mean anything, but when you started to put them together they became much more sinister.'

'Wasn't there anything you could do?'

Lydia shrugged. Nick's questions came in a calm, matter-of-fact voice that made it easy to answer him. *At the time there'd been nothing she could do.* Though it hurt to remember that. 'Izzy loved him. Or thought she did.' She wrapped a protective arm around her waist. 'He could be very charming when he chose to be. Do you know the kind of man I mean?'

Nick thought about some of the corporate bullies he'd met. The smoothly manipulative ones who would act as though they were your best friend before stabbing you in the back at the first opportunity. He nodded.

'Of course when I first met him I didn't know anything about his business dealings; I only knew I didn't like him.' She smiled that tense, humourless smile again. 'He didn't like me either, but I can't blame him for that. From the very beginning I was doing everything I could to undermine him. I advised Izzy not to live with him, not to have a joint bank account, certainly not to have a family with him.'

'Did he know that?'

'I imagine so. She told him everything.' She gave a sigh and continued, 'He managed to convince Izzy I was jealous of him—and of their happiness. I'd finished a fairly serious relationship about that time. It all sounded plausible enough.'

'Except you knew you weren't jealous.'

Lydia looked up and smiled. 'Hindsight is a wonderful thing. I don't even know I knew that for certain. I may well not have liked anyone Izzy became so intensely involved with so young.' She paused. 'Though, to be fair to me, I specifically hated the pressure he put on her to sell our parents' house.'

'Surely you needed to agree to that?' *If the house had been left to them jointly?* It must have been left in trust while Isabel had been a minor. His mind started to think of everything that should have protected a vulnerable girl from becoming a target of a predator like Daly.

Her voice broke in on his thoughts, unusually toneless and edged with pain. 'I didn't have much choice. Izzy was nineteen by then and Steven convinced her they needed the money for their future. I dragged everything out as long as I could. I "forgot" to give the tenants notice, I insisted on marketing the house at too high a price…'

Nick smiled. It was easy to imagine Lydia doing that. 'He must have hated you.'

'He had his revenge. He used it as an opportunity to drive a wedge between Izzy and me.'

'I can't see that working. She idolises you.'

'Now.' She shook her head. 'Not then. Izzy was twelve when our parents died and she went to live with my mother's sister and her family. I went to university. We hadn't shared a house for six years by the time Steven came on the scene. It wasn't as difficult as you might think for him to insinuate himself into her life.'

She reached out and brushed away an angry tear. 'Anyway, the house eventually sold and Izzy's share of the money was transferred to her account. It took a few months longer for him to persuade her to put everything in joint names.'

'And then he emptied the account.'

'Basically.' Lydia rubbed her hand along her arm as though she suddenly felt cold. It had nothing to do with the weather, which was still balmy and hot. 'Izzy didn't know and, even when she did, he managed to convince her it was a temporary business hitch. She certainly didn't tell me until weeks later, by which time he'd left her anyway.'

Another swipe at her eyes and she took a shuddering breath. 'I'm sorry. I don't know why I'm crying.'

Nick did. He would never have described himself as a particularly imaginative man, but he was having no difficulty at all in empathising with everything she was telling him. There was nothing he could do to help her but listen.

'Anyway, it was a life-changing experience. I've spent the last year or so concentrating on raising public awareness. Society needs to protect other women from men like Steven Daly.'

'It's been successful,' Nick observed quietly.

'I've worked hard. I thought I was focused before, but this has been more like a crusade. I really believe in what I'm doing. The fact that it's brought me professional respect is a by-product. I'd do it anyway.'

They walked through the narrow opening to the enclosed wall garden. Nick kept silent, instinctively knowing she wouldn't want anything else.

Lydia looked around at a kitchen garden that was still very much in the early stages of planning. He watched as her expression altered and she breathed softly. 'This is going to be amazing.'

Her eyes still held a hint of remembered pain, but she was back in control. The mask she wore to protect herself from the world was back in place. Even so, Nick didn't think he would ever be able to look at her again without remembering how vulnerable she could be. *The real Lydia Stanford.*

He looked around the kitchen garden which had taken him so many hours. It had been the place where he'd come to terms with many of his own demons. 'It's been slow going. When I arrived there was an old greenhouse on the site, which had been smashed. I've spent the better part of this year clearing away debris and picking pieces of glass out of the soil.'

Lydia's eyes followed the far wall with its fan-trained peach trees. 'It's coming along now, though.' She walked between two beds and stopped. 'I don't recognise this.'

'*Allium cepa "Prolifera".*' He smiled, watching the way she gently stroked the plant. 'It's a tree onion. I think it's the most decorative form of the onion family. The onions themselves are small but strong. Fine for pickling.'

He loved the way her eyes darted about the enclosed space. 'This is south-facing, isn't it?'

'Yes. It gets the sun for most of the day, until late in the afternoon, and the fact that it's so sheltered should make it highly productive.'

'You might be able to experiment with more exotic fruit and vegetables here.' She looked up at him and he felt his heart tighten so that he felt almost breathless. 'I must get a garden. I do miss it.'

Nick glanced down at his watch. 'We've given Wendy an hour. We ought to start heading back.'

With one last look over her shoulder, Lydia led the way out of the kitchen garden. As they left the enclosed space the summer breeze whipped at her hair. She caught it and twisted it into a loose plait.

Nick felt his stomach twist. Lydia was beautiful, intelligent and caring. It was hardly surprising that he should be attracted to her.

But a woman as vibrant as Lydia Stanford was never going to be interested in a man like him. A single father, tied to one place in one country. No adventures. No great causes.

They walked back across the lawn towards the house. What he needed to do was let Lydia get on with her job. She was here to see Wendy.

He had to remember that when she'd gathered all the information she needed she'd be gone.

# CHAPTER EIGHT

*NEVER cry all over a man—they don't like it.* Who had said that? Lydia returned with the tray of filter coffee and mugs and set it down on a low table.

She couldn't remember who'd given such sage advice, but she wished she'd paid more attention to it. Her third visit within eight days to Fenton Hall and Nick was noticeable by his absence. When she'd left after seeing Wendy the first time he'd been taking an important telephone call from Germany. On her second visit he'd been in London. This time he was expecting a conference call and was in his study.

It *might* be coincidental that he was never around, but if she'd been a betting woman she'd have laid odds on it not being. In her opinion it was beginning to look as if her arrival was his cue to disappear and she wasn't holding her breath in expectation of seeing him before she left today. When she'd gone to ask Christine for coffee his study door had been wide open and his computer switched off, but he'd been nowhere to be seen.

She pushed down the plunger. Perhaps she'd embarrassed him by crying? Maybe it had been information overload and he'd felt uncomfortable? Certainly she shouldn't have cried. She never cried.

She hadn't meant to. It had shocked her that he'd thought she would have deliberately used Izzy…and then she'd started talking and hadn't seemed able to stop. He hadn't seemed to mind. In fact, he'd been lovely. Surprisingly so.

Something had shifted the last time she'd seen him. It had felt as if they'd reached a new understanding, had begun a friendship. She shrugged. Clearly not. He'd obviously been marking time until his godmother woke. Anything else had been in her imagination.

Wendy put the sheaf of papers she'd been reading on the small table to her side. 'Are we done for today?'

'I think so,' Lydia said, lifting the coffee jug. 'You ought to have a rest after you've drunk your coffee…and I've got plenty to be going on with.' She smiled. 'Eighty-five thousand words, to be precise.'

'You know, it's depressing to think I was talking about all this twenty years ago,' Wendy said, indicating the papers at her side. 'I read the other day that the Amazon rainforest is currently being flattened at a rate of six football pitches every day. Six! And in some remote parts there's just one forestry agent to monitor an area four times the size of Switzerland.'

Lydia poured the coffee. 'I thought governments were now committed to stopping forest-clearing.'

'There's a big difference between what a politician promises before an election and what he delivers after it,' Wendy said dryly. 'Depressing, but true. It's complicated, of course. One can only be sympathetic to a country which needs agricultural businesses to keep expanding if they're to pay their external debt, but that's why I personally believe we should remove the debt…'

'Is something the matter?' Lydia asked as Wendy trailed off, her attention claimed by something outside the window. The elderly woman's face had lost its crusading fire and had become wistful.

'It's Nick.'

*Nick.* Immediately Lydia's stomach did a kind of belly flop.

'In the garden.' Wendy turned her head to look at her.

Lydia carried a bone china mug over to where Wendy was sitting. It gave her a perfect view of the sweeping lawn…and Nick. Nick and Rosie.

She watched as he swung his daughter round and landed her carefully, their faces full of laughter. Father and daughter. They made a striking couple. Nick in dark blue denim jeans and an olive-green T-shirt, Rosie in yellow shorts and equally bright cotton sun-top. They could easily have been part of a television advert.

'It's good to see that relationship building,' Wendy observed from her chair. 'Give him time and I think he'll be a fine father. Better than his own, anyway. Though that's not saying much.' She sipped her coffee. 'George was a cold man.'

Lydia glanced down at the grey head, hair neatly twisted into a chignon. She longed to ask questions. Her mouth twisted. It wouldn't be wise. Wendy was sharp enough to notice and she wasn't sure yet why she was so interested in everything concerning Nick.

He might be making great strides in building a relationship with Rosie now, but the fact remained that he hadn't done much in the previous five years. When she actually thought about it, that aspect of his character wasn't attractive at all.

So why did she feel this compulsion to see him, talk to him? Maybe she was piqued by the fact that he didn't seem remotely interested in her.

'Fortunately there's enough of his mother in him to make Nick worth bothering about.'

Lydia deliberately moved away from the window. It was almost painful to see how happy Nick and Rosie were together. Beautiful to see, of course, but she felt a stab of envy as she watched them. She didn't understand why that was, either. It all smacked of domesticity and she avoided that like the plague.

'Jennifer, Nick's mother, was a lovely girl. Died when Nick was a young baby,' Wendy continued as Lydia took her own cup and sat down again on the coral-coloured sofa. 'She had rheumatic fever when she was a child and was never very strong afterwards.'

'Did Nick's father marry again?' Lydia asked, trying to keep her voice light and neutral. It seemed an innocuous enough question.

Wendy snorted as though it were the stupidest of suggestions. 'It was surprising he found anyone to marry him the first time. Complete bore of a man, though very handsome. I never liked him. Thought he knew better than anyone else on any subject. Didn't believe it was possible for a woman to understand world market indices. After thirty years of arguing with him, I finally came to the conclusion I'd leave him in his ignorance.'

Even filtering that snippet of information through an understanding of Wendy, it still gave an evocative picture of Nick's father and, by extension, his childhood.

*He'd grown up without a mother.* That didn't surprise her. *And with a distant father.* She was even less surprised by that. Lydia sipped her coffee and wrinkled her nose at the bitter taste. She leant forward and spooned in a teaspoon of brown sugar. 'What's happened to Rosie's mother? Has she died?'

'Ana? Dead?' Wendy smiled grimly. 'No. Why did you think that?'

Lydia sat back. 'I—I don't know. I just wondered—'

'Rosie's mother is Anastasia Wilson. She's not dead. Though she's just about as much use,' Wendy added after a moment.

*Anastasia Wilson.* For one moment Lydia wasn't sure she'd heard correctly.

'She's a fashion designer. Has her own label now, I believe.'

'Yes, I know,' Lydia said. 'I love her clothes, but… *Anastasia Wilson* is Rosie's mother?'

Wendy gave her habitual snort of derision. 'Well, she gave birth to her, but she hasn't done much mothering. Left all that to her own mother.'

'Who's just died,' Lydia said under her breath, finally understanding why Rosie had come to live with Nick.

Wendy didn't seem to have heard her. 'As soon as there was the slightest possibility she might have to assume some parental responsibility Ana passed Rosie over to Nick.'

As though she'd been a parcel. *Poor little girl.* No wonder she'd looked so stiff and lonely when she'd first seen her. No one had even bothered to tell Rosie her grand-mother had died.

But...

Her mind seemed to have frozen on the one thought— *Anastasia Wilson had been married to Nick Regan-Phillips.* It had the same impact as if Wendy had said he'd been married to the Queen. It didn't seem possible.

They were two completely disparate people with, surely, nothing in common. Lydia had been at the same function as Anastasia Wilson several times without actually 'meeting' her, but she had read several articles about her in glossy magazines. Any visit to a dentist waiting room inevitably brought you into contact with one. She didn't remember any mention of Nick or of her having a child.

She frowned as she tried to pull disregarded information into the forefront of her mind. Anastasia, she was sure, currently lived with a man who Lydia would describe as having too much of everything: too tanned, too blond and too rich. And before that there'd been...Gaston Girard, the charismatic tennis star whose family had been involved in fashion for several generations. He'd seemed a better idea, but slightly too smooth for her taste.

But, a child? She couldn't remember anything about Anastasia Wilson having a child.

Most recently it had been about her fabulous new home in Jamaica and the inspiration she'd found experiencing a new culture. There'd been some mouth-watering photographs of her last collection, soft wisps of chiffon which had been turned into stunning evening gowns.

Without a doubt, Anastasia Wilson had an incredible flare for colour and a seemingly effortless ability to make the woman in her designs shine rather than her clothes. She was a brilliant designer. In fact, one of her favourites. But as a woman…

As a woman she came across as shallow, vain and rather silly. Everything she said was peppered with anecdotes of parties, people and places.

*Married to Nick Regan-Phillips?*

*No.* She couldn't believe it. Nick was fearsomely intelligent. Quiet and private. It just didn't fit.

Lydia wanted to ask so many questions. How long were they married? How did they meet? Why did they divorce…?

And then she remembered her jacket and cringed. Had Nick recognised it as one of his ex-wife's designs? *Who was she kidding?* Of course he had. It was unmistakable.

But she hadn't known. If she'd known who his ex-wife was, she'd never have worn…

*Anastasia Wilson was Rosie's mother.* That single fact pounded in her head and still she couldn't quite take it in.

'I'd no idea Anastasia Wilson had any children. I'm sure I've never seen any pictures…'

Wendy shook her head sadly. 'When Rosie was a baby there were plenty of photographs of them taken together, but in recent years…no.'

Lydia frowned.

'She's deaf.' And then, because Lydia clearly hadn't made the connection, Wendy added, 'Ana has a real problem with having a deaf daughter. She strives for perfect…and deaf isn't perfect. Not for her.'

Lydia swore softly. This beggared belief. 'Who taught Rosie to sign?'

'Nick asked Ana about that the other day.' Wendy paused to readjust her leg on the footstool. 'Apparently Ana's mother was very keen on it. There's some research to show that all babies, hearing or otherwise, do better intellectually if they sign pre-language. At least that's how she sold it to Ana. Makes me think a lot better of Georgina. I'd always thought she was a fairly stupid woman for giving birth to Ana, but...'

Georgina being Rosie's grandmother, Lydia thought, trying to piece together so many new pieces of information.

'...obviously not so stupid after all. She was also the person who insisted Rosie went to a nursery school with a deaf unit.'

*Thank God for Georgina.* But where had Nick been in this? Why hadn't he been the one insisting on the sign language and finding nurseries?

'So Nick hasn't told you anything about Ana?'

'No.' Lydia put her empty coffee cup down on the table. *He certainly hadn't.*

'Can't blame the boy for that. He should never have married her.' Wendy finished the last of her coffee. 'Though I doubt I'd have listened to me in his position. I've never been able to see much point in any marriage. I've always thought there had to be more to life than handing round hors d'oeuvres and having babies, so I'm no judge of what will suit other people.'

She lifted her leg off the footstool and reached behind her for the crutches resting against the chair back. Lydia was on her feet but Wendy waved her away. 'Have you ever used crutches?'

'No.'

'Can't wait to get rid of the things.' Wendy started towards the door. 'We're not meeting now until next week are we?'

Lydia shook her head. 'You've got an orthopaedic outpatient appointment tomorrow and I've got a book launch to go to the following day.'

'Until next week, then.'

Lydia resisted every impulse to help her, knowing how much that would be resented. She slowly gathered together all her papers and tucked them into her briefcase.

It really was impossible to think of anything other than the fact that Nick had been married to Anastasia Wilson. If she was being really rude, she couldn't quite get her head round the fact that an intelligent man had married a woman who talked in a 'little girl' voice.

Hadn't it grated? Or had he been completely mesmerised by her petite frame and cloud of jet-black hair? And with a spurt of jealousy she realised she didn't want to think about that.

Lydia put the final papers, the ones Wendy had been reading, in her briefcase and clicked it shut. She looked out of the window where Nick and Rosie had been.

They'd gone.

There was just that long expanse of lawn leading down to the weeping willow and on to a tightly packed spinney. There was no chance of seeing Nick today then. It was probably for the best, but...

She felt strangely purposeless. It would have been nice to have spoken to him. Seen Rosie. Lydia glanced down at her watch and debated whether she should make the drive home or stop in Cambridge for some retail therapy. There was so much she should be doing, but she didn't have the motivation.

Even though the sunlight had shone brightly through the windows all morning, the midday sun was something of a shock when Lydia walked out on to the stone steps. Heat hit her like a wall. She wrinkled her nose as she thought of the long sticky car journey home.

She crossed the front courtyard and unlocked her car, putting her briefcase inside, as the sound of scrunching gravel made her look up. Rosie came running round the corner as a streak of yellow. She looked bright, happy and very hot.

Lydia smiled, loving to see her energy and exuberance. It was what a childhood should be about. Rosie caught sight of her and waved a hand.

*Anastasia Wilson's daughter.* Now she knew she could see her mother in the dark curling hair and the almond-shaped eyes. A beauty—but not perfect enough for Anastasia. Lydia felt a wave of sheer anger at the ignorance and injustice of that.

Lydia shut the car door and waited until Rosie was near enough to sign. She wanted to ask where Nick was, but settled on asking where Rosie was running to.

The little girl's eyes shone with excitement. Her hands moved to show a square rug laid out on the floor and then she peppered her picnic with strawberries and cream, cheese, bread, small cakes and, best of all, crisps. They were her favourite and she'd picked them out of the cupboard herself, four whole packets.

Lydia laughed and told her she didn't like strawberries. After a moment of surprise Rosie signed that they also had bananas, but clearly she didn't feel they were as good. *She was an absolute sweetheart.* How could her mother not love and cherish her?

She saw Nick's shadow before she saw him. He rounded the bend and stopped when he saw her. Lydia instinctively smoothed down the skirt of her layered sundress. She waited while he crossed the courtyard towards her. 'Hello.'

'Hello,' he replied. And then, 'You've finished early. I thought you wouldn't be leaving for another hour or so.'

His words sharpened the suspicion that he'd been deliberately avoiding her. For a moment that hurt—and then she looked into his eyes and caught a glimpse of something that turned everything on its head. She saw a definite flicker of desire in their hazel depths.

And then she remembered something else. He'd said she was beautiful. With sudden clarity she realised he'd meant it and now she saw it in his eyes.

*So why avoid her?* That part didn't make any sense. Unless he still thought she was the kind of journalist who'd sell any kind of story. *Did he still think that?* It felt very important that he shouldn't still think that.

'We're going on a picnic.' His hand rested lightly on his daughter's head.

Lydia tossed back her hair, which was lying heavily about her shoulders. 'I know.' She smiled down at Rosie. 'And you've raided Christine's cupboards and taken four packets of crisps.'

'Do you think I've over-catered?'

Lydia felt a smile tug at her lips. 'Probably not.' Small lines fanned out at the edges of his eyes. *Gorgeous.* Absolutely gorgeous.

On some level, somewhere, she had to believe there was a very good reason why he'd not worked harder on being involved with Rosie's life. Seeing him with his daughter now it seemed incredible that he hadn't.

'Is Wendy tired?'

'No. Well, not particularly. She's gone for a sleep now, but we finished early because we'd got to a sensible place to stop.'

*In fact, they'd almost finished altogether.* Did he know that? Wendy had already been more helpful than anyone had anticipated. One more visit would probably be all that was necessary—and then there'd be no reason to return here. She might never see Nick again. All of a sudden it seemed incredibly important that that shouldn't be allowed to happen.

Rosie tugged on her dress and signed for her to come with them. She pointed out into the garden and Lydia would have loved to simply nod. Instead she glanced uncertainly across at Nick, not even knowing whether he would have understood what his daughter was saying.

His expression looked slightly rueful. 'Would you like to join us?'

Lydia bit nervously on her lip. Did he want her to join them, or didn't he? Looking at him now, she couldn't see the faintest trace of the desire she'd seen earlier and all her lovely confidence faded.

As though he sensed her uncertainty, Nick added, 'We've got plenty of crisps.'

Lydia smiled and held tight on the young hand in hers. It was all the encouragement she needed. 'I'd love to join you.' She looked down at Rosie and nodded. She was rewarded with a sunny smile before Rosie shook free and tore like lightning across the lawn.

'You'd think she'd be too hot to run like that, wouldn't you?' Nick observed beside her.

She had to ask. 'Do you mind me joining you?'

'Of course not.'

His reply was just a little too automatic. It made her wonder what he'd have said if he wasn't quite so 'British'. *What did he think of her?* She really wanted to know. At least she did if he'd revised his first impression of her. If not…well, if not she probably didn't want to know.

Lydia clipped her keys on to her belt. 'Do you want me to carry anything?' she asked, looking at the backpack, rolled up picnic rug and a purple-coloured plastic box.

'No. I'm balanced.'

She nodded and turned to walk with him across the lawn. It took an almost superhuman effort not to ask him about Anastasia, or Ana as he called her. She wanted to know whether there was any possibility of Rosie living with her mother again or whether she was settled at Fenton Hall for good.

Instead she asked, 'Is it Rachel's day off? I haven't seen her today.'

He nodded. 'It's a college day.'

'But she's happy here?'

'So she says,' Nick replied. 'Rosie's ecstatic.'

Lydia nodded and wondered what to say next. She looked about her, taking in the formal rose garden near the house. 'Do you have a favourite picnic spot?'

'Not yet. This is a first for me.'

*Of course he wouldn't have.* Lydia watched her feet as

they trod through the grass. He wouldn't have gone on a picnic because this was his first summer with his daughter. Seeing him with Rosie it was difficult to believe—and another thing she wanted to ask him about, but really mustn't.

'My preference today is for shade,' he said, looking down at her. 'How about you?'

'Shade's good.'

His smile twisted and then he asked, 'What was it you wanted to ask?'

Lydia gave a short laugh. 'How could you tell?'

He merely shook his head.

'Am I really that obvious?'

'To me.'

She looked away at the warm expression in his eyes. It scared her, but excited her too. The juxtaposition between the two extremes made it confusing. She hurried into speech without stopping to think whether it was wise or not. 'I was only thinking this must be your first summer with Rosie.'

'Apart from the summer she was born,' Nick agreed easily. 'She was nine months old when Ana left me.'

Anastasia Wilson had left *him*. That was a thought that was going to take a bit of getting used to. It didn't seem possible that any woman would prefer the overly bronzed playboy she now lived with over Nick.

*But it was now or never.* Lydia took a shallow breath. 'Anastasia Wilson. Wendy told me.'

'Did she?' His expression was inscrutable. It was really unnerving not to be able to tell what he was thinking, particularly when he seemed to be able to read her perfectly well.

'I—I asked her whether Rosie's mother had died.' She twisted round the gold bangle on her wrist.

'Ana?'

Lydia smiled. 'That's exactly what Wendy said. I'd not heard her referred to as anything other than "Ana", so I didn't know who she was.'

'Did Wendy tell you anything else?'

Lydia reviewed her options. She bit down on her lip. She could tell him Wendy's views on marriage, which he probably knew. Or that she hadn't liked his father, which, again, he probably knew. But that wasn't what he meant and she knew it. 'She said Anastasia isn't a natural mother.'

'That's true enough.'

Rosie skipped back and pointed at the ground before signing out the picnic mat.

'Over by the trees,' Nick said carefully, pointing a short distance in front of them. Then he looked at Lydia. 'What's the sign for tree?'

Lydia made the sign, splaying her fingers. 'It's an obvious one. Use your hand to make the branches, your forearm is the trunk.'

'I think I remember that one. It's more like charades.'

'Most signs are fairly straightforward. The knack is to think in pictures.'

'Such as?' They stopped at the base of a mature oak tree. Rosie was ready to help unpack everything. Nick laid a restraining hand on the top of her head. She looked up and he mouthed the word, 'Steady.'

He slipped the backpack off his back and set it on the ground. Rosie undid the buckle and struggled with the toggle which kept the top tightly closed. She looked up at Lydia, who stepped forward to open it.

Rosie reached in and pulled out a plastic box and unclipped the lid. Inside were tiny plastic Playmobile figures—a table, pram and assorted other things Lydia couldn't quite make out in the time they were held up to her.

Lydia turned round to find that Nick had spread out the picnic rug and sat down. 'Won't she lose the figures in the grass? Some of those pieces are very small.'

'I doubt it. She's incredibly dextrous and very careful. That box is part of an enormous plastic dolls' house she brought with her. She plays with it for hours. Far more than anything else.'

Lydia sat down on the rug and turned to watch Rosie as she set out tables and chairs among the tree roots and carefully balanced people in all the crevices. Quickly it began to take on the appearance of a little community and she moved her people around it, obviously lost in a world of her creating.

'It's amazing to watch,' Nick said. 'It's almost like she's directing an epic movie.'

Lydia turned back to look at him. 'It's very creative.'

'That's in her genes.' He pulled out a bottle of wine from an insulated bag and glanced at the label. 'Wine?'

She nodded.

Nick unscrewed the top and reached inside the box for a flask of coffee. 'We're going to have to drink from the flask cups, but since you're the guest I'll let you have the one with the handle.'

He poured wine into the first cup and passed it over to her. 'It's Australian. I've no idea whether it's a good vintage or not, but I like it.'

Lydia accepted the plastic cup. 'I would have thought you'd be a wine connoisseur.'

'I'm reliably informed I have no palate,' he said, pouring some into the second cup. 'My father was passionate about his wines. He had a cellar built beneath our house which was kept at the optimum temperature. I thought it incredibly dull and cultivated a taste for everything he thought most contemptible.'

'As rebellions go that's fairly mild,' Lydia observed, taking a sip. 'This is nice. I wish I knew something about wines. I hear other people talking about it and they sound so educated.'

The lines to the sides of his eyes crinkled. She loved the way they did that. 'I'm sure you can make it sound like you know what you're talking about. This one is "crisp and refreshing"'. He held up the bottle. 'It says so on the label.'

Lydia smiled. 'I've got no palate either. My dad used to make his own wine. We used to have oil-fired central heating and there was a boiler house just behind the kitchen. Dad used to say it was the perfect place to ferment wine.'

'Was it good?'

'Terrible,' she said on a bubble of laughter. 'If I'm honest, it all tasted a little bit yeasty. The absolute worst was parsnip, although he made a potato wine which was pretty unpleasant...but drinkable with cheese.'

Nick's eyes glinted across at her and she felt a burst of sheer happiness. She could get used to this. Lazy summer days, picnics with wine, Nick...

She could get used to Nick.

The way his dark hair curled at the back of his neck. The way he focused his attention on you when you talked and made you feel important. She loved his slow laughter and the easy way he moved. Lydia watched as he unpacked the food from the picnic box and laid it in front of the rug. It was companionable. Easy. There were so few days in her life when she did something for no other reason than it gave her pleasure.

'Explain to me what you meant about thinking in pictures when you sign.'

'Well…' Lydia glanced over at Rosie, still playing in the shade of the tree. 'Rosie might prefer you to use sign support, which would mean you'd follow normal speech patterns, but BSL is different.'

'BSL being what the interpreters use in the bottom right of the television screen?'

Lydia nodded. 'British Sign Language. If you wanted to sign a story about a man standing on a bridge you need to build up a visual image with your signs. If you sign "man" first you've got him in a vacuum which doesn't mean much.'

'So?'

'You paint a picture. You start by signing "bridge" because that's where it all happens. If it's important where the bridge is you fill in what's around it. Maybe put in nearby trees…or a stream. A castle, if that's what's there.'

Nick smiled. 'I've got the sign for tree.'

'You place everything in your picture and only then do you bring in the man. He can be on the bridge or by the bridge, walking across the bridge or jumping off it. Everything is shown by where you place your fingers in the picture.'

'Sounds complicated.'

She shook her head. 'It isn't. It's actually quite logical.'

Nick watched the light play on the myriad tones in her

hair. Streaks of gold, bronze, auburn and chestnut in a harmonious blend. Stunning. *She* was stunning.

He'd known, since that day in the kitchen garden, that he was attracted to her in a way he'd never been to anyone else. He'd thought he'd be able to control it if he didn't spend time with her, vanquish it. But he'd been wrong.

Nick watched as she unbuckled her sandal and slid her foot out to let her toes wiggle in the grass. She was unconsciously sexy. Ana struck poses, but Lydia simply was. Her long elegant fingers played with the gold chain at her neck and he saw the small pulse that beat there.

Avoiding her hadn't helped at all. Trying to keep away from her had only served to heighten his awareness of everything about her. She pushed her hair to one side and then twisted it round and pulled it through into a knot at the back of her head. Her movements were swift, practised…and sexy. Nick looked away, almost unable to cope with seeing the long graceful curve of her pale neck.

'It's hot.'

Nick glanced back. 'Don't you like the heat?'

'I'm the wrong colouring. Izzy and I both burn easily. Mum was a true redhead. We both missed out on the hair, but got the freckles.'

Nick looked closer and saw the fine dusting of freckles over her nose. Fresh, pale and beautiful.

Rosie brought over a small figure and held it out to Lydia, her hands flying as she told her something.

Lydia bent over the figure and then looked up. 'I can't do this.'

'What?' The vibrant colour of her eyes almost stopped him from breathing.

'The hat is stuck on too tightly.' She held it out and Nick reached across to take it.

He'd never believed it in movies when people seemed to imply a touch could be electric, but the merest touch of her fingers sent him into overdrive. Nick bent over the figure and pushed off the medieval headdress it wore, glad when the plastic moved. He looked up to see Rosie had settled comfortably in Lydia's lap.

Her beautiful hands lightly touched Rosie's arms and her head bent and softly kissed the top of his daughter's hair. Nick swallowed the lump that had settled in his throat.

*He was falling in love with her.*

*Please, no.* Never again.

If a miracle happened and Lydia could be persuaded to stay for him, it couldn't last. One day she'd wake up, just like Ana, and realise she was bored. There was no point pursuing something that couldn't have a future. Particularly since this time, he had the strongest feeling, he would never recover.

After a moment he held out the figure. 'Here.'

Rosie leapt up and quickly signed a thank you before taking the figure. It was unbelievable to him that he could recognise the sign as easily as if she'd spoken to him.

And all that was because of Lydia. If she hadn't pricked his conscience he might still have been locked in a completely separate world from his daughter. It didn't bear thinking about.

'Rosie doesn't look like she burns,' Lydia remarked, her face turned away to watch as Rosie carefully clipped on a different hat before balancing the figure. 'I always wanted that kind of olive-tinted skin. I always thought it looked exotic.'

Nick had to turn away. Lydia had no idea what exotic was. Exotic was the vibrancy in her hair, the mystical depths of her eyes, the way the layers of her ethnic skirt swung about her long legs. It was the tiny Celtic toe-ring she wore and nails painted in an extravagant shade of copper.

'She doesn't seem to burn, but I ought to put some more cream on,' he said, settling on the prosaic.

Lydia swung back to look at him. 'So should I. I never do remember and then I suffer later.'

'Use ours.' Nick reached into the backpack and pulled out a bottle of sun protection. 'It's got a factor of forty.'

Lydia took the bottle and squeezed a little out into her hand; it shone green in her palm. 'Is it supposed to be that colour?'

He felt his mouth twitch. 'It's so you can see where you've applied it. It fades.'

'So if I put this on I'm going to be green?'

'In the short-term,' he agreed.

Lydia looked at him doubtfully, as though she knew how near he was to laughing. Gingerly she smeared green streaks up her arm. 'You're sure this fades?'

'It's a brilliant idea when you have a wriggling five-year-old.'

'I'm not five!'

*No, she wasn't five.* Nick watched as she gently smoothed the lotion up her arms, across her shoulders, up her neck.

Gingerly she dabbed a faint smear across her nose and blended it in. 'Have I missed anywhere?'

Nick moved closer and reached out to touch her face. His thumb moved lightly across her cheekbone. 'There's a little bit…' And then his voice dried up. He couldn't think what he'd been about to say. He only knew how it felt to be touching her. Really touching her.

Her eyes were wide, flecked gold and stunningly beautiful. He saw her lips part softly and heard her sharp intake of breath.

*God held him.* He felt as if he was being drawn in as surely as a fisherman brought in his catch. It was inevitable. No escape.

He'd been fooling himself thinking there was still time to save himself from hurt—*he already loved her.*

And he wanted to kiss her. Make love to her. He so desperately wanted to make love to her.

There was no choice any more. He would settle for whatever she could give him for as long as she could give it.

'You're so beautiful.' He murmured the words against her mouth as his lips closed against hers. His hand twisted in through the soft knot at the back of her head and dimly he was aware of the cascade of hair that fell like a curtain about her shoulders.

Her lips trembled beneath his as though she was uncertain and then she relaxed into him. And for one moment all he could think of was her and how incredible it felt to hold her.

# CHAPTER NINE

ON SOME level Lydia had always known that Nick would kiss like that. Her heart hammered painfully against her chest and her skin tingled where his hand touched. She heard the soft guttural sound of triumph he made as he pulled her in closer and felt her own spirit soar in response.

Then he tensed. Lydia wanted to cry out in protest as he started to pull back...and then she remembered Rosie. Probably a fraction after he had.

*Rosie.*

Lydia looked across at Rosie, wondering how much she'd seen. Her dark head was bent over her game, her concentration totally focused on what she was doing. It seemed she'd seen nothing, but that could so easily not have been the case.

She cast a glance up at Nick. What had they been thinking of?

Nick's eyes travelled back from Rosie to her. 'I'm sorry.'

She shrugged, trying to convey an easy unconcern. It was just a kiss, she reminded herself, not a lifelong commitment. Lydia gathered her hair together in a long coil and twisted it back up.

*Why had he said he was sorry?* She didn't want him to be sorry. Sorry implied that he thought kissing her had been a mistake, and it hadn't felt like a mistake. It had felt...inevitable.

It was terrifying to look into his dark eyes and feel herself falling deeper and deeper into them. She'd never experienced anything quite like this in her entire life.

She was thirty years old, for crying out loud. She'd been in several reasonably serious relationships over the past ten years. She'd even, on two occasions, wondered whether she might have been in love. A simple kiss should have meant nothing, but this...intensity was outside her experience.

Lydia picked up her wine. It was the feeling of being out of control. Never before had she felt so vulnerable. This felt like walking out on a tightrope knowing the safety net had been removed.

When Nick looked at her he made her feel so many conflicting things at the same time. Part of her felt breathless and afraid, another part felt invincible, as though she could achieve anything.

And when she looked into his dark eyes she knew he wasn't sorry he'd kissed her, whatever he said to the contrary. She believed he hadn't intended to, any more than she'd intended to kiss him. But sorry? No, he wasn't sorry.

He'd pulled back only when he'd remembered Rosie. *As had she.* So now what?

'More wine?'

'I still have some.' Lydia put her cup down on the grass.

'Something to eat?'

Lydia accepted the plate Nick handed her and opened out a packet of crisps on to it. Every movement seemed as if it needed thought; even breathing had become unusually difficult.

She was aware when Nick looked at her. Equally aware when he looked away. And it was mutual, she was sure of it. The *frisson* between them crackled like a live thing.

*Had Izzy felt like that about Steven Daly?* The disquieting thought slid into her head with the same potency as the snake into the Garden of Eden.

It was a relief when Rosie noticed that the food had started to be unpacked and left her game to join them. Blissfully unaware of any undercurrents, Rosie concentrated on decimating a small fairy cake which had been filled with butter-cream.

Nick reached out and touched his daughter's hand, shaking his head when she looked up.

'Why do children do that?' Lydia asked, momentarily distracted by Rosie's uninhibited excavation of the butter-cream with her forefinger. 'I always used to eat the jam out of a jam tart first and Izzy used to lick the chocolate off a chocolate biscuit.' She reached out and took a large crisp and snapped it in half. 'I'd forgotten we used to do that. What was your childhood fetish?'

'I didn't have one.'

Lydia tucked her skirt around her legs. 'You must have.'

He shook his head before she'd finished speaking. 'I wasn't allowed any. My father paid for very expensive nannies whose primary role was to instil rigid discipline in me.'

Lydia gave silent thanks for her own childhood. There'd been times when she'd been ashamed of her parents, wished they'd not stood out from other parents—but she'd had no idea how lucky she'd been.

'That's sad,' she said, thinking of how much her parents had simply enjoyed Izzy and her. It made her ashamed she'd ever been ashamed. Grateful for the heritage she had without ever knowing she possessed it.

'The only subversive influence in my life is Wendy.'

Lydia looked up and smiled. 'She must have done her best.'

'Always.' His smile widened at some distant memory and then he said, 'I was never sure whether she involved herself in my life because she knew how much it annoyed my father or whether she really felt her role as my god-mother was a sacred trust.'

Lydia picked at the grass beside her. 'Perhaps a bit of both,' she said, thinking back to her conversation with Wendy earlier. 'If your father didn't like her, why was she asked to be your godmother?'

'Money.'

'I'm sorry?' Lydia said, not quite sure she'd heard him correctly.

His eyes glinted with amusement. 'The expressed reason, given at the time, was that Wendy was my mother's second cousin. Wendy's conviction, however, is my father had an eye to her money.'

Lydia immediately thought of Wendy's cottage with its antiquated kitchen and tired decoration. *What money?* She'd thought Nick culpable for letting his godmother live in such a way. Even after she'd got to know Wendy better, understood her proud and indomitable spirit, she still thought he should have done something to help her. But if Wendy was rich...

Nick seemed to read her mind. 'Don't let the way she chooses to live fool you.'

'But—'

Rosie's knee knocked her plastic cup and sent orange juice spilling out across the rug. Lydia lifted her skirt out of the way and accepted the pieces of kitchen towel Nick passed her.

'Has she got you?'

Lydia shook her head. 'Just the rug and the boxes.' She lifted one box up and carefully wiped the plastic bottom. Nick, meanwhile, refilled Rosie's cup.

'Now sit down this time,' he said slowly, making sure his daughter was watching his mouth. 'Careful.'

Rosie wasn't in the slightest bit cowed. She smiled and curled up against him.

Lydia balled up the damp paper towels. 'Have you got a bag to put these in?' He reached behind him and produced a carrier bag and Lydia tossed them inside.

She then asked, 'Why does Wendy chose to live in…?' She waved her hand about rather than use the word which came to mind.

'Genteel decay?'

Lydia nodded.

'She likes it.'

'But… Why would she…?'

Nick took pity on her. 'I've tried to persuade her to make the cottage more comfortable, but it doesn't interest her. She maintains she has considerably more than most of the world population—'

'That's true, I suppose.'

'And she doesn't care whether her decoration is this year's fashion or last.'

Lydia could hear Wendy saying it. Her lips twitched and she couldn't resist saying, 'Or from the seventies.'

'You haven't seen the bedroom. It's back in the forties.'
He took Rosie's cup from where she'd precariously placed
it and settled it in the middle of the rug. 'Like the kitchen,
which she tells me was cutting edge in its day.'

It seemed all her prejudices concerning Nick were falling like a pack of cards. *All her prejudices except one.* His
daughter curled in even closer and rested her head on his lap.

'She's tired,' Lydia observed.

Nick lightly stroked her curls. 'I suppose it's hot and
she's been running about most of the morning.'

Lydia longed to ask him about Rosie. Why had he had
so little say over her upbringing, so little contact with her
prior to her coming to live with him? She almost blurted
out a question, but stopped short. One kiss didn't seem to
give her the right to ask.

She watched the rhythmic movement of his fingers
through Rosie's curls and the sleepy way her dark fringed
eyelids closed. 'She's going to sleep.'

His hand didn't stop and gradually Rosie's breathing
slowed and her thumb found its way into her mouth. Lydia
looked up at Nick. The love on his face squeezed her heart.

'Has it been difficult organising your work so you can
be with Rosie?' Lydia asked softly.

'Very.' Nick's fingers stilled, but stayed buried deep in
Rosie's riot of curls. It looked almost like a benediction.
'I did it because it seemed like the right thing to do.'

Lydia nodded. She imagined Nick would be good on
duty, which was why she found it so incredible he hadn't
maintained some kind of contact with his daughter even
when his ex-wife had custody.

'I've been surprised at how effective I can be from

home…and just how few days I've needed to be in London. Long term I'll need to be there more than I've been there over the past couple of weeks, but I've learnt a lot about balance.'

*Balance.* She'd heard colleagues talk about a life/work balance, but it was a concept that was completely alien to her. For her, there was only work. It was her driving passion. The phone would ring, day or night, and she was ready to go.

She'd missed weddings, surprise parties, planned parties, even the presentation of her then-boyfriend's OBE. She never accepted any invitation without adding the proviso that she might be called away. Nothing had ever got in the way of work.

Except, perhaps, Izzy's overdose.

That event had sent a ripple through her life strong enough to send her off course—for a time. But there hadn't been any major conflict of interest. Nothing she'd had any difficulty in refusing, and before long she'd been on the trail of Steven Daly's insurance scam.

'The biggest surprise—' and Lydia could hear it in his voice '—is how much I've enjoyed it. I used to be on the motorway into London at around six and I'd never be home before seven on a normal working day. But being with Rosie…' he shook his head as though he couldn't quite believe it '—is incredible. I don't want to miss any more time with her than I have to.'

Lydia felt the same pang of envy she'd experienced watching them from the window. Seeing Nick, his hand buried in Rosie's rampant curls, she felt she was missing out on something important.

'What about you?' Nick asked. 'What's your five-year plan?'

Lydia pleated the fine flame-coloured cotton of her skirt. It was an interesting question because she didn't have a plan. She'd never had a plan and wasn't sure how to answer. She hadn't thought about doing anything different, within the next five years or beyond. She'd always go where there were stories to tell. It was her life. It defined who she was.

But why? She'd never thought about the why. Or even what she'd do if she allowed for the possibility of change.

'My plan,' she said slowly, 'is to go with the opportunities. On some level, I suppose, I still want to change the world.'

'And have a garden again one day?'

'Perhaps.' Lydia twisted the bangle at her wrist. 'It would be nice to think I will one day, but it's not very likely. I'm away from home far too much to make it practical.'

He nodded as though he understood what she was saying, had even expected it. She hated thinking he somehow thought less of her because of it. Why was it you had to sacrifice so much of one part of your life to make another part possible?

Would she, in the same position, have made the same choice Nick had?

She suddenly understood what it really meant not to have made any space in her life for the possibility of children—ever. It was a huge decision which, surely, warranted more thought than she'd given it? Was she really going to live her entire life without any emotional commitments?

At the core of every relationship she'd ever had was the knowledge that they would never hold each other back in their dreams. She'd absolutely bought one hundred per cent into the idea that relationships were secondary to careers.

She could honestly say she'd happily sent the men in her life off to report on war zones and to take photographs of Namibia—whatever had been their particular passion—without a qualm. And she'd demanded the same in return. It was what happened in mature twenty-first century relationships.

But…

Those relationships had floundered. The careers had pulled hard and eventually there had been nothing left to come back to. Ten years and there'd never been any sense of her being the centre of anyone's universe. She'd never been the dream.

And she'd never found anyone who could be hers. Maybe she was more like Anastasia Wilson than she cared to think.

'Will Rosie's mother see much of her?' Lydia asked.

'I doubt it. She'll come occasionally, probably bringing presents, but—' his voice took on a possessive quality '—day-to-day, no.'

'What did she say about Sophie leaving?'

Nick looked up. 'Nothing.'

'Nothing?'

'Her mind was completely taken up by the late delivery of some silk.' And then, as he saw her face, 'Ana never wanted to be a mother. I always knew she would have preferred not to have to juggle her career with raising a child.'

'But—'

'Rosie wasn't a planned pregnancy.' Nick looked down at his little girl. He should have fought harder for a relationship with her. Other fathers did. He knew of men who drove hundreds of miles to see their children every other weekend.

Nick looked up at Lydia, watching her wide eyes for some glimmer of what she was thinking. He blamed himself. Did she blame him?

'When Ana left…' He cleared his throat, his hand moving against Rosie's curls. 'Ana left when Rosie was nine months old…'

'I know. You told me,' Lydia said softly.

It would be easy to stop there, tell her nothing more—but he wanted her to understand. There *had* been mitigating circumstances and he wanted Lydia to know them.

'Ana left me for my best friend.'

There was some satisfaction in seeing her mouth part in shock.

His voice lowered. It was still difficult to put words on what had happened. 'Gaston Girard. I'd known him since we were seven. His mother had married an Englishman and we went to the same boarding school…until tennis took over his life. But we remained friends.'

Lydia shook her head, part sympathy, part disbelief. 'Nick, I'm…so sorry.'

'It lasted a year.' Nick swallowed. 'Slightly over. Gaston was on the international tennis circuit then. I tried to make trips to see Rosie, but it was…difficult and she was only a baby. With long gaps in between visits I could have been anyone.'

He stopped speaking and Lydia leaned forward to touch

him. Her fingers lightly brushed his forearm and Nick risked looking across into her eyes. So beautiful, they shone with unshed tears.

'I'm so sorry. If I'd known…I would never have… It must have been so….'

*Impossible.* It had been impossible. For months he'd steeled himself to make those visits; each one had been harder than the last, until he'd found reasons why he couldn't go.

The sense of betrayal had been so acute. Seeing Gaston… Just seeing the three of them together…

Nick swallowed painfully as he remembered how it had felt to see his best friend with Ana. Taking his place with Rosie. It had killed him.

Each visit had been harder than the last. Every time he'd seen it the reality had sunk in just that little bit deeper. It had been easier to pretend it wasn't really happening. He'd poured himself into his business. Had tried to blot it out.

'I tried again when Ana left Gaston and returned to England—'

Lydia's beautiful eyes never left his face.

'—but by then Rosie was two and hid behind Georgina's skirt. Georgina was Ana's mother,' he clarified.

Lydia nodded.

'After three or four times like that I stopped visiting regularly. I sent money, presents… The usual kind of things people do which means they don't have to invest too much of themselves.'

The hand on his arm tightened and he risked looking directly into Lydia's stunning eyes.

Some part of him had braced himself for rejection, but

all he saw was a compassionate understanding. 'You have her now,' she said softly.

'Yes, I do.'

*Unbelievably.* Back then, when Ana had decided to leave with Gaston, that had seemed an impossibility. But he did. He had Rosie. He would be the 'father' she remembered and the person who had the privilege of guiding her future.

It was the nearest he'd come to forgiving himself. He'd refused to talk about that time, but telling Lydia...seeing her reaction...had been cathartic.

In his lap Rosie stirred. Her young body uncurled like a bud and she sat up, her eyes sleepy.

Above her head Nick met Lydia's eyes. 'We'd better get back. It's late.'

'Yes.' Lydia's response had been automatic, but she glanced down at her watch. It *was* late.

It was time for her to head home, but that seemed even less appealing now than it had earlier. Her flat would be empty. Quiet.

*How had Nick endured that time?* She ached for him. Couldn't think of what to say—other than to apologise for her own self-righteous attitude towards him. She hadn't had all the facts. She'd had no right to judge...

Lydia stood up and shook the crumbs off her skirt. She looked up and caught Rosie watching her, her face curious. Lydia smiled and signed that it was time to pack up and go home.

Rosie nodded happily and then walked over to slip her young hand trustingly inside Lydia's. She led her towards her make-believe world at the foot of the tree and Lydia looked down at the intricate family groups. It seemed a shame to break it up and, for some reason, it made her feel tearful.

Carefully she helped Rosie fit the figures back in the box. She raked the ground so as not to leave behind a single piece, while behind her she could hear Nick packing up their picnic.

*How could she have been so sanctimonious?* Why had he allowed her to lecture him on his responsibilities as a parent?

She'd wanted to know why he hadn't learnt to sign for Rosie—and now she knew. But she hadn't expected how painful it would be to hear it. She knew the law was biased in favour of mothers, would probably have campaigned for just that bias, but... Nick had lost so much. That didn't seem fair.

They headed back towards the house. Rosie's short sleep seemed to have given her all the refreshment of a full eight hours. She scampered ahead, occasionally turning round to smile at them and check they were within sight.

Lydia glanced across at Nick and wondered what kind of relationship she could hope to have with him. Her tentative smile faltered. One kiss and she was imagining all kinds of possibilities.

Illogical.

Wasn't it?

Except it wasn't—and she knew it. She glanced down at her feet and watched the way her nails shone through the grass. There was something in his dark eyes that told her he would contact her when he was in London. They'd have dinner...

What then?

How much of a difference did it make if your boyfriend had a child? From what she'd observed from friends, they didn't usually introduce their children to their girlfriends until the relationship had reached the stage of a duplicate set of toiletries and at least one drawer in the bedroom. But they'd begun the wrong way up. She already knew she loved Rosie.

*Love.* Had she really thought that? Did she love Rosie? Lydia cast a surreptitious glance up at Nick. And what about Rosie's father? How did she feel about him? Just thinking about the possibility of loving him, being in love with him, turned her insides to marshmallow.

And it scared her. Love shouldn't feel like that, should it? Lydia frowned. What was she frightened of? And then she knew. *Love meant sacrifice.* Putting another person before you and trusting they were looking out for you.

She didn't do that. Ever. And Nick needed that. Listening to him talk about losing Rosie had made her realise that.

'How much longer will you be meeting up with Wendy?'

'We're practically finished,' Lydia answered, watching Rosie run down a bank, arms spread wide. 'I'll be here again on Thursday.'

'Thursday?'

She looked across at him and nodded. 'I've got a couple of articles to deliver for next week and a launch party to go to for Caitlin Kelsey's *Beyond Redemption*.'

Any moment he was going to ask her to dinner. She could feel it in the air. It was as real as the smell of summer carried on the gentle breeze. He'd arrange to meet in London. They'd have dinner and afterwards…

Her imagination was full of images. In an ideal world she'd simply have said 'yes'. She wanted nothing more than to know what he looked like in the morning, to wake with his arms wrapped around her. She wanted to surprise the laughter that transformed his face.

But Nick wasn't looking for the 'see you when we're in the same city' kind of relationship she favoured. He was too responsible to bring a steady stream of girlfriends through Rosie's life. He needed the sort of woman who would fit into country living and be a fantastic stepmother to Rosie.

If she could wave a magic wand and change her personality she'd do it. If she could be the kind of woman who got emotional satisfaction from a lemon-fresh toilet and a freshly baked tray of cupcakes…

If…

As he turned to look at her she heard her own small intake of breath as she took in the expression in his eyes. It was timeless. Unmistakable. *She wasn't ready for this. Didn't know what she thought yet.*

But even as the panic ripped through her she felt time slow down around her. Slowly, deliberately, his eyes moved to her lips and she knew he was going to kiss her.

For the second time.

Her breath seemed to catch in her throat. She wanted to feel his lips on hers. Coaxing a response. Making her forget that this wasn't a good idea. That she wasn't the woman…

The small distance between them vanished. *Dear God.* His mouth was warm and persuasive on hers. She could taste the wine and the strength that was entirely him.

For one brief moment she tried to be sensible. She pulled away and murmured, 'Rosie. We…'

His hands moved to cradle her face, his eyes seeming to read her soul. 'Knows the way home.'

Nick moved slowly, deliberately. He gave her every opportunity to pull away, decide this wasn't what she wanted, but Lydia found she couldn't resist any more.

Her hands pushed the backpack off his shoulders and she heard it hit the grass. She heard her own soft moan of pleasure as his mouth trailed up the side of her neck, the small whimper that begged for more.

'Nick.' His name on a breath.

Her mind refused to co-operate. She couldn't formulate the words, didn't really know what she wanted to say. He nipped softly at her earlobe and her head fell back, a mute invitation which she couldn't stop and didn't want to.

There was only the sensation of him and a slow warmth spreading through her body. His tongue flicked between her parted lips, coaxing a need in her she hadn't known she was capable of feeling.

His hands moved over her body and pulled her in closer…and then closer. Lydia could feel his arousal hard against her stomach and the soft answering ache settling low in her abdomen.

She wasn't strong enough to walk away from this. She wanted him. As perhaps she'd never wanted anything. She wanted him to push the straps of her sundress down, wanted to be naked before him. She wanted him full and moving within her…

She'd never felt like this. So completely abandoned, so…

'We'd better go inside,' Nick murmured, his breath ragged. His lips moved against her neck.

'Yes.' More groan than anything else.

And deep down Lydia knew she was saying 'yes' to more than walking inside Fenton Hall.

Lydia stretched languorously, her body warm and sated. She felt completely…new, as though this were the start of something wonderful. Unexpected, but completely wonderful. She rolled over on to one side and looked at Nick's sleeping face.

She'd wanted to know what he looked like in the morning. And he looked wonderful. The early morning sunlight worked its way through the partly opened curtain and shimmered against his bare shoulders. Lydia reached out and stroked along his collar-bone and down the smooth skin of his back. It was irresistible. He was irresistible.

Nick's eyes opened, his voice low and gravelly. 'Good morning.'

This ought to feel embarrassing, some part of her brain registered. She'd never…well, she had, but she'd never spent the night with a man she wasn't in a long-term, seriously thought about relationship with. But Nick…

Nick had been so sudden. Cataclysmic. Absolutely nothing she'd ever felt about him had been neutral, not since the first time she'd seen him.

That seemed a lifetime ago now. Standing on the roof of his godmother's cottage, with him so angry and disapproving below. They'd moved such a long way towards each other.

She let her fingers splay out on his back, loving the warmth of his skin. 'Morning.' Her voice sounded breathless.

Then he smiled, that slow unexpected smile that had always made her melt. 'I can't believe you're here.' He rolled over and imprisoned her beneath him. His hands pushed back her hair.

'I can't believe I'm here either. I don't—'

Nick bent his head and kissed the spot on her neck he'd discovered last night sent her wild and she let her hands curl into his thick hair.

'Don't what?' Lydia heard the teasing laughter in his voice. 'Are you sorry?'

That was an easier question to answer. 'No.' *Not sorry at all.* Her whole body was singing with remembered pleasure. Her limbs felt heavy and it was purgatory to think of moving.

He kissed her, a slow drugging kiss that made it even harder to say, 'But I do need to go home, Nick.'

In an ideal world they would have a lazy breakfast, the opportunity to make love some more, have lunch...

His eyes gleamed with passion. Nick bent his head and kissed her again. She loved the way he kissed her. She loved being with him. She loved...

*Being loved.* He'd not said the words, but that was how he made her feel. When he touched her she felt worshipped. His arms wrapped around her and she felt completely protected from all life's traumas. She'd never be sorry.

'Stay.'

That one word sent a spiral of desire coursing through her body. There was nothing she'd like more than to stay. She lifted a finger and traced it along his now roughened jawline. 'What's the point in our creeping around the house last night if I'm still here when Rosie wakes up this morning?'

Nick grunted and rolled off her. He laid back, one arm bent behind his head, his eyes glinting sinfully and his body completely relaxed. 'I hate it that you're right.'

Lydia gave a low husky laugh and flung back the bed-clothes. She picked up her sundress and looked around for her bra. 'Where…' she began before she noticed that Nick was openly watching her. 'Stop it!'

His smile stretched as Lydia held her dress up in front of her. It was too late for modesty, way too late. And strange, that after everything they'd shared, she should still feel shy.

'Rosie is your daughter,' she said with mock severity. 'It's five o'clock and time I was gone. What time does she wake up?'

Reluctantly Nick pushed back the covers. 'Six.' He bent down and picked up his jeans and flung them across the bed.

Lydia stood like some nervous virgin, envying how at ease he was with his body. So much for the British inhibition she'd thought an integral part of him. Total confidence. A man completely at ease within his own skin.

He flung a silk dressing gown around his lean body. 'When will I see you again?' he asked, taking her face between his hands and kissing her gently. It was the kind of kiss that gave comfort, made her feel incredibly special. He pulled back and looked into her eyes. 'Make it soon.'

Lydia felt her shyness recede. She reached out and touched his face, his stubble rough against her hand. 'Come to London.'

# CHAPTER TEN

LYDIA knew it was work the minute she looked at her mobile. The call hadn't been entirely unexpected. There'd been rumours that she might be given this particular opportunity because of her interest in politics and human rights. The recent journalistic award hadn't done her any harm either.

*Brussels.*

She was going to Brussels.

But the way she felt about it was entirely unexpected. She kept hearing Nick's words—'time away from Rosie is time wasted'. She hadn't really understood what he'd meant, but she did now. Time away from Nick felt like time wasted.

Lydia lifted her hands to her burning cheeks. She didn't want to go. For the first time in nearly ten years she didn't want to go. Seven nights and five days of Nick spread over three weeks and she didn't want to go.

It should have been everything she'd ever wanted. The chance to report on real issues that would affect Europe for the next decade and beyond. But a year…

Minimum. A year was a long time.

Lydia pulled a chair up against her wardrobe and stood on it to lift down her suitcase. She could still see Nick. She was being ridiculous. True enough long-distance relationships rarely worked, but that would be his choice. She could fly back to see him every few weeks. Perhaps he'd even find the time to come over and see her.

And Rosie. She'd be an excellent role model for Rosie. It would be good for her to grow up seeing women achieving things, being their own person.

*Brussels. The European Parliament.*

This was everything she'd ever wanted. She was going to be at the centre of things. It was what she'd been working for.

*So why did she want to cry?*

Lydia slowly opened her wardrobe and started laying out the clothes she'd need to take. A pair of well-cut black trousers, two brown. Two sharply cut jackets and a simple cream evening dress. She placed them in a pile on the bed.

It was just the thought of going. Once she was on the plane she'd be fine. Excited.

Of course she'd be excited. It was a completely fantastic opportunity. She was going to be at the hub of Europe, getting to talk to the people who were making the decisions.

Lydia put the first few things in her suitcase. This was what she'd wanted. Always. From the age of eighteen she'd wanted the excitement of change. She'd wanted the kind of career that meant a phone call could see her flying to a disaster area in Scotland and then the Olympics next. She wanted adventure. Variety.

She wanted the respect of other journalists. She still

wanted to change the world, be a force for good and the champion of the underdog.

Always. It was her lifelong goal. It was why she'd left Izzy crying in Auntie Margaret's small back bedroom and caught the coach to Cambridge all those years ago. It was why she'd pushed herself to get a first—because anything else wasn't going to be good enough to justify what she'd done to her sister.

Lydia sat down on the edge of her bed. So what had changed? If she didn't pursue her goal now it meant she'd let Izzy down for nothing.

The temperature outside was soaring, but inside she felt so cold. She felt as if she was being ripped in half, as though she was being forcibly torn away from what was really important.

How she was feeling made no sense. She'd always avoided emotional ties. Had never put down roots. She'd made sure she had no responsibilities, no children and no relationships she couldn't leave. It was different for her male colleagues. For them it was possible to truly 'have it all', but she'd accepted long ago that men rarely followed their partners around the world.

It was a simple choice. And she'd made it. At eighteen. She'd always known what she wanted. She'd never needed to put together a five-year plan—she had a mission statement.

It was *who* she was.

She was a career journalist, one hundred per cent committed to what she was doing. So why did she feel so…broken. No, not broken, more sick inside. Deep down, heart-wrenchingly sick.

Lydia pulled her Anastasia Wilson jacket from the wardrobe. Her hand hesitated as she put it in her suitcase, her fingers resting on the soft leather. She'd not asked Nick about why his marriage had failed. It hadn't seemed…appropriate to talk about his ex-wife and he hadn't volunteered the information.

It was another of those unwritten twenty-first century rules—never talk about past relationships. If they were over, then they were in the past and best forgotten.

*How ridiculous.* The ending of a marriage had to be something that shaped you, coloured the way you thought about your future. She hadn't wanted a post mortem on it, but it would have been useful to have known why. Perhaps Nick had found it difficult to be with a woman who couldn't put him first?

And Rosie, that inner voice whispered, she didn't need another career woman in her life. She needed a different kind of role model. She needed someone who would be there for her, loving her.

Lydia put in the last of her things and zipped her case shut. She couldn't be that person. Nick had to have known that.

By tonight she would be on the plane to Brussels. She would be fully focused on the opportunities and challenges ahead of her. It would be fine.

She glanced round her bedroom. One suitcase was probably everything she'd need for now. She could come back and collect anything else she wanted when she'd arranged an apartment.

There was just time to see Nick. She lifted her case and carried it out to the lift. It would be better to see him face to face. Explain. Say goodbye to Rosie. Then she could drive to Wendy's cottage and spend an hour or so with her before driving on to the airport. She'd have to leave the car in the long-stay car park for the time being, but all that could be sorted out later.

Her mind started to turn over the thousands of ways she could tell Nick she was moving to Brussels, but the journey to Fenton Hall wasn't quite long enough to fix on the perfect one. Confronted with him she made a mess of it.

His face, usually so inscrutable, showed surprise. 'You're leaving tonight?'

She nodded. 'Late afternoon. So I'm going to have to take a rain check on dinner.'

'Of course.'

Nick tried to look as though he was excited for her. She was obviously buzzing with it, loving the opportunity she'd been given—and he could see it was a good one. Lydia would enjoy being in Brussels and she was just the kind of journalist who needed to be there. She was passionate about what she did—and that was great.

It just didn't feel great.

And he'd only himself to blame. He'd known that what he'd found with her could only be temporary. That sooner or later she'd be off, chasing another story, searching out another wrong that needed to be righted.

He loved that about her. There was precious little he didn't love about her.

'I'll be back in a couple of weeks. Obviously I'll need to get my things,' Lydia said brightly. 'But there's no point dragging everything out at this stage.'

'What time is your plane?' He forced himself to ask the question. He was doing well.

'Four.'

He made rapid calculations. How long it took to drive to the airport, how long before she had to be there before she boarded her flight. *How long before she left him.*

'I'm packed and ready to go. I promised Wendy I'd stop by her cottage today. She's got some letters she wants me to have.'

*Lydia was going now.* Nick felt as if he needed to shout, hit something, walk for miles…

Instead he smiled. 'You need to get going.'

She nodded. 'I just stopped by to tell you I'm off and…to say I'll phone.' She smiled.

Nick felt as if his heart had been ripped out and stamped on. He loved her—and he was going to have to let her go because that was what she wanted. And he was going to let her go without guilt.

He'd known exactly what he was getting himself into. In the beginning, when he'd first met Lydia, he'd thought she was like Ana—but that wasn't the case. It had taken him a while to understand that.

Ana used anything and everything to build her career. She'd married him because he had the money she'd needed to bolster her fledgling business. She'd left him for Gaston because he could introduce her into the international jet-set world she wanted to be part of. With Simon Cameron she'd finally joined the establishment.

Lydia was completely different. She believed passion-ately in what she was doing. She truly believed she could change the world—and who was he to say she couldn't?

It was what Wendy had seen in her from the very be-ginning. The reason why she'd insisted on Lydia as her bi-ographer. His godmother shared the same burning desire to make her life count and she'd achieved so much. He admired her. He admired Lydia.

He loved the way she gave herself passionately to whatever she was doing and if he'd hoped he might become her passion then that had been entirely at his own risk. He'd known that from the moment he'd realised that avoiding her wasn't going to make the pain of living without her any less intense.

He turned as he heard Rosie's feet scurry down the hall. Lydia bent down so she could lip-read clearly, her hands moving in confirmation. Nick watched his daughter's face change. She was free to express what he couldn't.

Her hands flew, her movements were jerky. He hadn't learnt enough to understand what she was saying, but he got the gist from the expression on her face.

'I've got to go to work,' Lydia said, pulling her close and holding her.

Nick reached out and touched Rosie's shoulder. His daughter looked up at him, her brown eyes questioning. He nodded in confirmation of what Lydia had said. 'We'll see her soon.'

Then he looked at Lydia. Her excitement had faded and her face looked pinched. Maybe she wasn't finding this as easy as it had first appeared? Maybe she would find she wanted to come back to them? To him. But he had to let her go first. It had to be her choice.

Which meant he had to say goodbye—with Rosie looking on. It was up there among the hardest things he'd ever had to do in his entire life. 'I'll miss you.'

'I'll ring.'

He nodded. *He'd never told her he loved her.* It had

never seemed quite the right moment. He'd wondered whether it was too soon, whether it would put undue pressure on her. At least that was what he'd told himself. The truth was he'd been scared it would drive her away.

But she was going anyway. He should have told her. It would have made no difference to what was happening now, but he would have said the words.

Rosie pulled away and ran back down the hallway, her feet echoing on the wooden floor. 'What?'

'She said to wait.' He watched as Lydia took her lip between her teeth. She gave a gasping breath. 'This is so hard.'

'Lydia, I—'

She tried to smile and her mouth wavered. 'I'm sorry. I didn't think it would be this difficult…' She swiped at her eyes.

Nick just needed to hold her. He drew her in close and let his hand snake up to cradle her head. Her hair was soft against his arm and smelt of roses. *He loved her.* More than that, he ached for her.

For a moment they just stood there. 'I do have to go,' she murmured softly, her voice choked.

'I know.' Nick pulled back and looked into her incredible eyes. 'I know you do.'

Lydia reached out and touched his face and then she leant forward to kiss him. He knew exactly what her trembling lips were saying—it was thank you.

He felt the tremor pass through his body. She hadn't left yet and he felt utterly bereft. He would see her again. Brussels wasn't the end of the earth—but she knew and he knew she'd made the choice to walk away from them. It would never be the same.

They heard Rosie's footsteps coming down the stairs and Lydia instinctively stepped back. Every impulse prompted him to snatch her back into his arms, but he resisted. Instead he looked down at his daughter. 'What have you got?'

Her young face was very solemn as she held out a white envelope on which she'd carefully drawn a stamp in the top right-hand corner. Lydia took it. 'What is it?'

Rosie made a single sign.

Lydia bent down. 'Oh, honey, I'll remember you.' She made the sign. 'I'll remember you and I'll see you both soon.'

Then she stood up and left, without daring to look back at them. Nick watched her car snake down the drive until it had completely disappeared—and, in that moment, he knew how it felt to die.

If Wendy noticed she'd been crying she didn't say anything. She accepted Lydia's help in carrying the tea through to her small lounge and settled herself in the armchair.

'Brussels?'

Lydia nodded, trying to instil some kind of excitement into her voice. 'For a year.'

'What a marvellous opportunity.' Wendy's eyes seemed unusually observant but she didn't say anything more. She sipped her tea and then appeared to change the subject.

'Pass me those letters.' Lydia stood up and walked over to the sideboard she'd pointed at. 'I thought you might like these. When I'm dead they'll only be thrown away and you might find them interesting background reading for the chapter on the Sudan.'

'Thank you.'

Wendy sat back in her chair. 'I wrote them to Nick's

mother and I was very glad when George gave them back to me after she'd died. She was a wonderful correspondent, kept me in touch with what was going on at home. It can be very lonely saving the world.' Her mouth twisted in a smile. 'It's not for everyone, Lydia, my kind of life.'

Lydia looked up. She knew enough of Wendy to know she never spoke without an agenda. Often she spoke to stir up debate, but sometimes…sometimes she spoke because she wanted to be listened to.

'There are days now when I wonder whether I made the right choice. You know, people are more important than anything. More important than causes. I think I lost sight of that a little.'

Wendy paused to sip her tea. 'You have to know what kind of person you are. I prefer humanity when it's at a distance. I'm better at loving "people" as a whole than trying to love any one individual. But that comes at a cost.'

Her sharp blue eyes looked over the top of her teacup. 'Do you understand what I mean?'

Lydia nodded. She wasn't sure that she did.

'This is how I've chosen to live.' She looked round her dark sitting room. 'It suits who I am. I like not being answerable to any other person, but…I have chosen to be alone.'

There was a small silence and Wendy stretched out her hand. 'It's not my business to tell you how to live your life, but don't shut out other possibilities and other ways of being useful.

'Sharing your life with someone doesn't mean you can't make a difference. In many ways you can make more of a difference.'

Lydia felt the tears well up behind her eyes. She wasn't sure what to say. 'Nick... I—'

Wendy sat back in her chair. 'I don't need to know, but if you think I didn't suspect something was going on between you two you must think I hurt more than my ankle.'

Amidst the pain Lydia felt a bubble of laughter. 'I don't, I—'

'And, to tell you the truth, I envied you. I could have married, had a family of my own, but—' she shook her head '—I was never brave enough to risk my happiness on another person.

'I just want you to think about it. It might be right for you to live a life like mine. Maybe the causes you have will be enough for you. When you're my age and you look back on what you've achieved...what is it you'd like people to say about you? What is it you'd like to have done?'

*What was it she'd like to have done?* Lydia thought about it all the way to the airport. She thought about it as she boarded the plane and as she landed in Brussels. She thought about it as she checked into her hotel.

She cared about so many things. Justice. She cared passionately about justice. About fairness. About the starving. About the poor and oppressed. About the environment. About social deprivation.

They were the big issues—and in a way it was easier to care about them. There was distance in that. Lydia sat down on her hotel bed. She understood what Wendy had been saying about preferring humanity as a whole rather than individuals.

She had never thought about it before. Caring for individuals was more painful. Loving them was a risk. The things that had hurt her most had all been about individuals, when she thought about it.

University had been an easy focus to deflect her from grieving. She'd masked the pain of her parents' death by campaigning for 'big' causes. Her need for a career had had nothing to do with Izzy. She saw that now. Her sister wouldn't want that of her.

As an adult Izzy had told her she was glad she'd let her grow up with her cousins and not tried to hold it together alone. She hadn't blamed her for not rescuing her from Steven Daly. All that guilt she'd placed on herself.

*Why had it taken until now for her to be able to see it?*

She'd spent years hiding from her emotions. Her career had been a convenient focus. A shield.

When her parents had died…

When Izzy had taken her overdose…

Those were the events that had changed her life. Had altered her. Loving people came at a personal cost. When she thought about the people she loved or had loved she thought of her parents, Izzy, Rosie…

She wanted Rosie's life to be wonderful. She wanted to make sure her childhood was as perfect as it could be, that she grew up feeling loved and cared for. She wanted to make sure there was proper provision for her at school and that she wasn't stuck at the back of a class, only seeing a teacher for the deaf once a week.

She was passionate about that? *Was it wrong to care about that more than some international disaster?*

And she loved Nick.

*Nick.*

She loved him. Lydia looked at the cream-painted walls

of a hotel room that could have been in any city in any country of the world. *What was she doing here?*

Did she really want a life like Wendy's? Wendy Bennington, human rights campaigner, acclaimed by many, but at the end of each day she was alone. Did she really want that?

Lydia lifted her handbag on to the bed and pulled out the envelope Rosie had given her.

The stamp she'd drawn in the corner showed a sad face and squiggles to indicate the perforations. *It had given Nick time to kiss her.*

Her fingers shook slightly as she tore open the top. Inside was a drawing and a photograph. The photograph was of Nick and her. Lydia smiled and ran her fingers over his face. It was one Rosie had taken. The image wasn't central and she was slightly out of focus, but it was nice to have a photograph of Nick.

Lydia stood up and walked over to the kettle and propped the photograph inside the picture frame on the wall. Then she opened out the drawing.

Rosie had drawn a house with a sun in the corner of the picture. She'd coloured the roof in red and the door in green. It was a picture any clever five-year-old might have drawn, but in the foreground she'd drawn three people. One much smaller than the others and all three were holding hands.

Lydia felt as if someone had reached in and squeezed her heart until it cried blood. Rosie had drawn a family. *Them?* She'd said she'd drawn it so that Lydia would remember.

Then she glanced back at the photo—and at Nick's face. He was looking down at her, the expression in his face one of total love and acceptance.

How had she missed that? She felt the first tears start to fall as she reached for the telephone. She'd never been so unsure as to what she should do.

Her sister's voice sounded sleepy.

'Izzy, it's Lydia. I need to talk to you…'

Nick kissed Rosie goodbye and waved her off with Rachel. His life had taken on a strange pattern over the past few days. He felt listless. Lost.

No prizes for guessing why that was. Lydia hadn't phoned. She'd be busy sorting out her life in Brussels. He knew that. He had her mobile number and he could have rung it any time, but the thought of hearing her voice and not being able to hold her was torture.

He stood at the window and watched the rain come down in stair-rods. Was it raining where Lydia was? Was she happy? Missing him?

*Thinking about him at all?*

Then he saw her car. It was almost as though he'd conjured her up by thinking about her. He left the sitting room and went out into the hallway, almost not believing she was real.

Christine stopped him. 'Lydia Stanford asked for the gates to be opened. I've let her through.'

Nick didn't wait for his housekeeper to finish speaking. He walked out of the front door and stood foolishly in the rain, his face, hair, T-shirt quickly becoming soaked through.

Lydia saw him.

She sat for a moment clutching Rosie's picture. She'd come so many hundreds of miles and she didn't know what to say. She might be about to make a complete and utter fool of herself. She wasn't sure she could do it.

What if she'd misread Nick's expression in the photograph? What if she'd been a momentary diversion? What if…?

She looked up. Nick was waiting. He must be wondering what she was doing letting him get soaking wet. Slowly she opened the car door and climbed out. The rain poured down on her, but she scarcely noticed. Nick didn't move towards her, didn't say anything. He was watching, waiting.

'I couldn't do it,' she managed, her voice broken. She held up Rosie's drawing, now completely sodden but the wax picture still there. 'I opened Rosie's envelope and I couldn't do it. Brussels. I've told them I can't do it. That I needed to come…' *Home*.

She was crying, but her face was so wet with rainwater it couldn't matter. If he didn't speak soon she was going to wish the ground would open up and swallow her whole.

She tried again. 'It's a family…' Her voice broke. '*Nick*. She drew a family. She drew us.'

*Please understand,* she begged silently. She'd never felt so vulnerable as she did now. She had meant to tell him that she loved him, but she was too frightened to say the words.

*Help me*.

And then he moved, slowly.

His hands cradled her face and he reached down to kiss her. He must have known she was crying then because she could taste the salt in her own tears.

She was wet, cold, tired and…happy. Her hands snaked round him and held him close. He felt so reassuringly solid. Real. And he hadn't rejected her. He didn't seem to blame her for leaving.

Then he pulled her away and stared down into her eyes. 'I love you.'

She felt as if the floor had disappeared beneath her feet. Was it really going to be that simple? 'Why didn't you ask me to stay?'

'Would you have?'

'I might have done.' Then she thought. 'Probably. I think. I don't know.'

His mouth twisted. 'I nearly did, but I forced myself to let you go. I thought that was what you wanted. I don't want to be a compromise on the life you really want.'

'You're not.' And that was the moment Lydia knew Wendy had been right. She had a new passion, one that transcended every other passion. It didn't take away from the other things she could or would do with her life, it would only add to it. 'I love you.'

Nick put his arm round her and led her into the house. They dripped on the beautiful wooden floor.

'I must look a mess.'

'You look beautiful.' His words echoed what he'd said before and she smiled.

'I'm sorry, Nick.'

He gathered her close and she could hear his heart beating and feel the soft kiss he placed on her hair.

'I'm so sorry I had to go away to realise how much I love you.'

He tilted her face and kissed her. Then he smiled, that heart-stopping beautiful smile that made her bones turn to liquid, and carefully interwove his fingers through hers. 'I didn't want to hold you back. You've got such dreams and I…I didn't want you to ever feel you'd sacrificed too much.'

'But if it's what I choose…'

Nick lifted her up in his arms and carried her up the wide staircase as though she weighed nothing. 'If it's what you choose, then that's completely different—and I'll support you absolutely with whatever you want to do in the future.'

'Ditto.'

He set her down inside his bedroom. 'You're soaking; let me help you.' He reached out to peel away her wet top, but stopped to kiss her. 'Marry me?'

Lydia smiled. 'I've got every intention of marrying you, but not if you propose to me while you're taking my clothes off! I'm not telling my grandchildren that.'

Nick smiled that smile as he pulled her in closer. His voice was warm against her ear. 'Then lie.'

# Special Offers

Every month we put together collections and longer reads written by your favourite authors.

Here are some of next month's highlights— and don't miss our fabulous discount online!

**On sale 15th February**

**On sale 15th February**

**On sale 1st March**

# Save 20%
## on all Special Releases

## The World of Mills & Boon®

There's a Mills & Boon® series that's perfect for you. We publish ten series and, with new titles every month, you never have to wait long for your favourite to come along.

---

### Blaze®

*Scorching hot, sexy reads*
4 new stories every month

### By Request

*Relive the romance with the best of the best*
9 new stories every month

### Cherish™

*Romance to melt the heart every time*
12 new stories every month

### Desire™

*Passionate and dramatic love stories*
8 new stories every month